THE POOHMAN

WALTER S. ZALEWSKI JR.

For Inquiries and Book Orders:

William F. Zalewski and Family

456 Slateford Rd, Mount Bethel, PA 18343
Email: delaware.60psar@yahoo.com
Contact: 5704606897

ISBN: 979-8-9925178-0-4 (sc)
ISBN: 979-8-9925178-1-1 (ebk)

Thanks to all of Walter's family and friends, especially the Zalewski family, including his mother, Grace M. Zalewski, and his father, Walter Zalewski Sr. Thanks also to his brother William Zalewski, friends from Wall Street Financial, and the many loving aunts, uncles, and cousins in Walter's life.

CHAPTER I

The clouds were looking peculiar on this late Friday afternoon. *This must be what the weatherman describes as the mackerel sky, with that fish-back artistry in the cumulus,* I reflected. The temperature had been in the midseventies all day.

I was admiring a beautiful pink-rose sunset that only three minutes ago was yellow across the top and orange near the bottom. *It's a real sneaky chameleon,* I thought. A not-too-distant engine whistle was blowing, alerting all that the train was arriving to this Erie Lackawanna station I was diagonally across the street from.

The station doubled as a bridge, providing a walkway for pedestrians, connecting Union Place to Railroad Avenue, with two staircases inside that took would-be passengers to the tracks, thirty feet below. From my vantage point, the two-piece-suited husbands with briefcases and *New York Times* in hand (some would opt for *The Wall Street Journal,* while others would choose both papers; only a few rugged individualists would have the balls to be publicly seen reading the sports pages in the *Daily News* or the *New York Post*) would soon amble through the open doors, searching for that familiar-looking car driven by their wives, queued in parallel lines. Additional arrivals would rush to their own parked vehicles to go home, but an alternative group would detour to their favorite watering hole for some liquid courage after a tumultuous day of financial battles.

I was standing, alone, in front of one of these watering holes, the Summit Office. For some twenty-five minutes, I had already been inside, waiting for my buddy TJ to arrive.

Because of the stuffiness indoors and the sheer boredom of sipping club soda with lime, it was a welcome diversion to be breathing fresh air. It was too early to start tossing down brews, and besides, TJ and I would have a forty-five-minute drive ahead of us.

I glanced at my week-old Movado watch. The black-sapphire model was the one I had purchased. It glistened blue when light or the sun struck it at the right angle. This coruscant feature sold me. It was 6:35 p.m., and still no sign of TJ.

Watching the commuters across the way reminded me of when I was one of these commuting heroes, selling stocks on Wall Street. It was a three-and-a-half-year sentence without seeing any of the monetary rewards at the end of the rainbow. My mornings were spirited and optimistic, but my trips home were filled with anxiety. One consolation back then, suffice it to say, was at least the train had a bar car.

Taking one last drag of my nearly finished Winston, I discarded it on the sidewalk curb. Unfortunately, I enjoyed these things too much to give them up. I grinned. Having apparently killed enough time recollecting outdoors, I returned to the friendly confines of the restaurant, toward the bar, passing Don and Mike along the way.

Now, wanting a taste, I ordered a Coors Light from Bear, the bartender. Spying the freshly filled bowl of peanuts to the right of me, I generously helped myself to a handful. Bear brightened up when I inquired of the whereabouts of Horrible Honnible, but he was too busy for small talk because the crowd was already getting two deep in his area.

"It will be a godsend if TJ wants to drive down to John Henry's place," I murmured to myself, because I'd had it today, having driven to Sparta and back, with stops in between, failing to close a prospect I had been cultivating for seven weeks. Convincing myself that I'm as professional as an estate planner is something I don't have to do. I'm a good listener, and my client had needs. My pitch was soliloquized to perfection, going in and out with open and closed probes to handle all objections brilliantly. I had coupled assertion with persuasiveness in my former presentations. This was to be the final close. The only thing missing from the deal was a signature on the policy from my client, Mr. Bruder, a forty-one-year-old geometry teacher, who had inherited a sizeable fortune from his aunt Clare. Proudly, I had developed an imaginative customized annuity program to satisfy his early retirement needs. My stomach was tied in knots when he informed me he was not interested at the present time but to contact him in nine months. Hell, that's an eternity. He was more enthusiastic about his ninety-foot yacht purchase than in securing his financial future. He even joked about not being able to swim. Frustrated, I left his residence minus the $11,468 I would have realized in commissions. To me, that was serious money.

That was a lot of dough-re-me. *He would rather buy a fuckin' yacht!* I thought to myself. Mr. Bruder should have informed me long beforehand that I was wasting my time, I tried to sympathize. On the other hand, maybe I should have realized the warning signals that this deal was doomed from the start, I introspected. Well, chalk this one up for the war stories at the next regional sales meeting. I frowned. No one said selling was easy. This could have been my excuse to get a good buzz on, but I chose to nurse my beer.

Surprisingly, TJ had finally contacted me this past Tuesday at my office; I wasn't totally shocked, because he had never failed to miss one of our annual fraternity reunions, but because of his unique problems, I figured he would abstain this time.

There's a quartet of us, from our pledge-class days in college, living within an hour's drive in New Jersey. We get together on other occasions with girlfriends and wives, but this night was reserved just for the guys, because it was our once-a-year male bonding. Alexander Dumas would have been proud of some of our escapades.

The four of us are more like nonbiological brothers than friends, if that explains it properly. After we had known each other a few months, one of us pinpointed that there was a common denominator linking us together. In our respective families, we are all the only child. It's not important who made the discovery. He can remain in anonymity. Maybe we all had been vainly searching for that nonexistent sibling who had the same mode of expression as us, individually. Besides the camaraderie, we welcome the challenge and the competitiveness each of us imposes on the other, but we are most grateful for the genuine moral support we have for one another to succeed. There is no self-aggrandizement among us and "The hell with you, buddy" platitude that prevails in many friendships. Our little group puts to practical application a word most people can say and spell but can't understand: *loyalty*.

In a brief conversation where he did most of the talking, TJ informed me that he was okay and that he had started up a new business. He wouldn't elaborate on any details. Our celebration is always held on the Friday following the nineteenth of June. This year it happened to coincide with that exact date. TJ asked me where the guys would be going. I informed him that we were going to John Henry's uncle's tavern, down in Hunterdon County. What I didn't tell him was that I had my suspicions that our good buddy John Henry had a vested interest in the place.

In typical TJ style, short and to the point, he stated that he would definitely meet me at the Summit Office at 6:00 p.m. Friday to travel to the reunion together. You could never accuse TJ of being periphrastic. He was the best at expressing the most by saying the least. There was no reason not to take him at his word. I called up the other guys to let them know that TJ was alive but not necessarily well. Joe's worst fears were calmed to hear the good news that he would be attending.

John Henry was glad, too, but he tends to be more excitable. He chided me for not having more details to tell him. He babbled something about promising to organize a "swampy" posse to search for TJ had I not called him, but I didn't know what he was talking about.

Although there were a lot of unanswered questions, I was relieved just to hear TJ's voice. We were all worried about him. We had not seen or spoken to him since late January. My incessant phone messages left on his answering machine were not returned, and a month ago, I found out his telephone was disconnected. Attempts to get much information out of his uncle were fruitless. TJ, John Henry, Joe, and I are like brothers, yet he chose to isolate himself from us, shunning our calls when his troubles began and, subsequently, after his firing. The only logical reason for his withdrawal must be his pride, I supposed. He certainly came to the aid of others, but he didn't know how to ask help for himself; during this five-month crisis, you would have thought he needed a support boost from his buddies the most.

It saddened me to read newspaper headlines about his firing from Newark's city hall amid stories of improprieties involving construction bids and that he faced certain criminal prosecution for allegedly accepting bribes. Neither did I appreciate the gossipmongers spreading rumors about him, so I had a few choice words for those windbags who had nothing better to say. I knew TJ to be an honest man. Unless confirmed by him, I would not accept the lies or the "yellow" journalistic bullshit that was printed about his integrity.

Joe DeRenda telephoned my Westfield business office from his law practice in the capital. He read to me the brutal article in one of the Trenton newspapers concerning TJ.

"I'll tell you one thing," he angrily said. "When they're forced to print the retraction, they'll bury it on page 40, for no one to find." That was Thursday, April 21. Every time my secretary dialed TJ's residence, his line was busy. I debated whether he was home or had just taken his phone off the hook. Canceling the remainder on my appointment calendar, I left work early that day, going first to my home in Summit before driving to TJ's apartment, in the North Ward of Newark.

It was a paradox that only six miles away, down Route 78 East, I emerged from the aesthetic, safeguarded suburbs into the bowels of New Jersey's largest city, some sections still reeking from the carnage of its 1967 inglorious riots. To place the distinction in better economic perspective, in that short distance I was traveling from an area that has one of the highest family per capita incomes, not only in the state, but also in the country, to an environ that is one of the poorest in the United States. Newark has its myriad of urban agendas, preeminently crime, poverty, and squalor. The North Ward, though, has still retained, for the most part, its provinciality with its predominantly Italian American inhabitants, despite the sociological pattern changes in other sections of the city. The indigenous quality of its restaurants, bakeries, and small shops is incomparable.

I noticed that TJ's car was not in his driveway. As I anticipated, nobody answered the doorbell to his North Ninth Street apartment, but still I gave it one last long ring before taking off.

I deliberated whether to see George, TJ's uncle, who lived within a five-block proximity of him. He hadn't returned any of my phone calls either. I decided in the affirmative. After losing my bearing for twenty minutes, I found George's Rose Street address. An estate planner shouldn't have trouble with numbered streets, but this one had.

His was the light-gray house with the blue shutters, the first one in on the left side of the cul-de-sac. They didn't designate it as a court, but there was only one way out. Regrettably, I blundered. Over a year ago, he had relocated to North Thirteenth Street across from Columbus Hospital. Not being a native Newarker "user friendly" with these residential avenues, I decided not to take a chance getting lost again on unfrequented streets. Once I got to Keller Parkway, I knew it would turn to Franklin Street, running almost parallel to Bloomfield Avenue, intersecting two blocks above from the Garden State Parkway. Making the proper left onto Belmont Avenue would have saved me unnecessary distance and time, but that was in retrospect, after routing my complete MV. Fifteen minutes later, I made a right onto his one-way street. There was a long tidy row of brick two-family houses, all possessing a unique similitude. That was why I passed it the first time, having to cross over to North Fifteenth Street, forming the triangle back again at Bloomfield Avenue. I drove slower on my second attempt, pulling over at the correct street number.

He was peering through the window curtains when I got out of my silver-blue BMW, no doubt curious of his unexpected visitor.

I waved nonchalantly and walked up to his front door, where I was greeted.

"Come in, Stanley. I thought you were another one of those reporter types. They've been pestering us for weeks," he said indignantly. "My son—I mean my nephew—would never do the things they are saying about him. He's too good. Those bastards in city hall forced him out," George concluded.

Looking at George, I could see the consternation on his face.

He was choked up with emotion, and his eyes were tearing.

"That boy's strong. He'll get through this, all right. He has to get away for a while and think. He wouldn't tell me where he was going, maybe down South. I don't know. He told me to tell you. Excuse me. He told me to tell you that he would get in touch when he had all the answers. Will he be all right, Stanley?"

Putting my arm around his shoulder to comfort him, I replied, "Sure, you bet he will, Uncle George."

Even if I had thought the worst, I was determined not to say it. There are moments in life such as this where I could justify lying, I rationalized. Now my eyes were starting to water, and I felt uncomfortable enough to want to leave. TJ wouldn't want us to commiserate over him like this, so I turned down George's offer to make me coffee. If Uncle George needed me, I reminded him he had both my home and work numbers. He thanked me for stopping over. I said my goodbyes and left.

My car was parked a short distance ahead as I walked down the sidewalk. Notwithstanding the fact that TJ was my friend, Uncle George confirmed my belief in his innocence. TJ's dedication to the government of this city was nonpareil. I felt damn sorry for George too. His worsening right leg necessitated his getting about with a cane. For the eighteen years I have had the privilege of knowing him, George was always a pillar of strength. I felt compassion for him. I wish I didn't have to witness him stuttering his speech and crying. George was proud of TJ. He and his wife, Mary, raised him from childhood after his parents died; his was more than that of a father than an avuncular relationship. George's making a Freudian slip seemed appropriate.

CHAPTER II

Desirous for more substantial information, I drove to the Gondolier, the northern Italian cuisine restaurant that Uncle George formerly had a silent half-interest in. Two years ago, when his arthritis became unbearable, he sold his share to his partner's nephew, Louis Magna.

As I entered, it dawned on me that the last time I dined here was shortly after the New Year. Our happy party of four was nearly in jeopardy that evening if not for the intervention of TJ. My girlfriend, Samantha, was in the mood for Angelo's famous chicken savoy, which has no rival, excepting for Stretch's up at the Belmont Tavern on Bloomfield Avenue.

What gives the dish its special appreciation is that the chicken is brick oven baked in a special sauce composed of oil, vinegar, and wine with just enough aromatic spices to thrill your taste bud.

After gorging ourselves, TJ and I strolled over to converse with our buddy Louis at the rear of the bar, while Samantha and TJ's fiancée, Yolanda, chatted over espresso.

Middle-aged and definitely pear-shaped at about five feet eight, Louis always seemed to wear his trousers around his hips, allowing his cuffs to touch the floor. He would even joke that he was always dusting. His face was round, and a raised brown birthmark distinguished itself on the right corner of his upper lip. The dark bags under his tired eyes suggested he didn't receive enough rest. TJ said that Louis worked a double shift six days a week, and on his one day off, he took his family for a drive down the shore to see his wife's parents. No wonder he always appeared fatigued. Though he concealed any frontal scalp from showing with a low part by his ear, combing his thinning black hair directly across, he couldn't cover his exposed crown area. Louis didn't possess the engaging personality of his uncle Angelo, but there was a depth of sincerity about him that I liked. Louis was obliging to his good customers. Indeed, he was one of those people who would give you the shirt off their back, but with the manner in which he profusely sweated, you'd decline. Still, we called him our friend.

Louis focused our attention to an apparent ceremony that was about to commence; he had the insight, without asking, to bring us two frosted mugs filled with our favorite beverage.

"Hey, let me tell you guys somethin'. You'll never see this happening again. I've only witnessed this particular ritual twice before. The last time was eleven years ago. It's becoming as extinct as the dodo. You're going to be privy to somethin' as rare as testimony to an unassisted triple play in World Series competition, viewing the seventy-six-year reoccurrence of Halley's Comet, seeing a total eclipse of the sun, or being around for the coming-out party of the seventeen-year locust," he proudly vented in his bass-pitched voice.

I enjoyed the manner in which Louis briskly moved his hands to validate a particular point.

"Boy, you're on a roll, Louis!" TJ laughed. "Any chance of meeting the seventh son of a seventh son?"

"Not tonight," he answered.

Putting in my own quip, I added, "What about finding a two-headed rabbit or counting chickens' teeth?"

"Very good, Stanley," Louis jokingly declared. "We'll have to include that also."

Louis pointed to the coterie.

"That's Ralph Cizcero's entourage. He made reservations for a party of seven at eight o'clock sharp, requesting three booths in the back, away from any windows or doors, with the area roped off. He insisted that only Angelo wait on him," he said.

Two burly ones, who could never be accused of being handsome, confiscated the steak knives from the man and woman eating at the small table next to the Cizcero seating arrangements. The larger of the two goons whipped out a wad of bills you could choke Secretariat with. The couple's shock instantaneously turned to joy when he peeled off four semblances of President Ulysses Simpson Grant and stuffed them in the top pocket of the man's maroon sport coat.

"This will more than cover the inconvenience, with a little bit extra for a slice of rum cake," he directed with witless sarcasm.

Going past their table, he stopped dead in his tracks and did an about-face. He looked the woman over and spoke to the man.

"Hey, pal, that's a nice 'ting you're with. Let me tell you somethin'. Chicks like flowers. Buy it a nice corsage on me." He belligerently scoffed.

He tossed a folded "tenski" to the man and smirked as he waltzed by us.

"There's a lesson in assertiveness," I stated.

I was trying to evoke a response from Louis.

Without hesitation, Louis inquired, "That meek duo is masquerading as hitters? Those two gorillas are losing their marbles with paranoid precautionary actions like that."

He showed us his hands palms up.

Obviously, Ralph Cizcero was the flamboyant, in-his-late-fifties-looking character with the huge diamond on his pinky, bedazzling with enough gold to make King Midas covetous. His corpulent belly belied the presumption that he missed any meals. In his arrogant baritone voice, he was barking orders to Angelo and monopolizing the conversation around him.

Louis pointed with his elbow at the man.

"He's an agente beni stabli. That's a real estate agent. Ralph's also a maniffattore. That's a manufacturer. I think he makes bingo chips. They're the legitimate business fronts. Notice, I'm giving you guys the Italian lingo with the English translation where I know it," Louis proudly stated. "Hey, let me tell you guys somethin'. You can learn a lot from this. It'll be like watching *The Godfather Part 1* for real. Hey, it's no secret, he's a caporegime with one of the five families and soon to be crowned the new underboss," Louis expressed.

"Which family?" I curiously asked.

Quickly, TJ cupped Louis's mouth with his left hand, muffling his reply. Sternly he looked me straight in the eye. He stated rather emphatically, "We don't need to know!"

"My friend TJ is right," Louis endorsed approvingly. "I sometimes open a Pandora's box with my big mouth. Stanley, always remember the maxim 'Too much knowledge can be dangerous.'"

Louis flip-flopped his hands.

"You know. Hey, let me tell you guys somethin'," Louis candidly stated. "That Ralph Cizcero, he has no consideration for the rights of others. He's a pretentious bully, with the personality of a rattlesnake and the social graces of a weasel."

Louis squeezed his hands rather tightly.

TJ entreated, "What happened, Lou?"

"He gave me a bad case of *agida*. That's what happened. They came in here just when you guys were finishing your meal. Angelo was busy. Hey, you must realize, he has to attend to special preparations in the kitchen that require his undivided attention, so he implored me to greet Mr. Cizcero's party. He said to make him feel welcome.

"So with good intentions, I assembled most of the staff. I wished to inspect that they were wearing the proper attire. It was important to me to create the right atmosphere, showing respect for his patronage of our establishment. As co-owner, I extended myself, due to his position, and wanted to serve his gathering all the proper amenities due them, thus observing proper protocol. The last thing in the world I wanted was any purposeful slight, because of the repercussions," Louis alleged.

"Hey, I've heard rumors of Cizcero threatening to tailpipe a guy's auto as a reprisal because he suffered an indignation."

Louis explosively lifted his hands above his head.

"These stunts are predicated on morose determents to those soldiers who might otherwise think about challenging his orders. You must understand, the son of a bitch knows me. I'm sort of a relative, by marriage. My second cousin Marie is wedded to his nephew Anthony. He has the sobriquet—"

"We don't speak French," TJ and I interrupted mildly in unison.

"Tony the Tiger. Far removed from the depiction of the affable breakfast-cereal-commercial variety. He's away at 'college' right now. He's in his freshman year at the Danbury Federal Penitentiary for extortion. He'll graduate ahead of his class if he keeps on getting good marks from the warden. Maybe even with a degree in 'macho' from the other inmates. Hey, Cizcero shouldn't be treating me like such a lightweight," he voiced.

"Then, the snub happened. I offered my hand in welcome. He was ready to shake. Peeking over my shoulder, he pulled his hand back, sidestepping right past me, ignoring my gesture. I had my arm extended like a fuckin' marble statue, suspended in midair, for what seemed like a lifetime. I turned around. He was clasping hands and embracing with Angelo. Cizcero's group, having noticed the ruse, thought it very funny. Everyone was belly-laughing at my expense. I was embarrassed as hell, in front of all my help. Even Marco, that fool of a young waiter, was pooh-poohing me. I dismissed them, sending them back to work.

"Cizcero left me feeling humiliated in my own bistro. I was pissed, but I said to myself, Why get mad? I'll release my frustrations when I slice the citrus," Louis added.

Louis intentionally leaned over the bar, speaking directly to TJ.

"I'm in accord with DA. He, too, has no use for Mr. Ralph Cizcero. DA keeps rejecting his insulting offer of $25,000 to discuss 'business' for an hour. You know what he really wants, TJ. He begs DA's counsel for 'military tactics.' He would like him to reconnoiter the movement of 'enemy troops' bivouacking outside his turf. The greedy slob, he's already planning to be numero uno even before he's promoted number 2 man. Guys like him, they always covet the lion's share. The blockhead seems to be the last to know that DA and the Dangerous Don's brother Sal are like this," he demonstrated.

Louis illustrated by crossing over the middle finger of his right hand to the knuckle of his index finger, holding for a five-second count.

"If his true ambitions were leaked, he'd be swimming with the fishes in a cement bathing suit." He chuckled.

"My sides nearly burst when DA told Ralph that what he needed most was spiritual guidance. He could save money too. For only $1, he could light a large votive candle and say three Hail Marys at Sacred Heart Cathedral. Ralph, his complexion reddening to the point of explosion, left abruptly, whimpering like a spoiled puppy. Only DA could get away with that kind of talk, humbling a wise guy like him," recounted Louis. "DA, he describes Ralph best when he calls him the quintes—"

TJ replied, "You mean quintessence?"

"Yes, thank you. DA calls him the quintessential big shot. Ralph, he has earned my fear, but certainly not my respect," asserted Louis.

Louis's spirits were picking up, and he turned toward me. He pointed at me. "Excuse me, Stanley," he uttered, begging pardon, "I didn't mean to leave you out of the conversation. It's somethin' only TJ would understand."

"No problem, Lou," I responded.

Louis, now beaming with confidence, donned a small red beret he pulled from behind the bar shelf. He was assuming the role of impresario in this opera, going on to describe the other players since defining our protagonist, Ralph Cizcero.

Louis noted, "That's his wife and daughter seated with him. I'm glad my Carmen wasn't here to see the minks those girls came wrapped in. Whew! Big bucks! These gals don't wear no faux fox furs."

"That's his wife?" I voiced in astonishment, referring to the older of the two girls. "She's a vision of loveliness. The pair can easily pass for sisters."

TJ concurred, "She's a real peach, both of them for that matter."

"The wife's name is Gina. She's a bello signora. That means a beautiful lady. Mr. Cizcero took her as his bride when she was a mere child of seventeen. She must have been the spitting image of Theresa back then. Ralph found her when he was traveling through Italy on Giorno di Festa. That's a holiday. Oh, he's an enlightened one, Mr. Ralph Cizcero. He fancies himself as the great aficionado or the dilettante of the Renaissance Era," claimed Louis.

"On a lark, twenty-one years ago, he journeyed to Florence. As the story goes, he had a vision that he would die. Fearing imminent death, he must see Michelangelo's sculpture, which captures the contemplative mood of the duke Lorenzo de Medici, on Lorenzo's tomb in the Medici Chapel at San Lorenza. Clearly, he survived through the fantastic ordeal. While participating in the festivities of a local carnival, he cast his eyes on Gina, proposed, and married her within the week," he elaborated.

I was hoping Louis would cover Theresa next, but he didn't.

"The two goons standing, who intimidated that couple before, are his bodyguards. The shorter stocky one, I know, is Jimmy 'Long Nose' Cappicola. He's Ralph's donkey," he quipped.

TJ, noticing my confusion, explained, "That means he's the driver and he carries 'hardware,' sometimes a whole store."

I understood. Not noticing anything prominent about his proboscis other than its aquiline shape, I asked, "Where is the 'long nose' cognomen derive?"

"Oh yeah," Louis said with laughter, "thanks for asking. That's in reference to another part of his anatomy. Twenty-five years ago, he was all dick and no brains, and nothing has changed since."

I should have known better, I echoed to myself, shaking my head. Louis composed himself enough to go on with his story.

"The real name of the gargantuan-size character with the *cicatrice*, or scar, carved on that *faccia-brutta*, monster face, demeanor is unknown to me. They just call him Doc," he explained.

"All right, Lou, I'll play straight man again. I asked the unimaginative rhetorical question. Is he a practicing physician?"

"Of course he's a medico, a physician," stated Lou. "Oh, he's a specialist in his field. His practice is limited, and his hours are by appointment only. He makes private house calls stat. It is rumored that he has successfully applied his interpretation of the Heimlich maneuver to approximately fifteen to twenty unwilling patients who have ungratefully expired. He administers a slight degree of manipulation with steady pressure around the throat." Strangolazione, Louis prescribed, realistically chocking himself with his hands. "I'm soffocazioni!" he squealed out. "Some words don't need translation," Louis cried out, bursting with excitement.

TJ and I were in stitches over Louis's dramatization. He supplied us with two small bar towels and humorously commanded us to stuff them in our mouths if we couldn't control ourselves. It was ironic, because he needed the towels more than we did. TJ motioned me to look up. I saw that Doc was giving us the evil eye.

"What about the priest?" TJ asked.

I wondered about his role myself. It was a mystery to me why he was in their company, and Louis was unresponsive to TJ's probe. "That good-looking guy over there in the dark-blue double-breasted suit, with the sideburns, is Johnny Tangerine. That Johnny, he's something else. From a profile, doesn't he look like 'The King'?" Louis solicited.

I nodded. There was a slight resemblance to Elvis.

Louis stated, "The sole purpose of this get-together is for Johnny to get permission from Mr. Cizcero to date his daughter."

"Does he know what he's getting into?" I inquired.

Louis replied, "Hey, the crazy fool is in love with Theresa. She's Ralph's daughter and only child. Theresa's his globo dell occhio—the apple of his eye. Excuse me, TJ. The prete cattolico, priest, you inquired about will be interceding on Johnny's behalf. The two love birds met in St. Anthony's Church at the 10:30 a.m. Sunday Mass. Johnny's doing the right thing. He's very proper in such delicate affairs of the heart. Hey, let me tell you guys somethin'. Just look at that Theresa. She's only nineteen and already a great bella, beauty, just like her mother. They say whenever she's around Johnny, she's on cloud nine."

My eyes entered into a pact, time-sharing between Gina and Theresa. With her chestnut-brown hair brushed back away from her forehead, swept back at the sides, softened in a drape chignon, perfect lips, and soft hazel eyes chiseled on an angelic face, Theresa was both innocent and voluptuous in one breath. It didn't hurt with her having such a thin waist to possess such a magnificent set of breasts that certainly filled out her snug, seasonal colored V-neck sweater, presenting an unfair advantage to other girls her age. Her skirt was way too short for that time of year, but I'm sure no one was complaining about those shapely thighs. I was convinced Theresa was worth the risk Johnny was taking.

"That Johnny, he only travels first-class with the ladies. He's a good kid," Louis remarked.

"What kid?" TJ objected. "He's forty-four years old. Johnny was seven grades ahead of me in grammar school," he exclaimed.

TJ and I were amused with his declaration. Louis defended, "Hell, when you reach your fifty-second birthday like me, everyone seems like a kid." Excitedly, he stated, "Let's all calm down, before Jimmy or Doc comes over here. They're getting ready to start."

He was nervously pleading with us as his hands trembled.

"Louis, how do you know so much?" I teased.

"Hey, Stanley, TJ will tell you, sometimes it's like a fuckin' vegetable patch in here. The corn has ears, the potatoes have eyes, and the beans talk," he replied seriously.

We laughed.

I informed him, "Louis, you're too much."

I was thinking to myself, John Henry would have appreciated this twisted version of a fourth-grade personification of produce.

"Be quiet," he warned. "It's time for the opening curtain." Louis held up a single finger.

TJ whispered, "To laugh now would be insalubrious."

Though I didn't recognize the adjective, I understood its meaning. It wouldn't be healthy for us to snicker.

The priest introduced Johnny. Speaking on his behalf, he was boastful of all of Johnny's attributes for what seemed like minutes. The priest took a deep breath. He went into a prolix speech expounding on Johnny's genealogical chart. It was still hazy to me, but with the visual aid of a diagram with nomenclature, he attempted in theory to prove Johnny's ancestral linkage to Tiberius, second emperor of Rome. The exhausted father stepped back after he was through with his deliverance. Mr. Cizcero led the throng in clapping and cheers.

"Does he have the proper legal training?" Mr. Cizcero spoke. He directing his question to the priest rather than to Johnny.

The padre answered yes and something about a law degree from Detroit. Mr. Cizcero nodded.

"What was that all about?" I inquisitively begged Louis.

Louis explained, "It's a prerequisite for the courtship, and besides, it comes in handy when he picks up chicks."

TJ was disbelieving, and I was wowed.

"Hell, he hasn't practiced law a day in his life. He runs a pizza joint in Bellville with his cousin Rocco Gallo," TJ merrily replied.

We all chuckled.

"TJ, you're missing the 'ha, ha, ha' vital point," Louis proclaimed, pointing in his face.

"Which is…?"

"That Johnny, with his flowery elocution, would have made one hell of a mouthpiece," a grinning Louis symbolically assessed.

The boyfriend, who was a little fidgety from waiting, stepped forward. Mr. Cizcero permitted Johnny to touch his pinky ring.

Louis interpreted, "Oh, that's a good sign. That preliminary vote of confidence should make Johnny feel at ease. Johnny's reflex response without reluctance is his pledge of allegiance to Ralph. It's kind of like the promise the knight made to the king in the Middle Ages. What's the term I want to say, TJ?" he asked.

He answered, "You mean feudal oath."

"Thank you, TJ. Look, you guys. Johnny is getting ready to speak," Lou informed.

Johnny, taking his cue from the priest, stepped forward.

"I am privileged to make an introduction to this great assemblage," he proclaimed.

Johnny acknowledged the presence of the bodyguards. At first, they appeared ambivalent to his gesture, but after checking Ralph's happy face for tacit approval, they managed toothy smiles.

In a shrill, monotone voice, Johnny delivered, "Salutations, Mr. Cizcero. Thank you, noble one. I bring exaltation to thy name! Io! Io! Io! Of course, my exhilaration in meeting you is self-explanatory. I rejoice in this momentous occasion! May the stars that twinkle bright in the twilight bow to thy majestic aura! May the moon glow when you command and the sun gleaming bright at your pleasure create an iridescence at your whim! May the blue waters of the seven seas affectionately wave to say hello! May only the finest of wines exuberate the sensitivity of your palate! May your sumptuous meals always be lavish, epicurean delights! Henceforth, by order of royal decree, let only ambrosia and, exclusively, the sweetest of nectars be worthy staples for your impeccably good taste! May legends of trumpeters sound their horns triumphantly on this spectacular day! May the songs of the sirens soothe your savage spirit with joy! May pixies dance and harps play in perfect, melodious harmony! May birds of all specie sing praises to your name! I extend laureation elsewhere, from the animal kingdom, including the insect world, their only vociferous lamentation being their unfortuitous absence! Regretfully, for lack of time, I am unable to sufficiently expound on all the besetments yet to come! Summun bonum! Excelsior! Excelsior! Excelsior! Summun bonum! Hip hip hurrah! Hip hip hurrah! I offer tribute, my sovereign. Let me include any other exclamatories due!"

In my perplexed state, I looked at TJ for assurance that what my ears heard was real, Johnny's fantastic sesquipedalian address. His shell-shocked expression assented without words. Seemingly, Cizcero and his assemblage thought it swell. Everyone was exclaiming bravo and politely clapping, including the two goons. Louis reaffirmed my state of mind.

"Hey, I told you guys that this is a once-in-a-lifetime show. It's an extravaganza!" he proclaimed.

"That evoked memories," I cleverly related to TJ, after a moment of silent meditation. "I hadn't heard such a prosaic exclamation delivered with eloquence since my American Civilization II course in college, when Professor Davidhoff recited the oration of William Jennings Bryan's impassioned 'Speech of Silver in 1896,'" I proudly professed.

Not flinching for a second, TJ replied, tongue in cheek, "No, Stanley, it's definitely reminiscent of the rhapsodical oratories of Marcus Tullius Cicero, especially his letter to Julius Caesar dated around 47BC, where he praised Caesar's gracious benevolence in sparing the lives of his vanquished adversaries who had surrendered at Corfinium, or his pedantic entreaties to same Caesar between 47 and 44 BC on behalf of subjects desiring amnesty and permission to return to Rome after the civil war."

Obviously outwitted, but in my mind by only the slimmest of margins, I responded, "Touché." Louis was talking with his hands again, asking for quiet.

"Hey, you guys, that's a beautiful thing, especially that retort by TJ, and Stanley's concession, talkin' French, but if you two historical show-offs are finished, Johnny is trying to continue," Louis articulated.

"All exclamations bestowed on your lovely wife, the mother who bore this exquisite creature," Johnny continued.

With fixed attention, his eyes went from Gina to Theresa. He wiped off his moderate perspiration with a handkerchief before he looked lovingly to Gina.

"It gives me great honor to present Mrs. Cizcero with this baker's dozen long-stemmed red American beauty roses as a token of my gratitude," he emphatically stated.

The priest handed Johnny the bouquet. He offered it to Gina, and she accepted. Her gaze never left him.

Louis was busy counting the digits on his left hand. "That Johnny, he's totaling points now. You guys can learn a lot from this," he remarked.

"As wonderful as nature created this spectacular radiant efflorescence, these petals wither when compared to the splendor of your majestic beauty. You are a queen among women," Johnny complimented.

Johnny inquired, directing his question to Mr. Cizcero, if he could kiss Gina's hand. Ralph nodded his approval, and Johnny affectionately put his pursed lips to the back of Gina's palm.

"Hey, let me tell you guys somethin'. That Gina, she's blushing like a schoolgirl. She's enamored with Johnny's charms. Did you witness the passion in her eyes with those admiring glances at Johnny? She's hopelessly spellbound," Louis foreboded.

TJ pointed out, "Lou, I think you're getting carried away."

"Hey, fuckin' A, didn't you guys notice? Even a blind man can see that she admires his audacity and can't resist his virility. Johnny is unequivocally eager to show Gina all his masculine charms. Why shouldn't he? She still has a teenage body at thirty-seven," Lou championed.

TJ and I stared at each other. The wheels were turning in both our minds.

He reasoned, "That means Johnny is…"

At the exact time, we both deduced, "Older than the mother."

I tapped him on the arm first and informed him that he owed me a beer. He agreed reluctantly.

It was a game traced to our college days with a nice reward for the winner.

"Oh, so elementary, this pair of Dr. Watsons," voiced a perceptive Louis. "Next time someone steals my fuckin' bottle opener, I'll have to hire you guys as sleuths. Boy, Ralph's Gina is elegant, and she's oh so tight. That woman gives me fever, the likes of which malaria would be a blessing!"

In light of the moment, he wrapped a bar towel around his head. Moisture was starting to appear on Louis's nose.

"She's not wearing a bra. Feast your eyes on the outline of those capezzolos, nipples. Just keep watching. I'm waiting, in anticipation, for those poppe, breasts, to pop that solitary button on that sheer silk blouse that is clinging to those spectacular eggplants. She has perfect gambas, legs, and a cupcake deretano. Hey, let me tell you guys somethin'. Know what I mean?" Louis exclaimed.

Louis formed the silhouette of her petite derrifere with his cupped hands. He cracked us up. TJ and I had no choice but to put our heads on the bar, unable to restrain our laughter any longer.

TJ regained his composure, after catching his breath.

"Louis, you're starting to lose your marbles. You certainly have a vivid imagination," he said.

"Imagination, you guys? Okay, imagine this. My darling Gina is already a 10, right? I'm going to make her an 11 just for Johnny, because he's a good kid. I'll give her an extra mammella, teat. It seems quite practical to me that while his left and right hands are occupied, the mouth has somethin' to do. That way, no extremity may need to feel neglected," he predicted.

TJ and I were hopelessly helpless, holding on to our towels, heads bowed, as we listened to Lou's ranting.

"Yes," he joked nervously, "I realize I'm overstepping the boundaries of perfectly good taste, but I can't help myself. That Ralph Cizcero, he still has me all wound up. What is perplexing to me is, How can Cizcero be so naive not to be alerted to the attraction between Gina and Johnny? She desires him as her amante, lover, and Gina will play her role as the adulterine. Cizcero has served his purpose. Since his preoccupation with 'war games,' he can't devote proper attention to his youthful Gina. She's a young woman who has special needs that must be satisfied by a man with vitalita. To disregard his adoring wife and let her emotions rove, his mind must be in vecchiaia, old age. What the hell! I'll play droghiere, doctor, and that is my diagnosis. I'll send him off to the gerontocomio, home for the aged," Louis prescribed.

Utilizing two fingers from his right hand, Louis walked them in front of us on the bar.

"Let me get this straight. Are you suggesting an affaire d'amour," I quizzed, "between Johnny and Gina? I understand that the purpose of this meeting is because Johnny loves Theresa."

"Stanley, you and this other guy here, you both enjoy putting me on. Hey, you guys like bustin' my onions with this I-don't-speak-French routine. You ask about a love affair between Johnny and Gina? Most definitely, besides the one with Theresa."

"He loves them both, but Gina is a compulsively dangerous challenge," Louis replied with authority.

I implored to Lou, "I hope you're not suggesting the three are going to participate in a ménage…"

I knew the phrase, but I purposely wanted Louis to pronounce it.

"Cat got your tongue? I'll be daring. A ménage à trois? Now, you guys have me talkin' French. Johnny, the mother, and the daughter all in one bed."

Louis displayed three fingers.

"That would be risqué. Hey, you guys, I'm doing it again. I'm talkin' French. I know that Johnny has more brass than the rings down at the merry-go round in Asbury Park, yet I think that's too kinky, even for him. His forte would definitely be to give the girls separate but equal treatment. He'll probably work 'em both over and ride 'em like a champion. I don't know, maybe this Johnny is crazy like a fox and would chance it," he added after a second's muse. "You know, you guys, you can learn a lot from this."

Because TJ and I were totally losing our cool, we had to put those towels over our mouths to muffle our excitement.

Louis's forehead, I noticed, was beginning to perspire.

Relaxed again, I foretold, "Beware, even the fox can be killed, as in vulpicide."

Louis pronounced, "Oh, certainly, that goes without saying, especially if Cizcero should find out he's playing the cuckold. What do you expect? He's going to be generosamente, generous, with Johnny for making love to his wife? With his irascible demeanor over trifles, Cizcero would reach new heights of vindictiveness with such an embarrassment. He would requite the disgrace to save face with the other capos in the family. He would eradicate Johnny by probably having him emasculated. Then, poor Johnny would be rendered useless. He wouldn't even be able to soffocare, choke, his own polastro, chicken."

Louis shook his tight fist vigorously up and down.

"Hope, they say, can be eternal. Maybe, just maybe, when his hair begins to grow into a nice, thick-flowing mane and he learns to whinny, Johnny could enter himself as a cavallo castrato, gelding. He could try to qualify in the third race at Monmouth Park, in a mile and sixteenth," a straight-faced Louis replied.

He was playacting, as if he were holding on to reins.

Neither TJ nor I could handle this latest outburst. We hid our faces in our hands. My stomach was hurting so badly I couldn't take any more funny declarations.

"Hey, let me tell you guys somethin' else. Think you hurt? Pity the poor girls. Cizcero's unrighteous retribution would eventually filter down to them. They would have to be punished for goin' bad. Most assuredly, he would commit Gina to an insane asylum, for a long-term cure, till her mind got better, and force Theresa to enter a convent to repent, till he absolves her. If you think I'm sick in the head, well, that nut Cizcero can justify this punishment and his cohorts will slap him on the back because he is doin' the right thing. He has no respect for women. I once heard him taunting one of his recalcitrant lieutenants, 'If you were a fuckin' woman, I'd slap you.' Of course, this wild tale of the three lovers' doom is all academic should some young turk looking for advancement opportunities in the organization eliminate Cizcero, to be the main ghi, guy," Louis chronicled.

Lou unveiled a white hanky from his back pocket to pat the sweat dripping down to his cheeks. He took a deep breath and observed the Cizcero party. Lou informed us that Cizcero and the priest were still arguing a point of proper protocol. Attentive that our mugs were empty, he returned with two slightly overflowing, fresh ones.

"Hey, let me tell you guys somethin'. You might think I'm crazy for saying this…"

Both of us interrupted him and kiddingly assured him he wasn't insane.

"But if Gina, as beautiful as she is, came on to me bare-ass naked and begged me to make mad, passionate love to her, well, my erection would indicate my eagerness, but my fuckin' cervello, brain, would restrain me from going after the forbidden fruit," he confessed with all honesty.

Before Louis had a chance to repeat another sound, TJ was falling off his barstool. I went over to my pal with the intention of helping him up, but I was holding my rib cage, stumbling, then joining him on the dirty floor, intoxicated with laughter. I wanted to say, "Here we are, two so-called professionals, acting like blabbering idiots," but the words wouldn't come out. My sides were nearly bursting from all this laughing. We both pointed up at Louis, who was looking down at us, giving us the "Shame on you" sign language; the bottom of one finger was briskly rubbing the top of the index finger on the other hand, as if striking a match. We helped each other to our wobbly feet and back to our stools. Louis continued to sweat as he candidly talked about Ralph.

"I'll share a secret with you guys. I have overheard Cizcero talking when too much wine was getting to his head. He was boasting to his cronies about Gina, 'Only the Lord can take that woman away from me.' Imagine the conceit," he capsulized.

"Hey, let me tell you guys somethin'. I could get killed for thinking like this, let alone for speaking about it. Oh boy! Oh boy! A thought just whisked through my mind. I sure hope Cizcero isn't chiaro veggente, clairvoyant," Louis declared, his mouth agape.

Louis pulled out his hanky again to wipe his wet face. He placed his finger into his gin and tonic and then made the sign of the cross. Soon, Louis realized the severity of his act.

Realizing the severity of his act, he gasped, "Now I've done it. I have committed sacrilege. I'll have to get my ass up early tomorrow and go to Mass. I blame all my foolish behavior on that wicked Cizcero."

"You better go for a week straight," I scolded him.

TJ asserted, "Forget the week, Stanley. Louis needs a whole month."

Louis instructed us that the fine points had been worked out and they were ready to resume the ceremony. He wiped his sweaty face, again, but held on to his hanky.

"What are his intentions?" Mr. Cizcero blustered in a gruff voice, directed to the priest.

Johnny stepped forward. "My intentions are purely noble. I will treat her with proper respect. You may entrust her care with me. I assume the responsibility of protectorate. I will worship the ground she walks on," he concluded.

Johnny gingerly took a step back.

Mr. Cizcero jerked his head forward and downward, signifying approval.

"What is his request?" he demanded, displaying the same mannerisms to the priest.

Johnny, again, stepped forward. "I would like the honor of..."

His projection a little shaken, the good father patted him on the back for encouragement.

"I would like the honor of sharing a salad with your daughter. Her choice of dressing, per your discretion," he proudly expressed with conviction.

"Hey, Angel?" Mr. Cizcero softly inquired. His voice changing a few degrees in octave, trying to evoke a response from Theresa. It was hardly necessary. Her glow and wide-eyed smile confirmed her acceptance without saying a word.

Mr. Cizcero checked out Johnny, looked over at his daughter, and redirected his attention back to him.

Waving his finger at Johnny, he growled out of the corner of his mouth, his voice returning to normal, "No red wine vinegar mixed with her olive oil. She's not twenty-one yet."

There was an uneasy silence over the party, until Mr. Cizcero broke out with a big grin. He was laughing. Cizcero encouraged everyone to join in on the fun of his clever remark.

"Hey, let me tell you guys somethin'. Whew, it's acceptable. Johnny's in," a relieved Louis rejoiced. "Leave it to that Cizcero to keep the crowd in suspense with his attempt at humor," Louis ridiculed. "Boy, that was a beautiful thing, that request by Johnny. No way Cizcero could reject that. Johnny can breathe a sigh of relief now. He's in like Flynn. Everything to follow will be anticlimactic. I'll say it again. That Johnny, he only travels first-class with the ladies," he recapitulated.

Louis wiped his brow again, but this time with a bar towel, since his hanky was soaking wet.

Mr. and Mrs. Cizcero each took a pinch of salt and tossed it in the air while sobbing maudlin tears.

"She's no longer Daddy's little girl," Louis translated.

Mr. Cizcero gently pulled Johnny's cheek.

"What's that represent, Lou?" I interjected.

"Oh! That's just a subtle reminder to Johnny that if he 'goes bad' and ruins Theresa's reputation, he might as well commit suicide, because the pain inflicted will be worse, like I mentioned before." Then Louis whispered, "Here comes the pièce de résistance. Hey, I'm talkin' French again."

Mr. Cizcero and Johnny pulled apart a round loaf of sesame-seeded bread.

"Great!" Louis pronounced. "He personally accepts Johnny. It's consummated."

Everyone was congratulating Johnny. Angelo handed out cigars. Theresa stood to accompany Johnny to another booth. A sweaty-palmed Louis, not wanting to be left out, shook hands with TJ and me.

"You guys can learn a lot from this," Louis repeated.

TJ and I were so engrossed with the proceedings that we didn't realize the girls were standing right behind us. Samantha was hysterically laughing, and I was trying to discourage her from pointing to the Cizcero group. They were looking over, and she made it too obvious that her fun was directed at them. My heart jumped to my throat when Jimmy walked up to us with a minacious expression on his mug. I'd have to defend Sam's honor, I extolled quixotically. With three rapid-fired lefts, I imagined that I would stun him before he countered with a gun right out of his pocket.

His voice shook the place when he belted out, "What's with the fuckin' hyena? If you can't keep that dumb broad quiet, I'll—"

Before Jimmy could curse another word and before I could jump off my stool, TJ had the spunk to divert Jimmy's attention by pointing to Samantha while, at the same time, making little circles around his ear in the air with his finger.

Jimmy, speechless for a microsecond, blurted out, "Sorry, I didn't know she was fuckin' cuckoo. Just get her the fuck out of here."

He didn't have to say it twice—we were out of there. A nervous Louis was gracious enough to expedite our departure by putting our drinks on the cuff. The last thing I remember is Louis doffing his cap, waving, and his wishing epilogue, "Arrivederci, Parisians."

TJ and I were both shivering when we stepped outside, not because of the coldness of the twenty-degree temperature, but because we escaped the "heat" inside.

"Thank you, Odysseus." I was referring to one of the Homeric heroes in the *Iliad* and the ultimate warrior in the *Odyssey* who knew when cunning had a more advantageous effect than brawn. "That was damn close," I said. TJ concurred.

"TJ," I offered, "as ridiculous and unorthodox as this custom was, it was still very chivalrous on Johnny's part."

"No, it was heraldic," he replied.

My buddy was challenging me in a word-association contest, or more appropriately, he was verbally jousting with me on this theme.

I countered with, "Excuse me, his behavior was of errantry."

"Sorry, Mr. Jankowski," he pronounced with a mischievous smile, "not only was he gallant, but also valorous."

The wind was biting. The girls were scared, tired, anxious to leave, and I was stymied to get in the last repartee. Willing to concede to his perfectly timed double answer, I turned my back on him and unconsciously delivered a "Good night." "Good knight" instantly clicked in my head. I spun around. TJ was totally off guard, shaking his fist. I just didn't have the guts to inform him that my reply was just dumb luck.

"You, son of a gun, 'good knight'? That's the definitive. It's the mot juste, the precise word. Now, you have me speaking French or, as Louis aptly says, talkin' French. There is no more. Only you come up with that one. I'll call you to play some platform tennis."

"Good knight," he begrudgingly repeated.

We left in separate cars to go home.

After that evening, I saw TJ about three times before the scandal hit the papers.

CHAPTER III

I entered the doorway of the Gondolier. Louis noticed me as soon as I walked over to the bar area, where he was working. Weary-eyed as ever and slightly perspiring, he was slicing lemons and limes with a long serrated carving knife on a wooden board, and doing a rather neat job of it, I mused. After reaching for a towel to dry himself, he shook my hand.

"Long time no see, Stanley," he greeted me.

Teasingly, I voiced, "Yeah, Lou, I'm a sailor," thinking of the homonym *sea*.

My sophomoric pun went over his head, and just as well, because Lou wasn't his humorous self. Louis brought over a cold draft. He expressed deep regret that TJ had been implicated in such a scam.

"He's done a lot for Newark. I have my own axiom: 'The good die young, and the best get persecuted,' especially by the mayor and his henchman, Page," he voiced indignantly. "I'd like to see the day when both of them get their ears pinned back."

At that instant, Louis took the fifteen-inch, saw-toothed carving knife and stabbed a whole orange, impaling it, with the blade stuck to the cutting board.

"Don't mind me. Sometimes I get carried away with aggression, but I only release my frustrations on the citrus," he defended.

"Louis," I asked, "when was the last time you saw TJ?"

"Today is Thursday, right? I think…yes, I saw him Sunday night. Unfortunately, I didn't have much chance to talk to him, because he was busy, sitting at a table with DA," he informed.

"Louis, do you mean to say that the district attorney was here, questioning TJ?" I posed.

Louis seemed dumbfounded for a minute, and then he smiled.

"No. No. Dom over there," he stated.

He motioned behind me to my left. I swiveled around on my stool. Seated at a small corner table by himself was Dominic Anthony Salutini. "That's right, they call him DA," I said as I turned to say to Louis, but he had disappeared to the opposite end of the bar to wait on customers.

I recognized the distinguished, silver-haired septuagenarian with the courtly presence. Every strand of his thick head of hair was brushed back from his forehead neatly in place with the aid of a little gel. TJ had introduced me to him some time ago. His thin stature belied any lack of self-assurance. Dom simply commanded respect, and you wanted him to respect you. With a clear and articulate way of speech, it wouldn't surprise you if he said he did commentary on the radio or narration for films.

His voice was that good. Dom was TJ's political mentor of sorts. I can remember TJ excusing himself from our table at a fundraising dinner I attended with Samantha. TJ had a troubled look on his face and proceeded to buttonhole Dom in a corner for twenty-five minutes, but when he returned to his seat, he was tranquil.

"Dom just took the monkey off my back. I had to implement a delicate maneuver around certain people, who shall remain anonymous, in the mayor's policy office on an issue they opposed and I wanted promulgated to council. I wanted to avoid any imbroglio. Dom expounded ammunition for my prolepsis and instructed me on the skill of applying a 'political masse.' It was a real stroke of genius. That DA, he's something. He always has the uncanny knack for finding the right piece to the puzzle even when it doesn't appear to fit," TJ confided to me.

DA was a maker and shaker behind the scenes. He didn't suffer fools gladly, but those he chose to share his calculating advice with would come away with a vital strategy point previously overlooked. Having his political savvy on your side could be the difference, they said, in winning a close election. He was a player in Newark's prior commission form of government and now the venerated statesman from the North Ward. According to TJ, Dom was the man who refused to do business with the Mob. It was traditional to toast his good graces with a bottle of Möet & Chandon's Dom Pérignon-label champagne upon following his sage advice to victory.

Legend has it that one grateful politician, a former state senator, who was a dark horse candidate made up what seemed like an impossible stretch run, crossing the finish line after trailing by twenty furlongs (20 percentage points in the pre-election polls), presented DA with a rare Nebuchadnezzar gift (twenty bottles in one). Although I was in awe of him myself, I decided to go for it and brazenly walked over to his table. I expected him to brush me off in a condescending tone.

"Mr. Salutini, may I have a minute of your time, sir?" I beseeched.

He looked up after sipping his hot beverage. Thankfully, he was smiling. Mr. Salutini wiped his mouth with the linen napkin he pulled from his lap. He wore a wide striped suit, black shirt, and solid white tie held neatly in place with a jeweled tie tack. Mr. Salutini was perfectly attired for a role in *Guys and Dolls*.

"I have just finished indulging in a light repast," he answered. "It's remarkable. I now live in West Orange, but I still eat and play in Newark. I am very fond of terrapin soup. This is one of few places in New Jersey that not only lists it on their menu but can also prepare this delicacy well enough to suit my taste buds. Already, I have walked out of one of the so-called finer establishments because they tried to deceive me with mock turtle soup. I didn't leave, though, sans informing the chef that I was sorry…for him. Bless that dear George, all hobbled up. He still comes in here as a favor to me to prepare this exquisite creation. My grandchild Veronica likes to jest about my addiction. That little sweetie pie, she says to me, 'Grandpa, please don't eat too much turtle soup.' She's exceptional for only four years old. You'll beg my pardon. I have gone on too long," voiced DA.

He addressed, "Certainly, Mr. Stanley Jankowski, please pull up a chair."

I was astonished he recalled my full name.

Aware of my amazement, DA queried, "You're so surprised I remember your name? I'll share with you a valuable lesson. The most precious commodity a person has is his or her name. Even people living in an impecunious state all their lives have the dignity of their names. You give honor to a man when you say his name. It tells him that he is important to you." Dom then noted, "If you passed through here ten thousand people, all colors of the rainbow, that I had met on one or two previous occasions, I could recall the full names of nine thousand nine hundred and eighty-five. You must extend an old man an allowance for a small margin of error." He laughed.

Dom wasn't one to measure his words. He spoke calmly and confidently as he folded his arms across his body.

"The most interestingly profound names are the uncommon palindromes. These are words whose spelling inverted is identical to it forward, i.e., Harrah, Maddam, Miccim, Ravar, Peep, Soos. With the one-syllable words in this category, oddly enough, I employ reverse notation because I can't always define the root. A word of caution, though: if you come upon a rare first and last name which is a monosyllable double palindrome, such as Eve Nyn, please disregard my advice and punt on third down," DA joked. "Oriental names, I must concede, are the most difficult for me to recall, but at a wedding reception held in Fort Lee, I successfully associated all the names of the two hundred Chinese guests I was introduced to," he claimed, squeezing his chin.

I had a troubled look of misgiving on my face, and he was smiling.

"It's not so prodigious as it seems when you've been practicing it for over fifty-five years. Example: I've been in your company twice before, and your good friend has mentioned your name more than once. When I stumped for some of those political big shots, like ex-mayor Villani, and helped to make them prominent in the state, how was I going to get out the vote if I couldn't remember people's names? I study a man or woman's features, saying their complete name ten times in succession, and play a mental word-association game. I'll prove it to you with a practical application. Take for instance your name," DA said.

"Most people might think your name is difficult to recall with its Eastern European flavor, precisely Polish extraction, and educated guess that the origin is from the Kraków area, but for me it's easy. I take the derivatives. Stanley is baseball. One of my favorite players was 'Stan the Man' Musial, the former St. Louis Cardinals' slugger of the forties, fifties, and early sixties. Being Italian American, when I heard Jankowski, it immediately inspired me to think of the Roman god of gates and doors, Janus. The weather is cold and snowy in the month of January, and you've lost a cow on skis. Henceforth, I logically come up with Stanley Jankowski, the 'de rigueur,' to properly address you by," he instructed in an earnest tone.

DA had captivated an audience of one. I wanted to stand up and applaud his majestic performance of mind recall, but least of all, my purpose here was not for a sideshow.

"Mr. Salutini, could you please—"

Dom's interruption created an abscission in my request.

"Please, Stanley, call me DA. Forgive me for talking too much. Thank you for your patience with me. Sometimes I go off on a tangent," he pleaded, squeezing his clean-shaven chin. Dom asked sincerely, "You wish to find out about your friend Thomas, no doubt?"

"Yes," I answered him.

DA stated, "You are his closest friend, and it is good of you to want to know what happened. Concerning friends, I have my own aphorism: 'Good friends are like good wine, there are only a few vintage years.'"

A young waiter hustled over at the sight of DA's raised hand signal.

"Marco, bring two more of these," he said, pointing to his cappuccino cup. "Ditto on the Grand Marnier, please," he ordered.

"Mr. Salutini, shall I serve the liquor with the cappuccino?" Marco inquired.

Dom was slightly piqued, and his bushy gray eyebrows arched high from his pale blues.

"Indubitably, you serve them together. Are you in total disregard in comprehending that the Grand Marnier is my saccharine alternative to white sugar? Your lack of punctual service worries me. Go now, you are dismissed. Can't you see my guest is expecting to indulge his aperitif while antemortem?" he responded rather contemptuously.

Marco, starting to fidget, was just standing there in bewilderment.

DA smiled and pronounced, "Before he dies of thirst."

Now understanding, Marco ran off to the bar.

I could hear DA mumble "Distractions" under his breath while he shook his head.

"Let's get on with the business of men," he quoted after regaining his composure. "Rest assured, Stanley, Thomas didn't do anything criminal. His conduct was exemplary. He was setup, possibly as early as three years ago, when Darryl Page came aboard as the mayor's legal counsel. This was an attempt to curtail Thomas's overwhelming popularity, but I'll touch on that within its logical consistency," he solemnly declared.

DA scratched his chin, peering left and then right before continuing his narrative.

"Let's first preface the events of a month ago. I'm sure you're familiar with *The Star-Ledger*'s accounts disclosing corruption within Thomas's department. He had accepted the challenge of the newly formed Housing and Economic Development Administration, or HEDA. Concentrating his energies in the continuing Federal Green Acres Project for renovating city-owned properties, he delegated the responsibilities for securing contracts to his two assistants, A. Melvin Jackson and Leonard Minstein, duties that they performed under the prior directorship of Jess Monroe. He tired of the high-profile position as ombudsman with its endless disquisitions on urban affairs. Twenty-five months of handling the citizens' problems had become frustrating for him. Thomas was reacting too personally to every individual's difficult situation he faced, most of which were never going to be satisfactorily resolved. Here was a chance, afforded him, to get out in the field and do what he felt was a sense of accomplishment," DA said distinctly.

"Of course, I did not give my countenance for this move. Thomas was getting no plum. I was suspicious of the mayor's intentions. Jess Monroe, the former housing director, surprised everyone with his unexpected retirement announcement. Jackson and

Minstein worked for him, and Thomas inherited their employment. I shared with Thomas that sources close to me had hinted of improprieties taking place in housing. It was perceived, they said, that certain people were in other people's pockets. Blindly, he just ignored it as hearsay. Thomas jumped too impetuously at the mayor's offer of the housing director's title, and Taylor capitulated too easily to include the EDA. You have to remember that Thomas was devoted to the mayor and believed in his leadership. Unbeknownst to Thomas, the mayor had deliberately manipulated him into a corner. He could now be held accountable to the mayor, while with him as ombudsman, only a majority of the city council could relieve him of his duties," DA offered.

"What I can't fathom was the mayor's motive in making a move like this. Wasn't TJ at one time the chief adviser and still the campaign manager who had triumphed the mayor to three successive terms of office and a soon-to-be fourth?" I asked incredulously.

I looked into his pale-blue eyes, which seemed to change tint, expecting a direct answer.

"I will cover that in a minute. Let me continue," DA replied. "Thomas had unwittingly surfaced the kickback scheme of his two subordinates. Their modus operandi was exposed, as fate would have it, when Minstein returned from a Disneyland vacation with his family. His return flight was unexpectedly forced to land at O'Hare Airport due to engine problems. On top of that, heavy fog coming off Lake Michigan postponed all departures. He would arrive late for the bid that following morning. An unforeseeable car accident to Jackson on his way to work, rendering him helpless, initiated Thomas due to their dual absence to publicly open all sealed bids in the presence of vendors and undercover FBI agents posing as building contractors, clerks, and janitors. It was mere coincidence that Thomas was even there that morning. He had only come in for a minute to pick up blueprints and was walking out the door when a security guard intercepted him and told him of the two missing assistants. Naturally, he handled the bids," DA clearly noted.

"From what I heard, the room was chaos. Before he did, some vendors were challenging Thomas to open all the sealed envelopes in public, while other distinct voices were threatening him to take the bids back to his office. He couldn't understand their displeasure. Thomas, along with everyone else, was aghast when he discovered that two of the sealed bids he opened were found blank, although signed on each page by authorized company officials, one containing $40,000 in hundred-dollar bills, from the Wm. McBean Co., and the other $38,000 in smaller denominations from Komacozzi Brothers. Representatives from both companies, not wanting to explain the money or the blank quotes, stormed out of the room, hurling obscenities at Thomas. Fortuitously, they were charged with bribery and arrested shortly after getting to their cars. Upon later investigation, it was found that both companies were one and the same. McBean Co. was registered as a minority vendor. Reports from eyewitnesses who were on the scene described the atmosphere as absolute bedlam. People were screaming, levying accusations and pointing fingers in Thomas's direction. Not a newspaper photographer but someone who 'just happened to have a camera' took snapshots of a confused Thomas sitting at the bid table with all this money piled in front of him," Dom graphically stated.

"Little did he suspect that in the past, the two rogues would presumably take all the sealed bids back to their respective office, where behind closed doors they would presupposedly gloat over their illicit booty. Afterward, they'd divvy up the money. In this case, $39,000 each minus whatever 'slice' they were going to mail Jess Monroe, whose involvement I will cover later. What a nice day's bonus for two reputedly honest civil servants. After prices were compared, they would wave their magic wands, filling in the right arithmetic on the blank bids, reseal them, go outside, and announce the successful bidder.

"This way, they could adhere to the public opening of bids most municipal governments adopt. In retrospect, the fools' scheme was both ingenious in its cleverness and ingenuous in its simplicity. There were no midnight back-alley meetings to receive their payola. Their transactions took place publicly in daylight in the guise of a hand-delivered sealed envelope containing an unfilled bid. With two of them in on the take, there was always one of them present to control things. If a confrontation ever arose, they could simply reject all unopened bids that day. Still, they had no contingency plan, never thinking that circumstance might prevent both of them from being present. Minstein, I would venture, telephoned Jackson from the airport, explaining his dilemma about the flight not getting off the ground due to weather conditions. He never suspected a freak traffic accident would prevent Jackson from being present at the bid the following morning," he artfully intimated.

DA then related, "Not meaning to diminish the seriousness of Thomas's misfortune to be present that day, an amusing 'sidebar' added to the debacle. Minstein arrived about five minutes too late. He was unshaven, hair unkempt, and perspiring. He was dressed in a tropical shirt and safari shorts. Apparently, he abandoned his wife and kids at Newark Airport, taking a cab in a race against time to get to the bid room. When he realized that Jackson never showed up and the consequences to himself as to what Thomas had unmasked in front of all present, he started to shake spasmodically. Minstein started to pace the floor, incessantly rambling about Mickey Mouse, Donald Duck, and Pluto. Ah, he wanted his verbigerations to be perceived as a form of schizophrenia. Too bad. Even an amateur psychiatrist couldn't be deceived by his ploy of being crazy. He was just acting a little Goofy, knowing he faced a possible thirty years in the slammer," DA humorously remarked.

Massaging his chin with his right hand, DA looked about before continuing to talk. I didn't understand why.

"Thomas never knew that the bids were not opened at the 9:00 a.m. deadline," Dom said, "but maybe an hour or so later. He trusted his two underlings. Innocuously, Thomas had prematurely ended a federal sting operation investigating alleged corruption involving federal monies appropriated to cities for legitimate urban renovation, which the press cleverly dubbed *con*struction. Though the feds had sufficient evidence with informants, surveillance, and wiretaps to make their case stick, they were miffed that their operation was curtailed five weeks sooner than scheduled. They couldn't infiltrate and ferret out all the accomplices in the time frame they had allocated, thus untangling the scam on their own schedule," Dom relayed.

"The investigators charged that Thomas deprived them of adding more to their dossier. No way were they going to credit Thomas on his disclosure, or for saving the taxpayers money. Maybe they just liked being dressed up in their Halloween costumes a little longer. They were giving Thomas a rough time with his naivete. He did his best to cooperate with federal officials, going so far as to waive his right to legal counsel and take a lie detector test, but for five days a horde of assistant US attorneys interrogated him ad nauseum. Thomas pleaded his innocence, but the FBI regional bureau chief was an overzealous eager beaver on a holy war crusade, attempting to coerce a confession out of him. He threatened to lump federal charges of bribery, conspiracy to commit bribery, extortion, tax evasion, and failure to notice irregularities in the awarding of bids involving federal funds. Menacing charges on Thomas, for the murder of Cock Robin, would have been consistent with this type of nearsighted justice," DA told me.

"With the impending mayoral election coming due May 14, the mayor's political opponents seized the opportunity to cry corruption in his administration. 'Corruption in HEDA' became a banner headline. One magazine I thought fairly reputable, which was featuring 'Crime in Politics,' endeavored to do an exposé on Thomas. The material had a stench reminiscent of McCarthyism. Pshaw, some ignominious publishers will do anything to increase circulation," DA opinioned.

"The chief antagonist, Oliver Ramsey, the 'law and order' candidate, did all he could to sully the reputation of Thomas with front-page news. His aim was to attack the mayor through Thomas. He accused Thomas of malfeasance. Ramsey insinuated that Thomas was derelict in his duties as director not to have known of bribes. The obvious conclusion being that he must be in on the scam too. This was grossly unfair to Thomas. He had only been in his new position for less than five months. If the feds purported this criminal activity to have been going on for years, how then, may I ask, was Thomas expected to be so psychic? He was out of his office most of the day, supervising construction. To imply that he was derelict is absurd and fallacious," he deliberately stated.

DA continued, "On February 4, two days after the story broke, the mayor called a press conference at city hall. Taylor read from a prepared text, which was rather succinct. 'I do not condone the concupiscence of city officials who would stoop to purloin from this great commonwealth, engaging in erstwhile plots or in the future attempt to pilfer from city department coffers. It is the duty of the federal grand jury to purge these sectors of unscrupulous employees and those who seduced them with bribes. A man is also presumed innocent till proven guilty.' That was it. It was short and sweet."

"He remonstrated with the press for defamation of character and knocked his political opponents for traducing the good name of his friend of seventeen years and the city's friend, Thomas Jefferson Bell. It was a beautiful scenario orchestrated by the mayor. He despised crime and defended Thomas. However, the truth is, it was ignoble at best because this was all planned subterfuge," he charged, scratching his chin.

DA could sense I wanted to interject. I was confused with his last two statements. Before scanning the room, he held up a solitary finger for me to be patient and hold my thoughts.

"Thomas stayed on as director, but the two confederates were relieved of duties after their arrests. Then the bubble burst," Dom sadly relayed.

"On February 9, Jess Monroe, the former housing director, was found dead in his Mercedes-Benz, inside his Palm Beach, Florida, garage. The Dade County coroner's report read, 'Suicide by carbon monoxide asphyxiation.' He left a handwritten note confessing to absconding with $675,000, his share of kickbacks. Jess Monroe was the third accomplice in city hall I discussed earlier. He named names. Jackson and Minstein were scribbled along with…apparently, he expired before anyone else was listed," DA explained.

Dom went on to add, "My interpretation of Jess Monroe taking such a drastic measure is that the tormented anticipation of knowing he was going to be confined like a birdie in a gilded cage for the remainder of his years, compared to his retirement of the good life, was too much strain for him to suffer at the age of sixty-three. Jess didn't care to put on his bifocals to read the inevitable pica print about how he was an arrogant, greedy, corrupt civil servant who mis-used the power of his office to line his own pockets. Federal govern-ment authorities would have proved at his trial how Jess was guilty of a wanton misuse of his department for his own self-enrichment. So by some people's standards, he did the honorable thing. Others vili-fied him as a no-good squealer too afraid to take the rap himself. The fact, though, remains: he's dead. He left behind a legacy of shame. We'll never know, but I make an educated guess that Jess had to be the one who originally masterminded the plan. The other two were crooks, not mental giants capable of being so shrewd."

"On February 11, a scared Minstein did his canary yellow *tweet tweet tweet*," Dom implied. "After the feds promised to grant him partial immunity from prosecution. They painted a picture for him that Monroe could have been hit, since the two aforenamed con-struction companies were allegedly tied to the Mob. Prior to this exemption offer, he falsely labeled Thomas as part of the city official's triumvirate engaged in changing bids for building contractors along with company principals involved. He went so far as to sign a false affidavit. This was retaliation for not being named to succeed Jess Monroe. The dumb oaf didn't even have the brains to realize that his beef was with the mayor," DA emphasized. "Any good defense attorney will rip his testimony apart, because the man is a patholog-ical liar. The other guy, Jackson, in traction at St. Michael's Medical Center with a multiple stress fracture to his right leg, ill-advised by his attorney, clammed up. He should have taken off his muzzle, but at least he never corroborated Minstein's viperous testimony against Thomas," recalled DA.

"The next day, the mayor had Page conspicuously reassign Thomas out of HEDA to some dingy office in a remote section of the city hall building. Oh, it was a temporary stay, he was told, till things cooled down in the papers. Thomas was still being paid his director's salary, but without any responsibilities. The mayor was now eschewing contact with Thomas and had him in a very peril-ous situation. Thomas thought the mayor knew best. He remained steadfast, despite temporarily relinquishing his duties, he supposedly thought, even though people he had trusted for years were now turning their backs on him," DA divulged.

"Ramsey, attacking through newspaper articles, was relentless in his condemnation of Thomas and why Mr. Bell was still being employed at city hall. Thomas continued to repudiate all charges. Ramsey lambasted the mayor with charges of obstruction of justice. That was when the mayor started to do his 'tap dance.' Where he once took a harsh stance, he was now expostulating with the press," Dom informed. "Let me get back to your question."

I thought the silvery old man had forgotten.

"Like I said previously, Thomas didn't do anything wrong. A federal grand jury would have indicted him by now. There is not one shred of evidence to charge him on. As incredulous as it sounds, I feel he was set up as early as three years ago, when Page came aboard. Like I implied before, this was an attempt to curtail Thomas's overwhelming popularity. Of course, the mayor was grateful to Thomas in the beginning of their tenure. Thomas believed in the mayor's revitalization plan when others scoffed. That Thomas, he was brazen enough to engineer the mayoral campaign against the two-term incumbent, O'Neill, when it could have cost him his position in the Parks Department. As strange as it sounds, Thomas's success was his failure. The failure being that he had become more likeable to people than the mayor. There was never an attempt by Thomas to lessen the mayor's accomplishments or challenge his office. He graciously accepted his role, supporting the mayor's policy issues and working for the constituency.

"Even before getting involved with politics, Thomas was already a folk hero in this city. At St. Benedict's, he was a first-team selection Essex County football athlete along with being honored All-State Parochial. He was chosen All-City in swimming, anchoring the one-hundred-meter medley team. I think he even had the school record in the backstroke event. Thomas was captain of his debating team, and he went to the state finals with the chess club. Doubtlessly, his exploits on the gridiron in college are well-chronicled.

"More importantly, his decision to choose working for the public weal of Newark instead of a potential pro football career was admirable. The possibilities of fame and fortune were not as important to him as they were to other people, who could not understand his choice of public service. People in the know, such as the city council and influentials, knew Thomas was the man behind the scene responsible for getting things done in the city. The snide remarks Taylor overheard at cocktail parties filled him with umbrage. My word, did the mayor resent this. Thomas had become his enigma. He could not stand to share the kudos and accolades any longer.

"Although being a novice to the field of abnormal psychology, I can still deduct that the mayor must have been suppressing a deep-rooted hatred of Thomas for years. He is a psychoanalyst's dream come true: someone wanting to punish the person who has helped them the most."

DA then affirmed, "In baseball, you could compare the mayor to the captain of the team, the crafty ace pitcher of the staff who wants the credit for pitching himself out of a jam every inning and still drive in the game-winning RBI."

"As a purist, I'm a National League fan," Dom added, resting his chin in his left hand. "He's miffed if the young shortstop makes sparkling plays in the infield and cushions the lead with a three-run homer, thrilling the fans. The victory is unsatisfying to the pitcher because he didn't do it all himself. Not only doesn't he want that young shortstop on his team any longer or traded to another, he's also not content until he devises a way of banning that player from baseball for life.

"Remember when I mentioned subterfuge? Well, the mayor had to find the right venue for getting rid of Thomas. It is solely my opinion that the mayor knew all along about the FBI sting operation in HEDA. Try to follow this logic: the mayor gambled the scam would break months before the May 14 election. Thomas would be trapped in the scandal, and just when it became politically expedient, the mayor would dismiss him. The timing was perfect. The opposition field pitted against him this election was marginal at best. With Thomas out of the picture in disgrace, the mayor would accomplish his mission—that is, winning the election in a landslide without having to share the credit.

"He would come off as the philosopher king he imagined himself to be. He would be deserving of all glories due, and this would be in preparation of his ultimate goal, the ride to the governor's mansion two years from now. This, he felt, was his manifest destiny. It meant nothing to the mayor, exploiting his good friend Thomas, the loyal civil servant, who had championed 75 percent of his political victories with three consecutive wins." DA prognosticated all this.

I was trying to comprehend DA's story line, but I was still confused. He was rubbing his chin again and turned his head around. Dom uttered, "Let me put it in agricultural terms for you. Our gentleman farmer-friend would appreciate this." DA was alluding to John Henry.

"No, I stand corrected. I'll give you a livestock analogy: The mayor was the dirty swine giving orders. Thomas was the sacrificial lamb. Page, the city's attorney, was the Judas goat, who would eventually lead Thomas to slaughter. You shall see."

Now, I was befuddled. Marco, the waiter, had just brought us our round of drinks courtesy of Louis. He departed but was hanging around the table next to us, curious of our conversation. Now, I understood Dom's visual precautionary movements.

After taste-testing his newly served cappuccino, DA gave all indications of approval.

DA engagingly invited, "Does your fresh brew appeal to your taste buds?"

"It's great," I answered. "I especially enjoy the aroma and the flavor the cinnamon gives it."

"The cappuccino is meticulously prepared, and only the finest cinnamon in the world can complement that special aroma and tang. I have a penchant for exceptional quality, and my palate is very sensitive to the tasting of good cinnamon. Tiara brand is king. I can easily weed out all impostors to the throne.

"Tiara is packaged on the Isle of Malta and imported by select emporiums. Angelo grinds the quills, just as fresh pepper is ground in a mill. Commercial powdered cinnamon you purchase in a supermarket is usually adulterated with inferior cuts, such as chopped quillings, featherings, and mixed ground chips or blended with ground fruit, sugar, farinaceous, and dried fruit products, minced cassia bark, or worst of all, camouflaged surprises, such as pulverized nutshells. I'm no damn squirrel," DA amusingly insisted.

"The best is indigenous to the forests of Ceylon. During the rainy season, the monsoons, the bark is stripped from shoots on the bushes. Actually, it is an evergreen tree belonging to the laurel family, but they are pruned to never reach a height of more than four feet. The shoots curl into quills, known to the public as cinnamon stick. In true Ceylon cinnamon, the corky layers are scraped away and the quills are packed, one inside the other. The finest quality is pale in color, resembling a roll of dried paper, and the wavy lines are clearly visible. Tiara uses only the best Ceylon grade 0000. It has the best flavor and the perfect, pleasing fragrance. I have sampled the others with bitter disappointment. In my opinion, it is a myth that Chinese cinnamon, or cassia bark, as it is commonly known, is comparable to that from Ceylon. It is reddish-brown, and the bark is thicker and courser. It is pungent, not too sweet, and much less agreeable. Saigon cinnamon is gray-brown in color and has a rather-astringent taste. The crop grown in Brazil and the West Indies is weak, rather insipid, with virtually little or no aroma. As an acceptable change of pace when and where you can find a tin of it, the acrid proper-ties of Java cinnamon are at times pleasing. The combination of rich volcanic soil on the island, latitude 6 degrees south, longitude 110 degrees east, together with the heavy annual rain in the forests and the debilitating humidity ten degrees below the equator, has it's pri-meval effects on the crop," he said.

"Now you know, my friend, you are savoring the purest cinna-mon in a magnificent cappuccino, include the dominating orange characteristic of the Grand Marnier, and well, do I need to say more? The concept is clearly germane. You are indulging in ecstasy. I'll share a secret with you, my friend. My gumbas sing the praises of Disaronno Amaretto or Romana Sambuca, two cordials of very good quality. Not to embarrass their personal preferences, but their taste buds are not as refined as mine," DA endorsed.

I couldn't have agreed with him more, because the combination of ingredients was superb and, bravo, his classification of the spice.

DA was in quiet contemplation, relishing his drink. I hated to disturb his mood.

"Dom—excuse me, I mean DA. Getting back to TJ, again. Where do you gather all your information from?" I skeptically wondered.

"Ha! Ha!" He chuckled. "Where, do you ask? I have my eyes and ears throughout this great city. From the taxicab and bus drivers on the streets to the courthouse, the city council, the prosecutor's office, policemen, firemen, mailmen, sanitation workers, janitors, shopkeepers, restaurateurs, doctors, lawyers, street people, drug dealers, loan sharks, gamblers, bankers, building contractors, businessmen, and corporate executives, etcetera, etcetera. My sources are without limitation, extending their tentacles to the inner sanctum of Taylor's own office, where I've recruited my own mole," he proudly declared.

Marco was still malingering at the nearby table, feigning wiping off the condiment bottles. He was deliberately eavesdropping on our colloquy.

Dom, realizing it too, turned his head to the left, to face Marco. He waved him over.

"Hey, donkey ears. Why don't you pull up a chair, so you can hear it all much better? Don't you realize I'm engaged in a serious tête-à-tête with my friend Stanley here?" DA sternly warned.

A tongue-tied Marco was taken off guard.

"Mr. Salutini, I wasn't—"

Before he could utter another syllable, DA interrupted and cautioned, "Beware, Pinocchio, with every lie you tell, your nose will grow an inch. Begone with you, before I call Angelo or Louis over."

Marco hopped off like a stirred bunny-rabbit looking for cover, in the direction of the kitchen. Using his thumb as a potential hitchhiker would gesture, Dom pointed in the direction of the fleeing Marco.

"Stanley, he's harmless, but I have to be careful of what I say when he's close at hand. Picture this: He has even resorted to stooping under tables to listen to what I have to say. The lad only wants my counsel, but he's yet to earn the privilege. He's still wet behind the collar. He's entering his senior year in college next fall, and his mother has beseeched me on numerous opportunities to get him into the dental school here in the city. Though capricious at times, he's still a good boy. I suspect I'll have to whisper into the right ear to get him admitted," Dom espoused with conviction.

I shook my head in disbelief before partaking sips of my drinks. DA paused for a minute of contemplation before the Grand Marnier touched his lips. Something must have struck him as funny, because a sly smile took over his expression and his eyes became a deeper blue.

"You know, Stanley, in certain circles of academia, they would waive the credits toward a PhD in political science and a doctorate of jurisprudence for a student under my philosophical emeritus tutelage for a year. He would just have to pass an equivalency examination!" Roaring with laughter, he exclaimed, "Stanley, I'm just being facetious!"

I thought he wasn't kidding, but I didn't tell him.

"Let me expatiate further on Thomas's tribulations. I earlier mentioned Page, the city council. Somehow a pact between Page and Taylor was consummated over thirty-six months ago.

"Page's exponential reputation for smear tactics and character assassinations preceded his arrival in Newark from Charlotte, North Carolina. He earned his notoriety in Baltimore with his 'witch-hunting' expeditions of political opponents. His brand of behavior would have flourished during the stake-burnings in Salem, Massachusetts, during the late seventeenth century. Page ingratiated himself to the mayor to further enhance his career and readily accepted the dirty work in his emulation of Thomas. With his twisted mind, Page knew how to fester the mayor's neurosis of Thomas," DA enlightened me.

"As the weeks went by, cries of 'cover-up' and 'obstruction of justice' were launched on the mayor, and he pretentiously embraced it. Ramsey, the only real threatening mayoral candidate in the May 14 race, had fallen into his trap. He had abandoned the major thrust of his campaign, which had focused on the issues of street crime, drugs, and the escalating garbage disposal crises, to hammer solely on the theme of the alleged cover-up of the mayor in respect to Thomas. Successfully, he aroused residential obloquies. It was a colossal blunder. Was he ever injudiciously informed by his aides!" DA described.

Dom then narrated, "Thomas was now ready to be handed over on a silver platter to Ramsey. The timing was perfect. They had to make their move before Thomas was ever to be indicted or, for that matter, publicly exonerated, calculating that federal investigations take time. Page was sanctioned as the conduit to coerce Thomas into resigning. Not only was it unwise but also a monumental mistake of judgment for Thomas to have climbed into that car with that scoundrel Page. Thomas was meretriciously promised that he would be brought back as an aide after the election. After the storm passed, he would resume his duties back in HEDA. He would be reimbursed for his lost wages and any nominal compensation due him."

Waiting patiently for the proper cue, I interposed, "Why, DA? Why would TJ be so naive to accept this offer when he wasn't guilty of any wrongdoing?"

Dom abruptly answered, "Because the mayor smugly knew that Thomas's Achilles' heel was his heart. Speaking of Achilles, noblest soldier, bravest of the brave Achaeans, tragic hero of Troy, through translation he 'spake': 'Rather to be a serf to the lowest of yeomen than king in the land of the dead.' His words ring so dear to me. Clearly, I can see the modern symbolism, taking it slightly out of context with 'Salutini license,' applying it to Thomas's maelstrom."

DA was still playing with his chin. I simply nodded in affirmation, albeit not knowing why.

"He would sacrifice everything for the honor of the mayor and to preserve the welfare of this great metropolis. For that reason only, Thomas would deliver the beau geste," DA interpreted.

I wanted to purposely interrupt and tell him I don't speak French, but I didn't think it wise. DA took a healthy taste of his cappuccino.

Dom went on to chronicle, "That Page, he's a real piece of work. He created a lovely facade. Thomas's refusal to resign would be construed as letting the mayor down. He could be accused of not being a team player. The mayor was taking a good pummeling in the newspapers, defending the good name of Thomas. This implication of cover-up could cost the mayor the election. The emergence of Oliver Ramsey as mayor would not be a viable solution. The alternative: racism, at its worst, could rear its ugly head again and polarize this city. Thomas let himself fall into a 'Let's wiri one for the Gipper' syndrome. For my money, it was just another ploy in Page's assentation to Thomas."

I begged to know, "DA, why didn't TJ get an attorney for advice?"

"Stanley, I implored him to seek a legal opinion as soon as the scandal was uncovered. I had someone in mind who had a whole bag of tricks up his sleeve. Someone with the clout to fight back and ambush with his legal sortie. Thomas, he refused counsel. That's right, let me reiterate with synonymous rephrasing: he rebuffed legal expertise. No one wants to listen to the advice of an old man anymore. What the hell do I know? I only have a 957.75 batting average in separating political fact from fiction. He thought I was being jovial, but in all candor, I advised him to be wary of the 'Ides of March,' not realizing I was an augur of impending doom. Coincidently, on that indistinguishable date, March 15, 44 BC, Decimus Junius Brutus, not to be confused with Marcus Junius Brutus, who incidentally was also a conspirator, escorted his trusting friend Julius Caesar to his assassination," Dom historically recalled with bitterness.

He placed the fingertips of his left hand to his temple.

DA paused, then recounted, "If my memory serves me, Monday, March 18, the mayor called another press conference, just three days after Thomas resigned. You know it's whimsical, because the Sunday before, he marched in the St. Patrick's Day Parade commencing on Sanford Avenue and ending, making a left, up South Orange Avenue. Ostensibly, he was getting worked up for the following day's events.

"In his diatribe release, the mayor deviated 360 degrees from what Page had promised Thomas the Friday before. With the sequacious city councilor by his side, he went into a tirade at the bottom of the city hall steps. Let me paraphrase, as best as my feeble mind will allow," promised DA.

"'I will not harbor any criminals or be accused by my adversaries of using my office to suppress evidence in a criminal investigation. My concordance and concurrence with those who maliciously try to involve themselves in a conspiratorial attempt to defraud the public is purely non sequitur—it does not follow. If one is implicated then subsequently found guilty of corruption in office, violating the public trust, then life imprisonment is the only condign sentence. I can feel no compassion.'"

"At this point, the mayor took a deep breath and began to peruse his speech," Dom articulated.

"'In light of this unceasing eristic climate through the corridors of this magnificent structure, city hall, and echoing throughout the by-ways of this great city concerning Thomas Bell, I am forced to terminate his services.'"

"Here's the part where the mayor shed crocodile tears," he said.

"'Past friendship and past virtuous performance, notwithstanding, are inconsequential when the preponderance of circumstantial evidence purports misconduct in office. No one can be permitted to be above the law and be allowed to besmirch the reputation of my and your Newark.'

"Harshly, now.

"'I abjure my association with Mr. Bell.'

"Then stumbling.

"'It is with heavy burden I perform this sobering duty. To the citizenry of Newark, I implore…nil desperandum, never despair. Please, ladies and gentleman of the press, no questions at the present time.'"

Grinning, and shaking my head sideways, I wished I had half the fading memory Dom had at his age.

DA concluded, "It is truly remarkable that this nitwit got away with this gobbledygook of a canard, dispensing Latin phrases only academicians, lawyers, and priests could translate. Thomas was never fired. As I disclosed, he had resigned three days earlier."

My expression gave credence that I was still not totally coherent to everything DA had "gospeled," yet I understood the gist of his sinuation of events. DA had piqued my interest in this convoluted tale, which only he could decipher.

A sober DA asked me point-blank, "Stanley, do you ever play draw poker?"

"Yes, sometimes we have a game on Sunday nights," I replied. "But what does that have to do with this sordid affair?"

"As an amateur gambler, you'll better understand this scenario: Indeed, the stakes were very high, the mayoral election. Oh, it was a lovely 'sandbag' stratagem on the mayor's part. He checked, after drawing no cards, and invited Ramsey to raise when he defended Thomas and kept him on after the scam broke. Suckered into the nonbet, Ramsey shot his whole load. He abandoned his platform, throwing away a pair—the issues he could possibly win with—to attempt the odds against inside straight. He was too vain to realize the mayor was playing a pat hand. The mayor didn't need to draw cards. His sucker play worked, and he raised at the Monday-afternoon press conference. A notation to any player, be it poker or politician: contrary to popular belief, you don't always have to play the hand you're dealt, but for goodness' sakes, discard the right ones to give yourself a chance to win. Ramsey hadn't figured on the mayor's condemnation of Thomas and his not supporting his good friend till the end. The mayor fallaciously proved he wasn't soft on crime. Naturally, unknown to Ramsey, it didn't matter to the mayor that he would ruin the political career of his longtime ardent supporter, Thomas, with his salacious trickery. In Ramsey's case, he's finished. He'd have to reshuffle the deck to reorganize his position. Personally, it's getting too late. His only chance would be to solicit my help. I would have advised him, 'Never shoot your whole load,' but in the final analysis, he's lost all his chips," DA concluded, rubbing his chin. I laughed. As incredible as his analogy was, the pieces seemed to fit.

"Forget Ramsey. What did TJ think of your adventurous disclosure?" I inquisitively sought.

"You must understand, Stanley, in no uncertain terms, this is purely conjecture or supposition at best. I can't prove any of it, but remember, I have a certain knack with unscrambling these delicate matters. It's a matter of pride for me to be able to read between the lines. Oh, I pity Thomas. He's not prepared to accept the truth. Get this, he interpreted the mayor's speech as 'buncombe,' but I know it shocked him. He's relying on the mayor's word that he'll be brought back after the election. Thomas is usually imperturbable. Nevertheless, I could witness on his face a shadow of doubt he can't hide. It has to be mental anguish for him. He's counting solely on a thin veil of promises. I said to him, 'If you never pay attention to anything else I say, do this one thing for me as your good friend and adviser.' I begged him to leave town for a while so he could get a change of scenery, relax, and think of alternative strategies. Thank God he listened. He needs more time to sort things out.

"I am frightened with what I am about to divulge. I received a communique from one reliable source relating that the mayor, taking advantage of this turbulent atmosphere, had the subtlety to 'temporarily' appoint Darryl Chandelor, Page's uncle, as HEDA director, evoking the Emergency Employment Act. It is preposterous of Thomas to even consider his reappointment," a withdrawn DA disclosed.

I grimaced at the stark reality of Dom's disclosure.

"Stanley, did you notice that little gem in the March 21 paper down here?"

As I did not answer immediately to his question, Dom assumed that I hadn't. I couldn't recall the specifics of the caption in question that long ago.

"The article was on page 2, right column, in the paper. They had the heading 'Abdication in Newark.' Do they presume to be the fuckin' *London Times* of December 11, 1936, editorializing an unrealistic comparison to Edward VIII's forfeiting the crown? Stanley, please pardon me for that reprehensible, scurrilous expletive," DA pleaded. "Putting skepticism aside," Dom went on, stating sarcastically, "I'm sure when they're shamed into printing a retraction, they'll have the righteousness to bury it in the obituary column."

I offered, "Joe had a similar opinion about another publication in South Jersey."

"He has the mind of a good chess player, always thinking ahead, but excuse me. Feel this melon," Dom suggested.

He bade me to touch the half-melon that lay in a bowl to his right. I pushed its soft orange flesh with my finger.

He inquired, "How would you describe it?"

"The melon is ripe," I replied.

"It's ripe. Very good, that's the ticket. You catch on quickly. You are an excellent student. My theory is that the mayoralty was just like this melon here, ripe for the taking, this election, not by the field pitted against the mayor, but by Thomas himself. I did my best to persuade

Thomas not to play second fiddle any longer but to run for the office. With his image and looks, he's just what this city needs: a young, fresh, vibrant leader. Someone who can cross racial barriers and be endorsed by diverse coalitions. A candidate who has no allegiance to special interest groups. With me as his campaign manager, how could he lose? Thomas scoffed at my suggestion. He wanted to continue serving the mayor as part of his administration," DA sadly lamented.

"DA, maybe I'm slow to comprehend, but there're two serious points that still need airing. Why all this surreptitious behavior? Why didn't the mayor simply tell TJ straight to his face that he didn't want his political expertise any longer and work out an amicable departure?" I directed.

"Evidently, you have listened to every word I've uttered. See, I mentioned you are a good student. No longer are you a neophyte. You have an analytical mind. Your inquiries show insight. I know it is difficult to explain irrational behavior to rational people, nevertheless understand it as well.

"You'll appreciate this. I can offer you a one-word answer synonymous to both solicitations: *jealousy*. That's the key. Please allow me to elaborate. The natural tendency in most people's lives is to stay static. A handful change for the better, but way too many change for the worse. In the mayor's case, it was the latter. Oh, it goes without saying that he was an able, inspired man when he first took office, but he succumbed to the corruption of power. The taste of power swelled his head. Imagine this: The man doesn't even live in the city any longer. He keeps a fictitious address in the Vailsburg section. That's his 'red herring.' His ego needs prestigious dwellings. He resides in a beautiful house with his administrative assistant, Miriam, in Llewellyn Park, not far from me. It's a more suitable lair for 'His Majesty,'" Dom told me.

DA paused to sip both his drinks.

"The mayor wanted the pleasure of driving Thomas into the ground, thus ending his political career once and for all.

"What? You think he would allow Thomas to go to another comparably sized city and eventually become their mayor and outshine our bright star? No way, Stanley. In no uncertain terms would he permit that. That would be counterproductive.

"The mayor knew in all probability that Thomas would never work for any other city government other than Newark, but he wasn't taking any chances. As you invited, the gentlemanly way for the mayor to behave would have been to be aboveboard. Tell Thomas straight up that the time has come for a dissolution of their political union. The mayor should have shaken hands with Thomas and given him a 'golden parachute.' Two years' severance to find employment would have been grand. Better yet, find a position for him in government elsewhere and wish him well.

"Unfortunately, the problem with this 'once upon a time' fairy tale is that the mayor is no gentleman," DA argued.

DA asked, "Do you finally perceive with clarity the logical sequence of events that I have unfolded?"

"Yes, I think so," I answered.

"Good," he relayed, "because my mind is too frazzled to manufacture an extemporaneous parable to pound into your head." Dom was playful in his response.

He was holding his chin again, and if he rubbed it any more, he was going to put a hole in it. I smiled to myself.

DA had spun a web of gloomy entanglements a person shouldn't have to experience in a lifetime, yet in a few months, as TJ had to endure. I developed my own précis. Dom's tale had all the intrigue of a clandestine spy novel, except all the characters were real: the jealous, unscrupulous mayor; the boisterous hatchet man, Page; a slew of minor players caught in the plot; and our tragic hero, Thomas.

I drew my own conclusions. Where I was concerned about TJ before my talk with DA, I was now worried that he would never receive another appointment in the City of Newark again, at least not while the mayor held office. Thomas lost not only his job but also his career. Working for the city was the only position TJ ever had or wanted. Putting my government inexperience aside, I didn't have to be in a smoke-filled back room with political bosses to realize that a halo of suspicion would always hover over TJ's head even though he was innocent. It would be his stigma. Undoubtedly, there was little I could do. Regretfully for Thomas, he did not want to see his friends. I reached for my wallet in my breast pocket to pick up our tab, but DA wouldn't hear any of it.

"No, no, your money is no good here," he insisted. "Please say hello to the other two guys for me, especially that big son of a gun."

Dom was referring to John Henry and Joe respectfully.

"He's one of the few that can make me belly-laugh. I've expended honorary Italian heritage upon both of you. Thomas received my blessing years ago."

"When this problem with Thomas blows over, all of us, our women included, will have dinner. My treat. By the way, are you still peddling financial investments?" DA solicited.

I returned, "You mean estate planning."

"Yes. You contact me in a fortnight. My number's in the book. I have a new client for you, my nephew. He has a pending insurance settlement coming due. I'd be grateful if you would work out some sort of structured investment for him. I don't want him to blow his cash recovery on broads and cocaine. Young Alphonse is going through a stage where he's behaving a little wild in the mind," Dom pronounced.

I informed him that I would.

"Pardon me, DA, but what will TJ do if he can't return to city government?" I invited.

Dom answered, "Stanley, at this point, even I'm at a loss. I do predict in time that Thomas, just like the phoenix of ancient Egyptian lore, will rise from his ashes in greater splendor than before. But in the meantime, I own five dry cleaning stores and only have four sons to manage them. Why do you think I can devote so much leisure time to politics? The answer is simple: I don't have to work for a living. I offered Thomas a partnership in the remaining one with a reasonable buyout in five years, but he turned me down."

DA appeared forlorn but changed his mood to ask, "Did you marry that girl, Samantha, you were going out with?"

"No, not yet," I responded.

"She doesn't smile much for such a pretty thing, but sometimes she laughs at the wrong jokes," he presumed.

He was apparently referring to the finale of the Cizcero party.

"If it goes bad on you, my kid sister has a gorgeous daughter that would fit perfectly inside your arms. Let me know. I'll make all the arrangements," DA offered.

Out of respect, I told him I'd consider her. Angelo had come over to take care of the check.

"Stanley, it's been an honor speaking to you. You're a good boy, and you show respect. Let me give you, before you depart, a tiny piece of unsolicited advice you may employ in your business negotiations: think Yiddish and dress British, but be Italian," he enthusiastically voiced.

I expressed my gratitude to DA for his time and hospitality. Before I departed, I ventured over to the bar. I didn't see Louis, but pesky Marco was leaning there, gobbling a bunch of stemmed maraschino cherries reserved for drinks. Forcing a break in his feast, I asked him to extend Louis my thanks for his courtesy. Presenting Marco with a twenty-dollar bill, I instructed him that it was to cover the cost of a glass of Dom Perignon champagne for DA and to keep the change. I guess I'm a sentimentalist at heart, because some traditions are worth perpetuating, I believe. Then I exited and drove back to my office.

CHAPTER IV

My spine felt the jolt of a swinging arm. Being jostled brought my consciousness back to the confines of the Summit Office. Recollecting the tribulations of TJ was more mystifying than the classical Greek mythological account of Theseus battling the Minotaur in the labyrinth, except not as dangerous. No drastic changes in the rustic decor had occurred without me. My head turned sideways to confront my intruder. My unlikely attacker was a youthful-looking waitress who offered me a sincere but hurried "Excuse me" as she tried to "toreador" around the "bulls" who were selfishly blocking her path from the servicing bar to the diners' booths. I was indebted to her. She spared me the indignity of a free Chablis shampoo from the three carafes of wine she was precipitously balancing over her head on a tray. Staring at the volume of my Coors Light, I murmured to myself that repetitive question. Was my glass pessimistically half-empty or optimistically half-full? It was a marginal call at best, and I made the point moot when I downed the remaining contents.

I was checking out the strawberry-blonde with the San Trope tan in mid-June standing directly across the bar from me, a seat away from Michaelovitch and Walter. She must be a Short Hills debutante, all dressed up with no place to go but having the use of Daddy's Mercedes.

Her eyes had a soft blue hue contrasted by peach-glossed full lips that were very provocative when she smiled. Her sweet upper body was clutching a taut halter top, accentuated by a braided ponytail draped down her exposed back. This baby doll was good-lookin', but with an air of conceit bordering on narcissism. The perfect gift for her would probably be a vanity mirror, and she presumably already had eighty-one. She had the type of physical assets that could drive a man crazy. When you think you possess her, you don't, and when she becomes your obsession, you might as well put a ring through your nose, I contemplated.

I would have been content with just a little eye contact, but I was astonished, then flattered, by how easily she reciprocated. She was confident that I was not just wandering in her direction but my eyes were reserved for her only. She was enjoying my admiration yet playing coy with me. I received a demonstration of a multitude of slightly angled, over-the-shoulder poses. Her interest had been piqued, but she didn't want to be too obvious.

If I had the time, I fantasized that I would order a gigantic mimosa cocktail with two straws. Then, I would ask Bear to pass on a message to her that I'd rendezvous with her in a secluded corner where we could sensually sip our refreshment and anticipate the remainder of our evening together.

Much to my chagrin—I laughed—my baby doll had her calendar full. Three yuppie types were vying for her affection. I was trying to size up these suitors. This trio most likely worked at the same company together, and by appearance, it seemed as if they had the same tailored wardrobe and hairstylist, I deduced. It was funny how they were all copycats. These guys were alternating between flashing their teeth and patting back their overmoussed straight black hair. Without exception, they had shared a book on dressing for success, proudly exhibiting their striped Windsor-knotted power ties as tools of the trade. They had strategically surrounded her, with her back now facing me.

Before he stepped forward, clone no. 1 adjusted his tie and went into his act, making conversation, flapping his arms and hands in the process. He wound down, out of breath, and clone no. 2 took over. The first was very courteous, mind you, stepping back, giving way to his successor. Clone no. 2 fixed his tie before talking to her; he lasted longer than the first, but he, too, got winded. Clone no. 3 went through the same ritual, and then he expired. None of the clones had the foresight to anticipate that the baby doll needed a fresh drink until it was too late, then they all insisted on buying. The baby doll paid for herself.

She was holding court and loving every minute of it. I had to laugh. The baby doll was an incredible temptress, playacting as if each cookie-cutter cutout had her undivided attention, intermittingly touching each one as they conversed with her, still having time to flirt with me, and "Hellos" for every male passerby who happened to be wearing a suit. Not knowing her name, I dubbed her my darling Amanda because she was my idea of what I always imagined an Amanda would look like.

I tried to wave to Chris, who was hurrying out the door with a stunning brunette girl who, in heels, was at least three inches taller than him; the way he went through women, she was no doubt his new flavor of the month, and a double scoop at that.

The time was 6:45 p.m. and still no sign of TJ. Bear was engaged at the other end, forcing me to depend on a bow-tied bartender I'd never seen before to get a refill. After purposely ignoring my pleadings to pay homage to his regulars, he smugly inquired if I would like another libation. I politely informed him that I didn't speak French, and he rudely walked away with a scowl on his face. I wanted to instruct him that I was only being jocund, asshole. He pointed at me while probably discussing my family heritage with a lady patron he was serving next. I decided to put to good use the cliché "Let cooler heads prevail" and not make an issue of it. After all, I liked to visit this place every so often, and from the looks of him, I would unmistakably have had to define *jocund.* Maybe Louis could give him some tips on slicing the citrus, I mused. Finally, Scotty, a bartender I knew, came by to get me another "blast."

Behind me, standing were Courtney and Dave conversing with Dee and Mary Ann when I swiveled my chair. I smiled at them. I couldn't help not getting an earful of the chatter next to my left. Seated were two pleasantly plump, goose-faced, thirtyish-looking women talking with slight German accents about clothes shopping at the Livingston Mall. They were speaking loud enough for me to hear, facing me at times, knowing that I was in on their conversation. The pair was tittering at the mention of lingerie and what colors their husbands preferred. I was waiting with bated breath for Greta's response from Hildy about the arousal her Wolfgang would get when she modeled a lacey black number she demurely purchased today. Hildy tapped Greta on the arm, motioning to her that I was listening. Frankly, they knew I had been paying attention for at least ten minutes. Didn't I just know it, Greta switched to German, ruining the anticipated punch line for me. The gals were uncontrollably gaggling, and I was left with my mouth agape. Boy, that bugged me, when people who are bilingual pull off a stunt like that. One consolation: at least Wolfgang would have something to howl about tonight.

The ladies were better than the former occupants, who spent twenty minutes before being seated for dinner. They had been real swell. A pedigreed eighties couple climbing the corporate ladder hand in hand was what they were. He was Randy, and she was Mandy, or maybe it was the other way around. I smiled. The twosome, tall and thin, looked great together, but their appearances were deceiving. Both of them were real clothes horses. Randy's immaculate gray suit cost $800 or better in Brooks Brothers, and Mandy was outfitted with professional-looking apparel that was only carried in the finer ladies' boutiques. Easily, they could have been pictured on page 6 or 7 in some fashion magazine.

Their appealing physical impression turned ugly when they opened their mouths. Mandy was unappreciative about the apparently new diamond engagement ring that flashed from her finger. That rock was at least one full karat, but she criticized that the one Macey had gifted Stacey was nicer. She was nitpicking because her Dandy Randy didn't get her the best. When he ordered a domestic beer, she labeled his choice as dull. Randy got even when Mandy ordered a wine cooler and told her she was a "slave of the masses." She accused him of being boring and to lighten up more. Angered by her words, he countered with the fact that she was too domineering. Not to be outdone, Mandy hurled the accusation that he sometimes handled himself like a wimp and wasn't assertive enough in reaching his career goals. He cursed that she was manipulative. By the time they were on their second drink, they were building a crescendo with insults. The truth was coming out. The real crux of the matter occurred when he said that she wasn't as feminine as his secretary, Candy. That was the ultimate blow to Mandy's shallow ego. With unleashed furry, she called Candy a slut who was all eyelash and no brains and being a secretary to him was befitting her IQ. Furthermore, Randy was not half the man her boss, Andy, was. Andy was so masterful the way he demanded more "perks" with his recent promotion. It was dandy the way he treated his girlfriend, Sandy, showering her with trinkets and chocolates, but it was ironic that Mandy would say that Sandy was insensitive to Andy's generosity. Andy accused Mandy of being jealous of Andy's Sandy. They tried to get me involved in this verbal slugfest; Mandy was putting her arm around me, and Randy was offering to buy me a beer, but I refused to get suckered in with their pettiness and remained neutral. I wanted no part of this hornet's nest. Regardless of whom I sided with, I'd get stung.

Mandy grabbed one of the hostesses who had the misfortune to stroll by our vicinity, and demanded to view a menu right now. Hell, she was about to be called for a table any minute, but because of her attitude, she was going to be a bitch on wheels till then.

I'd say one thing in her behalf: she had a particular way with words when it came to food. Leave it to her to develop her own cutesy language to describe the bill of fare with an elocution delivered with falsetto. I could have been wrong, but I presumed she was trying to be "sheik" when she portrayed the soup as super. She might have the "super soup" as an appetizer together with a "silly salad." Mandy supposed that she and Randy might share a raw vegetable bowl, whereupon they would dip tangy tomatoes, crunchy cucumbers, curly carrots, and bushy broccoli into an herbal dressing. She was serious about celery and ravished the red part of radishes. For the entrée, she pondered over luscious, "lobby" lobster, succulent, "saucy" shrimp, or the incredible cracked crab from the crustacean class. Mandy struggled over sumptuous, sizzled steak, cheery curried chicken, or very vintage veal. She wouldn't order any turnips, however, because they were terrible. Mandy thought her last remark was hilarious, but I wasn't laughing. Johnny Tangerine would have complimented her selections, I thought. Randy just bobbed his head after her recital. He was being a verbally uncommunicative yes-man. Hidden from Mandy was my secret bet with her. If she favored fuckin' french fries, I was going to reward her with a hundred-dollar bill. Knowing her, she would have been appalled at the remark yet accept the money. So I kept silent.

Mandy excused herself to journey to the powder room, advertising to anyone within earshot where she was going, but before she left, she bade Randy to use his connections to get faster seating arrangements. Randy was noticeably agitated and babbled some unintelligible remark under his breath. He flipped his arms in the air and turned to me for a look of sympathy, but I just didn't have the inclination to feel sorry for him. He shook his head and replied, "Women."

With Mandy's vacant chair dividing us, I caught an unobstructed look at the profile of this knucklehead Randy. It startled me to realize I was almost watching my own mirror image. There were striking parallels. We both attracted good-looking, sophisticated types of women, but with different types of personalities. I certainly didn't have his pretense of affluence, because I had no such inclination to social importance. Though I'd resigned myself to dying a middle-class death, still we were both in unresolved predicaments that were heading nowhere except for trouble. The incongruity of his relationship was similar to my own; Mandy and he were politely tolerating each other and not growing. They were settling. Samantha, my girlfriend of three years, and I felt comfortable together, yet our ideals were starting to clash and our goals were becoming diametrically opposite. We didn't habitually air our dirty laundry in public like Randy and his fiancée, who predictably, with their surly dispositions together, approached bitterness when socializing with alcohol; we would never allow ourselves to be partners to such a fiasco, because we respected each other too much. Simply put, Samantha and I didn't complement each other enough to get married. She knew it as well as I, but neither of us had the courage to admit it. Both of us needed other partners to bring out the best in us. Randy and Sandy were in the same boat. They were ignoring the escalating differences and entering into a "mariage de convenance." Now, knucklehead Randy was making me speak French to myself. They would plan to have 1.5

beautiful children together and then wonder why, after three years, their wedded bliss was remiss and crumbling apart.

Joseph Cotton characterized it best playing the role of Uncle Charlie, as the "Merry Widow Murderer," in Alfred Hitchcock's 1943 mystery thriller *Shadow of a Doubt.* He stated to his niece by the same name, "Do you know the world's a foul sty? Do you know, if you rip the fronts off houses, you'd find swine?"

Whether to give Randy a five- or ten-cent piece of advice from an acquaintance experiencing a mutually unfulfilling relationship, I was unsure. After all, it was none of my business. The nickel opinion would be to simply have a heart-to-heart talk with his Mandy and just tell her that things weren't working out for either one of them and simply break off the engagement.

The dime suggestion was a little bit more complicated but could be worked out by all cooperative participants. Categorically, we had Randy breaking up with Mandy to court his true love, his secretary, Candy. Mandy, unhappy in love with Randy, really smitten with her boss, Andy. While Candy was receiving flowers from Randy, Andy was being plied with kisses and brandy from the enticing Mandy, finally receiving his own form of candy. Now, after Andy ditched Sandy, we had two perfect couples, Candy and Randy and Andy and Mandy, instead of the tolerating Mandy and Randy and the miserable Andy and Sandy.

Both couples could invite Macey and Stacey over for dinner. This way, everything would be dandy, excepting for Andy's ex, Sandy. Lest Sandy not be left unattached, I'd fix her up on a date with my friend Ignance. He claimed that he was very handy.

I ascertained that I was not a qualified lovelorn counselor. Though my judicial edict made perfectly good sense to me, I decided to keep my big mouth shut and let Mandy and Randy work out their own problems. Obstinate as Randy was, he wouldn't face the truth. He would have probably told me to go fuck myself, but on the other hand, Mandy might have listened, because she still got to share custody of Macey and Stacey.

Mandy returned from her primping in the ladies' room, and the two were escorted to their dinner table none too soon. The German gals commandeered their empty seats.

Back to espying my lovely Amanda. She was miffed at the attention that Mandy had given me, though she had added two more guys to her own ensemble. Like the ambidextrously skilled, she was dancing this string-pulled pair of marionettes with flair.

She exchanged my glance with pursed lips. The ubiquitous Bear had fortuitously come to my rescue and served me another without me having to wave my hands. With all the attention my Amanda was receiving, she was still bored. I pondered her turmoil. Should I snatch her away from her frustrations? We'd drive to Newark Airport, and I'd book flight for a Bermuda weekend, because nothing was too good for my Amanda. We'd stroll along the pink sand and in the surf, hand in hand, and I'd whisper all the right things because I was the right guy, I predicted. My dream state turned to reality when common sense hit me over the head, and I realized, she was too young and she was too immature, to go along with the fact that she wore phoniness on her sleeve as if it were an extra gold bracelet.

Twisting my body to the right ninety degrees, I caught a glimpse of someone who looked familiar. Yes, I was sure it was him. He was a grammar school pal I hadn't seen in at least twenty-one years. Frank Pecker was apparently with his wife and kids. He was a tough-fielding second baseman on our ball club. How cleverly apropos it was for Johnny McGhee, another fourth grader, to dub him Wood, and yes, he was red-haired. With that sort of imaginative perception at the age of ten, Johnny most likely wound up as an advertising executive on Madison Avenue. I smiled.

I was being entertained by the antics of the character with the mustache and rock-style-length locks clad in a taupe corduroy dress coat with the sleeves partially rolled to the forceps, rudely bumping into Austin. Twenty seconds ago, he had intentionally caused a scene over minutia. He had scolded Scotty for, of all things, pouring Chambord in his glass of champagne instead of crème de cassis to make a Kier Royale. The twit didn't realize that he received the proper ingredients for the drink that he asked for. In my view, it was an inappropriate cocktail to order at happy hour and this early in the evening. None of the women at the bar were imbibing in candy-ass drinks like that. What was his motive? To be the star at the bar.

Where was Ralph Cizcero when you needed him the most? I presupposed Mr. Cool Breeze was selectively hitting on the women across the bar. He was being very particular, because he only wanted to talk to the "pretty" girls. Whatever his rap, it wasn't working. Something he briefly told each woman made them laugh, but unfortunately at him. Though his line of shit wasn't effective, he was persistent to move on to his next female victim. He whispered phrases in Amanda's ear that made her blush, then she, too, shooed him away.

These three big guys standing directly behind me were getting me a little bit nervous. Mind you, in the dinosaur age, these gentlemen were at the top of the food chain, towering over us six-foot mortals. With their first couple rounds of drinks, their conversation was intellectually stimulating. Their banter was ebbing and flowing marvelously as they debated the Nixon administration of the seventies as a reversion to the Eisenhower mentality of the fifties. Without saying, it was a not-often-heard scholastic piece, and I was quite impressed with their political knowledge. I even volunteered a pragmatic Democratic Party comparison that met with consensus approval. After their fourth round of suds, their reserved, tranquil presence had been reduced to a foregone conclusion. They were boisterous on their fifth, and working on their sixth, they had become argumentative. Their neatly pressed sport blazers and tacked ties had been discarded for rolled-up sleeves. Oh no, these guys were displaying their beer muscles, and that was my cue to head for the john. I was leery of any punches being thrown in my direction by one of these tyrannosauruses. Whew, I was relieved when I saw that they had relocated to another area when I returned to my seat.

"Have you the time, sport?" inquired the female voice with the unmistakably Australian twang and yabber. I wondered if it must be international night.

"Five minutes after seven," I responded amid the commotion to the slightly built, white-haired lady with the cherubic smile.

Her asking was appreciated, because it had escaped my attention that TJ was this late. Out of respect for our friendship, I'd stick around another half hour, then depart for Hunterdon County without him. Deciding that this was my chance to be a gentleman today, I had the acumen to offer the lady my seat while she waited for her husband to park the car. Her uncommonly heard vernacular brought me back to bittersweet memories of a coed's voice so, so many years ago. "I was too damn irresponsible back then," I said under my breath.

Normally, I stand when I'm at a bar, and I was glad to stretch my legs. Not noticing when TJ entered the front door, I casually turned around, and there he was. We shook hands and exchanged brief pleasantries. He nervously stammered that he lost his gal, lost his job, and lost his Abe, but not necessarily in that order. My God, did he look awful! He had to be down to a hundred-forty pounds from a six-foot-two frame that usually carried a hundred-eighty pounds. For an occasion such as this evening, he would always dress resplendent, with a sharp-looking suit he purchased from Roots; sometimes, provided TJ made the effort, he even had the meticulous JC of JoS. A. Bank fame coordinate just the right sartorial splendor for him.

The reason would be JC's savvy golf tips. Son of a bee, whenever he returned from clothes shopping, TJ seemed to take three strokes off his game the next time we'd hit the fairways.

Tonight he chose to wear a soiled lightweight jacket; new, from their appearance, two-toned blue-green Reebok sneakers; faded Lee blue jeans; plus his trademark NY Yankee baseball cap.

His face looked gaunt, and his wire-rimmed sunglasses hid, until he removed them, sunken brown eyes belonging to someone who had just weathered a storm. Indeed, he must have, from what DA relayed. Not surprisingly, TJ appeared tense, and missing was his normal air of assuredness.

Harrowingly, going through his ordeal would have broken my spirit. TJ was a unique person; he always reminded me of a willow branch that always sprung back to form without breaking.

He was accepted at our college on an academic scholarship, declining free-ride offers to play football elsewhere. He made the varsity team as a "walk on," starting out as a defensive back, then as a wide receiver in his sophomore season. I knew he was good, but none of us realized how special he was till he was selected as an honorable-mention All-American the following year. Our football coach was flabbergasted when TJ decided to enroll in a city government program in lieu of playing his senior year. That was the career path for him.

The university's loss was the fraternity's gain, as TJ caught thirty touchdown passes from me for us to win the intramural touch football championship. It was impossible to cover him one-on-one. Just a simple "juke" with his head and he was gone. When he was double-teamed, he split the defenders, and when he was triple-teamed, I threw to Joe "Jugglin'" DeRenda or one of our other wide-open receivers. We made it look as easy as child's play, sometimes racking up six touchdowns a game. TJ always said his toughest catch was not on the varsity level but in our semifinal game against an independent team.

We set up a trick play, from our own ten-yard line, having TJ fake an injury and limp off the field, clutching his knee.

He had created the deception that he was lying in excruciating pain over on the left sideline with his trainer, John Henry, who skipped his varsity practice to coach our game. John Henry, in a performance worthy of *Hamlet*, was bemoaning the injury and ordered a new pledge brother to hurry for medical assistance. He acted as if he was going to call the first aid squad. In the huddle I had to tone down the squeals, because we didn't want the other team to catch on to the hoax. We had to execute quickly. I had two decoy receivers lined up wide right, who would both run short square outs. My other "wooden duck," Jugglin' Joe, was positioned as a left tight end. His assignment was to take his defender on a five-yard crossing pattern to the right. Mad Dog Monte's assignment as the fullback was to block, then also slide right, veering into a short curl route. My primary and only target was TJ, who had crawled his way inbounds far left. He had informed the referee that he was in the game. Set up in a shotgun formation, I didn't even want to glance his way until the ball was in my hands. Their safety read quarterback draw and came up to key on me. Salivating juices were flowing inside me. *Just don't blow this opportunity,* I cautioned myself. My worst nightmare was to throw a "wobbler." If I did that, I'd have to run, off the field and far away. When I received the snap, I pumped twice right, then screened over to TJ deep left, running his "fly" pattern. Nobody was even thirty yards from him. In a microsecond, I fired TJ a tight spiral he pulled in on his fingertips in full stride, and he galloped seventy-five yards down the left sideline for a touchdown. His only fear was that if he dropped the ball, John Henry was going to kill him as soon as he returned to the sidelines. TJ knew John Henry liked to keep his promises.

The now-faint three-quarter-inch scar TJ carried in his right eyebrow was partly my doing. It was first round of the playoffs. Though we were up by two touchdowns early in the second half, the going was tough against the Sigmas. We were facing a crucial fourth and five at midfield. We chose to go for it rather than punt. I had Jugglin' Joe covered one-on-one open by three yards down the right sideline. Joe's catch might have resulted in six points, but if he "flubbed" the ball, we would have been on our heels in poor field advantage, facing the sun. We needed a sure thing, so I opted to fire a strike to TJ, slanting seven yards over the middle. Bam Bam Bronski was patrolling the area as a linebacker. Not quick enough to intercept, Bronski held his ground on the spot TJ was arriving. TJ caught the football, but he also caught Bronski's lowered forehead. Whether the contact was flagrant or not, a free-for-all broke out. We won the fight and the game by forfeiture. The consequences were more stinging. TJ received fourteen butterfly stitches, and I earned a black eye.

I attended the pro-football combine with him down in Miami. He brought me along as his agent. He had the scouts salivating when he was timed in one forty-yard dash under 4.35. It was good enough to get him drafted in the third round by the Cowboys, and he didn't even play in his final year at school. As much as I and the guys coaxed him, he wouldn't sign a contract. He wanted to continue working for city hall and get a graduate degree in public administration at night, but look what it got him.

To simply imply that Thomas was altruistic would be as convoluted as pleading that Picasso was merely a painter. There isn't a proper synecdoche for either. An evolutionary process sequenced their learning. Since the time I first met TJ during freshman orientation, he had spoken reams of civic responsibility. Whereas Joe, John Henry, and I chattered about becoming millionaires before the time we were thirty, TJ was light-years ahead of us in terms of social consciousness. While he took an activist role in the dominant issues during our four years together—Vietnam, the ecology, preserving natural resources, and civil rights and justice—we did little more than to pay lip service, though we believed in the causes. He donated four hours a week in our university's community program to stamp out illiteracy, teaching basic reading and writing to underprivileged adults. It was because of his posturing that we got involved. Knowing someone like TJ, where values were more important than making a ton a money, comes once in a lifetime, if you're lucky. We needed a person such as him just to balance our overinflated ambitions and put us on a proper perspective of life. TJ was our barometer against keeping our own shallow egos in check from becoming too materialistic. He grasped, and made it sound worthwhile, the individual's singular contribution as a component in relationship to the whole. Accepting that life was imperfect and that slow, gradual change was a victory, you couldn't pinpoint him as utopian, like his namesake, Sir Thomas Moore, either. His reactions were caustic. TJ believed in practical solutions executed by decisive people.

His idealistic foundation was laid as early as grammar school, he claimed. Once, he confided to me that his father, whom he never got a chance to really, know perished while attempting to save the lives of others in a hotel fire. According to what Uncle George relayed to him, his dad happened to find himself at the scene. Not fearing for his own life, he just reacted because people were in need of help. TJ's father never received his chance to attend the police academy where he was admitted. It would have been excusable for TJ to go through life as an angry young man, losing both parents by the time he was five, having to move from Durham, North Carolina, three days after the funeral to live with relatives in Newark, New Jersey, he recalled dimly meeting only three times before. He also found himself in a new school with a new faith much different from his Baptist upbringing. A preacher dressed in vestments talked in a funny accent they called Latin, and on special occasions, the Sunday services were held in a gigantic house of worship they called a cathedral, if they weren't at St. Francis Xavier Church.

These cataclysmic events were unacceptable to him as a crutch, and he channeled his cheerful willingness in other positive directions. Some people called how he handled it intestinal fortitude, but I called it just plain guts.

He guessed that as early as ten, he was wrestling with fulfilling his dad's lost dream and satisfying his own inner desires for public service. It all came to grips and meshed together during an assembly at high school on career day, while listening to the speech made by the Parks and Recreation commissioner. The words "Making the commitment to first being responsible for yourself and then to others" stuck with him, and he understood the right path for him to take. At that precise moment, TJ swore an almost terrifyingly serene feeling instilled within him. Similar to men's spiritual calling to the priesthood, TJ knew his path was in the local government at Newark's city hall. This was his vocation. I recalled TJ playfully reciting, "It was as clear as a bell to a bell." The burden was taken off his shoulders of going into law enforcement for the sake of living his life for his departed dad. Any position in local government was all right, and if he could get into Parks, that would be a fine choice, because he would be helping to serve the community. Not compromising, he was at peace within himself and with his father.

Before the bow-tied bartender was about to ask TJ for a libation, I tapped him on the shoulder and explained that our server didn't appreciate the fact that we didn't speak French. TJ understood immediately, and he acknowledged the fact that it was time to go.

We've had a running joke about "not speaking French" for fifteen years, which we haven't outgrown, nor do we want to. It stemmed from the French I course both of us got stuck with first semester freshman year. We earned our Bs because we "aced" our written exams, but neither of us had an oral aptitude for the language. It was common for us and boisterously merry for the class to butcher our pronunciations. Imagine, our lab instructor insisted that neither of us would ever amount to anything in life because we couldn't speak French well in conversation. Since that day, any

French word that's been adapted for English usage that we hear or say, well, it's been ingrained in us that we inform the person in our company, "We don't speak French." We enjoy reminiscing about the notion. It can irritate certain people who can't draw an inference after they say a word they don't know is French derived. But that's the problem. Obviously, they don't have our sense of humor or didn't get stuck with French I in college.

We walked out the door of the Summit Office. I didn't want to get into a long dissertation about why I didn't want to drive, and fortunately for me, TJ just nonchalantly agreed to be the wheelman. He said he managed to find a parking spot on Elm Street. Missing from my friend's gait was that familiar bouncy step when he walked on the balls of his feet. Now he was walking flat-footed, with his head down. Instead of me finding his familiar customized Lincoln Continental Mark IV, he introduced me to a beat-up 1982 Chevy pickup truck. Though he couldn't keep up the payments on the Abe any longer, he stated not to minimize the effectiveness of this present vehicle, especially for his new business, but he offered no specifics as to the particular field of endeavor other than it was automobile related.

CHAPTER V

We traveled Route 22 West, heading in the Somerville direction. Some music would have been nice, if some crackhead thief hadn't popped TJ's radio; still, with the antenna snapped off, I doubt we could have played it anyway. It was fortunate that we didn't need air-conditioning, because TJ warned me that it didn't work either. No matter. The breeze felt good with the windows open, air waves naturally parting my hair. I always felt calm traveling in this area of New Jersey. Things just seemed more wide-open. I turned to face my driver.

He said, "I'm hungry enough to eat a horse. Well, maybe just a small pony."

I reminded him of the time we might have eaten horsemeat when we had lunch at a certain Spanish restaurant in the Ironbound Section of Newark, the name of which escaped me. The waiter kept asking if our steaks were tender. We kept hearing strange noises in the kitchen, and we were given the story that they were renovating and the chef had a cold. A week later, TJ mentioned that the place was ordered closed by the Board of Health for butchering live animals right in the pantry. A nice, fresh kill offered to unsuspecting patrons.

TJ chuckled. "I probably have had a filly steak or two, but not by choice."

Then, he corrected himself to "I'm as hungry as a horse." I was glad to see he still had a sense of humor to share.

"I don't understand it, Stanley. I'll go without food for days because I just don't feel like eating, then when I do get hungry, I'll devour everything in sight. My metabolism is in a rut, and I'm still losing weight."

I suggested that he have some tests taken, and he said that he was going to see a doctor in Newark next week, in hopes of discovering the right pabulum. Thinking, but not out loud, I wondered whether this was a good opportunity to question TJ on the events of city hall and find out what his new business venture was all about. After curt pondering, I decided, if I had to procrastinate about asking, then it was bad timing. When TJ felt comfortable, he would share his story.

TJ drove past the exit where we should have turned on the Somerville circle for Routes 202 and 206. Even though this wasn't the time and place for detouring, I didn't second-guess his presumed shortcut, because after all, he was my driver and still posing as a NY Yankee fan.

To pass the time, I recalled one of our road trips we took to John Henry's farm when we were in college. All of us consumed too much that day, littering John Henry's backyard with "dead soldiers." Not content with all that brew, we started to guzzle down gallons of John Henry's father's homemade apple wine.

Tommy Lynch must have knocked off close to a case of beer by himself before he climbed up the apple tree. He was swaying on a limb. John Henry made a big mistake and brought out his Winchester .22 rifle and a shotgun to show off his marksmanship. We were throwing tin cans in the air for him, and he hadn't missed yet. John Henry's father kept coming outside, telling him to put his artillery away for a sober day. We all wanted our turns to be the rifleman. Crazy Frank Cluarcy aimed the shotgun at the apple tree Tommy Lynch was in and fired. Tommy fell to the ground, and everyone thought that he was shot dead. John Henry knelt over his body. His father rushed out and, in the confusion, thought one of us blasted his son. He went back in the house and returned with a cat-o'-nine-tails. He was trying to whip us, and we were trying to restrain him. John Henry turned around and thought we had lost our minds and were trying to beat up his father. He made a bull moose charge and knocked us all down like bowling pins. It took all four of us to suppress him. Tommy got to his feet, and it was apparent he had dislocated his shoulder. John Henry's father put his face eyeball to eyeball with his son, started shaking him by the collar, then clutched his own heart and fainted. John Henry pulled up his truck to place his dad and Tommy in the back. He made tracks getting to a country doctor's office a few miles down the road. The road was bumpy, and everyone was trying to hang on. His dad's condition was fine, but Tommy had to have his shoulder popped back in place. The rest of us had sore ribs and bruises.

It was 7:40 p.m., and so far, we were on schedule. The scenery had been peaceful for TJ. He seemed more relaxed, and so did I. Farms were strewn along the countryside setting with a picture-post-card effect. Red barns confined to white trim punctuated the land-scape. One was serving double duty, advertising a July country fes-tival on its roof. Robins and other feathered fellows sojourned on a smaller gambrel-roofed barn as sanctuary within the same property. The Dutch door on the side distinguished by the two Roman numeral Xs exhibited functional practicality. Different barns we passed had silver-domed, ballistic-looking silos affixed to them, complete with narrow ladders the farmers must propitiously climb without experi-encing vertigo to reach the apex. Alongside one open-door barn was an empty corncrib that would be patiently waiting outside about six to eight weeks for the harvest.

The air smelled sweet. There were acres of planted fields grow-ing alfalfa, bib lettuce, corn, soybeans, and other crops. Vegetable stands seemed demographically spaced every couple of miles. One in particular caught my eye: "We've got your favorites, New Jersey tomatoes and asparagus." In one field, farmhands were tilling straw-berries. There were horse farms that had bleached-white picket fences leading to winding driveway entrances. One even offered a school for riding. We even came upon a goat and sheep farm perpendicular to a shrub nursery. There was a dirt road that led to an apiary that was proffering different varieties of clover honey, including in the comb. We drove past dog kennels and places that had country-fresh eggs and chickens for sale. On my side of the highway was a hand-printed cardboard sign wrapped around an oblique aluminum dowel, offer-ing "Bunnies 4 Sale." An antiquated ice-block vending machine notified motorists, "No 'kid'n', we have goats milk." TJ proceeded cautiously when we saw the metal sign warning "duck crossing"; over a small ridge on the driver's side, we viewed a man-made pond with mallards and their broods swimming aimlessly.

I had to share with TJ, "If people in the Midwest could only witness this region of our state, their fears would be unfounded about New Jersey only offering air pollution and gangsters."

When we traveled farther, one neglected tract of land was the only blot in our provincial sightseeing tour. The barbed-wire fencing imprisoning a ramshackle building, not destined for posterity, seemed inconsistent with the harmony of this beautiful landscape. A faded but still legible ten-by-sixteen-inch horizontal sign bill nailed to a rickety wooden post declared, "No trespassing." Who would want to? As an afterthought, I wondered if the Sahara Casino in Las Vegas would consider taking my "action" as a sport's bet.

After TJ knew that I had read the highway sign stating "Speeders lose licenses," he accelerated from thirty-five to sixty. He facetiously said he had to disprove their theorem and prove his hypothesis that his plates wouldn't fall off. I humorously chided him that it was *lose* and not *loose*. He obliged and slowed down to the limit.

There was little else to do but crack a smile and not restrain from burst-out laughter when the dusty bronze-colored El Camino with mud flaps, the confederate flag decal crookedly displayed on the rear window, and the "South of the Border" bumper sticker passed us on the right; sittin' pretty in the cab was a four-hundred-pound razor-back "porker" with a polka dot bandanna around her neck and sunglasses, watching the elevated "rubber ducky" antennae with the red pennant on top whip in the air. I wanted to yell out the window, "Sou-ie, sou, sou, sou-ie!" but my thought process was too lethargic to capture the moment. This scene was funnier by a country mile than the fast-traveling late-model Chevy pulling the two donkeys advertising on a sloppily painted sign "haulin' ass."

If the course TJ had taken was unfamiliar to me, then he didn't know where he was either. Maybe that was why he turned his cap sideways. He lost me turning right to Stanton. Of no help was the displayed highway billboard highlighting the course to Brennon's

Turkey Farm, second light make a left, three miles on the right, unless we were hungry for a holiday feast with all the trimmings. TJ was lost, but he was not sharing his secret with me. I was too tired to yell at him for being stubborn, so I suggested he pull over at the nearest gas station. He didn't. I wanted to look at a map of the area. Since he'd been doing a fine job as the wheelman up to this point, I had no choice but to trust his innate sense of direction, albeit I was crossing my fingers. Leaning back in my seat, almost wanting to drift off, I felt we'd get to the Inn eventually.

When we entered the Norman Rockwellesque hamlet that was half a city block long, I caught my bearings and knew we were heading in the right direction, especially with the aid of the rudimentary signpost with the swash letters pointing eight miles. The little town featured a general store with green wicker furniture on the front porch. Next door there was an antique shop, and juxtaposed to that was a store with a wooden shingle hanging in bright-red script, "Apothecary." On the second floor, above the drugstore was a haberdashery, emphasized with a majuscule *H*. Across the street, there was a barbershop complete with revolving candy-striped pole attached to its front. Other buildings housed a butcher, a realtor, a soda shop, and a law office. Not often that you got to see dingbats on shingles anymore, so it was refreshing to see arrows, pointed hands, and in the case of the advertised dentist's sign, a molar. TJ pointed out the chain-swinging signboard with hand-painted mocha Old English-style lettering on a pale-blue background spelling out *confectionery*. They sold homemade chocolates, fudge, sweetmeats, and other assorted sugary concoctions. On the village green where the promenade divaricated was a majestic gazebo where the idyllic visitor could seek refuge and rekindle lost memories of bygone days.

Visualizing as we were stopped at the light, I heard the uniformed brass band playing, the sounds of barking dogs, and the laughter of children; with deeper concentration, I could picture bal- loons of all colors of the rainbow and then some. Could even smell the aroma of beer-steamed hot dogs, fresh-buttered popcorn, and roasted peanuts washed down with the taste of an ice-cold barreled root beer, from what my grandfather had once portrayed to me as a child.

As we were leaving the business section, I counted on both sides of the highway about eight Victorian-style houses. They left an indelible imprint on me with their ornate detail and how well restored they were. One home even had a carriage house attached to it with a cupola on its roof featuring a Canadian goose weathervane. The sky-writing, cloud-climbing jet I spied in the hemisphere gave the anachronic impression that it didn't belong with this setting.

It hit me subtly that new construction had adroitly invaded these green pastures since my trip over a year ago.

There were new shopping centers, office parks, and neatly manicured town house complexes. It didn't deter from these pastoral surroundings, but it didn't enhance it either. I guess you can't impede some convenience and modernization, so long as it was limited to this to preserve the bucolic charm of the area.

I noticed TJ inhale a deep breath of country air in his lungs, then witness the hypocrisy of his taking a drag on a cigarette.

After I asked him if he wasn't defeating his purpose, he replied, "They raise tobacco too."

TJ hadn't lost his wit, I reflectively thought. He read out loud the sign atop a rustic John Deere tractor facing the highway along the edge of a field. It had furrowed its last field some several crop seasons ago. The sign said, "Get a lot while you're young." They were offering a two-acre parcel with a phone number to call. My driver made a right turn at the sod farm and asked if it was familiar to me. I remembered it and told him to continue on course. Had we made a left by the gravel road, that would have taken us in the direction of John Henry's residence. Here was the beginning of his property line, where the apple and pear orchard started. I recalled him pointing it out to me as his "line of demarcation," but that was a few years ago and in the daytime. Indicative was John Henry's dramatical caution concerning the boundary of the fruit trees.

He avowed, "I don't see any harm if someone swipes a couple pieces of fruit, and it's common knowledge that if you ask me, I'll let you pick a full bushel. Damn it, though, if I'll allow some vultures to filch a whole truckload of my Anjous, Bartletts, Boses, Cornices, Garbers, Hardys, and Kieffers, or my Cortlands, Cox's

Orange Pippins, Delicious, Granny Smiths, Jonathans, McIntoshs, and Winesaps again. Scooter Briscoe's white-trash pals got me good once. Ergo, they'll taste the pepperin' of a little rock salt fired from my pump-action scatter gun if there's a next time, or my new strain of honeybees will buzz them. Imagine the unmitigated gall. They sold my harvest across the highway eighteen feet up from my farm stand for three dollars less a basket than what I was askin'. If they were beggin' for a beatin', then that's exactly what I'd give them, and I did at a later date. Never hijacked from me since 'nd always consciously addressed me thereafter as Mr. John Henry. Law and order, I just love the way it works."

Because he must have repeated it to me a plethora of times, I retained most of John Henry's wrath. My basic instincts led me to believe that the town and the Inn were a few miles ahead in this direction. I hoped so. It was starting to get dark, and the rural road we were traveling didn't have any streetlights, just red plastic reflectors spaced every so often. The full moon tonight was our only beacon of light.

Jokingly I told TJ, "Follow the moon. I wonder if they'll be any werewolves out this evening as a result of this entire lunar mass."

"Maybe just a few weird wolves," he countered.

We were passing a grove surrounded by trees, and in the opening I saw a huge solitary tree stump with a mist hovering above it. Perched on the stump was the biggest crow I had ever seen in my life, and its call was a strange "caw" I'd never heard before, admissibly human sounding. The black bird was as tall and thick as the short-winged puffin, except with a much-larger wingspan. Intrigued, I implored TJ to back up the truck. The scene looked eerie to me, and he agreed to because of his own curiosity.

"Perhaps this unhallowed ground is where the Jersey Devil resides," I offered quite candidly.

"That's just a silly superstition, and you have your geography confused," TJ corrected.

There was an unmistakable trepidation in his voice.

"The devil myth originated down the shore or in the isolated Pinelands."

"This place is isolated too," I said.

TJ was meditating.

"Confidentially, there's a chill in the air, but this spot is definitely colder. It sends shivers up my spine," I sincerely admitted.

I noticed the pimples of fear and the bristling, erect hairs on the arms of TJ's rolled-up sleeves. Taking advantage of his present calamity, I allowed my imagination to roam.

"If my memory serves me correctly, the legend has it that a guy and his girlfriend are stranded on a deserted road because he runs out of gas. They're parked underneath a tree just like the one we're under. The guy goes for help and tells his gal to lock all the doors. He's gone for hours, and it's pitch-black outside, just the way it's getting now, and she can't see a thing. She's freezing and scared. She wraps a blanket around herself that she finds in the back seat. Next, there's ungodly screaming and howling. Someone is trying to open the car doors, and it's not her boyfriend. She puts the blanket she's wrapped herself in over her head, and her body is shaking uncontrollably. Her heart is thumping a mile a minute when she hears wild scuffling sounds on the roof of the car. The poor thing has screamed herself into a frenzy and is frozen stiff from nerves. She finally collapses and passes out. Repeated knocks on her window awaken her from her sleep. She recognizes men's voices asking her if she's all right. Trembling, she peers through her blanket to notice it's daylight. Looking in the direction of the callers, she sees blue uniforms, and then two friendly, concerned faces. 'Help me.'

"'Please help me,' she cries. 'Where's Fred? Have you seen Fred?' she entreats. The officers assure her that she'll be fine. They implore her to open her passenger door, but she can't, because her hands are shaking violently. One of the officers goes to the squad car and comes back with a device to pick the lock, but it's not working. The officer is frustrated, and the lady is frantically begging them to release her from her tomb.

"'Miss, we'll get you right out. Pull the blanket over your head,' he states. As she covers herself, the other officer kicks in the driver's-side rear window. They open the door and pull her to safety. Both officers beg her not to view the top of the car. 'Miss, please don't look up,' they persist. Unable to control her curiosity, she looks up, and then…I forget what happens next."

TJ had listened carefully to every word I spoke and was in anticipation to the climax of my story. I turned his way with a full grin on my face.

"He forgets. He forgets," he was mumbling to himself.

TJ reached over to open my door and playfully swatted his cap at me.

"Maybe, if you would walk the rest of the way to the Inn, it might jog your memory!" TJ shouted with conviction.

"No, no, that won't be necessary," I hastily announced.

Apparently, TJ didn't appreciate my suspense game, but he always enjoyed a good laugh when he pulled the stall ploy on me.

"Start driving and I'll try to remember. Well, as I previously mentioned, the two Coast Guard officers told her not to look up."

"What the hell is the Coast Guard doing there? You were talking about two cops," TJ interjected.

"Wanted to see if you were paying attention, pal. Just keep your eyes on the road," I said, smiling. "Right, the two cops are walking her to their patrol car, and she is compelled to look up at her car. She lets out a bloodcurdling scream when she views, hanging above the car, the remains of her boyfriend, Fred. Poor Fred, he was hanged from a rope, his eyes were pecked out, his face was half-chewed off, his hands were missing, and the scuffling sound she heard before she fainted was his shoes brushing against the roof of the car. Claw marks were embedded all over the finish."

TJ confessed, "If you told that stupid tale in Newark, I would simply laugh. But out here in the sticks, even though I know the story is folklore, I'm not laughing. It's spooky out here, and I'm glad that my gas tank is three quarters full."

When we drove up to the crest of a hill, on the corner in the valley below was the white Presbyterian church with the lanterned steeple and the graveyard right next to it. Across the stream from the edifice was a multicolored stone gristmill replete with waterwheel.

"Where the road forks, turn left," I instructed TJ.

A quarter mile later, we were in town. It was a similar small village that some would call quaint. The buildings all had outside shutters, and not a brick or stone was out of place. I could see the sign for the Inn, in Gothic letters, down the end of the block. In front, three horses were actually tied to a hitching post with nickel rings. Upon our entrance into the side parking lot paved with Belgium block, the only vehicles other than the one sharp-in-appearance hunter-green Corvette with DAR on its plates were Jeeps, pickup trucks, and vans. It was peculiar not to see any cars. I teased TJ that he brought us here right in style, in his paneled rig.

CHAPTER VI

Pleasant sounds of country music could be heard inside the Inn as I tried to decipher the embossed Roman numeral date on the corner stone, MCMXXVI. TJ opened the oak-wood door with the copper hinges. Through the small foyer, a sign above our heads read, "Surrender all guns at the bar or we keep urn." As we walked in through the maple swinging doors, angled to the right of us, our line of sight immediately came to grips with the authentically carved Mohawk warrior wearing full-feathered headdress and vigilantly offering us the hospitality of his wooden cigars. My leather soles were being introduced to the maple-grained hardwood floor. I was slipping in one spot where it was slick and wet. We were treated to the immortal Hank William's "Jumba Bali" by Jake Jewel and the Jayhawks, who were on a small stage, dressed in powder-blue suits with rhinestones. An oyster-white Stetson distinguished Jake from the rest of the band, who wore black, I reckoned.

I took in my surroundings. It was reminiscent of what I pictured in a Western movie. A bar was to the right. Adjacent steps were leading to a second-floor landing, where customers watched below from wood railings. Perpendicular to the band was the biggest stone walk-in fireplace I'd ever seen, measuring six feet high and five feet across. Directly in front of us, people were dancing, and those standing were clapping and stomping their feet. I peered between two shirtless, overalls-with-suspenders types wearing Mack Truck caps to get an unimpaired view of the rear. In another room I saw people sitting at round tables and some funny-looking men tossing doughnut-shaped objects. The place had cathedral ceilings and the type of clustered lights in brass that you could swing from if you jumped off from the rail of the balustrade, like the motion picture cowboys do in fight scenes. Spaced on the walls was an appropriate number of elk heads whose antlers doubled as coat and hat racks, and an eight-foot-high taxidermic grizzly bear with paws raised in the corner, all by his lonesome.

A couple of the local tinhorns were staring at us, especially the squinting, mean-exterior hombre with the handlebar mustache and the silver-linked band encircling the brim of his cowboy hat. We reciprocated in the same manner, giving them the snake eyes. They probably thought we were just a couple of mavericks. Certainly, they'd like us to leave. I suggested to TJ that we belly up to the bar and get ourselves a drink because we weren't vamoosing for anybody. Still, I kept my eyes peeled for bushwhackers.

Laughing, I said to TJ, "Tenderfoot, this bar *ain't* big enough for the two of us. I'll give ya exactly one minute to mosey out of town, or I'll come a-shootin'."

"I'm tired of runnin', so I'll be a waitin', Ringo," he answered, as from a stale B shoot-'em-up script.

We proceeded to slither through the dancers and the onlookers, who knew we were strangers.

"It's your choice. Either we can act smart and don't look stupid or we don't act smart and look stupid," I razzed TJ as we were walking.

The mahogany bar had accommodations for nineteen stools across, with four more in each corner. The matching wood liquor shelves in front of us were beautifully handcrafted with ornate leaf designs, and there was a mirror covering their full length.

We situated ourselves in the corner opposite the stuffed bear. TJ kicked something metal on the floor when he went to move a spare stool out of the way. Upon investigation, he grinned when he found out that the object was a spittoon, or, for the more refined upper crust, a cuspidor. Someone had dropped change in it, and you didn't have to be Albert Einstein to surmise that sticking your hand in the cylinder for a few quarters and dimes wasn't worth getting slimed.

Alongside the shelves, ornamentally crisscrossed were pairs of Civil War swords and sabers. Displayed on trileveled shelving was an array of handsome English pewter and sterling silver tankards, one toby, and some eye-catching German steins, a few of which had arabesque patterns.

TJ brought to my attention the glass drinking containers the patrons were being served with. They were utilizing sixteen-ounce mason jars as mugs, and the idea seemed perfectly appropriate with this decor. To the right, where TJ was standing, were gallon jars of pickled eggs and pigs' feet. Yours for the taking, if your stomach could take it, for forty cents and seventy-five cents apiece, respectively.

Two farm boys alongside me were guzzling down brews and sampling the homemade chili that was served in its own steaming little cauldron. Other orders were coming out sizzling in their individual skillets, which included attached handles.

The fast-talking wiry bartender gladly fetched his train engineer's cap when one cowpoke presented him with a big tip I couldn't see the denomination of; possibly, it was a sawbuck. Maybe it wasn't. There was a full-scale Lionel train set perched on top of the shelves, which I presumed was a stationary display. To our surprise, the bartender pushed the throttle and the train took off, smoke rising from the engine on tracks hidden from view. I timed the journey it took for the five-car train with caboose to circle the anteroom and the back dining area in eighty-five seconds. Coming back to home base, she was greeted with two-fingered whistles and "Yahoos!" The front-toothless farm boy nearest me shared, "She can make it under seventy-five seconds if he wants to."

He pointed to the gray-haired bartender in between a mouthful of chili.

Even though TJ and I stuck out like sore thumbs, especially me in a two-piece suit and tie getup, even without my filbert-brown Indiana Jones wide-brim skimmer, I was feelin' down home, and TJ was tappin' his fingers to the rhythm of Jake Jewel's current tune.

After he'd finished his song, Jake encouraged this young pig-tailed girl wearing a calf-length yellow dress to step onstage and sing. Backed by a throng of backslapping well-wishers, she climbed up the three-step flight, slipped off her heels, and broke into a rendition without prodding of "Stand by Your Man," which brought the house down. People leaning against the railings above us were parachuting dollar bills in response to her performance. She curtsied and shyly walked offstage, collecting her money in the doffed hat of a helpful cowboy. Finally realizing our presence among the regulars, Mr. Model Train Enthusiast came over to serve us.

Before I could order a bottle of Coors and get TJ a double Stolichnaya on the rocks, the bartender playfully suggested, "You boys better fess up and tell me where you're from, 'cause I know you're not from here, but welcome anyway. What can I get ya?"

After we confessed to who we were, the bartender's nonchalant countenance turned into a sheepish grin.

"Why didn't ya tell me in the first place, boys? Happy to meet your acquaintance. Welcome to my place. I'm Uncle Miller. Put away your money. It's no damn good here."

He gave us amiable handshakes and said he'd heard a lot of good things about us.

He grabbed TJ's hand and pronounced, "Don't let them suckers get ya down. We're all your friends in here. I'll go fetch your host. He's hangin' out with Joe in the back."

Uncle Miller skipped over to the opposite end, where there was a service bar, and instructed a dimpled, neckerchiefed brunette waitress clad in Wranglers and straw hat to go fetch John Henry. The band was on break, causing a distinct lull from the previous goings-on. Uncle Miller took advantage of the moment. Unable to wait patiently for his nephew's arrival, he projected his voice in the direction of the back room and bellowed out, "John Henry, come and greet your guests!" Excitedly he rushed back and informed us John Henry was making his way through. He asked us how we liked the place and claimed he decorated most of it himself with a little help from his nephew. The conception of the train set overhead was something he had once seen in a picture book. Kiddingly, TJ inquired if he had confiscated any guns tonight, like the sign past the entrance suggested. Turning serious, he looked down under the bar and returned with three revolvers and a miniature handgun: a .25-caliber Beretta with a two-and-a-quarter-inch barrel, a .32 S&S special, an easily concealed .22 Walther, and a deuce-shot Remington derringer.

"No, we didn't have to. These are all volunteers. Funny thing is, they belong to three women. One gal was packin' two pieces," he declared. "We don't hang up a board with a bunch of painted words sayin' somethin' we don't mean. There's no double standard around here. Not more than two nights ago, I was forced to frisk a woman I suspected of carryin' two pointed .38s under her sweater. Thank goodness it was a false alarm. I sincerely apologized for the inconvenience, and she thanked me for the pleasure, but I insisted that the pleasure was all mine, ma'am. Hubba hubba," our spry host acclaimed.

He gave us a mischievous wink and unforgettably brought us our round of drinks.

It wasn't hard to spot John Henry lumbering through even though his golden shoulder-length locks had been sheaved for ten years. Presently, he was sporting a shorter, neater cut contrasted with a darker-shaded full beard, screening his recognizable cleft chin.

He scaled in at 275 pounds, 25 less than his playing weight, and measuring at slightly over six feet, seven inches tall. The astonishing thing was that he carried only 6 percent body fat. Imagine, with his unusual height and weight, I watched him do twenty-eight consecutive chin-ups. I witnessed an amazing feat, and he implied that it was nothin'.

After all, with his massive chest muscles and possessing super-abundant arm strength, he could do serious damage ripping apart a Manhattan telephone directory when he truly wanted to test himself.

As our titan defensive end on the varsity football team, he was a consensus All-American two years in a row and unofficially compiled thirty-nine quarterback sacks his senior year. Had they kept such stats in those days, it might have been an NCAA record. He boasted his dual Academic All-American honors with a 3.8 cum in biology.

John Henry had the pro scouts drooling with his superior strength and quickness. It would have been a dream come true for him had New York selected him with their fifth pick in the first round of the draft to bolster their aging defensive line.

Instead, they went with a linebacker out of Texas. Why? No one knew. Naturally, the Chargers, moving up in the draft via a trade with New Orleans, picked sixth that year and scooped him right up. How germane it was for a team that had lightning bolts on the sides of its helmet as a logo would choose John Henry. His acquisition bolstered a position that was already laden with fine talent, but from their point of view, he was a no-brainer choice because he was the best available athlete left in the draft.

From the inception of his rookie season, he was an opposing coach's nightmare when he came in to the game on long yardage, causing havoc with their passing plays. During minicamp of his third professional season, the offensive coordinator was perceptive enough to ask John Henry to scan the left tackle's obligations in their playbook. Prior to camp, the career of one of the starting offensive linemen abruptly ended due to a fluke eye injury resulting from a boating accident. Not only did John Henry scan, but he also had the proclivity to study and master all the blocking schemes. Though he was still going to play defensive end that fall, he scrimmaged as a left offensive tackle to see if he felt comfortable with the stance and footwork at the position. He couldn't believe that it felt so natural for him to block. His technique was flawless. With the advent of big strong defensive tackles like Buck Buchanan, opposing teams needed offensive tackles of equal size and strength. John Henry broke the mold at six foot eight, weighing 300 pounds. His measurements became prototypical to the position. At times, he tipped to 308 pounds after indulging on barbecued ribs and fried chicken meals.

When he sought my advice at that time, I told him that fans perceived offensive players as more intelligent than defensive ones, and aside from the quarterback's responsibilities, left tackle was the most difficult position to learn because of the complicated pass-blocking assignments. I have always reminded him that I helped prolong his career and that interest was still accumulating on top of my unpaid agent's commission.

All joking aside, the big guy was always generous to a fault with his buddies. He provided tickets for the three of us with guests for any away East Coast trips, insisting on paying for the shuttle flights too. We flew out to Northern California once a season to view a home game. We would be issued sideline passes but were obligated to "key" on him during the Chargers' offensive series, at least part of the time, to critique him on how well he was playing. We didn't mind.

He pestered TJ to get a tryout, even introducing him to the Chargers' receiver's coach. "Wait till you see him catch a slant over the middle," the big guy promised. John Henry's intimation fell on deaf ears, however, because TJ was predisposed not to play in the league. The rest, as they say, is history, but in John Henry's case, it was geography too. He fully converted the following season, playing ten more years at left tackle. As his career wound down, John Henry became the cagey veteran who remarkably went unscathed, sustaining only stretched ligaments in his right knee and minor injuries. It wasn't until his twelfth campaign, when he had already announced his retirement, that he suffered a broken fibula the second-to-the-last game of the season. He was carted off the field as the fallen hero. The home crowd, standing as one, cheered wildly as the befallen John Henry gave the fans his last trademark raised helmet above his long matted-haired head with both hands. This time, though, he was lying on his back. The brutality and honor of pro football should transcend from the motto of Spartan soldiers of antiquity regarding his shield, "With it or on it," but there are some flagrant similarities even today. During a serious conversation about pro football, John Henry once confided to me that very few players get to leave the game on their own terms.

Financially, in his best years, he was making about 105,000 dollars, providing he made bonuses for reaching achievement plateaus and making the playoffs. It was great money when compared to the public at large, but John Henry was underpaid compared to football's glamor positions: the game breakers and touchdown makers, whom he had to create holes for or protect. Nevertheless, he used his earnings wisely, namely increasing the acreage of his family's farm.

Long before it became supermarket fashionable, John Henry was in vogue, experimenting with organic vegetables. Cross pollination, hybridization, hydroponics, and working with plant interbreeding became second nature to him as part of his everyday vocabulary. He even had a laboratory built on his property so he could conduct testing on the growth patterns of different crops using different fertilizers and producing new strains of varieties not indigenous to New Jersey's soil and climate, along with other projects he had in the works.

The crowd was parting for John Henry as the Red Sea did for Moses, excepting for the two crew-cut, overalls types who were blocking his path. He simply divided and conquered, snapping the 195-pounders aside like twigs. Next, he gently karate-chopped the fellow with the Panama-styled hat and beer-bellied physique, who was chewing away on tobacco. The poor guy swallowed his chaw. He waddled his way to the bathroom, hurling obscenities while covering his mouth. John Henry was too oblivious to realize what happened. He detoured slightly off his course, to the edge of the dance floor, taking the time to give a hand spin to this slender, smiling, auburn-haired girl sporting a French braid, accentuated by a prim azure bow. He roved twice more, tendering courtesies and salutes. Finally reaching his destination to us, he let out a wild yell in his classic baritone voice. Practically shaking our hands off, he gave TJ and me bear hugs that would have warmed the heart of the petrified grizzly had he been alive. He introduced us to the bar crowd as his best friends, and we were immediately greeted with cowboy yells and Indian war whoops. People were slapping us five, and I nudged TJ on the arm. I told him to cup his hands for all the money that was going to shower on us from above. He laughed at my remark. Accepting his celebrity status, he waved to his new "relatives."

Needless to say, John Henry was ecstatic that we had finally arrived and guided us in the direction of the back dining room as we dodged through the heavy dancing traffic. TJ was walking in front of me as we passed that grand fireplace. On the chalk-white stained mantle were color-patterned German steins and pewter mugs. Above that was a five-foot-long Revolutionary War musket with attached bayonet and powder horn. A foot away, housed in its own humidor encasement, standing upright was a rarely seen blunderbuss with shot. Impressive to me was the notched almost-pristine pair of Colt .45 pistols eight inches away from the rifles.

TJ wasn't quick enough, and certainly not big enough, to intercept the behemoth that put his arms around John Henry from behind. The Vandyke-style bearded one, with Mack truck cap worn catcher's style, must have been four hundred pounds and wore a leather vest with a T-shirt underneath. Only a man of his enormous girth could spin John Henry around like that. He was grunting, displaying all his horselike teeth, fish eyes bulging to the point of madness, with worm-size veins popping around his thick neck, from where a cowbell was hung. Those ham hock-size biceps were trying to squeeze the living daylights out of our big friend. Oddly, with this hubbub, the people nearby were not scared for his welfare. Coming to the aid of his frat brother, TJ picked up a wooden chair, but John Henry simply shook his head sideways, not wanting him to intervene. John Henry yelled out, "Guernsey!" and operating his two arms like pistons, he was striking the man in the solar plexus with his elbows. When he loosened the behemoth's left arm, he grasped it. Raising the arm and walking underneath, he reversed and pulled straight back with full extension on the man's limb. The attacker went down to his knees in pain, slapping his free right arm against his leg to concede defeat. John Henry was in a position to snap the man-beast's arm if he so desired.

Hollering to the behemoth, John Henry demanded, "Guernsey, ring that bell and moo like a cow."

To TJ's and my surprise, the rotund fellow rang that cowbell and recited his bovine chant as commanded. John Henry let go of his hold and helped his adversary straighten up. Both of them were laughing and affectionately hugging each other. John Henry thanked Guernsey for the fun. It was all a big contest.

The now-docile Guernsey, looking over TJ with the wooden chair frozen shoulder-length in his hands, implored, "Put that thing down, Hoss, before someone gets hurt."

Then, he waddled back to his table.

We resumed our trek to the back room, where to get by one last blockade, John Henry used the ruse "Make way, lady with a baby." The people turned around and smiled when they saw it was only the big guy. Apparently, they were used to his wangling antics.

This room, slightly smaller than the main barroom, jumped out at you with Frederic Remington reproductions of the Old West hanging on the walls. Joe DeRenda proudly stood up to greet us, dressed in black, pointed Frye boot finery, with roweled silver spurs, when we arrived at our table. We passed the strange-looking men who were tossing rubber disks in the corner. Joe must think he was an ole weekend ranch hand paintin' the town red, I reflected. He remarked what we thought of the place, and virtually in unison we answered, "Unbelievable." When I asked Joe what part John Henry had in financing this little saloon, he playfully winked.

Careful to look around before he spoke, Joe whispered to us, "He made an old man's dream come true." Joe humorously pointed out, "That the men's restroom is the double horseshoes facing down, not the ones facing up."

He classified, "You won't believe it. I don't know where they got it from, but they have something similar to a damn cattle trough in there. It's a fuckin; community urinal with no dividers!" he insisted.

Joe asked, "What took John Henry so long to get us?"

I replied, "He suddenly stopped to play tag with Guernsey."

"Oh, that's what all that commotion was about, and I thought this guy was running for office," Joe commented.

With the blink of an eye, Joe scanned me, then TJ, then returned back to me. He winced, after realizing the ramifications of what he just voiced, and shrunk in his chair, but fortunately TJ's thoughts were occupied with this room's ambiance. TJ readjusted his NY Yankee cap, which had not left his head since we arrived. He was paying special attention to another less gigantic stone fireplace directly behind him, where suspended above was a painting of Jefferson Davis, with an inscription below it reading, "Only presidential portrait not hanging in the White House." Joe changed the subject to John Henry's relatives.

Looking at John Henry, Joe heartily expressed, "It must be family reunion night in here, because everyone you greet, you're calling cous."

To get my direct attention, Joe slapped me on the arm.

"The latest rage in the rurals. His new mass epithet. A fad soon to come to the suburbs. Cuts down on name recall," Joe sniggered.

"Yeah, we're one big happy clan around here," offered a beaming John Henry. "And, Joe, mind your own business," he good-naturedly chided. "A country boy is allowed the privilege of adopting a few new idioms."

TJ inquired about how the place was doing.

Grinning, John Henry replied, "We've got the best little stud farm in New Jersey. We just purchased a prize bull from a farm in Lancaster, Pennsylvania, and he's driving the cows crazy. By the way, my Sally is pregnant again."

A now-attentive TJ deducted, "From the bull?"

Joe and I congratulated TJ on his well-timed jab, and John Henry, caught off guard, thought it was funny too.

"I'm sure Sally will think that's marvelous. Maybe she'll reconsider suggesting that you be the baby's godfather. She had testing done, and it's gonna be another boy. Sally thought the responsibility would do you good. Now, we'll have to take that upon advisement, and I know how much you hate that phrase."

"Oh, it's one of my favorites," he wagered. "It's a cheap cop-out in government and the preferred junior corporate executive answer for someone who can't think on their own two feet or someone who can't admit they don't have the authority to make a decision," TJ purported.

Now, TJ was off guard. We could tell he was honored the way his eyes rolled.

"When's the last time you ate, cous?" John Henry implored to TJ. He added, "Your shrivelin' away to skin and bones. Stay down on the farm with me for a couple of months and we'll fatten you up like a blue-ribbon Holstein heifer."

TJ answered back, "I have a healthy appetite when I decide to eat."

While John Henry and TJ were exchanging jibes, Joe took the opportunity to ask me about TJ.

Joe did a double take when I explained in a low voice, "TJ hasn't volunteered anything to me yet, and neither did I try to probe him. He's told me nothing about his new occupation, other than hinting it's something automotive related. That's too broad an area to speculate on. I don't even know where the guy is living," I acknowledged.

Joe agreed, after a pause, "Maybe that is the best approach to take, and I won't ask TJ any questions either. Stanley, I'm forced into making an admission to you. I'm stymied about how to open dialogue with TJ concerning this subject. It makes me feel troubled that I can be the tiger in the courtroom but a church mouse about broaching the subject of my friend's problems with him tonight," Joe conceded.

"Because you care about TJ's well-being, as John Henry and I do," I said, patting Joe on the back. "There's no onus on you to do anything. The important thing is that we're all here for him. Believe me, the ride coming down here was no piece of cake for me either. He drove." I laughed. "You know how easily it is for him to go off the beaten trail when he's exposed to country surroundings."

"You're right. When he's comfortable in our presence, he'll eventually open up, but damn, the guy looks terrible. I wish there were something more we could do than this," he suggested.

Joe discreetly passed me a thick envelope under the table that he took out from inside his sports jacket pocket.

"It's from the big guy and me. We had to do something. Give it to him after you guys leave for home," Joe requested.

Even though TJ and John Henry were occupied talking, I somehow had a sixth-sense feeling that TJ knew that Joe and I were discussing him. Purposely raising my tone to create a diversion, I inquired of Joe what the doughnut game was that the funny-looking men were playing in the corner. Joe gave me a blank stare.

"They're pitching quoits. You don't remember playing the game down at the farmhouse? It's somewhat similar to horseshoes, except that it's played with a rubber disc that's flat on one side, eliminating the danger of ricocheting iron flying at you, and the distance between posts is markedly shorter. The object is to pitch the quoit on the metal post surrounded by circles in the middle of a slate board slanted about twelve degrees. The game is still played to 21 points. A ringer is worth 3 points, a leaner worth 2. Quoits on the board closest to the post are worth 1 point. John Henry and I were a team earlier against his real cousin Emmel and some grotesque, jaw-projecting character they call Toady."

"Those guys, because they play all the time, beat us, badly. Every other quoit they pitched was a ringer. John Henry's pretty good, too, but every time he pitched a ringer, Toady would top it with one of his own. John Henry had the guy guffawing, calling him Eagle Eye, but he still wasn't missing," he said.

Priding myself with having a detailed memory, I certainly had a momentary lapse about quoits. Maybe because I didn't have a knack for the game. I couldn't get a rubber quoit to lie flat on the slate board without bouncing off.

A happy-faced, perky waitress, twenty extra pounds plump, accompanied by Uncle Miller, walked over to take our food order.

"Boys, I'm happy to inform you that tonight you have a fine choice of entrées: possum potpie, goat liver fondue, or lame brain stew," he seriously projected.

Leslie Ann was shaking her head.

"Sorry to have to disappoint anybody. I'll have to nix the lame brain stew. Lame brain is always plentiful, but today we are out of brains. I know it's kind of a contradiction of sorts, but don't try to make sense of it. Sure as blazes, you're all feelin' effervescent melancholia about that pitch," he guffawed.

"That's one of the better oxymorons I've ever heard. Certainly better than the hyperbole you uttered near the bar," TJ revealed to me, in a toned-down voice.

"I'll make up for it. If you're all a-willin', I can rustle up a potpourri consisting of sow belly, poached eel entrails, and ewe tripe complemented with our especially prepared dill sauce, or if you push me to the limit, I'll flambé turkey buzzard gizzards with sherry, mint sauce, garishly sprinkled with sprigs of edelweiss I went all the way to the Alps to retrieve," he boasted. "What will it be?"

We were all a little dumbstruck with our host's unpalatable selections.

I whispered to TJ from the side of my mouth, "These good ole boys must eat anything."

"Except their women," TJ replied, more vociferously than he wanted to.

My mouth went O-shaped, but the rest of our party hadn't paid attention.

"To laugh now would be insalubrious," I reminded him in a low tone.

He winked and tipped the bill of his cap. John Henry, pretending agitation, looked up at his uncle with a basset hound frown on his face but turned it into a broad smile when he couldn't keep up his masquerade.

"Don't take my uncle so serious," John Henry offered, slapping TJ on the back. "He's just having fun with the college chums. Anyway, those innards selections were the Thursday-night specials. He knows what we're havin'. Some real good gruel—I mean grub. Cousins, my uncle serves only the finest black Angus beef from the Hudson to the Delaware River, give or take a tributary stream or two. I'm ordering for everybody. Five prime ribs, and have them served medium rare, or when they're done mooin', whichever comes first."

The smiling-faced waitress interrupted John Henry to inform him that there were only four of us.

"Leslie Ann, darlin', please put the extra right in the middle of the table for the winner," he replied. "A giant tossed salad everybody can share, and country vegetables. If your servin' succotash tonight, bring some out so the city boys can see what it is and let them say 'How ya doin'' to some rutabaga and prove to them that it might put some hair on their chests and not bite them on the ass. If you don't eat it, we'll wrap it up and you can take it home as a pet," he raved. "We'll have baked potatoes, and bring us each a half-dozen ears of Luther Hill corn. Cousins, these are hybrid dwarf ears, and they taste as sweet as brown sugar. Sweeter than honeydew melon, if you're lookin' for multiple comparisons. They're grown in a greenhouse by yours truly. They'll try some shoofly pie if no flyin' dipterous insect marauders have perpetrated its contents. If they still have room in their bellies, then bring out Jersey-grown rhubarb baked in a delicious, mouthwatering pie crust your aunt Edna would have been proud to serve if they had only known how. Bar none, that woman's the best cook in the book. Top it off with fresh, homemade black raspberry ice cream. But first, bring us a dozen bottles of beer iced down in a bucket. Surprise us with some mixed flavors, Bud, Coors, Heineken, and Miller. And a nice bottle of apple wine for starters."

TJ poked me when John Henry gave our waitress a pleasant pat on the rump. We expected him to get slapped. But she didn't seem annoyed. Apparently, she was used to his boyish charms.

Walking over to our seats, seemingly knowing what we were thinking, she admitted in a soft voice, "Sometimes I pinch his too."

"That's exactly why he's our hero," TJ exchanged in jest.

The three of us laughed at his remark. When I shared the fun with Joe and the big guy, they were smiling too, especially John Henry.

The dinner was everything John Henry promised, not to mention the "countryfied" presentation, which was more. The prime rib must have been two-pound cuts of beef, and indeed, it was tender. Shouts of "Tasty!" from our table became the optimum word. Everyone was in gastronomic splendor. Joe and I couldn't finish our portions of meat. Because our two voracious buddies with the bottomless stomachs tied, they were without dissenting vote declared cochampions, thus sharing the remaining piece.

They were in the process of consuming forty-eight ounces of beef apiece. Our carnivores' esophagi must have managed somehow to work overtime.

It almost slipped my mind to ask John Henry about the new construction we passed on our ride down.

"Cousin…" John Henry paused between chewing a mouthful of rib steak. "That's a woebegone subject with me. This new generation think they're a bunch of genteel farmers. Many of their land holdin's originated with their great-great-granddaddies, who toiled long hours and hard years to pass on the fruits of their labor, the legacy of the property that they presently own. This new breed are a lackadaisical bunch. Puttin' it mildly, or, since you're in farm country, expressin' it 'sheepishly,' they want to live off the fat of the lamb without tendin' to the grazin' of their potential mutton.

"Imagine that, a tiller not wantin' to get his hands soiled. They seek to become instant millionaires. With the price of land bein' high right now, the real estate people are offerin' a lot of money to farmers to sell off parcels or entire farms. It seems simple enough, but when farmin' is in your bloodline and all you've ever known, it's difficult to do any other work. Some of my brethren have been seduced by the land developers, who promise riches beyond their wildest dreams. They'll entice you to go into partnerships, usin' your property to build on.

"No-risk ventures employed the labor force and offered the expertise. They'll ask for seed money to cofinance the project. A few have done all right with this type of arrangement. They'll reap the profits on some good-payin' rentals, as long as they stay occupied. Others didn't fare as well. Some construction was halted because the developer went belly-up or didn't comply with buildin' codes. That left some farmers holdin' the proverbial feed bag.

"One young farmer I know cast conventional wisdom aside and financed a whole project himself after the contractor bailed out with his seed money, forcin' him to put up his entire farm as collateral. He couldn't keep up his note payments, and the bank was goin' to have no choice but to foreclose. Instead of havin' aspirations to be the next shoppin' mall tycoon, he should have taken his seed money and purchased real seeds, planted them, and worked his fuckin' farm. Fortunately for him, he has a good woman in his wife, Amy. She was able to secure a loan from her parents in Vermont to save the estate. What a woman. She takes care of her own land, minds the kids, and works here a couple days a week. You know, cousins, she's a better farmer than her goofy husband.

"Don't get me wrong, I'm all in favor of progress, but how many shoppin' centers do you need? The people who live in town houses are travelin' fifty to seventy-five miles one way to work. There's very little heavy industry in this community. Those people live for the weekend. They'll be hard-pressed to sell when they want to relocate," he predicted.

"The epoch I envision will be culture shock to us dirt diggers. Maybe I was born in the wrong era. I like preservin' nostalgia with independent shops in a town settin', and I prefer an agrarian way of life. Let me tell you, cow tippin' ain't no general pastime 'round here unless you're some college flunky with a warped sense of humor not able to hold more than three Budweiser beers under your belt without gettin' tipsy. Not only is it disconcertin', it's downright sacrilegious in these parts.

"They fly with the same birds of a feather who smirk at improvin' the head, heart, hands, and health, the ideals of our Four-H Club membership. To them, Four-H stands for 'Four Hooters' from Hunterdon. Don't be whistlin' that tune around me unless you can back it up with more than your fuckin' big mouth," John Henry defended.

"Proud of my membership in the NRA. Own over twenty pieces. Legally, people own guns and learn to shoot early in this neck of the woods, regardless whether for collection, huntin', sport, or defendin' one's own castle. Trust me. I believe in the creed 'Better to be judged by twelve than carried by six,'" he testified.

"Well, cousins, I don't hide the fact that I'm worth a few dollars, except it's tied up in farm equipment, predial property, and financin' the renovation of this joint. I have some money in the bank, but I'm cash poor and land rich. People say, 'Look at all the dinero you would have if you sold out.' Where would I live and where would I go? Farmin' is all I know. I went to college not to play football but to learn how to be a better farmer, blendin' a scientific approach with the commonsense method I was raised with. If I did nothin', then I'd want to die. I can't live being crowded in. I need breathin' space and elbow room. Around here, when I get the hankerin', I can walk around my backyard in my birthday suit, naked as a blue jay, without my next-door neighbors gawkin' at me. Sally thinks I'm flippin' my lid when I go outside au naturel, French fans, but the kids think I'm a laugh riot. You do that stunt in the suburbs or the city and you'll be arrested for indecent exposure. The nonvoyeurs will turn you in," the big guy addressed.

"Remember me havin' that scarlet-colored Jaguar XKE I purchased after my rookie season in the pros? I had to have that sports car. To break it in properly, I drove from California to home, expectin' my father to treat me like some big deal, patronizin' my choice. His reaction was soberin'.

"'What's a farmer need a mousetrap like that for?' he snapped. 'Foreign newfangled gizmo nonsense is all it is. It's too small to haul or pull anythin' with. That thing's as useless as teats on a bull.'

"He's bemoanin' the fact that I didn't buy a made-in-the-US-of-A Chevy or a Ford truck. Somethin' that was useful yet bein' patriotic," John Henry voiced out.

"'Besides,' my father teased, 'the farm animals will laugh at you.'

"Remember now, I was twenty-two years old, makin' bacon or great money in those days playin' ball, and my dad was still referrin' to me as a farmer and tellin' me I made an idiotic purchase. Damn, I hated to admit that he was right. He helped me focus back to reality. I was a farmer who was lucky enough to also play football. To make peace with my pa, I sold the car shortly after and got myself a maroon pickup truck with fancy racin' stripes, just to be a little sporty. Dad was right on the money about everythin', exceptin' one, only the barred Plymouth Rocks and the Rhode Island red hens made fun of my Jag. They'd peck at the spokes and make peculiar hieroglyphics with their spurs around my wheels. It got to be tiresome shooin' them away," the big guy recalled.

"When I stop into 0 Days Feed Store, Charlie, the proprietor, is always bendin' my ear about takin' Sally travelin' here or there. His boys operate the water-powered mill that grinds grain for livestock feed. Mind you, cousins, I've known him almost all my life, and he's never left the friendly confines of Hunterdon County. Charlie's afraid, if he leaves, we might get gerrymandered by the folks in sprawlin' Burlington County. He's too pigheaded to accept that politically correct Mercer County serves as a buffer in between. All he does is collect vacation brochures to places he'll never visit. He certainly has the money to sightsee any place in the world, yet he pesters me to go tourin' the United States and plannin' trips to exotic lands. Well, cousins, I was taught as a youngin' to respect my elders, so I yes him to death. If I really wanted to explode on him, I would answer that I'm fuckin' tired of travelin'.

"For the almost-fifteen years that I played ball, in both college and professional ranks, I've traveled to almost every major city in the country multiple times, and then some. I'm sick of hotel rooms, hotel food, and flyin'. We maintained two residences in my playin' days, and my Sally's a saint for havin' the patience to have put up with it. I haven't been on a plane in five years and have no intention of ever gettin' on one again. No place in the US is that far away I can't get there by automobile or train. I'm satisfied to visit eastern Pennsylvania and New York City every once in a while, but most of all, I like to hang out on my farm. If I'm away too long, I get lonesome.

"Now, I'm lecturin' on this matter, and I made a sanctimonious commitment to Sally I'd finally take her to France. I've hemmed and hawed about goin' for years, but I'm goin' to be a dutiful husband because I received an ultimatum about who rules the roost. She helped sway me by tellin' me I could learn an object lesson from some of the French farmers. I'm goin' over there with the intention of studyin' their artichoke and asparagus growin' techniques. My Sally is sometimes too smart for her own good. It doesn't hurt either that I've bought some time for the fur surroundin' my face if I'd agree to go. Damn, matrimonial concessions, I call it!" He laughed.

John Henry pulled the air on his well-kept beard.

"You two cousins wouldn't know about those sort of things, would you?"

Naturally, he was referring to TJ and myself. Both of us displayed toothy smiles, and I gestured for him to continue his story.

"We're goin' sometime around next spring, a few months after the baby is due in January. As you might deduct, we're goin' via ocean liner, because they haven't figured out a way to lay railroad tracks from here to there as of yet."

John Henry scanned our faces.

"The intellectuals among us," he purported, "will be enriched knowin' that I'll be travelin' with the works of Shakespeare, as in manufacturer of fishin' poles. Always wanted to cast off the quarterdeck. Could even catch myself a mackerel. TJ, please be prepared when I return three weeks later for me to tutor you in a little foreign language lesson. Maybe I'll even teach you to sing the 'Marseillaise.'"

"TJ," he said, facing him, "don't be surprised if Stanley winds up makin' this trip with us. Look at him cringe. He doesn't know what I'm talkin' about, and I've sworn not to let the cat out of the bag," he stealthily foredoomed.

I drew my own conclusion. He didn't know what he was talkin' about.

"If I had my way and I were independently wealthy, I'd buy up all the land that's goin' for sale and make a deal with anyone willin' to farm it. Wouldn't make them croppers either. They can keep all the profits minus whatever I pay on property taxes. That's a more than fair deal. Or they can buy the property from me for what I pay for it. There would be a secret covenant, of course, included, like those Fancy Dan private clubs use, exceptin' that mine would be non-discriminatory. The property can only be used or sold for farmin'. Farmland lyin' fallow is bad enough, but worst of all, I hate to see useless construction that has no place around here. When asphalt and cement replace green grass and soil God intends for pasturin', I'm irked. I just want to preserve the integrity of this terrain. This earth around here used to be the stereotypical American Gothic, exclusively a large farmin' culture."

John Henry was flexing his muscles and poking his chest with his thumb. It was a tip-off to those that knew him that he was agitated.

"On the horizon, I can only hope there exists a professional gentry cult who will supplement their incomes workin' small tracts growing specialty crops and offering their staples directly to the public. They'll begin the new wave of a cottage industry.

"Myself, I have no other place to go. My roots are here along with kin and kith, present company being included in the former. My farm is what I bequeath to my three children as their inheritance. I hope they'll continue the tradition. Sally knew a long time ago the epitaph I want chiseled on my tombstone: husband, father, and farmer. If she wants to include 'Hall of Famer,' I won't be mad. Won't be in much of a position to be vigorously perturbed six feet underground. If Canton sees fit to enshrine me…

"Shucks, I'm only pullin' your legs. Hey, albeit, I wasn't as good as the best—Dierdorf, Donovan, Gray, Kenn, and Walters—I still played hard and well. Russ Washington, who played with the Charges, was great, but he was a right tackle. When I broke in, no one but no one was better than Art Shell, and then Anthony Munoz made his presence felt. He redefined excellence at the position. Just call me lucky, right? My career happened to overlap two of the all-time greats who happened to play in the fuckin' American Football Conference with me. Still, I made five Pro Bowl selections as an alternate. Humph. On second thought, maybe an asterisk containin' the following watercolored words, brush-painted with aquarelle, would suffice: 'Pending election by the NFL Hall of Fame Committee.' Something temporary that would wash off with a March drizzle or a good April shower." The big guy chuckled.

"You brought the subject up, cousin. It wasn't my idea to filibuster on this topic. I'll get off my podium now and finish my meal," he poignantly acclaimed.

The three of us had been listening attentively while John Henry vented his anger, placing our forks down until he finished. We were all solemn after his declaration of convictions. It wasn't often that you see him so serious for more than a few minutes, and he moved us with his impassioned pontification eulogizing Hunterdon County husbandry. Insomuch as I know him and, however unlikely, John Henry's proclamations were anarchist, he would attempt to lead the bloodless counterrevolution back to agriculture and agronomics.

Dismissing his ambiguously loony assertion about me being coaxed into taking a three-week trip next spring to, of all places, France as ranting, I refused to allow myself to explore it further with him. I wouldn't dare dignify it with a remark, because that was exactly what he wanted me to do.

It finally caught my attention that Joe was wearing glasses. I mentioned to him that he looked like a Princeton attorney now, whatever that meant. Possibly because he had monogrammed every article of clothing he wore. Joe was one of the most knowledgeable people I've ever known. A little to our chagrin, he was probably slightly smarter in some areas than his three genius friends. If the four of us were ever temporarily stranded on a desert island without the benefit of our womenfolk—and of course, I chuckled—they would tell us what to do. Pure logic prevailing, Joe's genre would be to think out the best workable, synergic solution; John Henry would contrive the means to carry it out to fruition; TJ would keep the group in harmony with his inspirational leadership; and I would be left to physically do the work. No doubt, I would devise some noteworthy improvisation, plus offer other suggestive improvements if they let me.

Joe is three inches shorter than me, but at least ten pounds heavier. He graduated number 2 in his Rutgers Law School class and was a partner in a hotshot law office. His practice is an old established firm catering to a blue-blood clientele in the state. When Joe was accepted to law school, TJ transposed an HRM to an *F* in his last name and penned the tag Joe DeFenda on him. With Joe's clout on his side, TJ could have positioned himself better during his catastrophe, but he offered Joe no return calls either. I glanced in TJ's direction. He was still busy working on his second helping of prime rib. John Henry insisted on everybody having an after-dinner drink even though we still had beer and wine on the table. Too impatient to wait for our waitress, he lumbered over to the service bar area and returned with three different types of hard liquor and substituted six-ounce mason jars for shot glasses. He bragged that he had everybody's favorite Jack: apple, Daniels, and Yukon. The big guy proposed that we all drink a toast, after pouring four big shots.

"Don't get unnerved, cousins," he calmly replied. "This way, my wrist doesn't get worn-out refilling."

He was proud of his explanation and let out a good belly laugh for all other onlookers to notice.

John Henry started chanting at our table, "Toast, toast. Let's have a toast!"

He picked up the volume to be heard all over our room. Not satisfied, John Henry stood up and gestured with his hands, working the other patrons to join in with his demand. They were eager to obey their master, needing little encouragement. Soon, chanting men and women had taken up John Henry's challenge and were demanding a toast, clanging mason jars on their respective tables and stomping their feet.

Instinctively, I knew the obligation was with myself or TJ because of our past experience with impromptu ceremonial witticisms on the dais. I took out a quarter from my pocket and asked TJ to call it as I flipped it in the air. He called heads, and the coin hit the table tails. He lost. It was my choice, and I bestowed the honors on him because I couldn't think of anything clever to say. TJ shook off a peeved expression toward me before harmlessly swatting me with his Yankee cap.

He rose from his chair, asking John Henry to remain standing, holding his drink in raised fashion.

Looking straight into the eyes of our cohost, he recited, "Let me make a toast to one of the nicest guys I know…"

The big guy stood there, proud as a peacock, waiting to hear his name finish TJ's salutation. With the skilled timing an LA comic would admire, TJ uttered, "Me." Poor John Henry's jaw dropped, and his face blushed to an even-darker shade of red already flushed from booze. He stood there looking so innocently ridiculous as uproarious laughter filled the air.

TJ put his cap back on and received a clamorous ovation from the room.

A smiling John Henry, feigning a tight fist to TJ, had to admit, "Damn it, that was good, cous. Damn it, that was good."

He lightly slapped TJ on the back. The big guy mumbled something about seein' a man about a horse and swaggered off in the direction of the men's room.

I asked Joe, who was conversing with TJ, what time he had. He told me it was time to go.

"Actually, Stanley, it's five minutes to eleven," he answered. Joe relayed unclearly, "I promised Mary that I would get home early. My kids have the flu, and I'll be caring for them all day tomorrow. Otherwise, I won't get a chance to review a brief for a case I'll be going to court with on Monday. Let me leave now, while the coast is clear."

He was referring to John Henry's temporary absence.

"The big guy will never let me leave. He'll tie me to my chair," Joe declared.

I coughed at his remark. Joe was right. John Henry would do just that. He bade us good night and said something about seeing us in two weeks.

"He's a great guy," I relayed to TJ, regarding Joe. TJ seconded my opinion. John Henry came back to join our table and inquired of the whereabouts of his cousin Joey.

"He had to go home," TJ volunteered.

John Henry jumped up and down. Acting as if Joe had done something tragic, he started cursing, "That fuckin' bastard…he had to go. We only get together once a year like this, and he can't stay all night. That sneaky son of a bitch. He had to go home! I should have tied his ass down to that chair."

TJ and I both smiled. TJ pointed to John Henry's empty glass. Being the closest, I poured another shot of Jack Daniels for my big cousin, to keep him chipper. We had seen this act before. He never wanted any of us to leave. He was like a big kid who couldn't get enough of our company.

"Hey, cous, we're still here," TJ said in solace.

"Damn right. Dam right you are!" he exclaimed while pounding his fist on our oak table. "We're the Three Musketeers. I feel better already. We'll all see Joe at the shindig I'm throwin' next month. We're havin' roast sucklin' pig, barbecued on the spit. You boys don't have a choice. It's obligatory."

I told him it sounded good to me, but TJ wasn't sure if he could make it.

"I'll let you know," he answered.

"Let me know, hell! You'll say yes right now," the big guy commanded.

TJ agreed without much choice.

"Then it's all settled. You're all coming, and I'll put everybody up. Sally will be thrilled to have overnight guests," he said.

John Henry knocked off the rest of his shot, and I could tell he was in one of those sentimental moods.

"I miss the frat parties and coaching the touch football team. Remember the trick play I designed?" he asked.

"You designed? In your wildest dreams! Earlier tonight, at the Summit Office, I ran through that play perfectly again because I originated it, cous," I insisted.

"Hmm, hmm," TJ sounded, trying to clear his throat. "You're both wrong. I was the architect of that play."

So we were all guilty of hamming it up. We laughed. John Henry refilled our "shot glasses" and was contemplating another toast.

"This time it's my turn," he slurred.

He motioned us to stand with him. In a powerful tone, he instructed everyone in the room that he wanted their undivided attention. Even the strange-looking quoit players stopped their game on John Henry's directive.

"Ladies and gentlemen, to the fraternity. And to my two favorite cousins, Stanley and TJ."

The crowd was enthusiastically cheering nonstop. It was a beautiful thing to experience. Now, TJ and I were the embarrassed ones. I observed clapping and whistling, the likes of which I had never seen before, even at sales rallies. People from the other room were pouring in to join the frenzy. When the excitement died down, I overheard TJ ironically suggest to John Henry that he should run for mayor. He should practice what he preached.

He answered him, "Why, cous, in this one-horse town, there's room for only one horse, and that's my uncle Miller, who's the mayor."

I teased John Henry that for a biology major, he sure talked funny.

"Talk funny! I've talked this way all my life, cous. When I went away to college and would come home on break, folks thought I had developed a foreign accent. They blamed it on them Communist-ideological, blasphemin' professors. Down home, folks here just tend to start phrases and everyone else picks up on them. For instance, my farmhouse from here is 'a yell and a holler.' That's one and a half miles. Years ago, farmers would yell across fields from one another. They didn't own phones and didn't have the luxury of time to walk over," John Henry concluded.

TJ added, "The farmers must have had a great set of lungs."

"Sure as hell did, cous, sure as hell did," John Henry agreed.

I smacked TJ on the arm.

"This good ole country boy here is a piece of work and a fraud," I said tongue in cheek. "Everything is just one homespun cliché. John

Henry, we know you minored in English. You've read the classics, everything from Homer to Will Shakespeare, with a little Austen, Camus, Cooper, Dickens, Dostoyevsky, Hugo, Scott, and Stevenson in between, yet you insist on espousing a cracker-barrel dialect and philosophy."

John Henry was squirming as he looked for a way out from me, his accuser. He flexed and poked his massive chest muscles with his thumb. Our big cousin tried to signal Uncle Miller, and when that failed, he attempted to get the attention of a passing waitress, but she didn't see his distress call. He scanned from me to TJ. His bloodshot eyes returned back to me, with an alley cat grin perched on his face.

He expressed, "Cousins, when in Rome, do as the Romans… and in here that means havin' some more apple wine."

He proceeded to fill up our glasses, again.

"Hey, be careful, cousins, this apple wine is a sneaky concoction. Just when your brain falsely convinces you that you can drink this like cider, it sneaks up on you and puts you on your ass," he insisted.

I said to myself, John Henry just took himself off the hook, and I let him do it. He was the only person I ever knew who could play any crowd and make others feel comfortable while he did. He could entertain for hours with stories as an ex-pro jock, show his intellectual side if the situation warranted, educate us all regarding past and modern farming techniques, or play his ingenue role of a good-timin' country boy just wantin' to have fun.

John Henry, to me, was the modern epitome of Rudyard Kipling's poem "If."

CHAPTER VII

The three funny-looking men were still playing darts in the corner of our room. They were dressed in suspendered baggy green jeans with rolled-up cuffs, displaying heavy black work boots on their feet and wearing flannel long-sleeved shirts buttoned to the collar. All three had a scruffy, four-day-old beard, but what made them appear conspicuous, even in this crowd, was that they were all wearing checkerboard Montero hunting hats, with the flaps down, covering their ears, in the summertime. The trio brandished those foul-smelling, crooked, wine-soaked cigars. They were continuing to gawk at our table.

That was when TJ voiced, "I know I'm not paranoid, John Henry. What's with them? Those guys have been staring at me all night. They're the nerdiest bunch I've ever seen. Look, they're all tins of snuff and packages of beef jerky and Slim Jims sticking out of their back pockets. Must eat that junk like candy."

John Henry answered, "Don't pay any attention to them. They don't get to see many Afro-Americans."

"And I thought I looked Swiss," TJ shot back with barbed tongue.

We smiled at his remark.

"Some people just pooh them. Other folks call them illiterate riffraff, but in actuality, they're swampies. They live in the swamp perimeter about five yells from here. They stay mostly to themselves and live off the land, fishin', huntin', trappin', growin' a few crops, and doin' odd jobs. The swampy womenfolk make and sell beeswax candles. Since I provide the hives, I give them all the wax and we split the honey. These swampies can come in here as long as they behave themselves. We don't dare serve them any vodka. It makes them too crazy. These swampies can handle other booze. They can knock off a fifth of redeye or rotgut whiskey apiece. They're not brand-conscious. Splash it down with a dozen beers each and they're perfect little lambs, but allow them to nip a little vodka and they want to wreck the place. They become two-shot commandos. Take a good gander at that group over there. Collectively, they have the mental capacity of an acorn, but they're still good ole boys. It took the patience of Job for me to constantly petition them not to bring their shotguns when they came to the Inn. Now they congenially leave them on the racks inside their pickup trucks.

"Notice that they all carry a Bowie knife at their sides. Those things have a dimension of between fifteen and eighteen inches long, separated by a handguard with a short handle made from horn. Some swampies elaborate the lower part of the hilt with scrimshaw. Practically speaking, the freakin' thing's a half-sword. They would cry like babies whose rattles you just took away when I'd confiscate those blades. I'd always give them back at the end of the night, but they claimed they felt naked in public without them. They can handle one of those knives as expertly as my aunt Hannah is with a needle and thread. I wasn't about to entertain any excuses after one swampy might slash another, because Toady was cheatin' at darts and the accuser didn't know the knife was 'loaded.' So I compromised with them, affixin' a proviso. As long as they kept their 'Arkansas toothpicks'—that's what the swampies nickname their knives—sheaved and snapped tight, they can wear them. Otherwise, my edict stands: they're banned for life. And for the locals in these here parts, the fun begins and ends here at the Inn. Damn, those Bowies are as sharp as razors, and they curve concavely to the double-edged point. I hear tell the swampies even shave with them to cut down on health-care product expenses," John Henry finished.

While I engaged in meditation, it struck me how John Henry's swampy "posse" term derived. I inquired the origin of the swampies.

John Henry pondered for a fraction of a minute. With one of his huge fists, he was gently pounding our table.

"As I recollect, from what Grandpa Edwards used to tell us, the swampies migrated up from an island that's part of Virginia, where incestuous behavior was the norm and outsiders were scorned. Others say they came from the poverty-stricken Appalachian coal-minin' regions of West Virginia. No one knows for sure. Seems like it was the familiar tune of moonshiners runnin' away from the revenue man and eventually settlin' in these parts down in the swamp. Grandpa owned the land and gave them permission to stay. Henceforth, they acquired squatters rights to the bog, under the law. Grandpa felt sorry for them. He remembered his own unpleasant encounter during Prohibition with treasury agents over his applejack and wine distillery, the recipe of which your samplin', still exists today," he claimed.

"The swampies have been known to intermarry, and you talk about being generous, if a swampy takes himself a common-law wife, he's obliged to share his bride with his single brothers. It might surprise you, as homely as some of these guys are, the quality of lovely-lookin' women that take up with these mangy swampies. When their libidos start workin' overtime and they get the 'itch to get hitched,' the prospective grooms put on their courtin' duds, spruce up their pickups, and go truckin' off to the Blue Ridge Mountains in search of a young wife to bring back with 'em. The swampies call it huntin' for two-legged deer. The womenfolk are a sturdy lot. They're doin' chores from mornin' till night besides carin' for the children. The brides, usually in their teens, and though children themselves, are presented an opportunity to escape an even more impoverished environment at home, so they settle to start a family of their own. They know what to abjectly expect, and I've never heard of one runnin' away yet."

John Henry chaffed, "Some of the swampy children go to school, while the others receive their 'cultural education' at home.

"Everyone else carried .20-gauge pump-action shotguns firin' size 8 loads, exceptin' me, 'cause I squirrel with a not-often-seen single-barreled .28 shotgun, and I brought my .22 Winchester along for target practice. We had strayed off the south end of my property, crossin' farmer Billows' fallow field through the grove, scramblin' and fightin' our way through the briar, where Zach said we would find gray squirrel nests onto a red oak clearin' that was county owned."

John Henry took a brief time out to guzzle down the remainder of his beer.

"We had gotten our shots off," the big guy continued to narrate, "and bagged two nice, furry ones. My cousin Emmel, or Ole Dead-Eye as he prefers me to call him durin' huntin' season, had a kill that was exceptional. The first one he scoped, a ground squirrel, dodged away among the protection of the trees. Persistence does sometimes give you a second chance. Never losin' concentration for a moment, Emmel drew his sights in on a second one, apparently a flyin' phalanger sailin' in at nine o'clock high. Ole Dead-Eye seemin'ly on a swivel, wheeled, aimed, fired, and dropped the acorn marauder. One of the best demonstrations of riflery I've ever seen." This he swore.

"Cousins, I'm a good shot, and I'd have to classify the Jones as marksmen, but Emmel—excuse me, Ole Dead-Eye—is in a league of his own. At forty yards away, he can knock the eyelid off a black-eyed pea goin' downhill…on roller blades," the big guy flourished.

"Now, it was one of the swampies turns. Zach, who answers to the reptilian name Turtle, said he would shoot next. He earned that moniker, I'm told, for bitin' off the head of a live box turtle. Chewed it a bit, then swallowed," the big guy disgustingly described.

TJ feigned vomiting by sticking his fingers in his mouth, and for a queasy minute, I thought I was going to barf for real.

He recounted, "Turtle caught sight of a squirrel about twenty yards to the right of us across the stream. The nut-gatherer was a big gray one who had come out of a thicket and was standin' up, showin' off his white undercoat, in front of an oak tree, havin' a snack. The bushy tail sure was a cute fellow with his front paws holdin' on to seeds while his tiny jaw muscles went into high gear, chompin' up those morsels."

John Henry grabbed one of the remaining diminutive ears of corn left over from our meal, using his table knife to slice off a couple wedges of kernels; he cupped his hands to his mouth and proceeded to do his best pantomime of a human being eating like a squirrel, going so far as to exaggerate the rapidity of his bites and puffiness of his cheeks. When he expected our expressions of mirth, John Henry was surprised to find agitation. His way-off-Broadway performance didn't get the rave reviews he was seeking from us.

"Well, cousins, before you start gettin' too sentimental, let me inform you, down in these here parts, game dinners are a way of life, and squirrel is good eatin', not mindin' the stringiness, especially if it's marinated in red wine and cooked properly. I don't kill what I don't eat," he defended. "As I was sayin', Turtle raised his shotgun, took aim, and was ready to squeeze off a round, but his older brother, Big Clemson, brushed his barrel aside."

John Henry peeked over his shoulder at the swampy table, near the dartboard. John Henry hesitated for a few seconds, grinned, and said he could duplicate the proper voice inflection of the swampy brothers' dialogue.

"'Whad ya do that fur?' Turtle begged of Clem.

"Big Clemson answered, 'Wanna see ya use your toothpick.'"

TJ looked at me in befuddlement, and I mildly kicked him in the leg.

"'Betcha all the hind legs when Ma cooks 'em,' challenged Clem."

John Henry paused theatrically during his monologue to take big sips of his apple wine. He sneaked another look at the swampies. Lowering his voice, he motioned us to lean forward. With choir-boy innocence, he rested his chin in his left palm, elbow on the table.

He proclaimed, "They think there's some sort of aphrodisiac in those hind legs. Now, this is the gospel truth, they swear that after savorin' these parts, they become absolutely irresistible to women."

After the giggling and ha-has ended, TJ poured us all another round.

John Henry beseeched, "It's true, cousins, grown men wantin' the hind legs of a roast squirrel will fight one another at the supper table like spoiled children demandin' their birthright to the Thanksgivin' Day gobbler's drumsticks."

Unable to control my laughter, I made the mistake of gulping my apple wine and shot out a spray through both my mouth and nose. John Henry arrived to my belated rescue by slapping me on the back.

"Easy, cous, come up for air."

TJ, obviously knowing that I was all right, interrupted, "Save him later. What happened next?"

The big guy, working on TJ's curiosity, replied matter-of-factly, "I forget the rest."

"Stanley tried to play this game with me on the ride down. Maybe this beer bottle boom-boom side of the head will jog your memory," TJ, clowning, fired his verbal salvo.

"Don't get exasperated, cous. A guiding-light beer just gave me total recall," John Henry snapped back. "Well, cousins, the swampy that was taking aim, Turtle, grinned, displayin' every rotten tooth in his mouth, noddin' approval. Don't ask me why. It was a ridiculous bet for him to accept. The shot with his .20 gauge from that distance was a cinch, and the squirrel was his prize for the takin', but remember these swampies want all the hind legs for themselves. Without question, he was the reincarnation of Jim Bowie, I told him, if he made that throw. My words sounded good to him even though I knew he didn't understand what I meant. Turtle proceeded to lay his rifle on the ground.

"He unbuttoned the Bowie knife from its thick-leathered hide scabbard and pulled it out. Thirteen inches of cold blue galvanized steel and well-balanced. He asked his brother to be quiet and waved us off to the left of him. Turtle carefully stalked up about four yards. Checkin' for wind velocity, he wet his thumb with saliva. It seemed as if half a minute had gone by while he was starin', to judge his distance. I was thinkin' to myself, 'He's wastin' time, and if he wasn't so fuckin' selfish, he would have been goin' home with that squirrel carcass two minutes ago.' I snickered when he planted a kiss on his Arkansas toothpick. The swampy kicked his right foot back and held that knife with his right hand cocked back, like you're pitching a quoit. Mind you, that blade is over a foot long and one and a half inches wide. Takin' a deep breath, with right hand and foot moving forward as one, Turtle let go of his Bowie with a wild swampy scream."

"Now, cousins," John Henry insisted. "I was watchin' intensely, and in that exact moment, a speckled trout jumped out of the stream. The whirlin' steel ripped as easily as apple butter into the underbelly of that fish, penetratin' his gullet, carryin' him off. To my disbelief, an off-course ruffed grouse intersected the same flight path, where he, too, was speared through, explodin' tiny greenish tertial feathers in midair above the stream. Now that Bowie with two animal trophies already impaled was zoomin' in for a bull's-eye on that ole gray squirrel. He was just munchin' away, mindin' his own business, not payin' attention to his impendin' doom," the big guy maintained.

John Henry stood up to walk a few paces and stretched his arms and legs, looking over the entire room. Bewildered, TJ and I were just sitting there, waiting for the climax of this yarn. Rejoining us, he started whistling, staring at empty space. He knew that we knew that he was working us pretty well. Before TJ could interject, I decided to break our minstrel's tune.

Sarcastically, I implored, "Don't tell us, cous, that the swampy got the squirrel too?"

TJ, echoing my sentiments, pleaded, "Say it ain't so, John Henry, say it ain't so."

"No, the squirrel scattered, relinquishin' his position to a nosy eight-point whitetail buck who came ramblin' out of the woods with his head lowered. The trajectory of that knife cracked him right in the skull. He dropped deader than a stone, with the grouse and the wiggleless trout packed tight on that blade, landin' DOA. We raced over to the bank on our side of the stream for a closer look-see. I was jumpin' up and down with Emmel. I was clamorin'. 'It's a miracle! It's a miracle!' I got down on my hands and knees and said a silent prayer. I'd never witnessed anythin' like that before in my life, and certainly, I never will. Stanley, you're good with math. What are the odds of that happenin'?" he sincerely queried.

Before I even had time to even think about calculating a statistical ratio to this phenomenon, John Henry blurted out, "A zillion to one."

I curtly smiled and kept my answer to myself. He was on a roll. Who was I to disagree?

He affirmed, "The four of us waded across the stream at the rift point, a little farther down, for an up close and personal look at this 'hunter's smorgasbord.' Emmel and I were gapin' at this catch of the day with envy. You could even call it the catch of the century. I had to rub my eyes to make sure they were not deceivin' me. My cousin was scratchin' his forehead. He recalled an article, which he thought was in *Field and Stream Magazine*, he read some time ago about a target shooter who killed two small game with one pull of his bow when they jumped in his line of sight. I could appreciate the logic of that happenin'. Could even make an argument for a cross- or longbow and certainly usin' a high-powered .30-30 rifle, but to spear through three critters with the flick of a fuckin' Bowie knife? That's impossible."

"Turtle, the happy knife-chucker," John Henry upheld, "was proud as a peacock. With a strong thrust, he recovered his weapon, nonchalantly wipin' the blood on his left trouser leg and returnin' it to its proper leather home. This was celebration time, and I would have been remiss not to have brought my flask filled with black-berry-flavored brandy on one of these wild-game huntin' trips. Very selectively, I chose only the Leroux, Jezynowka, brand. Stanley, I blame you for introducin' it to me. It's the one with the slogan on the label that says, 'Made specially to the Polish taste.' Well, my Dutch, German, and Scottish taste buds prefer it too. Emmel and I were tra-din' blasts with Turtle. Clem turned a deaf ear to my hospitality offer. We were backslappin' and yahooin' with the other swampy.

"The three of us were behavin' like kids splashin' in the stream, playin' a game of ring-around-the-rosy, but forsakin' the all-fall-down part. We had Turtle convinced that sportsmen from all over the country would want to have a Polaroid snapshot picture of them-selves with the 'big game hunter.' Famous people will insist on hirin' only Turtle Jones as their huntin' and fishin' guide because he knows where the really big ones are. He wasn't positive if we were funnin' with him or not, but Turtle liked the notion of his soon-to-be celeb-rity status. By golly, measurin' his swills, he was also strikin' up a plea-surable acquaintanceship with the liquor in my silver-plated vessel. Turtle had acquired a sophisticated taste for my premium blackberry brandy, as he chugalugged the remainin' contents."

John Henry said with unfailing continuity, "As excited as his younger brother had been, Clemson was actin' like an amnesia victim to what just took place. His lackluster expression hadn't changed. He had been as emotionless as the fuckin' cigar-store Indian we feature near the entrance, but with one arm akimbo. Clemson was tracin' with his eyes the wondrous zigzag escape route the squirrel took to the woods, to elude a possible second shot.

"Being incoherent to my first plea, I repeated, 'What do you have to say about that?'"

"Clemson recurred but, thinkin' I was his sibling, answered, 'Ya lost the bet.' When he realized his mistake, he turned to his brother. He added, 'I'm a-gonna go home and tell Pa I won all the hind legs.'

"Then he skedaddled through the woods in the northwesterly direction of the swamp. I was stunned by his response. Evidently, it didn't faze him what Turtle had accomplished, and this was as per-plexin' as the marvel I was a spectator to only minutes before. Lookin'

Turtle square in the eye, I challenged, 'I suppose Clemson won't tell your pa what happened?'" John Henry foretold.

"Turtle immediately replied," John Henry distinguished, "'No need to. He won fair and square. Clemson was so excited about win-nin' the hind legs that he forgot he came a-ridin' with me in the truck. He don't win many bets. The only thing is, he's gonna be awfully sad,' Turtle grieved."

"'Why?' I asked.

"'He ain't gonna get no hind legs 'cause we didn't shoot any squirrels,' he stated."

TJ looked at me with a blank expression, and I offered the same response back at him.

"Well, cousins, remember me mentionin' about them not havin' the mental capacity of an acorn?" he reminded. "After Turtle's pronouncement, I said to Emmel, 'Let's get out of here before extra-terrestrials kidnap us.' He didn't get it, and I didn't bother to explain what I meant. We helped the swampy load his catch to his pickup. Emmel asked if he was interested in barterin' for the squirrels that we shot. I said no. They were his as a present from us. Gratefully, he offered to skin the deer on the spot and share the venison with us. Cousin Emmel and I thanked him, but we insisted he take everythin' home to his pa."

"We are highly disappointed that you think we're that naive after knowing your capers for almost twenty years."

TJ and I shook hands in self-congratulations.

Prolonging the comical admonishment, TJ playfully rebuked, "The punch lines in your anecdote were okay, but if you don't mind, let a professional like me tell the jokes."

After I gave the angled guillotine sign across my Adam's apple, TJ slapped me five.

John Henry held up his hand in the manner a traffic officer would gesture at a busy intersection to stop cars, save the tempestuous style. He rolled his short sleeves up shorter, showing off his hardened biceps and clenching his hands.

"If you are finished, cousins, if you are finished. You have embarrassed me in front of family and friends. You have besmirched my reputation for sincerity. You have desecrated a decent rural role model. I understood you two to be like brothers to me, and after twenty years of friendship, it hurts me to no end that you don't believe me. As everyone present can attest, I sometimes embellish the truth, but I never lie," the big guy defended with lamentation.

John Henry proceeded to unbutton his shirt, revealing his massive forty-eight-inch chest. Dangling from his neck was his ostentatious display of two thick gold chains. One chain was adorned with a proof-quality South African Krugerrand coin, while the other had an insignificant-looking copper coin attached.

"May lightnin' strike me dead," he declared, "right through the heart, if I'm lyin'."

Following TJ's suit when he ducked his head under the table, we were mirthfully reacting to the big guy's oath.

Not taking himself seriously, TJ voiced something from below. "Gold is a good conductor of electricity, isn't it? And button up that shirt, will you? Are you practicing to be a Benny, bare-chesting for the beautiful, bouncy, bubble-gum-ball blowing, bosomy, bronze bimbos bathing on blankets, in bikinis, on the beach at Belmar?" he alliterated with brashy baselessness.

John Henry's rebuttal to our actions was swift. "That was over fifteen years ago, and you were there too. If my cousins are through bein' foolish, maybe we can make a small wager, so I can preserve my dignity."

In a voice loud enough for everyone present in our room to hear, he appraised his two 18K gold chains with one South African gold coin and the trifling copper coin at a conservative value of $3,000, not including sentiment. He offered to bet his treasures against TJ's cornelian stone ring and my new watch to prove he was a man of honor. TJ and I huddled. I offered my opinion in a cautious voice that John Henry was bluffing. He assented without words and added in a whisper, "John Henry is full of shit, a lousy poker player, and we can't back down now."

"John Henry, let me get this clear," I said. "You're betting the jewelry around your neck against our possessions that you're telling the truth. We're going to need conclusive proof that the story is real, and we make the final decision. If you agree to those terms, then you have a bet."

Even with my mind cloudy from too much beer, wine, and a couple of shots, I was proud of the way I collected my thoughts. TJ gave me a thumbs-up sign. Without hesitation, John Henry verbally agreed to the deal and sealed the pact by shaking hands with us.

Thinking he reacted too swiftly, John Henry was pondering the situation, talking to himself out loud.

"I would like to reconsider my bet. We've all had too much to drink. Let's make the wager next time we're all sober. I'm riskin' my best jewelry against your rinky-dink crap. I made a mistake. All bets are off," he vainly disgorged.

I didn't even have to glance TJ's way to let John Henry know in no uncertain terms that we were not going to let him weasel out of the wager, and besides, I didn't appreciate him mocking our valuables.

"John Henry, you made a bet in good faith, and I expect you to live up to your obligations," I demanded in a voice loud enough for all present in the room to hear.

The hometown crowd was shifting to our side too. They were goading him to keep his word.

"Okay, cousins, okay. Everybody has convinced me to reconsider my position. I'm only doin' it for one good reason: to redeem my good name your vile tongues have trampled. If you want positive proof, then I'll just have to give you positive proof," John Henry promised.

He barked out, "Uncle!" in the direction of the bar and beckoned him to come over to our table.

I watched Uncle Miller relinquish his bartending duties to the attractive, raven-haired girl with the cascade of waves and the good set of legs I had noticed earlier. He hurriedly trotted over to join us, shaking his head in disgust.

While raising his eyebrows and squinting his eyes, he scolded, "Damn it, boy, you know I'm busy. This better be important. What the hell do you want? Excuse my bad manners, boys." He directed his apology to TJ and myself. "How did ya like them steaks?"

I don't think he paid attention to our reply of "Great," because he continued to chastise John Henry.

"Mr. Highfalutin, I've got a mind to give your ears a good pull, but I'm in a generous mood tonight," he threatened.

John Henry just sat there gravely with his head bowed down, taking his verbal punishment. Both of us were silently glad to witness his reprimand, our sympathies lying with Uncle Miller, because we felt guilty to have taken him away from his chores with our foolishness.

He screamed, "If every time I had to stop to see what this big lummox wanted, I'd never get my work done! I slave like a mule seven days a week. I'm tryin' to operate a business, not be a damn confidant. It don't pay anythin'!"

John Henry attempted to get out, "Why are you so grouchy and tryin' to be so orner—"

Uncle Miller cut off his unfinished interrogative sentence and was scowling.

"Don't ever sass your elders, boy," he scolded. "Ya may act and get treated like a big deal elsewhere, but not in here. When ya visit my place, ya put your pants on, one leg at a time. Same as I do, and same as everyone else, I reckon. Let that be a lesson to ya."

"You don't…," John Henry expressed excitedly. "You don't seem to understand—"

Again, the big guy got cut off at the communicative pass.

"I understand that my nephew, who is supposed to be a smart college fellow, is talkin' like a man with a paper asshole," he dared.

I witnessed the big guy do a quadruple blink, and his eyes seemed to roll back, confounded by his uncle's latest outburst.

At present, TJ and I didn't appreciate John Henry taking so much abuse. We had welcomed a little chiding, but we were annoyed that Uncle Miller was heckling him so. We were feeling remorseful for making the damn bet.

"Now, like I said, John Henry, this better be pretty damn important, 'cause I have to give Amy and Suzy a hand with preparations. That new assistant cook, Murphy, is causin' a hullabaloo in the kitchen and threatenin' to quit," Uncle Miller mildly forewarned.

John Henry, pouting sheepishly, responded, "I'm sorry, Unc. I wouldn't have called you over if it weren't very important."

"Well, spit it out, then, boy, and stop bein' so damn mealy mouthed," Uncle Miller required.

"Uncle," the big guy said, "I recollect it was about five years ago come this late November when Emmel and I went squirrelin' with Turtle and Clemson and that freak event happened that you are aware of. We need you to settle a little bet. Unc, I want you to tell these boys what happened, and I can't give you any coaxin'," John Henry stated.

"Well, I hope to high heaven no one bet the crown jewels. If no one is laughin', that's supposed to be a joke, fellows," Uncle Miller implied.

TJ looked at me for a response. In silence, I addressed him, "Yeah, I don't fuckin' get it either."

"Nephew, ya know better. I disapprove of wagerin', especially at the Inn. It's the devil's doin's. Ill-gotten gain is just not righteous," he ecclesiastically justified.

Uncle Miller was deep in thought. He had his arms folded around his chest and was intermittingly pulling the dapple-gray whiskers on his neatly trimmed pride and joy perched on his upper lip.

With the conviction of a judge ready to pronounce sentence, he profoundly addressed, "That was when that swampy fellow killed a trout, a game bird, and a buck with one thrust of his knife. Boys—"

John Henry interrupted, "Unc, these boys thought I was lyin' when I told them that story."

"Boys, I hope ya didn't gamble too much, because my nephew is tellin' the gospel truth. Third biggest thin' to happen in these parts, other than the Lindbergh kidnappin' trial and Grandma Fargo givin' birth to quadruplets at the age of fifty-two. I was just a youngin' then, and the year was…well, if I say that, then I'll give away my age, so I won't," he clamorously explained.

"If I may be allowed for a second to comment on the Lindy baby kidnappin'. The jurisdiction for the legal proceeding took place at the ole courthouse in our county seat, Flemington. It's a stone's throw from here…"

"I'd stand on my head for that. Someone hurling a small rock about seven miles," I doubtingly rejected, hinting to TJ.

"So would George Steinbrenner," he lowly poked.

Uncle Miller glared at us for three seconds' count. He was trying to reproach us as if we were two whippersnappers in his peanut gallery.

"My uncle Owen Frankfurt back then was editor in chief of the local *Courant*," he resumed. "He held to the very singularly unpopular belief that Bruno Richard Hauptmann, tried by a jury who only heard circumstantial evidence and convicted him of the hideous crime, was actually railroaded for lack of a better suspect. His editorial dissent from the mainstream opinion at large cost him a broken car door, a broken window at his home, and a broken arm at his office. Owen damn nearly got himself lynched, if it weren't for the intercession of his cousin through marriage, the sheriff at that time, who later became a justice of the peace, the Honorable Jesse James Sturke. It wasn't uncommon for rural law enforcement officers back in the 1930s to tie down their holsters to their leg for a more comfortable pistol release, and Jesse did just that. His six-shooter piece is still intact with the five notched ivory handle, placed on display in the dining room," he apprised. "Beggin' your pardon, boys. Sorry to harp on with trivia from my ancestral roots. Ya have other pressin' thoughts on your minds." He smiled.

TJ's and my forlorn expression indicated we weren't too happy with Uncle Miller giving credence to John Henry's account, much less a possible abortion of criminal justice, and maybe still an unsolved mystery.

"With due respect to Uncle Miller," I insisted, "John Henry, you give us some more valid proof. Right now, it's our word against yours."

TJ backed me up.

The big guy replied, "You're forcin' me to introduce some evidence and another witness to substantiate my claim."

He stood up and pointed to the area of the room where four men were playing darts.

"Cousin Emmel, borrow you a minute?" he called out loudly in that direction.

The man walked over and tipped the brim of his Ryder truck cap to us. Uncle Miller introduced us as John Henry's school chums. He asked him if he needed another cold one to wet his whistle. Cousin Emmel declined the offer, stating he had a full bottle of beer back at his table.

"Cousin, I'm sorry to interrupt your game. I need your help in settlin' a small wager. Over yonder, what's hangin' above the dartboard where you're playin'?" John Henry plainly questioned.

Cousin Emmel was noticeably fidgety, and from his sluggish thought process, you wouldn't classify him as a rocket scientist.

"Well," he carefully said, "every fool knows that's a buck's horns hangin' overhead. Are you funnin' with me?" He asked the last in a hoarse-sounding voice.

TJ and I had no idea where John Henry was going with this line of questioning.

"No, you know better than that. You gave me the right answer. Now, I have one more question to ask you, and then you can go back and finish your dart game. The final question has a slight degree of more difficulty to it, but I know you'll do fine. Think carefully and tell everybody, What's tied to them antlers?" the big guy plainly asked.

For a minute, I thought we were part of the audience of a game show and the emcee was asking the contestant, "What was Simple Simon's first name? Think carefully before you reply."

Cousin Emmel answered, unfaltering, "That's too darn easy. There's a fish tail and feathers. You know that."

Upon that pronouncement, John Henry's smile turned to a grin.

His cousin was happy with his good answers. I was anticipating a siren to go off. The model of the show comes out, gives Emmel a big kiss, and presents him with his booby prize.

"Gentlemen, excuse me, cousins," John Henry appealed, "I just presented you with exhibits 1, 2, and 3. There's your proof from that incredulous day. What more do you guys want?"

With that testimony, I was almost willing to concede, until I looked over to TJ. He rose from his chair and boldly summoned to cross-examine the witness. TJ hadn't anticipated John Henry's objection. He indicated his impatience by flexing his chest muscles. Uncle Miller couldn't hide his fret either when he covered his mouth with his hand.

TJ petitioned, "Emmel, isn't it true that you're John Henry's blood-related cousin?"

He replied yes but sneaked a peek at John Henry for assurance.

"Emmel, I have only one other question." Then TJ asked, "What's the craziest thing you ever heard about in this county?"

Aware that Emmel was shifting his eyes to John Henry for guidance, TJ insisted that he answer the question without looking to his cousin for help.

Fidgeting again, Emmel remarked, "I guess Grandma Fargo havin' all those babies at her age."

"Well, there you go, cous." TJ and I both chuckled, telling John Henry he had lost the bet. "He didn't back up your story, and Emmel was supposed to be with you that day, cous."

We both had our right hands opened palm up to each receive our new gold chain.

John Henry was aghast.

"Wait a damn minute. Not so fast," he said as he thumped his mason jar on the table. "Let's return to a little order and decorum in this here court," John Henry lectured.

TJ fired back, pointing a finger, "Cous, you can't get away being both judge and defense attorney."

"All right, then, Unc behaves like the Ole West's Roy Bean. Let him play judge," the big guy conceded. Staring at TJ, he smiled.

"Counselor, that was a shameless attempt to badger my witness, and you tried mighty hard to confuse him. Your tryin' mighty hard to razzle-dazzle the jury with smoke and mirrors, but it isn't workin'. This isn't the big city, where you can get away with any hocus-pocus chicanery," he rebuffed.

"I recall Emmel Andrews to the stand. Emmel, you just answered what the craziest thin' you ever heard of was. Now, I'm askin' you to tell these good people what's the craziest thin' you ever saw, and damn it, boy, I was with you. Take your time to think."

Without hesitation, Emmel responded, "Well, why didn't ya say so in the first place? You were there with me when Turtle nailed them three critters with his Bowie knife." Pointing above the dartboard, he asserted, "Those are the souvenirs from that day."

Holding his left thumb cocked with his right hand, he pointed his left index finger above the dartboard.

"Thanks for your help in straightenin' somethin out, cous. Your group is wavin' over for you. It must be your turn to throw, so I'll let you resume your game," a grateful John Henry declared.

"It was a pleasure meetin' ya, and I hope ya didn't lose your shirts," Emmel said before departing.

TJ's mouth dropped, and John Henry haughtily expressed, "Case closed."

I begrudgingly acknowledged to nobody in particular that the story must be true. I looked to TJ for a response, but he answered me with silence.

Stone-faced Uncle Miller, standing with his hands still folded, revealed, "Boys, I hate to pour salt on your wounds…"

Not finishing his statement, he rushed over in the direction of the bar. Returning immediately thereafter, he had with him a glass-enclosed picture frame.

"You boys believe in newspaper accounts, don't ya? Now, I'm not talkin' about that sensationalism crap, but honest news reportin'. Here, take a gander at this," he politely offered.

Before I had a chance to scrutinize the contents, TJ snatched it from me.

"We're dead ducks," he gravely said. "Everything they've said is true."

Grabbing it back from him, I perused the contents of a newspaper clipping printed by the *Hunterdon County Quarterly Fish and Game Review*, dated December 12, 1983. It gave an account confirming their wild episode. Turtle Jones did what they swore to, as witnessed by Clemson Jones and two cousins, Emmel Andrews and ex-professional football star John Henry Andrews. TJ flipped his ring on the table, and I did likewise with my Movado watch.

"Cousins, I pleaded with you to believe me. It hurt me to have to prove with witnesses and exhibits that I'm a man of integrity. Winnin' your jewelry is nice, but it's less than satisfactory if you both don't entertain me with a sincere apology," he callously disparaged.

Both of us genuinely professed our sorrow for doubting his word. Competitive as we are, neither TJ nor myself liked to lose, especially possessions we personally valued, and especially to John Henry, who would gloat over his victory. There was no one to blame but ourselves for making such a stupid wager. It would teach us a good lesson. There's no such thing as a sure bet unless you're positive that you're the winner. We had accepted a less-than-perfect chance to be right, and the stakes were too high. In retrospect, I should have realized John Henry's colorful story line was too bizarre not to be true. He had more to drink than we, so we couldn't even accuse him of plying us with liquor. Even though I could purchase a new watch such as the one I possessed until a second ago, I didn't want to. I liked my former, and besides, John Henry wouldn't appreciate its coruscant feature as much as I did.

Poor TJ. His cornelia stone resting in a gold setting left to him from his father was one of the few mementos he had to remember his dad by. Forget the monetary value; John Henry and I understood the sentiment that ring had. That was the first time I ever saw TJ take it off his finger. So if we chose to behave like two sad sacks in the depths of pathos, about ready to weep, instead of two grown-ups taking their dose of medicine like men, that was our prerogative.

John Henry started to guffaw. Next, his uncle, along with the crowd surrounding our table, started chiming in. Even Emmel came over with his dart buddies to join in the merriment, at our expense. It was bad enough that John Henry was getting a vicarious thrill out of our malady, but to have his relatives and strangers poke fun at us, too, with their glad-handing, thigh-slapping, knee-jerking bodily movements, was more than we should have to tolerate. From our perspective, we couldn't understand all the commotion caused by losing a simple bet.

TJ whispered to me, "I've seen less exuberance exhibited at political rallies where delegates were cheering and clapping on cue."

Taking advantage of the lull on the noise level, I managed to blurt out, "Is it our misconception, or did we indicate we're two hucksters from North Jersey?"

Before I could make another statement, my eardrums were reverberating from the spontaneous combustion of uproarious laughter. Both TJ and I threw our hands in the air in an attempt to ease our frustration of not knowing why. Didn't they grasp the intelligibility in what I tried to say, or were we among a group stricken with "moronic plague"? As I mused, a ridiculous thought swam to my head. Had we entered, turned stage left instead of right, and been given the ignominy of nondimensional, surrealistic players in Ionesco's Theater of the Absurd, sans lucidity? The play was being revisited in my mind. "Exit stage…"

I watched as Uncle Miller slapped John Henry on the back and kissed him on the forehead.

"You're the best," Uncle Miller advocated. "It's time ya tell them," Uncle Miller begged in between horse laughs. "Give these boys some peace of mind."

Sweeter music was never heard when John Henry distinguishably offered, "Keep your belongings."

In our haste to collect our sentimentals, I grabbed TJ's ring and he took my watch by mistake. During our sloppy exchange, we dropped both items into drinks. With that deft show of coordination, we brought the house down for the third time. During this state of glee, John Henry contracted the hiccups and remedied his trauma by shrewdly drinking from the mason jar filled with apple wine containing my Movado. He thought he'd recovered, but he couldn't get the words out he wished to say to us. Finally, he'd recuperated enough from his ailment to lean across our table and told both of us in our faces that we'd been duped. At this discovery, I felt my face turning a bright shade of inferior claret wine, and TJ would have blushed if he could have. Emmel and his smart-aleck dart buddies were literally laughing their heads off, and for a microsecond, I wished they physically did.

Emmel received John Henry's attention and asked, "How'd I do, cousin? How'd I do?"

The big guy returned, "You did real fine, cous. You've become a real thespian of sorts."

"John Henry, I'll take an oath, right here in front of everyone. I've never dressed up in women's clothes ever in my whole life," he defensively denied.

"Don't get flustered and discombobulated, cousin, and please, for heaven's sake, don't go double-jointed on me," he explained. "It's just another word for an actor, and like I said, you played your part well."

Incredulously, our usual extraverted personalities were now taciturn. Uncle Miller was standing between TJ and myself, with his arms draped around our shoulders, trying to offer us comfort.

He stated honestly, "Boys, don't feel too stupid. We've fried some bigger fish than you with this tale. I helped concoct the whole idea after John Henry told me what really happened. Those antlers are from a buck I shot myself in Moscow, as in Pennsylvania, upon Route 435. It's about thirteen miles away from Lake Wallenpaupack. We hung them above the dartboard, tied some bird feathers I found in the parking lot, and attached a fish tail I cut off in the kitchen. My nephew Larson is editor of the *Chronicle*, and he ran off the bogus account on his press.

"We attract to the county some wise guy travelin' salesmen and smart-mouthed city types lookin' for antique bargains. They like to have sport with us dumb country bumpkins. Lester King, a dealer who's here tonight, gets them in his store all the time, tryin' to 'get over on him,' but it's Lester who turns the tables, doin' the bamboozlin',￼" he jawed.

"They like challengin' us to a war of wits, but it's them who get battle-scarred. Maybe we don't offer the vivid color and pageantry of a Barnum and Baily Circus act, but we can dramatize a fairly good ole dog-and-pony show of our own, and with pizzazz. When I spot a good fish who's gettin' plastered on booze and talkin' trash, I let John Henry cast his line and hook 'em. Our Emmel reels 'em in, and I put 'em in the net after I bop 'em on the head. We bring in a fairly good catch for a bunch of so-called rubes."

He started shrieking again.

"Ya boys were cagey fish. Ya nibbled on the bait for a long time before ya got hooked. My big nephew was ready to jump out of his skin, TJ, when ya started to cross-examine Emmel. The poor boy memorizes his lines. He doesn't know how to ad-lib.

"Your tactic surprised us all. No one had ever tried to do that before. We may have had to place an emergency 911 call. With the evidence we've fabricated and the down-to-earth believability of our witnesses, the loudmouths are shamed into admittin' they've lost. Golly-gee, even Supreme Court Justice Sandra Day O'Connor would be hard-pressed not to support our claim. Like I said, we've fried some bigger fish, but you boys take the cake with the expressions you had on your faces. I had to hold myself back from bustin' out laughin' when ya gave up your things and apologized. Let me assure ya, we never keep the suckers' jewelry. That stuff's just too darn sentimental. It would make me plum restless, sleepin' at nights, knowin' I had possession of someone's granddaddy's heirloom pocket watch. We let them sweat it out for a while. We make 'em cough up with cash or a check to square their losses. It makes me sad I can't inform 'em they've just received a good country fuckin'—I mean education."

John Henry interposed, "We conferred extraterritorial privileges on you. It's a country-bumpkin dispensation."

While winking at his nephew, he replied, "Thanks for the comment, smarty-pants." He continued to us, "If you're wonderin' about whether we keep the money, well, we don't. It gets donated to the widows' and orphans' fund in the county. We tell 'em straight up where the money's goin' to. On top of it all, the suckers don't realize they're makin' a tax-deductible contribution and it's for a good cause, besides. If I take a check, I tactfully warn'em good. I also hold the title of town constable. If the check bounces, I'll get a warrant for their arrest and they can tell all their social set friends how they paid off their debt workin' on my chain gang in zebra uniforms. Naturally, they get so scared at that declaration their pockets get mysteriously deeper and they find the dough on their person or authorize a wire transfer. Works like a charm every time," he delineated.

"Question, Unc," John Henry implored. "What was the cock-and-bull about me talkin' like a man with a paper asshole all about? You better be careful with your reply."

"I just needed to add a little zip to my script," he cavorted. "Oh, I was tryin' out some new material and do a spoof on ya in the process. Keep ya on your toes. I've got news for ya. My unbiased opinion is to leave it in the routine, because it brings ya unexpected sympathy and allows me to briefly play the villain. Ya know, after numerous performances, I get tired of bein' typecast as the affable and congenial uncle. I needed to broaden my horizons, so I took the liberty to expand my character's role and give him new definition," he shared with a bearish grin. "My biggest dilemma right now is decidin' whether to be the cranky ole codger or just a plain testy ole man," he offered with histrionics.

I was afraid he was going to, and then he asked, "What do you boys think?"

TJ and I just bobbed our heads, as if we were apples in water. Under his breath, I heard an indistinct, "Whatever." John Henry pointed a finger.

"Unc, you've got me worried. I think you're tryin' to steal my thunder," the big guy challenged.

"Oh, don't fret. No one could ever play your part. You've been blessed with the gift of gab. That's why your such a storytellin' wonder. That gene must have come from your father's side, because my sister, your mother, didn't have your knack to make such good bullshit deliveries." He cackled.

"Unc, the apple doesn't fall too far from the tree," John Henry theorized.

He was staring at his uncle.

"What have I done to ya, boy? Ya'll be the death of me yet, but at least I'll die laughin'," he jocosely admitted.

Uncle Miller walked over to his storytelling nephew, who had just laid a big egg of a practical joke on us, the college chums, I said to myself regretfully. With clenched-tight fist, he delivered a soft uppercut blow he held prolonged to John Henry's chin.

"Boys, as he was holding back between gasps of air, still, my favorite part is when I threaten to pull his ears," he finally managed to expel.

John Henry countered, "Yeah, Unc, I'm glad you don't take your Lee Strasberg method actin' so seriously."

"Ya sure are," he stated, then repeated, "Ya are the best." When our eyes caught, he demonstratively inquired, "Stanley, don't ya know some big wheels in Hollywood? 'Cause we just gotta nominate him for some kind of Academy Award."

With that petition, TJ and I merely shook our heads and joined the howls of merriment along with the big guy and Uncle Miller. As our host and cohost stood for yet another toast this evening, they interlocked arms and allowed themselves to drink out of the other's mason jar and harmonize an invariably colloquial slogan, "Happiness is bein' the only hick, ridin' the only horse in a one-horse town."

"You know, Unc, just bein' one of your favorite nephews is enough honor for me. Is this the week that I'm the favorite?" the big guy jocosely supplicated.

Uncle Miller responded, "Ya know how I hate this kind of sentimentality. Next thing ya know, I'll be bawlin' my eyes out in front of your college chums, and damn ya, boy, if you get all syrupy and start sayin' ya love me. We'll…I'll have to haul off with my right fist and pop you one on the kisser."

Uncle Miller informed us, "You've been great sports to take all the jabbin' so well. That's why you're all best friends. Don't let my nephew get too uppity, 'cause remind him that paybacks are a bitch, and if you're real unlucky, you marry one. Thanks for the fun, and I'll see ya a bit later, 'cause I really do have to get back to the kitchen."

Both TJ and I were staring at John Henry. TJ decided to break the code of silence first.

"John Henry, you are a bastard," he chided.

"Well, you're right, cous, I am," John Henry countered, "but I'm also a pretty good amateur raconteur."

I invited, "That was a damn good 'Gullible's Travels' routine you guys rehearse for the big-city ignoramuses."

Meditating, I hadn't remembered participating in a "Gullible's Travels," another game traced to our fraternity days, in over a decade, and I offered solemn apologies to Jonathan Swift double that time period for messing with his book title. This so-called intellectual exercise, apart from our regular horseplay, was conceived in the minds of Joe and TJ. They rationalized that they were shielding our frat's chapter from mediocrity. Usually, they were elaborate, well-thought-out schemes and stories. Other times, the simplest tales could be the best. Most often, Joe, John Henry, TJ, and myself were the players. There were occasions where there were group dupes, such as a three-on-one, a two-on-one, a two-on-two, and infrequently, a dueling challenged one-on-one. Sometimes the four of us shared wits and ganged up on another fraternity brother. It wasn't any fun to dupe somebody you didn't know well. They just wouldn't appreciate it. The help of subplayers could be enlisted, such as other students, faculty and staff, university personnel, or even a stranger's services might be required to perfectly pull off a charade. The rules were fairly simple: You couldn't cause physical harm to anyone, no morbid themes on the person being duped (i.e., you couldn't feign someone's illness or a death for sympathy to gratify your ego), you couldn't allow anybody to sweat it out for more than sixty hours, and most importantly, when you were told that you were duped, you couldn't get mad. You had to laugh it off. Your revenge was sweet, by brainstorming and carrying out an original dupe of your own.

"John Henry, if your story was fictitious, as you admit, then we technically win the bet because you lied. Fork over the two chains, cous," TJ boldly required.

Applying my two cents' worth, I concurred that TJ was absolutely correct.

John Henry returned to his seat. He had reversed his chair, allowing his arms to straddle the spoked back. TJ and I sat normally.

"Before you two get too carried away with victory by acclamation, let me remind you that I only expressed to you guys that you were duped. Never did I erroneously admit that I lied. Forget the gold coin and chains. Losin' them wouldn't matter one iota, but this dull copper coin is invaluable. It's a Fugio. That was the first coin authorized by Congress in 1787. My great-great-great-grandfather passed this through generations on to me. Do you really think I'd risk this on some half-assed bet I knew I couldn't positively win? No way, cousins. Mitigatin' circumstances at the time prevented the complete story from bein' told. Remember when my uncle said, 'After John Henry told me what really happened'? Well, cousins, truth is stranger than fiction, and you would only accuse me of insultin' your intelligence if I spoon-feed you the truth. It's anticlimactic to the published version," the big guy dared.

Recalling the exact statement Uncle Miller had said, I realized it bothered me at that time. Unlike Oedipus, who solved the puzzling "the riddle of the Sphinx," and less stressful, my disposition was to ask John Henry straight out, "What really happened?"

"Bein' cognizant that dependin' on how you view the unblemished details you may find them preposterous, I'll trace my steps back to where I'm methodically studyin' Turtle's warm-up to his knife throw. Everythin' I aforementioned, up to the point where he released that blue steel, was factual. Moreover, Turtle's action was an infraction of the law. Under New Jersey States Annotated, Title 23, he was subject to a fine of between $100 and $500 plus the court cost the municipal judge would impose killin' small game with anythin' but a shotgun," he assured.

"Before continuin', I wish to make you aware that there are only four witnesses to this spectacle. Along with the four, there are two people I shared this with, my wife, Sally, and Uncle Miller. Now, you two are included in my inner circle. Not even Joe's known of this occurrence, because I've been afraid that the excitement might exasperate him," he intimated.

Disbelieving, I listened for more. TJ puckered his lips, caricaturing John Henry.

John Henry, unaffected by TJ's new, wrinkled demeanor, revealed, "Never have I considered myself an animal rights advocate, but when that swampy planted a smooch on his Bowie, my conscience started to ask me, 'What if?' Rememberin' Turtle as a virtuoso handlin' a blade, I accepted the inevitable, that he would hit his squirrel target. But what if he only maimed the furry guy because he was throwin' a knife and the poor animal was writhin' in pain? My stomach was churnin' into knots, and I just couldn't afford to take the chance of there not bein' a quick kill. Within a fraction of a second after Turtle's fling, I discharged my .22 rifle six inches to the left of the squirrel, with the intention of hopin' to scatter him away. The Bowie was slowed down because it did, indeed, harpoon the trout and the grouse, who crisscrossed the flight path. Fortuitously, my bullet arrived first, alertin' the fortitudinous bushy tail to shift his balance like a gyroscope to his right. Not that damn renegade buck, but a doe, who debouched herself from the woods, was struck by my shot," John Henry certified parenthetically.

"The force of the extra weight of the bird and the fish attached to the onrushin' steel conked the squirrel unconscious when it brushed against him. That impact, collidin' with the gray squirrel, reversed the animal-carryin' projectile, causin' the blunt handle to strike the oak tree in the background. The knife caromed off and upward, whirlin' in the air and reverberatin' like an out-of-control propeller blade. When it returned to earth, the Bowie sliced the throat of an unsuspectin' brown rabbit who had strayed out of the brush. Now, cousins, we have five critters lyin' on the ground. Four are dead, and one is incapacitated. One was mistakenly shot by a gun, and the other four, amazin'ly enough, were brought down by a fuckin' knife. Even I had to do a double and triple take to fully accept this metaphysical happenin'. Havin' mixed emotions, I rushed over to resuscitate my squirrel.

"I was delighted that he was alive but disgruntled that I'd shot a female deer and not a fully racked stag out of season that I wasn't even aimin' at, with all things, with my .22 rifle. But I'll get back to her later.

"My priority was with the squirrel. Luckily, he just had the wind knocked out of him. Turtle was as happy as a hog in shit because he'd won his bet, but there was no way he was goin' to collect. He wasn't goin' to get his mitts on my new pet. Enraged enough, I was willin' to fight both him and his brother over a dumb rodent. Two mangy swampies both fully armed to the teeth with Bowie knives against me. Doesn't sound like a fair fight, does it? Yeah, for them. I would have unleashed forearm shivers, crackin' into their temples, separatin' their heads from their shoulders, and elbow smashes fracturin' their ribs, includin' the floatin' ones, to save the life of my *Sciurus carolinensis*, gray squirrel. Insane, I know, but that was my mind-set. The Jones boys could sense it, too, because they know too well that crazed look I get in my eyes when I'm agitated and what a peck of trouble I can be. Them hopin' to stop me would be like tryin' to pour hot butter up a pole cat's ass without gettin' sprayed. No hind legs were worth gettin' a good thrashin' from me. They knew I'd make them floss with their own Arkansas toothpicks. They were unaware of my impetus. My anomalous hostilities were being directed toward them because I was still ticked off for killin' that damn doe, not a renegade buck, seven days before the law allowed.

"Thank goodness for me, no outsider was around to call the 800 number for Operation Game Thief. You talk about fines. Under the provisions of the Fish and Game Code, Title 23:4–48, I was subject to owin' a bundle of money. Five hundred maximum for killin' a deer out of season. The second and subsequent offenses were subject up to a thousand dollars each. Slayin' the wrong gender and usin' my small-bore Winchester, instead of a 12-gauge. To top it all off, I'm subject to another three hundred dollars to a grand in penalties for bein' in possession of a missile larger than number 4 shot while huntin' small game. I could have gotten hit twice for bringin' along that damn .22 for target shootin'. If I could have made an incantation, 1, 2, 3, abracadabra, to make that six-pointless disappear, or some other mumbo jumbo, I would have, but unfortunately, I wasn't mystic. A confluence of thoughts were goin' through my head. My loyalties were divided between tellin' everythin' as it happened and what a great article it would make or to put a lid on it, so to speak. No one was goin' to believe I didn't purposely shoot that doe with my fuckin' .22, besides her bein' out of season. I didn't give a damn about the fines. I was concerned about the notorious publicity I would receive in print from my accidental indiscretion. My mind could picture the negative blurbs.

"The actin' captain, Bureau of Law Enforcement, for the Northern Region, which includes Hunterdon County, who's no kin of mine, and thank heaven for that, 'cause' I can choose him to be a friend and I choose not, would have attempted to put me in handcuffs and railroad me off to the nearest calaboose, charged with poachin'. It slipped my mind that he now calls himself a conservation officer instead of a game warden, but he's still a screw to me, even though he reports to the director, Division of Fish, Game, and Wildlife. Knowin' him the way I do, I'm convinced he'd arrest his own grandmother. The captain's not content just collarin' downstaters. That's hunters from the big-city environs who have a total abhorrence of the law. He has to harass home boys like myself, who would never do no wrong in the woods.

"Sure, we have a few local malcontents who blatantly shoot from within their own trucks, practice night-lightin', and go over the bag limit. They should be fined and their huntin' privilege taken away. The good, law-abidin' hunters don't condone misdeeds. Though the intent was absent, I did in fact, as Turtle had done, violate the law. Without the slightest doubt, I knew he would have denied my served writ of habeas corpus *Cervinae*, deer, on him. And what do I know about legalese?

"That high-muck-a-muck has more laws to back him up than do our local and state police. A conservation officer can search without warrants and make more types of other arrests that cannot be legally performed by our county officers. He takes advantage of his gestapo-like authority. I'd be damned if I was goin' to explain myself to him and beg for mercy while he maligned me. Exempt from usin' polysyllables, I'd have to break down the story to him usin' mono words, without any colorization. He'd force me into repeatin' myself, expirin' from absolute boredom. I'd be talkin' a blue streak for naught. If you boys think I'm joshin', then you're dead wrong. The expression 'Madder than a wet hen' applies here, maybe because my pullets, the bantam, silver-spangled Hamburg hens, have won the egg-layin' contest in our local fair the past nine years and he comes in a distant second place. At the arboretum, where they perennially host the tricounty flower festival, my rhododendron exhibits have no equal, while his chrysanthemum entries finish an unlucky seventh and eleventh. He held no grudge? Cousins, the guy would have loved the chance to discredit me. He'd misuse the power of his tin badge for his self-interest. Wasn't goin' to be his whippin' boy. He wouldn't be content just to hang me in effigy. He'd like to do it for real!" John Henry claimed.

"If a national wire service picked up on the story, and you betcha it was newsworthy, my goose would have been cooked well done. It's not that I'm a household name, but I do command respect in some circles. I would have been the laughingstock of all my ex-teammates, players, coaches, and the enemies I had in the professional ranks and at the college level. Bein' barraged by unflatterin' telegrams from fans and practical jokers who would ballyhoo me with stuffed animals and toy guns in the mail isn't the same as playin' an intellectual trick on some friends. Think of the joy on their faces when I'd attend an honoree dinner or a testimonial roast and the master of ceremonies and guests would jibe at me. Unmercifully, they'd give me the 'raspberry' treatment. It was too excruciatin' for me to imagine," John Henry foreboded.

He hesitated dramatically, wanting for reactions that never surfaced.

"Gettin' back to my squirrel," the big guy sadly expounded, "I planned to take the little critter to the office of Martha Peterson, the nearest veterinarian. Sally would take good care of him after that. She's very good with animals.

"Now, cousins, you met Emmel, and I realize his thinkin' process is sometimes a little slower than molasses drippin' down the side of its own bottle. Now, I'm not bein' condescendin' when I admit that I do most of the talkin' and thinkin' for him, and I'm not patronizin' him when I admit he was blessed with other noble attributes other than brains. He's one of a kind. Explainin' the necessary vicissitudes of the circumstance, Emmel displayed complete loyalty to any way I wanted to handle it. My cousin returned with a gunnysack for the immobilized squirrel. I had to make overtures to the rambunctious Jones boys to lessen the impact of the vicious circle I was about to get myself caught in. I *dictatorialized* to Turtle, 'Not only are you not goin' to keep the squirrel, but you also have to forfeit the braggin' rights to what you have accomplished.' His reaction? He jumped up and down, angrier than a hapless chimpanzee disobeyin' his trainer, spoutin' rigmarole. Never did it sink in to his brain that he was subject to stiff penalties. It could cost him forty bucks for the two small critters he slew and twenty extra to include for the attempted murder of the squirrel with his Bowie. It's classified as an unlawful contrivance. He doesn't get away scot-free for stickin' that fish either, just 'cause his fishin' license was current. An additional forty dollars in fines could be levied for catchin' trout out of season and usin' an improper method other than anglin' with hand line or with rod and line.

"If they really wanted to be sticklers, Turtle could be subject to owin' another fifty bucks for bein' under the influence of my blackberry brandy," he assessed.

"I thought he'd be understandin' to the country parable 'Even though a blind chipmunk finds a coconut, it might be too big for him to cart away.' I thought wrong. Knowin' I was goin' to have a minor insurgence on my hands but not a full-scale revolution, I anticipated the swampy reachin' for his sheaf on his right side. Quickly I placed thumb pressure with both my hands on his wrist and turned it clockwise in front of his body as an effective reasonin' tool.

"I heard the sounds of a war whoop. Not wantin' to be left out of the fracas, cousin Emmel recklessly bowled over Big Clemson with a flyin' above-the-knees maneuver, keepin' him pinned to the ground with a figure-eight leg lock to prevent himself from gettin' bit or eye-gouged. It was a brave and beautiful thing to behold since he was outweighed by forty or so pounds. I was perceptive that Emmel was not tryin' to achieve nirvana, let alone understandin' what the hell it meant, and he started to spin around, and around, and around, before he took to flight. He was a regular whirlin' dervish. Luckily for him, dizziness didn't prevail. Finally, he planted his left foot, leaped in the air, and threw his right hip into the cross-body block as I used on 'trap' plays. Rollin' three times in succession, he finished the move perfectly.

"When Turtle was calm enough to listen to me, I pledged to him the two squirrels Emmel and I had shot earlier, along with that stupid whitetail. As a bonus, I was also goin' to throw in a quart of vodka apiece for him and his brother. In exchange for these terms, he couldn't repeat what had actually happened. When he grasped the meanin' of my words, Turtle grinned, displayin' every rotten tooth in his mouth, noddin' in approval. I completely lessened the hold of my grip on him, and Emmel attempted to do likewise with Clemson. Turtle and I were laughin' 'cause the two of them looked like a fuckin' pretzel, all twisted together. We helped them get untangled and up to their feet. Clemson was semihappy with the conditions I put on the table, offerin' figuratively.

"The brothers parlayed for a few minutes by themselves, bickerin' my offer. Damn good Indian traders, those boys are, 'cause they came back to me with a counterproposal. To cement the deal, they wanted included two more quarts of vodka and the right to drink their liquor together at the bar.

"Aware that I had made a great deal, I cussed and swore anyway, even goin' to the extent of kickin' out clumps of dirt in the process to make them feel they had hoodwinked me good. Got better divots than I've ever made with a nine iron.

"Deliberately, I accused them of takin' advantage of my generosity, but if they were willin' to drink their shots handcuffed, then let's shake on it. They obliged graciously.

"Done deal. Rather than to try to penetrate their thick skulls with complications, I strictly reminded them that anyone snoopin' to find out details had to go through me and it would help matters out if they stayed sequestered in their marshy domain for about ten days. My wish was that they start barbecuin' venison steaks as soon as possible and throw the antlerless head in the swamp.

"The method in my madness was for them to devour the evidence. New forensics methods used by game biologists the captain would have at his disposal could determine whether my doe had been dead one hundred and eighty minutes, twenty-four hours, three days, one week, or one mouth. Any unnecessary chance of allowin' prima facie evidence couldn't be afforded. The four of us were conspirators. We were all guilty for failin' to report the event.

"So in theory, everyone came out a winner. The swampies received their just deserts, or to put it in proper perspective, their squirrel hind leg supper and my armor went untarnished. Uncle Miller, as he said before, helped piece together the faulty re-enactment along with auxiliary materials to justify my claim. Occasionally, I get a twinge of remorse for Turtle not gettin' his total 'day in the sun,' but he's still the hero of our edition," John Henry exhausted.

"Myself, since that unforgivin' day, I've contracted buck fever, meanin' I just can't pull the trigger anymore. Hate to admit it, but I'm a damn impotent huntsman." He sighed.

"Cousins, in conclusion, around these here rural parts, when the facts blend to legend, it becomes trivial and you perpetuate the legend," the big guy supplemented.

Stretching my arms out to their limit, I intentionally yawned before acquiring a more comfortable posture in my chair. TJ, in a reclined position, would have been focusing on the ceiling if he didn't have his fists covering his view. Not accepting implicit obedience to this now-avowed probability aside, in the solitude of my mind what was not being discussed between TJ and I was John Henry's attempt to condition us as if we were the white rodents in Pavlov's theory. First, he deliberately knew we wouldn't believe his story. Secondly, we were falsely convinced of the supposed truth. Thirdly, we were told that the truth was really fiction. Finally, we were informed that the legend was not the truth and the truth could only be shared by a few "rats." This was behavior modification at its worst. He had run us through his maze without TJ or myself getting a bite of the Brie. Hopefully, we were too smart to go sniffing for any more cheese.

Having two questions of entrapment to John Henry's revised interpolation of the truth, I implored earnestly, "Whatever became of the squirrel?"

Animatedly rolling up his eyes for TJ's benefit, the big guy replied earnestly, "Of course, you are talkin' about my pet squirrel Cody. As I conveyed earlier, we took him to the vet's office, if you think I don't remember everythin' I say. Sally nursed the poor little fellow back to good health, and we domesticated him. I sawed a half-circular porthole on the bottom of the kitchen door, and he learned to come and go as he wished. He greets people when they enter that way, then scampers off to his abode in the pantry.

"Watchin' the bushy tail shuck peanut shells is a sight to behold. He's real neat and leaves the discarded debris in a nice, neat pile in the corner. Cody's a regular connoisseur when it comes to apples. He prefers my Golden Delicious variety. Ever see a squirrel eat an apple?" he asked.

Even though TJ and I shrugged our shoulders, we still said, "No."

"Cody picks up that apple, mind you, which is one-third his body size, with his tiny paws, the same way you would if you used both hands. There's an appreciable difference. He spins the cord and chomps his way through like a little squirrelin' buzz saw. It's a comical scene worthy of a *National Geographic* layout. Cody's popular among his arboreal pals in the neighborhood, goin' to the extent of invitin' them over for afternoon snacks, the classy host, he is. Sally's labeled his friends the lunch bunch, or the bunch who come over for lunch. I call them bushy-tailed slobs. It's not a pleasure for me when they ersatz bad manners for etiquette, rumpussin' all over my linoleum floor, chasin' one another's tails with their blusterin' and insatiable desire to jump on my kitchen table and countertops. They're a messy lot, leavin' shells all over the kitchen for my wife to clean up. It's worse than a jamboree. The last straw was one day, when all pandemonium broke loose and they went to snoopin' into the cupboards and found my honey almond cereal, gnawin' off the cardboard lid, feastin' without askin'. They were playin' with the hidden puzzle before I had a chance to tinker with it."

Stealing my thunder for the second question as by osmosis, TJ posed, "Hey, cous, what about the hind legs as a love potion? Is there any validity to that claim?"

"I was wonderin'," John Henry cheerfully rebuffed, "why it was taking so long for one of you ladies' men to question me on those delectable parts. Years ago, when I first heard about it from the swampies, I ignored it as a silly wives' tale, until I saw what it did for Toady. He's kinfolk to Turtle and Clemson, a second cousin once removed.

Poor Toady. Try as hard as he might, he couldn't get himself a purdy girl. Toady would come up empty-handed every time he went huntin' for two-legged deer. Now, mind you, cousins, ole Toady didn't receive that amphibian appellation because he resembled Prince Charmin', but rather the contrary. They talk about plug-ugly. Garden slugs I'd seen in top soil seemed to be enjoyin' better sex lives than ole Toady, and even salamander-like newts had a thumb's-uppish on him. Slimy skinks felt the same way. I'd go so far as to say that I've been mooned, double hog-back growlers that are profoundly better-lookin' than sorrowful Toady. You boys remember one, I'm sure."

Before I had a chance to face TJ, I was coughing up my swallow of beer, and my watery eyes caught TJ spraying out his apple wine, including through both nostrils. He was banging his fist on the table, laughing. Undoubtedly, we knew what John Henry was comparing ole Toady, to and it wasn't a pretty sight. Only a farm boy could really appreciate it. The first and only time I witnessed this unholy spectacle took place second semester, freshman year. It was either late March or early April. I don't recall the exact month. Our big cousin had invited Joe, TJ, and myself along with pledge brothers Crazy Frank Cluracy and Machine Gun Mulligan out for pizza. Thank heavens I never had one of those weird nicknames labeled on me. That meant five pies, two with the works, three with extra cheese, and to top it off, the big guy was paying. As the six of us walked the fifteen blocks to Luigi's, we strolled by the newly opened deli with the neon rainbow sign. The eatery had a picture window, and diners could sit at a table, front and center, to people-watch the passersby. Who would imagine that seated right at the window were those two assholes on the fencing team, Brent and Bradley Hopkins, with three cunts from that snobbish sorority who thought they were too high-heeled to date a member of our frat.

"If I had known before bein' inducted that those beauties would never go out with me, I would have chosen a classier frat to pledge," John Henry would wisecrack whenever one of the superficial "sisters" was in earshot.

The Hopkins, besides being real brothers, were members of our archrival fraternity. Not only were these two hated by brothers in other fraternities, but they were also strongly disliked by their own frat brothers. These "brothers from hell" purposely ran scams on students for their own brand of kicks. From phony fifty-fifty basket of cheer raffles where one of them became the winner, to dabbling in phony term papers, to knowingly selling the wrong answers to midterm and final exams and celebrating with "Ha, has" after the deceived students flunked. John Henry said that even though we were freshmen, we couldn't pass up the opportunity to teach these two assholes a good lesson and show the three cunts somethin' so disgustin' to behold they would have to call up their daddies to explain it to them. We stopped around the corner to powwow. All we were told was that the big guy was going to "moon" them country-style. Our mission was to shield him till he got his pants back on from any sidewalk walkers, especially those dressed in blue uniforms, carrying sidearms, and answering to "Officer." After he did his thing, we'd divide our group into twos and take different routes to the pizza parlor.

It was a rather nicely conceived plan.

We converged at the café's window and formed a phalanx with John Henry in the middle. He dropped his drawers and, to our disbelief, pulled his penis and testicles back to his anus. We were in hysterics, because from a frontal view, he had temporarily displaced his "jewels." Before he squatted, John Henry placed his index finger and pinky parallel in the form of horns. He shoved them in the same region. Finally, he pressed his entire perineum up against the plate glass, grunting porcine snorts. John Henry, for our fraternal edification, best explained this rear view as a wild warthog pokin' and sniffin' his snout somewhere it shouldn't ought to belong, with the added bonus of a hangin' wattle from a white Leghorn rooster, all only separated from their viewers by a half-inch transparency. The tusks were optional. Who said a country boy couldn't be graphic?

Our audience was in shock after they noticed our rapping and tapping. The quintet went bug-eyed, spitting out whatever form of food or liquid they had in their mouths. One girl ran shrieking to the bathroom, but not before slapping Brent. Another "sister" was suspectedly forcing regurgitation while merely dry-heaving. The other turned around in her chair but was curiously playing peekaboo as her fingers masked her face. The "hot shot" brothers did their ostrich imitation, burying their mugs into their arms for the remainder of the fourteen-second, double hog-back growler. They weren't stupid enough to want to take on the big guy.

By 2:00 p.m. the following day, upperclassmen and women he knew and didn't know walked up to John Henry and congratulated him on what he did. The saga of his raw heroics proliferated on campus, and those that hung out with him got popular too. So not wanting to mess up a good thing, we stuck around him, as he would say in farmese, "snug'r than peas in a pod" the rest of the semester. After all, we were determined not to go through four years of being nonentities on campus.

"They say one woman's molehill is another woman's mountain, and Toady needed the right niche to be elevated to the higher mass. Now, mind you, those swampies are a resourceful bunch. The menfolk of the clan decided they'd go squirrelin' and donate all the hind legs to Toady 'cause of his precarious situation with findin' himself a wife. His mama stewed up a whole cauldron of those varmints just for him. Lo and behold, he returned from his huntin' trip with a gorgeous gal who could easily pass for Miss Virginia, Miss West Virginia, Miss Tennessee, or represent whatever Southern state she well damn pleased. When they're seen in public, that woman holds on to her ole man, Toady, tighter than wet rawhide lashed around a fence post, dryin' in an Albuquerque sun," he noted.

TJ was playing with the rim of his mug, but still attentive.

He inquired curiously, "Did you ever eat any of them, cous?"

"Well, cous, I've shared so many firsts today to cleanse my soul I feel like I'm in a confessional," he cathartically wisecracked. "I admit to having an exclusive supper of squirrel hind legs twice in my life. The first time was 2 BS—that's two years before Sally. I was datin' Emmy Beth Olson at that time.

"She broiled a whole pan full of them rascals for me. If your wonderin' whether or not I noticed anythin' different in my performance that evenin', the answer was no, because I'm always good," John Henry euphemistically flaunted. "The strange and disturbin' things occurred when I ventured into town the next day. Good-lookin' women I'd never seen before were followin' me around like stray dogs, sniffin' all my private areas," he bemoaned.

TJ, frolicking too hard, nearly fell off his chair at that revelation.

"It took every ounce of strength I had in me to fight them off. They couldn't accept the fact that I had me a steady gal. For a couple of months after that, I wouldn't go out in public unescorted by Emmy Beth until that damn scent faded away," he doggedly told us.

"The second time I devoured those critters, this time devoid of curiosity, I was performin' an act of mercy. It was midafternoon of the day I had my first date with Sally. That obstinate woman must have turned me down at least five times, till she finally agreed to go out with me. There was a slight condition attached to it, though. She agreed to dinner if I would stop sendin' flowers and never ask her out again. That woman drove a hard bargain. She purported that I, of all people, was a sycophant and a no-good womanizer. She was about to be engaged to Billy Bob Turner, whose family owns a fairly good-size goat ranch in the county. In addition to knockin' my socks off, that woman just got under my crawl, 'cause no one had ever labeled me a sycophant, and I acknowledge that I had to refresh myself with the *Webster's Dictionary*'s definition to remember that it meant 'a servile flatter.' After that episode, I was determined to make her mine. I didn't want to subject her to a lifetime of bein' Mrs. Billy Goat Turner. It just didn't sit right with me, and I had to take desperate measures. Prior to our goin' out that evenin', I stuffed myself on pan-fried you-know-whats. Two days beforehand, cousin Emmel and I went to squirrelin', mind you, out of season. Emmel handled the particulars, arrangin' for us to get a 'special' vermin permit. The law allows if you're a farmer or fruit grower, and I'm both, to make an affidavit that gray squirrels have caused injury to your livelihood. So what if it was double-dealing?"

TJ and I were laughing.

"Do I need to remind you, cousins, all is fair game in love and war? We returned, gettin' us a good dozen. I must have forced down over twenty hind legs. If this squirrel mystique was goin' to take effect again, I wanted it to work real well. Remember, she only gave me one shot to be Mr. Wonderful.

"That evenin', I took her to a ritzy restaurant in Frenchtown. I don't remember the place's name and whether or not it still exists. Assuredly, Sally would skin me alive if she knew I had forgotten the identification of where we had our first date. One thing's for sure, I ordered chateaubriand for two and a superb bottle of wine. Even their maître d' replied, 'Excellent choice, sir,' when I ordered a 1977 Louis Jadot Pouilly-Fuisse white burgundy table wine. Suffice it to say, a little voice inside guided me in my selection process. Payin' no attention to proper wine selection parlance, I ignored my waiter's advice on champagne. Didn't want to come off both predictable and tacky to Sally. Unsolicited, our server suggested a cabernet sauvignon. I took exception to his choice as gauche. The whole idea was to leave my imprint on Sally that I knew my vintage bottled grapes, even if I didn't.

"Durin' our meal, I could barely pick up my fork and lift my glass 'cause I was so full from my furry lunch and I could feel my belly lettin' out volcanic-size eruptions. Any minute now, I was frettin' that I would be belchin' out lava all over the fine-bone china and the fancy teal linen tablecloth. Barely ten sentences did I converse in that night. My sad contention was that the whole evenin' was a total disaster. Bitter disappointment set in the form of heart palpitations. Knowin' I had blown my only chance to make a good first impression, I feared the worst.

"I couldn't wait to get out of there even though I knew I'd be draggin' my tail between my legs. As I dropped Sally off, I expected she would callously exit, sayin', 'Good night, John Henry, I wish you a great life…except without me.' Incredulously, Sally told me at the night's conclusion that she was impressed that I was an attentive listener, a superb conversationalist, and that for a big man, I was a dainty eater. Imagine me, a dainty eater? In all my life I can't recall anyone ever sayin' that to me before. I don't think I was dainty even when my mommy was breast-feedin' me. In a gentle voice I couldn't refuse, she pleaded me to pencil her in on my busy calendar. When she said that, I felt as happy as a colt in clover."

TJ held up a finger and smiled.

"If I may be allowed to make a salient point you're failing to include I'm sure you'll regard as trifling. As I recollect, at that time you presented Sally that night with one of your gift-wrapped Chargers game jerseys with number 75 on the front and sleeves and 'J. H. Andrews' printed on the back. Hopefully, you thought, if she wore that out in public, no punk would bother her, because your woman was wearing your brand. Also, you were boastful in the fact that you spared no expense on your 'hot date' and you drove up to Sally's house honking in that red 'mousetrap,'" TJ annotated.

"My dear interruptive cousin," John Henry rebutted self-reliantly, "the uniform jersey was just a simple token of my affection, and those other things were solely window dressin'. You're forgettin', my color-blind friend, that my 'mousetrap' was scarlet."

John Henry picked up the conversation where he left off.

"I knew I should have broken down there on the spot and pointed out to her that the only reason she was attracted to me was that I ate squirrel hind legs earlier that day," John Henry persisted. "Strangely coincidental that Sally would flip-flop in one day from bein' in love with Billy Bob and ignorin' me to thoroughly enjoyin' our date and exclaimin' how I was an unexpected pleasure. She had anticipated me bein' my normal self, a rude dude, dominatin' the conversation with 'I, I, I, I, I.' I'd be drunk and sloppin' down my meal like a classless pig. Rationalizin' at that time, if I had told her the truth, she would have most certainly called my bushy meal culinary quackery. As I said, I pulled the wool over the lady's eyes, 'cause after all, I am a sycophant.

"That night, I must have set a land speed record racin' from Sally's back to our spread. I was as proud as the peacock we had on the farm. Jumpin' out of the Jaguar without openin' the door, I started flappin' my arms, struttin' my stuff like a barnyard rooster, cock-a-doodle-doin' 'round the chicken coop. Next thin' I knew, lights were turned on in the entire house and faces in the windows were lookin' at me make a fool of myself, but I was so happy I didn't seem to mind. Figurin' he'd be irritable, I'd say my sorries to dad the next mornin' for wakin' him up, but he was too excited to care, because the hens set a new egg-layin' record that night. Two weeks later, Sally was my steady, and I've never heard her purposely mention Billy Bob's name again. So, cousins, under false pretenses, Sally only became my girlfriend, and later my wife, all 'cause of a swampy panacea for love."

John Henry falsely sniffled while dabbing the canthus of his eyes with his thumb. "Presently I feel contrite, because I seized the opportunity to prey on her naivete. I've never breathed a word of this to her to this day." He heartily laughed.

TJ started to laugh, and I was forced into the zestful merriment too. We'll never know if there was an ounce of truth to anything John Henry alleged so far this evening. Anyway, this was all in fun. We were all having a great time, so it would be fuckin' brash for me to call our cohost mendacious, even though I'd like to. TJ and I still owed him a "Gullible's Travels" routine of our own as a payback, and I might even conscript the services of Joe DeFendo into our stealthy army to pull it off well. I poured another round for everyone and proposed yet another toast to John Henry. As Uncle Miller said, "You are the best."

TJ agreed.

CHAPTER VIII

As I turned my chair to get a better-angled view of the dancing in the barroom, TJ gave me a slight tug on my shirtsleeve to get my attention. Before I could make a comment to him, new company had arrived at our table. Two identical pretty-faced women of elephantine proportions surrounded our cohost, interchangeably hugging and kissing him in between giggles. Alerted to our gazes, he took time to come up for air.

"Not a bad way for a man to die, to be smothered by affection," he said, romping amusingly. "Cousins, let me introduce you to the lovely Bea sisters. They're twins, as you probably guess. Honey's on my left, and Busy's on my right. They're growers for wholesale florists, but more importantly, they are 100 percent certified women, not the skinny, meatless things you guys like. These gals will keep you warm in the winter without investin' in a goose down comforter and provide enough shade on a sunny day that you can throw away your beach umbrella. If I weren't happily married to my Sally, I'd choose one of these big babes to be my missus," he declared.

The girls cooed and sighed at his pronouncement.

John Henry vaunted, "But not to fret, girls. I couldn't allow myself to designate one of you as second best, so I'd marry both of you in a double-ring ceremony. There's plenty of lovin' in me to share."

"The big guy is waxing sugarcoated phrases," TJ offered robustly.

The happy-faced waitress stopped by to efficiently clear away empty bottles and mason jars, sincerely commenting, "He talks that talk to all the single girls. It's bullshit, I know, but John Henry has a way with words that a girl knows are especially meant for her ears only." She hurriedly uttered softly, "I can't help it if I'm smitten too."

The portly sisters grabbed the poet laureate of Hunterdon County by his sleeves and marched him off to the dance floor.

"Do a little favor for me and a big one for them by showin' us a little Hunterdon County ass," John Henry petitioned the twins before departing to kick up his heels.

The gals, giggling again, responded by turning around. With their backs facing us, they bent over to pull their dresses high above their thighs. Inspecting a mountain range of quivering exposed cellulite might make weak men faint, but not TJ and me, because after all, the big guy said we were ladies' men. A shrill two-fingered whistle was offered courtesy of our big cousin, and we found ourselves clapping and cheering the sideshow.

Nature called, and I seized the opportunity to hit the bathroom, with TJ following a pace behind. Exiting, we shared some "Yucks" about the plumbing system in the lavatory Joe had alluded to. When we returned to our table, we were standing, watching John Henry and the two sisters bop to a rock and roll tune that Jake Jewel's band was playing. When the song was completed, Jake encouraged the shy—until she got a microphone in her hand—pigtailed girl to join him in a duet. They broke into Patsy Cline's classic ballad "Crazy," after Jake informed the crowd that not known to many, it was written by Willie Nelson. Improvising as only he could, John Henry was waltzing, one arm around each girl, with him in the middle, slowly moving this protean mass counterclockwise. When he turned to us, he cavorted, wall-eyed, and curled his tongue for spectacle. TJ was getting a kick out of his latest spoof.

"Now I know where I've seen this before," he predicated. "This is the modern version of Cerberus, who in Greek mythology was the three-headed dog who guarded the portals of Hades."

Before getting a chance to sit down, I felt a gentle squeeze on my arm.

I half-heartedly veered to my right.

"Hello, Stanley, I'm Daphne Roussant, Sally and John Henry's friend. Nice to see you again," she diffused.

Her voice was the most lovely-sounding French accent this side of the Seine. Was my peripheral vision out of focus, or was this the same honey-doll John Henry had given a twirl to en route to the back dining room? I asked myself. Something was different, and my mind was racing to figure out what. Her eyes burst a radiant emerald green, exceptional from what I'd ever encountered; even though they were sincere eyes, they still engulfed a mischievous Siamese cat-like quality I was fascinated by and yearned to know a whole lot better. I was smiling back while ruminating a few moments. If she was attempting to hypnotize me, I'd just stand there and enjoy it. Eureka! It struck me. She had let her wavy locks fall to her shoulders in a sweeping, tousled mane fashion that made her look dreamy. The lady could assume different forms. Nevertheless, she wore the same ribbon bow for poignancy.

Her luscious lips were *purr*fectly pink, and her lustrous smile seemed to broaden, highlighted by dimples at both ends.

Upon my expert survey, her other personality traits included a slinky 35-22-34 body on a five-foot-nine frame. Her firm buttocks protruded ever so amiably from underneath her tight tartan plaid skirt like two prize cantaloupes. Those long curvaceous legs were dressed to the nines in opaque ebony stockings with minute diamond patterns. At point-blank range, my feline friend had left me speechless. Daphne looked at TJ for assurance that I was all right.

"Oh, he's just fine. It's not every day that he gets to meet a genuine angel. I'm Thomas, but my friends call me TJ. From all indications, it appears as if you'll be a friend sooner than he realizes it," he said, trying to restrain his chuckles.

She acknowledged TJ and shook his hand, still gazing at me lovingly. My solid 170 pounds, blue-gray eyes, and medium-length light-brown hair must have appealed to her. At least I hoped it did. Thinking to myself, even if she directed every vulgarity in the book at me, it would have sounded good. Taking one too many sideways steps, I awkwardly jarred our table, but I was oblivious to anything else but her.

Phonetically, I wanted to sound like Mr. Smooth, but I came off as an insufferable buffoon when I finally blurted out in a voice that didn't sound like my own, "Hi! You can call me Stanley. Oh, Stan is just fine."

I didn't know what I meant. Then I said something dumb, like, "Call me…anytime."

Nodding, she smiled at me encouragingly and told me I had a sense of humor too. I extended my hand to her, and when she reciprocated, I placed my left hand over the top of hers, bringing the entire grasp to my lips, offering a gentle kiss. She was genuinely impressed. TJ stepped closer to us, and I hadn't released my hold.

With my attention fixed on this angel, I vaguely recalled him saying in his brusque fashion, "Two's company, and three is getting to be too much of a crowd…for me. Your galaxy only has space for two planets, and your telescopic vision is focused on one heavenly body. Excuse me, I'm going over to the bar and mingle with the locals. See ya."

Apparently, TJ had just delivered some form of space analogy, but I was too busy to retort. Disingenuously, I placed my hands around Daphne in dance position without ever releasing my touch from her body by simply circumnavigating my route. She was enchanted with my aplomb. As we danced slowly, Daphne was holding on to me tightly, playfully making tiny ringlets with her fingers where my hair tapered at the nape. Not making much sense, I whispered things in her ear. She laughed a laugh that was distinctly sweet. *I can't do any wrong,* I thought to myself. I should have pinched myself, because I must have been tarrying in a dream sequence of some made-for-television sitcom. Smiling while taking a step away, she swayed her head back, tousling her hair. Daphne allowed me the pleasure of admiring her graceful neck, understated with a fine string of baroque pearls, from arm's length. She was a paragon of exquisite beauty.

It had always struck me as silly—that is, love at first sight. To me, the idea of it was always something reserved for drugstore novels. The concept at worst would be to have a chalky feeling in your stomach, and at best it would be to have butterflies in your belly. Honestly, I felt both. It was childishly cute the way she was mildly biting her lower lip while slowly etching the contour of my profile permanently in her mind. Daphne took her finger and physically traced the outline of my upper lip ever so smoothly that it tickled.

"Sally has said so many good things about you that I finally had to investigate for myself. A woman's intuition," she coolly said.

What possessed me, I didn't know, to certifiably phrase in the best French pronunciation I'd ever phrased, "Chacun a son gotit. C'est selon, mademoiselle." Each to one's own taste. That depends, miss. Astounded, I thought to myself, *I just seriously spoke French to this woman.* Unexpectedly, she rushed into my arms and kissed me tenderly on the lips. I returned her advance with ardent pleasure, offering a long-lasting passionate kiss as we were still dancing. When she pressed her seductive body to mine, my psyche was throbbing and I felt a warm, tingling sensation all over. Disregarding the presentation of my au jus-stained tie, I jettisoned my suit jacket more nimbly than the contorting Harry Houdini ever did to fully appreciate her brassiere-less ample bosoms jubilantly pushed up against my chest. With rapid succession, Daphne planted kisses all over my cheek, and with finesse, she swished her tongue in my left ear. When she duplicated that procedure, I felt as if my heart pulse was skyrocketing all the way past the rings to Saturn.

Needing very little encouragement and not lacking initiative, I wanted to impress her with my own repertoire of bodily movements. Affectionately embracing the corners of her mouth a centimeter away where the laugh lines began became more gratifyingly sweeter than Godiva chocolates. Fervently I French-kissed her, connoting the serpentine versatility of her protrusile organ. Navigating on course, I proceeded to space kisses generously around her neck and shoulder blades. Making both my hands transpositionally serviceable, I tenderly caressed her entire back and rubbed her taut hips.

'Silly boy, stop it, that tickles!" She gasped. "It's making me feel too…too…good." What a pity for my poor, sultry swan. I was causing trembling goose bumps all along her arms and collarbone.

Ignoring her mild protest and her feeble attempt to shift away, I continued with the business at hand, because she knew that I knew that her erogenous zones were begging me to continue. Daphne, with due credit, was burning an impassioned flame in my loins. This was the closest I had ever felt like I was making love with my clothes on since high school, and I wasn't even grinding.

As the town crier, I wanted to make a proclamation about how good her warm flesh felt in my arms and how intoxicatingly fragrant her body chemistry was, but selfishly I kept my felicity to myself. Barely trying to be romantically loquacious, I sprinkled extemporaneous "Babys" and "Darlings" into her aural cavity and snappy double entendres she convulsively relished. Brushing aside Daphne's bouncy, luxuriously satin-to-the-touch hair, I exposed her petite mouselike ear antithetical to the sparkling, dichromatic sapphire stud in her pierced lobe. "Oh no," she foretasted before my torrid breath blew into her canal, possibly penetrating the sanctum sanctorum of the eustachian tube. Unquestionably, I even fogged up her gemstone. As I nibbled gently on the circumference of her outer auris, covering the helix to the lobule, Daphne's body shook from the titillation going down her spine. Again, she weakly attempted to escape from my nonexistent hold. Pertinent to Daphne's ultimate emotional surrender was when the androgynous-featured busboy carrying a too-full, heavy tray of dishes, unmindful of my darling's jerky movement, startled her, boomeranging her back to my arms.

Undauntedly, I whisked her away from any other nonstationary, unstable equilibriums or foreign objects.

Pleased with my nimbleness and expertise in handling a crisis, she clung to me tighter, if that was possible, sobbing while avowing in a shrill tone, "This is where I always belonged and should have stayed."

What she just expressed seemed dumb, but I was glad she said it. Unimportant to me was the question, Was I committing a faux pas? More importantly was that she had gotten me speaking French not only to her but to myself as well. I felt so comfortably in sync with this woman. Not caring that I was acting sophomoric, and excluding the tinge of guilt from my thought flash to Samantha, I continued my assault, but on Daphne's other, neglected ear.

Whatever music Jake's band was playing was way overmatched by the symphony conducted by my saline tongue. Orchestrating as the consummate maestro, with affettuoso and grazioso, its length seemingly traveled the entire inner labyrinth, concluding at the cochlea. It went in and out ever so slowly as in diminuendo, changing cadence to allegro, reverting to slower, with meno mosso, adding variety with spiritoso, and blending in arpeggio, capriccioso, and tenuto, accordingly. Without the aid of a metronome, I conducted an up-and-down movement, then substituted a rhythmic sideways motion for diversification, including modulation, to sensitize and saturate inside her folds where the pinnate areas of the antihelix, concha, triangular fossa could be located, not excluding the humped section of the antitragus. The tip of Daphne's ear was pulsating from ecstasy. Concealed by a curtain of curls, Daphne's bottom lip was quivering, and with her mouth agape, she panted "Oohs" and "Aahs" with rapture. I could have been mistaken, but I also think I heard one good "Ooh la la."

Practicing medicine without a license, but instead with a big grin, I assured her that the artificial tinnitus (buzzing sound in the ears) she felt was only temporary. She looked at me in amazement, then laughed that sweet laugh when I broadly smiled. Daphne knew I had been teasing with her. She actually thanked me for making her feel giddy and wonderful all over.

Dare I say to her that she was the cause of the atrophy that had set in my arms and legs? The moment was too precious to ever let go as I held her. Pulling out a hidden napkin, almost out of nowhere, she expertly wiped away the perspiration on my forehead and my liquid mustache. It was a sleight of hand trick performed by an artist.

My imagination didn't have to roam too far to deduce that if she felt so sensual with her clothes on, what would she be like in the buff? This time, our once-more, long-lasting erotic kiss was interrupted by the oversize *tap tap tap tap tap* of a human woodpecker at my back.

"Excuse me, Romeo, for cutting in," John Henry jokingly blustered. "You two remind me of a couple of Bogalusa bayou teenagers in heat. You'd both be obligin' to me if you took your act to some motel room or, better yet, to a country inn with a vacancy. Our cash-payin' customers might think that I was runnin' some type of bordello," he quipped.

Daphne's fresh complexion transferred to burgundy, and I got a little red in the face also. The big guy implied that I needed a cold shower and to shake a leg with Honey Bea while he had a few minutes dancing alone with Daphne. I couldn't tell if I was jitter-buggin' with Honey or Busy, but who cared which of the full-sized gals I was with? No way could I tell them apart. Regardless of which sister, she was very light on her feet as we swung to Elvis's "Don't Be Cruel." Lip-synching at the song's conclusion, Honey gave me a thank-you squeeze for the dance that I thought cracked my back.

John Henry juked over to us, grinning as if he were the Cheshire cat in *Alice in Wonderland.* Our "Eagle Scout" was using semaphore signals with his handkerchief. He proceeded to point at me with his index finger and offered a hitchhiker's thumb over his shoulder in Daphne's direction. He followed it up with a double thumbs-up.

"Even if you can't decipher the code," he said, "you're in. I don't know what you did or said to that sweet girl, but you have her meltin'."

He put his arm around my shoulder.

"Now, cousin," he cautioned, "it's most likely the strong buildup that I gave Daphne about you, and I won't discount the possibility of your debonair personality and semigood looks, but if you want to keep this good thing goin', you'll let me rustle you up an elixir of squirrel hind legs before you see her again. Think about it." He offered it jocosely.

My back was turned to John Henry. Because Daphne was my magnet, north in front of me, I didn't need the benefit of a compass to find my direction to her. The big guy was whistling the French national anthem to needle me, but he only rated my snicker. It had been just a few minutes since I'd held Daphne, but it felt as if an hour had gone by. Feeling nervous as I got closer to her, I wished I could hide my anxiety better. As I approached her, my glimmering spirits subsided, because she had been breathlessly awaiting my return. As I took her hand, she kissed me tenderly, abating all my inner turbulence.

Two cute blondes in skintight Levi's with cutouts on the knees, who couldn't be a day over twenty-two, were arguing over whose boyfriend was who. One was freckle-faced, and the other was pallid-skinned with her hair cut in a Dutch Boy style. The object of their agitated affections was an acne half-pint-size cowpoke with a ten-gallon hat on his head acting as if he were accustomed to the tigresses fighting over their man. Before the girls could spit any more fiery insults (e.g., *bitch*, *shithead*, *slut*) and start clawing and scratching each other over "Junior," I escorted my smiling new friend to a secluded inglenook, where the atmosphere was less confrontational. The catfight had been a blessing in disguise, because it gave me an opportunity to be alone with Daphne, and I wanted to know everything about her.

I sat alongside her in the booth, where we could chat and still privately watch the cash-payin' customers partyin'.

"Would you quarrel over me that way?" I playfully asked.

I was trying my best to restrain my amusement. Daphne put her hands around my neck, interlocking her fingers purposely, moving her face slowly closer to mine. She came to a halt an inch away from kissing range, staring into the blue-gray windows of my soul.

"Stanley, you would enjoy seeing me behave foolishly that way over you," she sternly offered. "The reply to your question is nondescript."

Daphne's words stated indifference, but her eyes told me something else, smarting indignation. Her arms had not abandoned my neck, but she moved her face six inches farther away. She was contemplating. Any moment, I felt Daphne was going to give me a piece of her mind.

"I will, though, answer you inquiry," she angrily said, "in a manner I think you'll understand."

She removed her arms from their hold on me.

"One of me is more woman than you could ever want or deserve. C'est la guerre"—it is war—"if a man can't give 100 percent attention to a tantalizing woman of foreign intrigue. It is unacceptable behavior to me," she scoffed.

She was pouting and sad-eyed. My choice was simple. I would rather be punched squarely with shots to the bread basket by a loan shark's enforcer than to be slapped verbally by a woman I cared about. The pain was less traumatic.

She was acting capriciously, I said to myself, so I was going to have to make allowances. No malice was intended in my solicitation, so I had nothing to apologize for. Apparently, I had struck a nerve. Winning a war of words now would make me lose later. If I responded saying the wrong thing, her tear ducts would explode in a brook down her cheeks, so I refrained from uttering with a faux French accent, "Au contraire"—on the contrary—"my little kumquat, you look so beautiful when you are mad." She would have accused me of mocking her, left our table crying, and walked out of the Inn, leaving me behind as the villain. So I didn't.

Honestly, she looked wonderful in her distressed state. The moment could best be described as compassionate, seeing her so femininely vulnerable. She was one of those rare women that would look beautiful heedless of her mood, but I would have given anything to see her happy again. Yeah, damn it. I would have even parted with the Movado watch the way she just touched my heart. Oh my gosh. What was I saying? Was it because I had too much "sauce" this evening? No, I'd still do it even stone sober. Never would I intentionally hurt this lady. It would be perverse. The two of us must be kindred spirits. Still, she still sneered at me, but at least it wasn't jeers.

Right then and there, I had a penchant to call her Daffy to break the ice, and I did just that, smiling all my pearly whites. She was startled, but not piqued by my pronouncement.

"Only my brothers," she softly voiced, "are allowed to call me by that pet name. Next thing I know, you'll have some eider, canvasback, or hooded merganser suffix attachment to it."

"Daffy Duck." I chuckled.

She laughed that sweet laugh of hers. She poked a gentle hand thrust into my rib cage with her knuckles.

"You are a conceited brat," she offered, "who's taking advantage of the fact that I like you. Didn't you realize that those dizzy girls only wanted that young man's old-style Western chapeau? You didn't notice the poor boy's awful complexion? He badly needs the services of a good dermatologist."

I laughed with Daphne when she finished her faux interpretation, though her emotions said something quite differently. Suddenly, she hugged me. Then she rested her head on my shoulder, scratching my back. Chuckling to myself, I realized Daphne and I had just had our first fight. I had let her win, and we weren't even dating. I liked her style, ergo, in making up. Her body language implied that all was forgiven. I was still currying her favor even though Stanley was a conceited brat. At least I was a conceited brat that she liked. Daphne slid her right arm athwart my waist, making herself comfortable crossing her leg over her left knee. My left arm was around her shoulders. I was servicing as a cushion, because her left foot was balancing on my left shin. Our free hands entwined in fingers, shaping a tepee. Whether John Henry was being honest about Sally saying he was a good conversationalist on their first date, even though he barely constructed a paragraph, I was going to put that creed to practice displaying a quiet reserve, allowing Daphne to ramble on with the story of her life.

CHAPTER IX

Bubbling with enthusiasm, Daphne related that she was born in Chantilly, France, where lace was made and exported. Her parentage was mostly French. Her mother, one-eighth British, hailed from Toulon, while her dad was a native Marseillais, a descendant of a long generation of fishermen.

"The pounding of hooves on turf and not a life at sea were in his blood," she disclosed.

She paused, and my thoughts momentarily meandered. I knew I promised myself to remain silent, but I couldn't help it.

"Daffy, if I'm out of line, please tell me. Do you mean to say that your father likes to fully indulge in betting a few francs at the track?"

"Oh no. Nothing of the sort." She laughed. "You think my papa is a professional gambler. Nothing could be further from the truth. Wait till I inform him what you said. He'll be amused and want to meet the rogue. I'm sorry if I didn't make myself clearer. He breeds and trains horses that compete in the British and French derbies. One thing you may have heard is that horse betting is a popular pastime in France. Nevertheless, you are quite the comedian, regarding my papa."

Funny, I expressed to myself. I wasn't trying to be entertaining. She continued her biography sketch. Her mother's father was a commercial produce farmer in Monteux, which was east of Avignon in southeastern France, department of Vaucluse.

Daphne lived such-and-such miles south of her grandfather's place in Le Thor.

"I bet—now you have me gambling. You're a very bad influence," she offered humorously. "You wouldn't guess that I'm a country girl at heart?"

"No," I answered, "not by the way you look."

"Let me assure you," she told me, unerring, "that some very lovely girls are raised on farms. Even a few not-so-pretty ones can become attractive later on," she assured.

I didn't understand her last statement, but I smiled anyway.

"Let me guess," I speculated somewhat securely, "that your grandfather grew…yes, your grandfather grew artichokes."

"Had you wagered me, you would have lost. He never grew them. Most are grown up north in the Paris Basin. My grandfather planted turnips as his staple crop, which are fed to cattle in sliced form," she corrected. "The memories of my childhood that I'm most fond of took place on his farm during weekends and summer hiatus."

Daphne appeared eager to discuss her adolescence. As for gambling, I didn't want to admit that I had enough games of chance for one evening.

"Besides, with a name such as Andre Morel, it would be ludicrous if he didn't harvest a few mushrooms. As in the stock market, he liked to dabble, but in his case, it was fungi. Because of his name and his occupation, competitive farmers and merchants liked to have sport with him when he came to market. He wasn't partial to their theatrics," she told me.

She had piqued my interest on this topic, and I was slightly annoyed she didn't elaborate. Skipping over, she went on to stress that a year of her formal childhood rearing was in one of those stuffy British middle schools, before she returned across the channel to complete her education. Her parents had separated for a while. At that time, Daphne and her mother were living with an aunt in Yorkshire. Obviously, this was a sunder she wished to address to me.

"England is charming, but France is my home," she confided.

Please don't interrupt her, I disclosed privately, but a fusillade of curiosity prevailed.

"Daphne, what did you mean by your grandfather dabbling in mushrooms? Tell me more," I implored earnestly.

"I didn't think the subject would interest you. Apparently, I was wrong in my assumption. Maybe I was afraid of coming off as a disingenuous bore with truffles—I meant trifles," she pleasingly remedied.

"Never you," I quickly said, gliding my hand over her silk sleeve as a vote of confidence.

I would have lobbied to muster up a bunch of votes for her if I had to.

"The white mushrooms that were served with your meal earlier, the *Agaricus bisporus*, were one of the varieties he grew on his farm. It is one of the easiest types to be cultivated and accounts for the majority produced by commercial growers in the States and on the continent. *Agaricus bisporus* are always a welcome concomitant to prime rib or any cut of beef," she lectured.

"Grandfather was favored to have good clay soil rich in nitrates on his property. That's very beneficial to a good mushroom 'flush.'"

Catching myself ready to burst laughing, I turned askance, as if watching the crowd, before returning to her eyes with a smile.

"You must forgive me. It struck me as funny when you said 'flush.' As if I was calling my hand in a poker game, declaring an ace high-mushroom flush," I digressed from what Daphne was trying to explain.

She didn't understand the connection at first, but when it made sense to her, Daphne shared my fun. She even congratulated me with a peck on both cheeks before calling me a rogue again. This time a likeable one.

"Daphne, what, pray tell, is a mushroom *flush*?" I rebounded inquisitively.

"Be assured, it has nothing to do with seven-card stud," she smilingly insisted. "After the initial harvesting crop, several successive yields of mushroom sprout every two to three weeks. The first three to four produce the most dense crop, while following flushes give sparser yields. Do you now understand what is meant by the term *mushroom flush*?"

"Yes. Especially when an expert presents it so clearly," I responded.

"If your intention is to try to flatter me, then you have succeeded. I shall continue. Grandfather was systematic in crop rotation and perennially exercised the use of different types of fertilizer. To cultivate his white mushrooms, Grandfather built greenhouses. These are necessary to control humidity, temperature, and ventilation. They serve as a deterrent to insects and disease organisms. Mushroom-growing is a rather-risky business, and cultivation cannot take place in the open fields."

"Daffy, maybe this a stupid question, but when and where did cultivation first take place?" I pryingly asked.

"Stanley," she said, digging, "there are no stupid questions, just dumb answers."

"Touché," I responded as I kissed her hand. "Hmm," I murmured to no one in particular. Twice I'd called her Daffy and she had let it go by without incident. She took the hand I had been holding and placed it under her chin in contemplation.

"By the looks of your broad-smiled countenance, you resemble the pussycat that swallowed the scarlet tanager," she remarked.

Of course, I offered no response, even though I knew that the goofy cat swallowed a canary! At least she hadn't mistaken the type of bird for a grackle. I simply whistled the melody of the first tune that came to mind, and for some reason, it happened to be "Ding Dong Bell."

"Mushrooms have been around Europe," she continued, "since the days of the ancient Greeks and Romans. The scientific approach in France started in the early eighteenth century, if I'm not mistaken. The area around Paris with its caves and abandoned quarries was always a hub for mushroom horticulture. The cold, damp environment encourages fungi growth, and the temperature in deep shafts most often remains stable. My grandfather cited that the mushrooms grow right on the floor of the caves. It is frankly the best natural enclosure. Unlike other vegetable production, which demands rich soil, sunshine, and water, mushrooms require organic nutrients in the form of compost. Unfortunately, my grandfather didn't have the luxury of having a cavern on his property, thus utilizing the best man-made alternative. Caves, he said, have their disadvantage, particularly when it came to preparing the mushroom beds and harvesting the fruiting bodies."

"First and foremost in cultivation is the germination of fungi spores. My grandfather, a self-taught horticulturalist, was adamant about producing his own master culture. Sure, he had his peccadillos, but that's what made Poppy—that's what I called him—so special," she relayed.

Daphne placed her hand over her mouth in awe.

"I haven't recited that to anyone in years. His first name was so beautiful, Andre. Stanley, you make me feel very comfortable."

"I'm glad," I responded.

I wasn't expecting her compliment.

"Instead of working with tobacco-processed spawn or rye and wheat grain, as is typical of mushroom growers, for a specific purpose, Poppy used barley mixed with calcium carbonate as the culture medium. His reasoning was that taste wouldn't suffer from increased yield. Next, a compost was prepared. Unconventionally, Poppy preferred a composition of sheep manure with straw rather than a horse-manure mixture." She laughed.

Sharing in the frolic with her, I implored, "How did you handle the smell?"

"I would always wear nose plugs," she answered, "and most of the time, he wouldn't. The odor on humid days could be awful." She playfully pinched her nostrils.

Still laughing, Daphne repeated that the manure was mixed with straw.

"We would pile the manure in long heaps, to allow natural fermentation to take place. During the beginning of the second week, Poppy meshed in turnip skins to the compost. I'll never know if he was joking when he claimed that the addition led to good mycelial growth. The time frame for this process took about two weeks," she explained.

I offered her a cigarette from my pack, which she refused. Instead, when mine was lit, she took a drag.

"The preparation of the 'beds' follows. There are no sheets or pillowcases," she said to mimicked me.

Attacking her pun, I knew saying I didn't get it would have served no purpose, so I laughed heartily.

"Preparing the beds is called filling. Poppy would place the fermented compost in twenty-six-centimeter-deep trays, from what I remember. For your edification, that's about ten inches. Sometimes I forget that in the States nobody other than engineers and scientists can convert to the metric system. Poppy would stack the filled trays in tandem. Another week of fermentation took place, allowing for more chemical changes in the compost, thus eliminating bugs and any bacterial disease," Daphne informed.

"Continuing in sequence, we arrive at spawning. If my memory serves me, at a temperature of around twenty-nine degrees centigrade, the barley spawn was measured in teaspoon-size portions and pushed into the 'beds' about six inches apart. Some growers double the length. For the next two to four weeks, this period, known as the run, allows for the growth of the mycelium throughout the compost. In the cultivation process, this was a period of idleness for Poppy. All he could do was check temperatures in the beds and greenhouses and spray for insects. It allowed him to devote the majority of his labors to tending to other chores or his turnips," Daphne recalled.

She's so beautiful. I was nodding at her every other word, sometimes shrugging my shoulders, determined to be quiet and not interrupt. I enjoyed the way she gleefully expressed this botanical preparation in chronological order, without mishmashing numerical accuracy and not missing a beat. Further, I could listen to her for hours. Daphne's English articulation was pleasantly sounding, especially when she stressed her consonants. Recited by her, a sonnet would receive its proper justice.

"The last phase in the process is called casing. When the master culture, the mycelium, has permeated throughout the compost, the beds are moistened. Poppy used only natural mineral water from his well. Here was where mystique played in. From a leather pouch hidden in one of the greenhouses, Poppy sprinkled a coarse white powder directly on top of the compost. He followed this procedure by spreading a sliver-thin layer of his rich clay soil on top of the bed. He repeated my prior description with a final covering of white powder on top, moistening again," she imparted.

"That totals five layers," I volunteered.

"Correct," Daphne said. "However, the distinguishing thing was that all the layers combined were no more than an inch and a quarter thick. Poppy claimed that no other grower in France knew of this method of adding the white powder. As I implied earlier, he was truly a nonconformist. When I would inquire of the contents of his 'magic bag,' he would merely laugh. His name for me was—and please don't laugh—Daffodilly."

I did laugh, though expeditiously and slyly.

"Stanley, I'll allow you to call me Daffy in private, but never Daffodilly, nowhere and nohow," she pleaded. "Poppy would only say that the white powder was his secret to the recipe. It was essential to the yield and the excellent taste his mushrooms favored. Oh yes, I once recollect him having a conversation with Papa about it. He attributed that the systematic arrangement of the white powder was broached to him from a Basque planter he befriended in Spain many years ago, during the war.

"It certainly worked for him, because while other farmers produced three to four good flushes per tray if they were lucky, Poppy would receive six to eight excellent ones. The first three flushes make up 75 percent of the mushrooms that farmers take to market. The remainder is kept for personal consumption. Other growers could only envy him. He would suggest to them that they didn't sing sweetly enough to their mushroom beds."

"What do you guess was in the pouch?" I questioned.

"Remember, Stanley, I was so young. My answer is only speculation. If I were to guess then, I would say the powder was fish bones. Codfish bones, specifically, that he pulverized. That was his favorite seafood. Not all Frenchmen savor escargot or frogs' legs," she revealed. "Grandmama would go to the fish market every other Thursday to purchase his craving."

"Daphne?" I called.

I moved my face closer to hers.

"Yes, Stanley."

"It's all so axiomatic. The answer is right in front of our noses. Your grandfather wasn't drying to raise mushrooms, he was attempting to make lasagna with all those layers," I zestfully insinuated.

Daphne nodded in agreement and told me I had made an excellent parity, but not before she grabbed my knee with one hand, applying some pressure and dispensing what she labeled a French monkey bite.

"The purpose of the top soil layers is to encourage primordial growth. That is the elemental stage of the mushroom. Roughly twenty-one to twenty-eight days later, voilà. The fruits of the labor have appeared," Daphne detailed.

"So the whole process takes about ten weeks before you can pick your first mushrooms," I deducted.

"Stanley, you listen quite attentively. You pay close attention to details. I'm impressed. I like that quality in a man. I'm glad that I came here tonight," she smilingly emphasized.

Had she been talking to DA? I wondered.

"What about the exotic species of mushrooms that you hear France to be so famous for? Did your grandfather cultivate any of those?" I was curious to ask.

"No doubt, monsieur," she teased, "you're inquiring about *Amanita caesareas*, chanterelles, and truffles, to name the most impressive ones. You more than likely have eaten some that are produced mainly in the Orient, which are the Padi Straw and the shiitake mushroom. Chinese and Japanese restaurants complement these varieties with mixed vegetables. For the first three, there are no tried and true scientific methods that I am aware of that can grow these delectables on a full-scale basis. It's basically hit or miss and a cash crop only few in Europe can rely on. Along with the difficulty of obtaining a master culture that will form a symbiotic association with an indigenous medium, you compound the problem with fungal disease, weeds, and insect control, particularly flies."

"Varieties are found in deciduous woodlands because they adapt well to sylvestral environs. These fungi are the ones that my grandfather speculated with. On the purlieu and about Poppy's property were scatterings of oak, beech, birch, and chestnut trees," she communicated.

Daphne laughed that sweet laugh of hers.

"Stanley, please don't ask me," Daphne warned, "which specie of mushroom is the best. We—and by *we* I mean we French connoisseurs—have a habit of trying to insist that the type of mushroom we personally like best is all of France's favorite. I suppose it's patriotic culinary license.

"The first type I spoke of, *Amanita caesarea*, or Caesar's mushrooms, which they are called, were the favorite of the Roman emperors. They described their taste as 'fit food for the gods.' They do have a magnificent flavor. To illustrate their historical perspective, it is alleged that Emperor Claudius Caesar was fatally poisoned by consuming what he thought were safe and edible *Amanita caesareas*. The plotting subversives probably administered a destroying agent, such as hemlock, into the unsuspected mushrooms," she guessed.

I silently clutched my head and opened my mouth wide in mock respect for the departed luminary. Daphne couldn't help herself from smiling. She enjoyed my pantomime.

"Getting back to the seriousness of your lesson," she begged. "*Amanita caesarea* can be identified by its orange caps and yellow gills. We would find them in the clearings of oak and chestnut trees. They are a good choice raw in salads, creamed, or in a thin pink sauce, with sun-dried tomatoes over egg noodles or linguini. Oh, a note of caution: proper care must be taken not to confuse this fungi with the poisonous *Amanita muscarias*, or the fly agaric, as it is called. The cap is close to the same color, and its identifiable warts are sometimes washed off when it rains. Although it is not poisonous, it is hallucinogenic, and unless you're into psychedelic 'tripping,' it should be avoided," she cautioned.

For a fraction of a minute, I thought it a bit diverting, until Daphne explained that the competition among growers and pickers was intensely keen. Reputation for selling quality to market was all important, and one mistake could ruin one's livelihood. An amateur hobbyist supplementing his income could confuse the two mushrooms. Deadly classifications, such as the Death Cap, do associate themselves, along with the edible varieties, in deciduous woods, particularly near the beeches and oaks.

"Since we are wandering on the subject of poisonous mush-rooms, Stanley," she demurely informed, "I am forced to make an admission to a most despicable act."

Everyone tonight, it seemed, had made a form of admission to me of some confidentiality. Why should Daphne be any different? I mused. Reading the lady's character as I knew, what more frightful crime could she have committed other than to deliberately step on the pavement cracks of the Avenue des Champs-Élysées in Paris?

"If you despise me, then that is what I deserve. Why I am about to reveal this to you, I don't fully understand, other than not want-ing to keep any secrets from you but to be honest and forthright. I am too old to play woman of mystery games. What you get is what you see. Granting that we are to become better acquainted, I would expect the same courtesy from you," she implied. "Stanley, I admit to being confused. I don't know where to begin. Possibly, I'll just begin at the beginning."

"It's always a good place to start," I augmented.

"Maybe it was three years ago or four. Who cares? He came up to me in Regine's, a popularly trendy nightclub in Paris."

"Who was *he*?" I asked.

"He," she pronounced disdainfully, "is Jean-Luc Sorac. He was a textile exporter. Not terribly good-looking, but masterfully confi-dent and rich. A regular bon vivant. My intuition upon meeting him was to stay away, yet I didn't have faith in the bad vibes I was receiv-ing. We reached a common ground from my merchandising studies at college. He liked some of my ideas and stated that he wished to incorporate them in his business. I was fooled in more ways than one. A romance blossomed after eleven weeks of dating, and I con-ceded to be happy. Jean-Luc enjoyed my presence at his fencing com-petitions. He distinguished himself with the pee, though opponents questioned his sportsmanship.

"I was gullible to believe he was a widower. His spouse and including his two small children were fatalities in an airline explosion over the Tyrrhenian Sea. He said that a woman with my compassion-ate personality was his life's search since their cruel departure from this life. How could I not pity the man for his loss? And over the following months, I admired his strength in the manner he shouldered his bereavement.

"Then I found out the painful, ugly truth from my papa. Because he had suspected something sinister about Jean-Luc when they met, Papa had hired a private detective to gather information on his background. There was a very much alive wife and two wee boys living in a terraced villa overlooking the Mediterranean Sea on the Italian Riviera in San Remo. Apparently, they had made a miraculous recovery from death.

"Having three residences, with one a secret hideaway in San Marino, a tiny country situated within the boundaries of Italy, including headquartering his business in France while his family dwelled on his seaside estate in a neighboring country, Jean-Luc was slick at covering all bases in his deception, to the extent of engaging the lies of his associated cronies. Having the obsessed determination of Joan of Arc, but with condemnation for his callous deceit, I sought to teach him a valuable lesson for repudiating his family and deceiving me. Never would I have dated him if I were aware he was married. Wanting someone else's husband is not my style. My affectation for revenge was all-consuming as I conceived the perfect recompense."

She paused a bit.

"I held a soiree, a dinner party, at my Paris apartment, inviting two other couples who were aware of his licentious guile. Unbecoming to him, I granted the condemned man his last meal but prepared it with my own diligent fashion. It was the guest of honor's very favorite. I rotisseried skewered poussin, wrapped in bacon and stuffed with wild rice and lapin, rabbit, sausage. Basting with marsala wine every ten minutes and slowly cooking at 315 degrees, it seemed like a millennium for the birds to get done. The cretin or debauched monster, in terms as I reticently thought of him, would never dare let me ersatz guinea hen again or squab when I had difficulty locating poussin at the meat market. The parvenu would debase me and sulk. "'The flesh does not have the succulence and is not as tender,' he would state.

"Jean-Luc was stalwart in his insistence that I only purchase sel de mer coarse, crystallized sea salt. A common iodized version would be found picayune.

"He flatly prescribed that his epicurean palate demanded choice ingredients and proper attention to details."

Another pause.

"The fraud, I'm positive his food selections were bland during his earlier humble milieu and not the refined taste buds he claimed. Assorted vegetables were served as an accompaniment to the fowl, including petit pois, peas, for color. Precipitating the main course, pâté de foie gras canapes were offered, as well as lobster thermidor croquettes," Daphne impeccably detailed.

"A very special mushroom salad with vinaigrette sauce and a splash of sauterne was prepared exclusively for the beast—I mean Jean-Luc. While my other guests were dining on shaggy ink caps in their salads, he was unawarely advocating the culinary pleasures of the common ink cap. The only problem with this almost-similar type of mushroom is that there is a severe cross-reaction when alcohol is consumed to promote gastric poisoning. So being the perfect hostess, I made sure his wineglass was always replenished with more port, and even popped open a bottle of Georges Duboeuf Beaujolais Nouveau I had been saving for the occasion. I so much as insisted he finish the remaining contents of the Cointreau bottle and help himself to the Chartreuse, which he did. With a drink in hand, he praised my skills in the kitchen to the rest of my guests, but the only 'cooking' I was interested in was the simmering in his stomach. Bon appétit, Jean-Luc. The mixture would never kill him, just give him the champion of all bellyaches later that evening or by the next morning," she confirmed.

"As I confronted him with the truthful existence of his family by presenting an unretouched photo in the presence of my guests, he merely stated that he wished not to burden me with such gruesome details. He showed the heart of an assassin. Then, I showed Jean-Luc the door to leave…forever. Instead of playing a game of charade, dominoes, or piquet, my other guests tried and convicted him in mock absentia, a bas, down with, Jean-Luc. Exiled to the former penal colony off the coast in northern French Guiana, lie du Diable, Devil's Island, would have been too kind," she abjured.

"By seven o'clock the following morning, he telephoned, cursing that I had caused injustice to his digestive tract. Half-asleep but cognizant of his worry, I inquired if he had partaken of any 'destroying angel' mushrooms, usually fatal if ingested. They are rarely found in Europe, but I didn't share that tidbit with him. My bitter outcry to him, 'C'est un miserable.' He is a scoundrel. 'S'il vous plait'—if you please—'call the gendarmes,' I dared before hanging up my receiver," she informed.

Breaking down, Daphne was shielding her eyes from me, sobbing sincere tears.

"I suppose now…you'll think…I'm uncouth. He cost me…he cost me eight months of my life. Why was I so naive?" she stressfully delivered, sobbing. "I don't know," she successively answered herself with remorse.

"Daphne, you were very charitable to the slob," I offered in consolation. "You could have been justified requiting his actions in a far worse way."

While she wiped away her tears with a tissue, I was grasping her right hand with both of mine. Her voice was a little strained, yet she laughed that sweet laugh of hers. Noticing her trepidation, I assured her that everything was fine, and she continued to describe the other mushrooms.

"Only lecture on the 100 percent edible ones," I warned her teasingly. She smilingly accepted my remark.

"The Chanterelles, or *Cantharellus cibarius* as they are identified, are my preference," she ratified. "They resemble the flowering bloom on a pumpkin, orange-yellow in color and funnel-shaped. When the flesh is dried, it has the distinctive smell of apricots. When I've sautéed Chanterelles in olive oil, with chives, garlic, curly parsley, lemon, and scallions with three healthy wrist pours of chardonnay, allowing to simmer for five minutes, the dish manifests itself into becoming indescribably savory morsels. A trace deviation within the parameters of à la grecque," she calmly outlined as a devout epicure.

"A very tempting meal is boeuf bourguignon. This time we add bacon, cubes of choice beefsteak, and onion to the already-cooking mushrooms. Ditto the volume of wine, ersatz white for red and, voilà, a final statement in fine dining," she devoted. "You may see Chanterelles sold dried in markets. If I wasn't at his farm on a particular weekend, Poppy would always save me a few Chanterelles he might locate near beech or oak trees."

"When climate conditions would be perfect for the prize, usually late September, my grandfather would take me on treasure hunts. Equipped with a small trident pitchfork, a trowel, a sharp penknife, a sturdy wicker basket, and a well-trained dog like his Clement, we would pack a lunch, including a full skin of Bordeaux wine, with us to go searching for our booty, truffles. Our expeditions could either take us somewhat west, well over a hundred miles, in his canvas-covered Labourier truck, where Poppy knew there was limestone in the soil near a population of oak trees. Here we looked for signs of the black Périgord truffle, and if we ventured northeast toward Turin, Italy, we were exploring for the white Piedmont truffle. Both are named for the areas where they are mainly found," she echoed.

"Frankly, Daphne," I broke in, "I have sampled Chanterelles with much pleasure, but I know little of truffles other than they are found underground. Aren't you supposed to look for them with a trained pig?" I cleverly interposed.

"Apparently, you possess a little more knowledge than you care to admit to. You've done a little homework on French agriculture. The answer to both solicitations is yes, yet the second is not so resounding, as it is a misconception on the part of Americans. Don't feel too badly. You're in good company," she said gladly.

"Being subterranean in habitat, truffles form their own order of fungi. They don't even faintly resemble the type of mushroom most everybody is familiar with seeing and enjoying. They're oval in shape, having tubular projections a lot similar to a petite russet potato, including wrinkle lines on the skin, but instead of eyes, truffles have warts. Normally, they have half the size and weight, and the black Périgord can even have a reddish tint to it. Unless botanical science has progressed, the only haphazard method that I am aware of to cultivate them is to simply plant acorns or germinate some with particles of truffle to increase an oakwood's yield. The process must be perennial, because as the trees age, the harvest dwindles. Since they are so scarce, it means that truffles command the highest prices at market. Hiding places and amusing methods of finding locations are passed on to the next generation. Growing four to six inches below the earth's surface, they propose a precarious difficulty to the adventurer who wishes to dig them up.

"What I recall is that Poppy would look for nature's fluctuation signs in our pursuit of edible buried treasure. He would show me how to observe ground discolorations, soil erosions or disturbances, and swarms of flies hovering in the air. The truffles permeate a scent that sometimes attracts a certain type of gnat that oviposits directly above the soil of the fruiting body. As coming to near in proximity to crushed skunk cabbage would give off a rather-unpleasant, pungent odor to flair the nostrils, the black Périgord has the characteristic aroma of mild cheese. They argue in France that the smell is closely Camembert, or definitely Roquefort, while the white Piedmont discovered mostly in western Italy has the hint of Gorgonzola. It's a silly embracement of nationalistic pride but nevertheless said. Once a suitable location could be found, Poppy used to say, 'All one needed was a good pair of eyes and a keen sense of smell.' He had the twenty-fifteen vision, and I had the sensitive nose. That's why we made such a terrific team of explorers," she proudly remembered.

"Getting back to your trained pigs," she said, laughing. "It is true that pigs are used to dig up truffles. Can you imagine a pig on a leash? Well, I have, firsthand. They are disgustingly terrible to coax and divagate from where they're supposed to be sniffing. Eating is the only thing on their minds, and if they locate a truffle for you, the chances of them devouring it are excellent. After all, it is food to them, too, and they're the ones that found it," she cheerfully said, raising her voice an octave higher. "It would be better to train deer because of their acute sense of smell, or even squirrels I've surveyed excavating potential truffle sights. They have an innate partiality for this underground vegetation."

"Cody," I blurted out enthusiastically, not being able to control my silence.

"Pardon me, Stanley. What did you say?"

"Oh, it was nothing, Daphne. Please continue."

"I have seen goats being used to locate truffles and have even heard stories of muzzled bears being employed. A well-trained dog is still the best hunter for man. It was provident for Poppy to have Clement during our treks. He was a pedigree Kerry blue terrier who was unflappable in his ability to pick up the essence, dig, 'go to ground,' and retrieve the prized truffles. Never did we have to worry about him consuming the fungi, because awaiting for him when we returned to the farm was his reward, a nice, thick-cut lamb chop," Daphne relayed.

I nodded approvingly. It might be my preference also. She didn't realize that her hands were toying with my matchbook cover as she spoke. It was being passed back and forth without slipping out.

"During the thrill of the hunt, I have observed French gentlemen clad in their best country finery. Ensembled in ascots, berets, chamois jackets, and waterproof gloves, clearing their nostrils and sensitizing their mucous membranes by inhaling spirits of ammonium carbonate or some other decongestant, they began sniffing the terrain like a forest animal. Two others held on to his legs, pushing him like a human wheelbarrow in pursuit of the scent of truffles, while the 'holdee' grappled with the slick leaves. They all take a turn. It was a sight worth the price of admission, preeminently, if one of the two holders tripped, knocking over the entire wheelbarrow," she unfolded, giggling.

"I have watched explorers, firsthand, with makeshift divining rods looking for the black Périgord, much the same way a prospector might be diluted to think they can locate an underground brook with sorcery. Scientific types, better suited to attending a symposium, would go trampling through the oaks with makeshift Geiger counters in tow. Did they think that truffles were radioactive? Poppy would squirt his wine down his throat and smirk at their antics. Idiots. They think they've established an art form. Probably, they got lucky once, found a mushroom, and this nonsense is all that they know, he would say."

I relished her anecdote.

"Truffles are an expensive delicacy that inhibits splendor to any gourmet meal. A prerequisite for a Sunday dejeuner—a late-breakfast—feast is, voilà, truffles and eggs over lightly. Filet mignon broiled to order with diced garlic and black Périgords is most lavish for a late-evening meal," she attested for any devotee.

"When he found some that suited their requirements, one particular posh five-star restaurant in Versailles, Poppy would ship truffles by rail to have them immortalized on their bill of fare. The establishment would flambé the black Périgord with exotic mixed herbs and Rémy Martin King Louis XIII, thee champagne of cognacs. After rolling the mixture into a delicate crepe, they would present the aflame masterpiece on a bed of watercress. The à la carte selection was their pièce de résistance.

"It was honorifically titled 'truffles à la de Rothschild.' Equivocally, you paid through the nose, but the dish was decadently delicious. It became the rage of the Parisian social set. One requesting this nicety attained instant celebrity status at his table. Other diners cheered and marveled."

I clapped politely in jest.

"Can you believe the minister of health in Vichy tried to ban truffles à la de Rothschild from one swanky, highbrow-café menu? There was public outcry, to serve this crème de la crème creation. It has been said with discretion that a couple who dine on this luxury will enjoy amorous gratification," she excitedly divulged.

"Earlier tonight, I heard of a surefire love remedy that's considerably cheaper and not as scarce as your truffles," I revealed.

"What is it?" she inquired, tugging at my collar.

Not wanting to appear foolish rehashing the ridiculous "squirrel hind legs" theory, I got out of my self-made trap by claiming I needed to experiment with it first before I could explain it.

Espying a mood of sudden disturbance about Daphne, I was ready to offer words of comfort. She was clenching her teeth, and her poor eyes were sullen. Daphne ran her fingers down the side of her face while her other hand was still clutching on to my matchbook. Hastily, she jumped from her seat.

"Sacrebleu," she vigorously said out loud. *Confound it.* "I nearly forgot to discuss the cépes. Pardon me. Getting volatile has a tendency to make me speak my mother tongue, as you have no doubt witnessed. It would be a monumental failure not to talk about that variety of mushroom. I would despise myself as a Frenchwoman if I didn't include them," Daphne offered seriously.

"Whew, that's a relief. I thought there was something wrong," I added with concern.

"No," she said, "only that I almost committed a mortal sin in French cuisine if I neglected to give the cépes their just due. You could only appreciate the blunder being French. They are a handsome, cocoa-colored, thick-based fungi. Near beechwoods would be the best place to find them, but you can also locate them. My having been able to stir French words in with my English and you still understanding is refreshing."

"You're too kind," I replied, "but Sally is so right. She's such a great judge of character." I laughed. "Daphne, from what you shared with me, it sounds as if your grandfather was quite a fellow."

"Oh, that was definitely the case. He was aloof, even to the point of being a recluse at times. From what my papa told me, Poppy never fully recovered from his feelings of being spurned by the French government after the Second World War. Like many other fearless patriots fighting the Nazis with the Maquis, Poppy was overlooked when de Gaulle was awarding the Legion of Honor to underground resistance fighters. Papa said that weekly he risked his life liberating displaced Frenchmen conscripted by Laval's policy into the German labor force, smuggling downed Allied pilots and Jewish refugees across the Pyrenees into Spain. As I informed you before, he was the brunt of jokes when he did come to market, so he avoided the task when he could. He became misanthropic, and large crowds always bothered him. Sometimes I think that his demophobia was passed on to me," she said in a soft tone.

"As it worked out, Grandmama was more stingy with the purse-strings than him, and a terrific haggler. She would insist on top franc for his produce in Carpentras and had the ability to escape unscathed using language Poppy would have been rebuked for using.

"Socializing for Poppy was with his family or his only friend, a nearby farmer, Jaques Durant. His seclusion quirk had its benefits for me. His granddaughter received his undivided attention. The grandsons, my two older brothers, were never very interested in mushrooms—just give them a football, what we French call a soccer ball or the reins of a horse, and they were content. Oops, I forgot to mention them, and I'm sure they wouldn't be happy about that. Henri is thirty-four, five years my senior, and Pierre is thirty-one. They're both involved in the horse breeding business with my father. Too bad Poppy kept so mum about his cultivation techniques. Because he kept them only in his head and not written down anywhere, they were never passed on. Shortly after he died, Grandmama sold the farm and she moved in with us. I'll never forget the little bit he taught me," she declared with reverence.

"A little bit. That's definitely underevaluated. I would state that you retained quite a lot. Your coverage of fungi is cyclopedic. You were speaking volumes," I qualified exuberantly.

"Are you being sincere or just very generous with your compliments?" Daphne accusatorially requested.

"Both," I responded with a grin.

She shared my smile and laughed that sweet laugh of hers.

"That's a shame the farm had to be sold. Daffy, when was the last time you visited the area?"

"Not since my midteens," she sadly rejoined. "Come next spring, however, I'll be accompanying Sally and John Henry as unofficial guide on a holiday cruise to the South of France. Nice will be our port of entry. After a brief stay, a train will take my deluxe tourists to the original horse farm of my father, where I was raised."

Before Daphne could offer another dainty tidbit, three dots, three dashes, and three dots transmitted through my brain waves. This was John Henry's apocalyptic notion about me going to France he was haranguing about after dinner. I'd been set up, I silently told to myself, but indeed, what pleasant company as Daphne to be coupled with. I was smiling, and she didn't know why.

"We'll go on from there," she protracted, "to Poppy's former land. I've already made the necessary arrangements with the absentee proprietor, so we will not be trespassers. John Henry is excited about me introducing him to French farmers, and one of them, Maurice Lippet, will play the role of translator. While he is sojourning in the south, doing his cultivation thing, Sally and I will hop a plane to

Paris and explore the City of Lights from a native's perspective. That John Henry, he worries me so."

"How?" I asked.

"In a roundabout way, sans the billowing, brassy mannerisms, he reminds me of Poppy. They share the same stick-to-itiveness," she confided.

"Whom do I remind you of?" I happily investigated.

"With that sly smile on your personage, not minding your pointed ears," Daphne jovially said, "you remind me of Clement. Good boy, do you know where the truffles are?"

For a pausing reverie, I told myself that the lady was spunky to take such liberties.

"Yes, but I'm not telling you, unless you prepare thick-cut pork chops for me. I'm abstaining from lamb."

"Stanley, are you inviting yourself over for dinner?"

"No, I was only in character. I'm not sure. I don't know what I meant."

She had caught me off guard.

"If we still know each other in the spring, why don't you think about…?" she said.

Daphne bowed her head, hiding her eyes from mine, allowing me to digress. I was glad she didn't finish her statement. My reply wouldn't have been fair either to her or to me. After all, we just met less than an hour ago. How can I make plans with someone nine months from now who I wasn't even dating? Even with a woman I was seeing steadily, I'd never made plans more than three months in advance. Too much can unexpectedly happen in between, where unions fizzle and future arrangements go in disarray. Possibly, this French maiden knew more about my psyche than me, I pondered. Fat chance. This beautiful, finicky feline sitting alongside me could be fickle. Next time we meet, Daphne could feign a total memory loss regarding our conversation and our "hot-necking" because too much wine swirled her head.

In any event, there was the perplexing predicament of Samantha. Thirty-eight months of a semicomfortable relationship couldn't be just shoved out the window on a whim.

We were going out to dinner tomorrow night. Although our alliance was on shaky ground to consider marriage in the near future, Samantha would never want to suddenly, without warning, lose me, even though on her evaluation chart from 00 to 10, I measured a bawdy 9.15. Yes, she and her friends and family could actually rate a guy a cipher or a double zero. I smiled.

Wearing cut-rate designer labels can plummet you there along with rubber-soled shoes. In her world of formality, a woman without the proper boyfriend languished in social insignificance, but my score seemed to continually beat the competition off in her disillusive quest to meet the ultimate gentleman. My main problem was that if I would only remember to place the toilet seat back down, I might attain a new milestone, 9.3 status.

I snickered at the thought because now I did things that annoyed her on purpose. Arriving late, driving beyond the speed limit, and excessive smoking and drinking had become the foibles. Since my shrewd chat with DA, I'd developed a fondness for cappuccino, bolstered by a Grand Marnier on the rocks. It was difficult to find establishments that carried the Tiarra-brand cinnamon, save putting them on notice of its favorability. Unbiased changes were surrounding my life. Who could imagine me patronizing French liqueur? Samantha wouldn't be so tolerating of me telling her I just met the love of my life yesterday, who was French, and I'd agreed to go on a cruise with her to the south, married to "dorks," and with them, it was hard to pinpoint who was dorkier. From what Sam confided to me, Stephanie's dorky husband, Wesley, actually had the television set shut off on him by her during Super Bowl XVII, causing him to miss John Riggins's second-half forty-three-yard run around left end, on fourth and one. The dork capitulated to polish the silver. He was definitely the dorkiest. To make matters worse, Stephanie wouldn't allow him to take up golf.

The females in her family only wanted the best for Samantha, so they pondered, Why was she withering away with me the last three years? Perish the thought of them being my in-laws too.

Duh! Maybe if she told them she was on a schedule of two to three times a week, because she had very special needs in the "sack" department, that they couldn't substitute me for. The mother and two sisters were three thorns in her side that she needed removed. Those backstabbers had tried to exert their asymmetrical, overbearing influence on Samantha to conform to their critical view on what was proper.

Before me, they judged her initial dates' character flaws so harshly that there was never a second or a third outing. Thank God they were all away on a month's vacation in Wales when Sam and I met. They were touring the scenic beauty of Barry, Cardiff, Porthcawl, and Tenby on the Bristol Channel and visited St. David's on the western St. George's Channel side. By the time they discovered my swarthy presence, it was too late. She didn't want to give up her weekly schedule. Reprehensibly, perhaps that was all there ever was between us.

Even her own father, Harold, advised me after one too many Cutty Sarks and water doused the flames in his mind.

"If you truly love Sam, you'll relocate. I can't take back my mistakes with her mother. Once every so often, I visit this prostitute in the city who's a dominatrix. There's no sexual fulfillment. I only allow her to put a muzzle about my face and a spiked collar and leash around my neck, walking me naked on all fours around her apartment like a fuckin' cocker spaniel. She offers biscuits when I'm a good doggy and reprimands me when I'm bad. This is the way I deserve to be treated. Do you believe I actually pay good money for this abuse…and tip her besides?" he confessed.

My uneasy response was no. He was austere when he made his admission, so I was absolutely unsure whether or not he was lying. Funny thing, after this weirdo's confession, he found me with scarce time to play eighteen holes with him anymore. I couldn't take the chance of him barking when I'd start my swing or his getting the urge to retrieve my fairway shots, ergo, fetching the golf balls in his mouth. His stupefied advice, though, was solid, if I was in love with his daughter. The only problem was, I was not. Anyway, my business, my family, and my friends were in the area, and I was not about to forsake them. The only relocation would be me distancing myself from Samantha and her family. In the long run, everyone would be happy.

Gladly, I aborted my melancholy funk and resumed my approving countenance. I looked in Daphne's direction, my steady gaze becoming a stare and transforming from there to a fractional trance, wondering if this special lady was psychic. Surely, Sally had enlightened Daphne on the qualifications of Samantha, yet it was spooky that I perceived her knowing exactly what I was just musing. Purposely, she had refrained from bringing up Samantha. She would like very much for me to bring up her name to the table. Thinking too hard was making me cynical. In any event, Leslie Ann, the happy-faced waitress, had arrived at our seating.

"If I had my druthers, I would have waited on you sooner, but I didn't want to intrude on your conversation. John Henry gave me strict orders. 'If they don't look like they're dyin' of thirst, then don't bother them,'" she relayed. "May I get you folks a couple of drinks?" Daphne ordered only her second Campari and soda for the evening. So much for my dumb theory about her numbing her senses with too much alcohol. I, of course, wanted DA's favorite orange liqueur on ice.

Before leaving, Leslie Ann stated, "It's only my observation, but you two really get along swell together."

Both of us thanked her for the compliment, and I promised to double her tip.

When our drinks arrived, we touched glasses and Daphne replied, "À votre santé." To your health.

CHAPTER X

Some eighteen minutes later, I was digesting the experiences Daphne had just relayed to me before pardoning herself to enter the door with the upright horseshoes to powder her nose. The continuance of her biography sketch was either good novel material for an international writer or the background a lackluster female postgraduate student would covetously plagiarize for *Who's Who*.

The second time she arrived on American soil was right after high school graduation, she said. Daphne had been accepted to Vassar and was enrolled for the coming fall. She was so excited about arriving in America again. She was happy, too, that her Mama had stopped coddling her and had accepted the fact that her daughter would be thousands of miles away on foreign soil, getting an education. It wasn't as if Daphne would be totally isolated, because there was a scattering of friends and relatives who lived in the New York Metropolitan area. Papa had sanctioned her decision because the experience abroad would make her poised. She would spend the summer living with her older cousin Claudine Laurent at Claudine's New York City apartment she shared with a roommate who would be away through September. Those preceding months before school, Claudine had secured her a position as a kitchen helper in a Westside Pub. On her day off, and time in between permitting, she took in the many cultural and historical aspects New York City had to offer. Two weeks before the start of classes, she was walking to the front entrance of the Metropolitan Museum of Art to view a new exhibit.

"The Metropolitan is a grand museum. It's not the Louvre, but then again, what is? The comparison isn't fair," she uttered honestly.

Daphne relayed, she rushed over to a senior citizen who had slipped on her assent up the flight of steps and tumbled downward, apparently hurting her side. The woman's expression writhed in agony. People were walking right past the poor darling, ignoring her cries for help, she said. Daphne assured her not to worry. She had the where-withal to notify the person at the desk who she suspected as being the concierge at the museum that an elderly lady needed emergency medical assistance. She calmed the woman by singing a lullaby ditty in French and holding her hand until an ambulance arrived. Noticing that during the interim of her seeking help the lady's pocketbook had been stolen, she unselfishly gave her three extra dollars she held in reserve. The final act she recalled was the old lady gently squeezing her cheeks and inquiring her name. Upon the lady's insistence, she offered it twice. Little did Daphne realize at that time that this incident would later affect her career and lifestyle, as she told it to me.

At Vassar, she was mortified. It was one big mistake. It was a lonely place because she couldn't make any friends. Her prestige-conscious classmates mocked her upbringing. In their ascorbic ridicule, she was the "peasant who wished to dine on pheasant." They were uncouth, devoid of any sensitivity, even snubbing her equestrian skills. She did not appreciate them telling her she couldn't have intellectual pursuits. She might be from the French countryside, but she also had a mind. Her guidance counselor had never warned her that she might be misfit for such a school and be branded from any cliques. It was very depressing, Daphne remembered, going to classes, eating meals, and studying at the library all alone, holding from family that her new educational adjustment was not fine. She cried herself to sleep every night, praying to St. Bernadette for calm. She hated the college, the United States, and its stupid flag, which she had previously always admired, she told me.

When the pressure became unbearable in early November, she came back to New York City to inform Claudine she was predisposed to dropping out of school and returning, ashamed, home to France. Claudine's support was always there for her in ways she said she'd never forget. Though Claudine expressed a mutual susceptibility for her, she still grabbed Daphne by the shoulders and shook her violently, as she recalled.

"You will not be a quitter. I will not allow it, nor will you. You're not going to waste your grandfather's money that was left to you for studies or lose this semester's credits and go home a failure," Claudine shouted to Daphne. "You can transfer to another university next year. While you're in Poughkeepsie, I'll research schools having your area of concentration, send for applications, and together, we'll find the right fit. Just believe in yourself and trust your cousin. You are fun to be with. You show empressement. You'll make many friends during your stay here. Americans are no different from people in other countries. In certain circles, your acceptance depends on your wealth. Don't blame yourself. Those stupid, swinish snobs only ostracized you because you were not born rich. So you're not a member of America's 400 Club. Congratulate yourself. Can you imagine any of those golden-spooned snips having the heart to leave family and friends going overseas to the Sorbonne as fluently bilingual, as you came to a prestigious American college and adapting to their new surroundings and customs as easily as you fared? It would be a soul-searching lesson in prudence. They'd rather welcome deportation." Claudine laughed. "In another month and half, you'll never have to face those people ever again."

Daphne kept praying to St. Bernadette while she gutted it out at Vassar. She finished the semester making the dean's list. In late January, she would begin classes at Mount Saint Vincent College in Yonkers, New York.

Everything came to pass as Claudine had promised, save the fact that existing on three hours' sleep during a four-month period had finally taken its toll. Daphne had suffered from exhaustion. She celebrated the Christmas holiday and three weeks more in the hospital. It was goodbye, Mount Saint Vincent, for the spring and hello to $7,047 in medical bills, for which she had no health insurance. She only had coverage while as a student on campus.

Her mama, papa, two brothers, and a slew of other relatives took the trans-Atlantic flight Air France to visit her as she convalesced.

Papa took care of her charges. Her family wanted her to return home, except for Claudine, who wanted her to stay. She reminded them that Daphne would have to enroll for summer classes to catch up on her curriculum. Since her ex-roommate had relocated for a position in Minneapolis, there was now a vacant bedroom for Daphne, and furthermore, she could help with the rent. Daphne was incensed to stay and would not defer to any other opinion. Inner strength had overcome one obstacle, and her illness was just a temporary hurdle for her to jump. If she left now, she'd always regret it. She wished to earn some money, too, to reimburse her father. Her family couldn't help but notice this maturation, and her girlish looks were taking on the curves and shape of a taller young woman. As long as she got healthy, they decided she could stay in America.

She was thrilled to be around the company of Claudine and her older friends, shopping and going out in the Big Apple. A month later, she was strong enough to resume work, where she was hired back by the pub, working part-time in the kitchen and waitressing lunches when it was feasible.

He struck her as obnoxious, the squat, husky man with the fat face who chain-smoked in her customer area. Noticeably uncomfortable in his seat, he kept squirming to find the desired position. He addressed her by Daphne Roussant and stated that he had spent a lot of time and dough for ad space in the classified section of *The New York Times* to offer a reward to hunt her down. She had never seen him before in her life. It seemed to Daphne that in one fell swoop he snapped a life-size picture of her with his pupils.

"My mother was right on the money. Even at her age, she's still a good judge of talent. Not only did she describe you as bright-eyed, having an innocuous smile and good cheekbones, but she also felt the magic. Truthfully, the perception is there for me too. So much for schmaltz," she recalled him brusquely saying.

"Is that accent real, or are you making it up?" he demanded.

Daphne was leery that there might be something mentally wrong with the stranger. Occasionally, she waited on people like this and was told to just humor them. After all, she was working in New York City with its assortment of personalities.

He explained that he was the son of the lady she helped seven months ago at the Met.

Daphne still was not clear of his meaning. She thought he might be referring to American baseball.

He quizzed Daphne about helping an old lady who fell down the steps at the museum.

She answered yes. "That was your mother?" she inquired. "How is she doing?"

"My mother is doing fine," he answered. "Thanks to you. She had to have a hip replacement, and she is in Palm Beach, recuperating nicely. The warm weather is very therapeutic for her, he offered. To assure himself that Daphne was truly his mother's helper, he asked her to describe what happened."

She did in detail but omitted the money part. He wanted to know if Daphne gave her anything before his mother was transported away. Then, she remembered the three one-dollar bills.

"I'm sorry," he said. "I just had to be positive. For a thousand dollars, there were fifty people claiming to be you, except that only the genuine Daphne Roussant would only know about the stolen purse and the three bucks. A regular customer at your bar called the number that was published and implied you fit the description that I had given. My mother remembered Daphne but, in her excitement, confused croissant with your last name. He gets the grand. You never told anyone what happened?" he asked, confounded.

Daphne assured him that she gave the money freely. It was not a loan and a situation she had kept private for no particular reason.

He introduced himself as Maximilian Weiss, president of the Weiss Agency, but insisted that Daphne call him Maxi. She said that he hated his first name. The grateful lady that Daphne helped was Ruth Weiss, who founded the business some forty-five years ago. They were talent agents for actors and models. His mother instructed him to find her, and at forty-eight years of age, he was still listening to his mother. He wasn't just here to thank her or give Daphne her money back but to give Daphne a once-in-a-lifetime opportunity to be a model.

"Don't worry, I'm not promoting prostitution," he assured. "I'm no stereotypical, pink-Cadillac-driving pimp with leopard-lined seat covers. This is a legitimate career opportunity. Don't get me wrong. I'm not a very nice man. I'm a cold, calculated businessman. Nobody gets solicited by us. Models are referred to our studio. Photos are sent to us. If we like any of them, and that means my sister Myra, who handles the modeling division, we want to set up an appointment to see the girls with a professional-photographer-quality portfolio and with a current work history. Nobody but nobody gets to see Maxi until you're on the payroll. Even my wife and kids can't make an appointment to see me, because I'm too busy making deals so that they can enjoy the best that my money, 'shmoney,' can buy."

To set up all that could cost a girl $5,000 or a lot more with hairstylist, makeup artist, wardrobe, and modeling school before they'd made a penny in the business, Daphne recalled him saying.

Since he broached the subject to Daphne, he wanted to touch briefly on modeling schools. He said he wished they would only remain as a figment to one's imagination rather than reality.

"They serve only one purpose: to fleece a pretty girl's parents into believing that their daughter is beautiful and potentially famous. American Express, Discover, Mastercard, and Visa are acceptable ways to pave the way for the dream."

"What a bunch of bunk!" he declared. "You can either chew gum and walk or you can't. A girl is either beautiful or she's not. Pretty doesn't cut it in the fashion world," Maxi professed. "He himself was potentially handsome, yet he never reached his potential at all."

"It's not at all debatable semantics." He snickered.

"After a girl graduates, what kind of placement can the school offer?"

"None," he promised, answering his own question. "One defunct modeling school in Vero Beach, Florida, had the chutzpah to promise their students' assignments in the motion picture industry. What they delivered was borderline mishmash. Attractive girls clad in drab usher uniforms making minimum wage, carrying lit flashlights, were searching for discarded empty popcorn boxes in the aisles of movie theaters owned by the guy's brother-in-law. The bottom line was that the girl graduating from such a school still needed an agent. She could have saved her parents and herself all that money and disappointment," he boisterously recalled.

He mentioned to Daphne that the prospect was a rarity but possible that a cover girl could be found in a modeling school, but the discoverer was usually an agent or a photographer who had affiliations with an agency.

"A brassy girl who knows she's beautiful and is not sensitive to rejection could march uninvited into one of the fashion offices of *Allure, Bride's, Cosmopolitan, Elle, Glamour, Harper's Bazaar, Mademoiselle, Mirabella, Red Book, Town Country, Vanity Fair, Vogue,* or *Wedding* and be given an assignment right on the spot, even without her own book. It's happened for a few relatively flawless models, but the chances are slightly less better than winning the New York State Lottery," Maxi wisecracked.

"We reject nine out of ten sets of prints. When we interview, we pass on four out of five. They may have the look, but not the intangible. That special quality. Myra's very good, not the maven I am, but nevertheless, she's excellent at determining character. She's my righthand man. My sister knows who's soft and who won't want to work hard. She can weed out the weaklings. Those girls who are inclined to party all night with booze and drugs. Myra knows the ones who have pastry fetishes, mainly the box of doughnut for lunch queens. They splurge, then have to purge. Like lead, it finds its way right on your backside. Self-determination not to be chunky in the ass is sacrosanct in this business. Anything else is a death sentence. She can diagnose anorexia and bulimia better than an MD.

"For each model in our employ, Myra sets up nutritional guidelines with a physician. The tiresome method of counting calories is outdated. Our girls watch their fat content intake. Believe me, it will make life a lot easier for you, especially when you get out of your teens. While other models from competitive agencies are starving themselves on the latest fad diet, popping pills, and upchucking their lunch in the bathroom, you'll be satisfied on three to five small- to medium-size well-balanced meals per day with room for snacks. You won't be susceptible to headaches, dizziness, and fainting spells.

This type of supervision allows you to binge on your favorite ice cream and cake once in a great while. If you were told that you could never have it, then you'd question the sanity of being in the business. What a lackluster mind-set that some models are so disciplined into depriving themselves that they feel guilt over eating a grapefruit or a head of lettuce because of the stupid calorie content," he forcefully reminded. "Myra will break it all down for you. You'll meet her. She's a little frumpy now, but that's four kids and three husbands later. In her twenties, she was a Venus. My sister was a top ten model in Chicago, Los Angeles, and here. She'll work with you. You'll learn from her all the pointers on exercising, dieting, hair and skin care, plus how to angle and posture your body the right way.

"On every floor of every sky-rise office building in Manhattan, there are ten pretty faces aspiring to be models, and they'd all throw their boyfriends out the window for the chance. The shame is, 98 percent of them are schlemiels."

"They have no class, and they didn't come to the rescue of Ruth Weiss."

Maxi implied that from what his mother relayed, she could have tumbled further if it weren't for Daphne's adroit intercession, thus preventing further extensive bodily damage and maybe even, "Oye," kicked in the face. For someone who was a foreigner and in this country for only two months, Daphne had "moxie" in reacting so quickly to the situation, he commented. That was why she was being offered special treatment that he wouldn't afford his own daughters.

"My mother's from eastern Europe. She immigrated to the United States with her Kiev-born parents from Hungary when she was only twelve and couldn't speak a word of English other than ordering a knish. She shares a kinship with you."

Maxi petitioned if Daphne had any goals. She told him about the debt to her Papa and starting classes next fall at Mount Saint Vincent's. He suggested that she might want to consider taking a few part-time evening courses at one of the city colleges, because if things worked out, her demanding modeling schedule would be hampered by distance and academic workload. At that time, she didn't appreciate a stranger making assumptions for her.

Next, she reported that he boldly vouched that she would be paid eighty-five dollars an hour to start, plus any miscellaneous expenses.

"The sky is the limit from there," he positively assured.

That was more than fifty times what she had been making in a sixty-minute period, including tips, Daphne mentioned.

"You'll be pampered with us to the utmost. No schlepping for buses or subway. The client will provide the transportation from your doorstep, to and from."

Maxi voiced that it was ironically droll for him to say that he wouldn't promise she'd model the latest Paris creation, nor would he lure her with the dazzling of her "kisser" on the cover of a trendy ladies' magazine. Other than that, she would have plenty of good, solid work assignments. She would pay her dues all right because she had nothing but hard work ahead of her, he assured.

He also predicted that in about fourteen months, her shyness would be wiped clean off her face. Maxi confided of his "borscht belt" connections he had with advertisers, in the garment center, and with manufacturers, marketing agencies, and public relations groups. He said that he wouldn't bind Daphne to an exclusive contract with Weiss. Maxi didn't approve of that, but that was his mother's wish, and he always listened to his mother.

"You'll be afforded the freedom to freelance with anyone else other than a Weiss client. After you get a little seasoning, with your appeal and shape, I can almost guarantee that Ford and Casablancas will come knocking at your door, trying to woo you away, with the Wilhelmina and Zoli Agencies not far behind. That's your decision, but you'll never get lost in the shuffle with us."

"Frenchy," he took the liberty in calling her, as he would always call her because he had a difficult time annunciating Daphne, "after twenty-seven years, I know this business like the back of my hand."

Then, to her astonishment, he recited a number and recalled exactly before he flipped it over the amount and shape of the prominent veins on the back of his left hand, including the convex-shaped scar.

"Very soon you'll be able to do that with any part of your body. It makes for a nice parlor trick," Maxi cavorted.

He ended his pitch by giving her his card and reminding her that he was bound by everything life had promised because he owed her a debt.

"So call me soon to make arrangements to be photographed. Don't be a schmuck. Ignoring my mother's gift could be cataclysmic for the rest of your life. Bring companions along," he welcomed.

She said, he left, but not before leaving Daphne with a one-hundred-dollar tip.

Daphne replied that at that time she should have been overwhelmed but wasn't because she hadn't taken Maxi seriously. Not anyone before this had ever thought of her in terms of being beautiful. Certainly not her papa or any of her boyfriends thought she was. Now, out of the blue, at eighteen years old, outside her own country, she was being afforded the chance to actually be a model at the crazy rate this stranger, calling himself Maxi, had offered. It was absurd.

Her fellow work associates congratulated her on her newfound patron but cautioned that she didn't give up her real-paying job. After all, they said this was New York City. If it sounded too good to be true, then it probably wasn't.

As sedate as she was over Maxi's disclosure, Claudine was astounded for both of them, Daphne implied. Claudine had Daphne in stitches, she said, with her frolicking, sauntering about the living room, modeling every chair, pillow, sofa, and wall poster for her younger cousin's amusement. As much a skeptic as Claudine was, she believed that this new career offer could be destiny and not a farce as she substantiated the Weiss Agency's listing in a Manhattan phone directory.

Daphne replied to me, even with that proof she was still uncompromising to make the appointment with Maxi. In her assessment, the whole affair was still a wild hoax, and deep within her, she was terrified to embark on something so fantastically glamorous. During the ensuing week, Claudine resolved to uncover the truth. She took the liberty to pool from her sphere of friends contacts who could supply resource material to support the credibility of the Weiss Agency. What she researched was supportive. No filings against them from the Better Business Bureau. They purchased advertising space in *Variety*.

Established in 1935, they were in good stead with the Chamber of Commerce, and the agency was, indeed, started by Ruth Engldowicz Weiss. An acquaintance of an acquaintance of her boyfriend knew an actor represented by them who auditioned and was offered a part in a daytime soap opera.

Before Claudine could share the happy results of her networking with Daphne five days later, she broke the sad news to her older cousin that she was caught in a layoff. She sadly said that she was told by the day manager that the Amber Pub was closed until further notice. One of the cooks had told her that the reason was for failure to pay New York State sales taxes. Claudine was overjoyed. The day of reckoning had arrived for Daphne. She couldn't afford not to visit Weiss's studio, especially at the risk of losing the huge per-hour rate Maxi had offered. Claudine promised to go on the appointment with her, as her security blanket, and make sure no contracts were signed. Daphne shared with me the fat she reluctantly, with tears, agreed.

On March 23, they arrived twenty minutes early for her ten o'clock photo session at Maxi's East Fifty-Second Street midtown address, she recalled. Daphne didn't deny she felt badly that Claudine had to call in sick from her translator job to be with her that day. When the receptionist offered them a choice of juice or coffee, her cousin replied that it was a good sign. Daphne remembered that she grasped her hands so tightly that her clammy sweat was bonding them like glue.

When they were permitted entrance to Maxi's office, what was to greet them was a mannequin lookalike of him seated at his desk. Maxi was supine by the side of the furniture, looking at them from a reflecting mirror "jerry-rigged" to facilitate seeing his visitors sitting in their chairs.

"Don't mind if I don't get up," she remembered him saying. "Since my unsuccessful disc surgery four years ago and my constant pain, I took up working from on my posterior. It may seem unorthodox to you, but not to my back. Only my arms get tired. My seven-year-old came up with the idea for the likeness. Forget modeling. She'll be a marketing genius. One of those think tank people," he seriously stated.

"This is just too unreal," Daphne recalled, saying to herself as secretarial help perambulated Maxi to get his okays and signatures on documents.

"When I first worked in this position, the hardest blemish to resolve was finding a brand of pen that could write upside down." He laughed. "I never warn anybody, because the shock on first-timers is priceless. They think I'm meshuggener." Crazy. "Meshuggener Maxi. I like the sound of it. They get used to it, as you will," he insisted.

Maxi went on to ask Claudine if she had any questions.

Daphne expected a whole battery of questions from her, but intimidated by the posh surroundings, she inquired only of his mother's name. He expressed Ruth and begged Daphne to pick her out on some of the pictures on the wall, which she did. Claudine was confidently pleased.

Myra was aloof upon meeting them at first, then she warmed up. She was studying angles of Daphne's face. She stated that she would supervise the cosmetic wizardry that would transform Daphne's image: a manicure; applying natural makeup; a haircut, highlighted and styled; and a wardrobe selection. It would take four hours to prepare her, prior to the photo layout, so Claudine could go and return at 2:30 p.m.

"She'll look stunning," Myra promised.

"Preparation such as this would become an everyday part of her life," Daphne said.

Once she accepted the inevitability of her situation, the hyperventilating and nervousness dissipated and the wondrous feelings emerged. As she was being prepped and primped by Myra's staff, Daphne was being coached about the dos and don'ts in the modeling profession. She was riveted by Myra's diatribe on the darker side of the industry. Maxi's sister was a wealth of information, she relayed. From her matter-of-factly demeanor, Daphne accounted that Myra didn't suffer fools gladly. (Maybe, she also knew DA.) She was a perfectionist, and only those who showed promise would be allowed to tap into her experience. After completion, Daphne was enraptured by her new recreation.

"Simply put," Myra replied, "the look was definitely becoming to her."

Claudine was aghast with embarrassment because she didn't at first discern her younger cousin from the rest of the models present. She was highly approving of the transformation.

"This before-and-after preparation is the allusion. The developed proofs will be the illusion. You'll look even better," Myra foresaw.

She did. A bright future was on the horizon, Myra predicted.

Everything that Maxi had promised with Myra's spit and polish coaching came to fruition. Particularly, Daphne acknowledged, she paid her dues. Her first assignments weren't modeling but merely looking good at sales convention booths, grand openings, seminars, and car and boat shows. She was the lure for potential buyers to see the product, but at forty-five dollars an hour for these bookings, she didn't mind.

She never breathed a word to her parents about this sudden career or how much money she was making. She would surprise them at the right time, when she was convinced she was established and had staying power to model. Claudine was sworn to secrecy.

The initial article of clothing she modeled, she recalled, laughing, were kelly-green galoshes with smiling frog faces on the toes.

How fitting for a French girl, she interposed. Because she did well with that item, she showed off glow-in-the-dark rubber boots four days later. Then came belts, Cape-Cod-fishermen-styled slicker raincoats finished with a sou'wester, umbrellas, slippers, bathrobes. Myra later booked her for appearances in minor catalogs and consumer retail chain magazines.

By July, she almost doubled her per-hour rate and was working steady six days a week. She inferred that she had become a modeling workaholic. Feeling homesick, she flew to France to visit her family, bringing presents and the news of her good fortune. She said her mama and papa could not believe their eyes and ears on how beautiful she had become and the fantastic story of assisting Ruth Weiss that evolved into her present success.

Her father had tears down his cheeks when Daphne presented him with eight thousand dollars in cash.

She enrolled at Marymount College on East Seventy-First Street and Third Avenue for part-time studies locally. Mount Saint Vincent's was unreasonably far away, and she couldn't afford to pass up the amount of money she was making. She related she enjoyed living in the city and Claudine's company and friends.

Spoiling Claudine with clothes and trinkets was a pleasure for her, and at nineteen she was paving the way for her older cousin to go to graduate school.

Within two years in the business, Daphne was now starting to be featured in teen fashion magazines. Unlike other models in her age group that she got to be friendly with, no work assignment was beneath her. It wasn't in her vocabulary. She was only in the business by fluke, never having aspirations to be a top model, so her ego never got into the way of not modeling the latest designer's high fashion. So what, she said, if she wasn't making five to ten thousand dollars per shoot because a thousand dollars, sometimes a day, was great money to her?

The competition with models who aimed that high was fierce. Enticements of who could drop ten pounds quicker in that same number of days to get the next European assignment in Paris or Rome was not uncommon. Quite frankly, she had been to those cities already several times before, so they weren't a carrot held out to her, but to American models who had never been out of the country, it was adventuresome and romantic.

The models knew each other's imperfections, and a few playing the role of spies gossiped on who had plastic surgery work or who received silicone injections. Daphne commented that she knew models who totally abstained from food of any kind because they were twenty to thirty pounds less than what their body types called for. Their metabolisms were out of whack. They popped drugs and diet pills like vitamins. She relayed that they were always depressed and had very low self-esteem. A lot of them suffered from burnout just as she had experienced a few years earlier, but theirs was not from lack of sleep.

She laughed that sweet laugh. She admitted that it took about forty times or so before she adjusted to being dressed and undressed by someone else. Even today, she was not totally comfortable with the experience. It depended on who the fitter was, she conceded.

I smiled, and it took all my restraint, biting my tongue, not spitting out what carnal thought my mind was thinking. I'd like to change places with the fitter for a week, a day, or an hour. When my devilish grin persisted, she pulled on the hairs of my wrist.

She had been lucky, Daphne admitted. Largely, through Myra's circumspect advice, she maintained a regimented health plan: working out forty-five minutes daily, cross-training with exercising, jogging, racquetball, riding a stationary bicycle, swimming and yoga; following her low fat diet for life; drinking water, eliminating caffeine; taking a multiple vitamin; and limiting alcohol to moderation. Three quarters of the models she knew got by on crash diets.

She said that she paid heed to Myra's counsel when going out to lunch or dinner with a client: "Decline and eat alone afterward, or if you must attend, order consommé and a small garden salad with lemon, because regardless of what selection you choose, they will qualitatively and quantitatively dissect your meal. Rumors start spreading of you eating too much. Your hefty appetite is the cause for having the fitter to let out that dress in the back, making for extra nips and tucks that weren't necessary when the garment was on the hangar," she voiced.

Against Maxi's and Myra's best wishes, she once filled in for a sick friend who was a runway model. She said that she was assured that the designer's contemporary line, though alluring, was all in good taste. Modesty, as such, didn't prevail during the last quarter of the showing. Taking the risk to wow the attendants, the Italian designer had the models paraded out in an avant-garde collection created in Venice, not intended to be part of that showing. Fully exposed cleavage surrounded by panache, optional boas, and geometric cube-cut outslits on the derriere was the chic style, maybe appropriate with the French Riviera jetsetters and with European models, but not with most American girls or parochial-schooled Daphne.

"It turned out to be more a sizzling Parisian nightclub revue, complete with wolf whistling, sans the cancan, than a fashion statement," she recalled.

Because "runway models" were treated as meddlesome trouble-makers if they balked at wearing such apparel, they kowtow to the designer's demands. The designer could cite them with the cliché of trying to break up the continuity of his show.

Outraged, they could have models "blackballed" from ever working the runway circuit again. Daphne's wits would not let her panic, because Myra had prepared her with what to do in such a perilous crisis. Refrained from any bootless banter, she had the gumption to forcibly expunge the soda crackers she had eaten as a snack by swallowing the emetic she always kept in her purse. She sneaked out of her dilemma, not even bothering to be compensated, Daphne conveyed. It was the last time she would do a work-related favor for another model, she swore to me.

Daphne mentioned that she had had a reputation for being a hard worker ever since she fell into this crazy business. Designers could count on her for being on time and maintaining a constantly trim, lithesome figure, allowing their clothes to look great on her.

Her only imperfection, they said, was that her breasts were too big.

Thus, when she started modeling, her boobs were bound; six years later, when bosoms "evolutioned" full circle and were in, the same designers told her she was perfect. Photographers said she was fun and easy to work with. She wasn't a prima donna, so they referred her for other shoots.

Despite her demanding schedule, Daphne continued her limited course studies at school, sometimes doubling up on credits during the summer. She would pass up on copious paying bicoastal assignments if they interfered with her Tuesday-night class.

She'd skip once in a while but didn't like to make it habitual. Regional work, even if it paid less, was her preference, she explained to me.

Financially speaking, at only twenty-two years of age, she had made oodles of money. Enough, in fact, to invest in her father's business, which he relocated to Gournay, selling the family horse farm in Le Thor. Daphne was chagrined that he couldn't keep up both, but she knew the impossibilities for such.

Now, two of the favorite places she knew growing up belonged to others.

She was young, energetic, personally pleasing, successfully juggling time for her studies, happy with her boyfriend, popular in several different social circles, and her career was humming. Through Maxi's good offices, she was booked to do a major cover, and when a top model's agent overpriced his client, Daphne was offered to pose for yet another magazine's overlay. She was catapulting to new heights in the profession in the United States, from where she had begun.

Everything had been going well, maybe too well, and within four months, her emotional infrastructure began to crumble. When Claudine married Harold, she had expected them to live close by at his apartment, but when he was promoted to assistant director of marketing at the Atlanta, Georgia, office, it was an unexpected disappointment for the girls. They had grown accustomed to being around and doing things with each other on a daily basis, and now they were severely distanced. They communicated by phone, but the sisterly companionship was severed by nine hundred miles. If they had the necessary brick and mortar, they could have symbolically built their own "Wailing Wall" with the grief they shared together before Claudine's departure.

Then Louise and Robert moved across the river out of the city to buy a condo in Hoboken, New Jersey. Frances took a new curator position in the New England area. No more than five blocks from her, Rachel was wantonly murdered in her loft. They had been close friends. She had no known enemies. There was nary a clue. On the police blotter, it was an unsolved crime. Paula, a fellow worker from her Amber Pub days, was robbed and beaten unmercifully one night awaiting her subway train. Unable to mentally erase the trauma, she moved back home to Lexington, Kentucky.

Gissele, a model Daphne's own age, from the Elite Agency, was going to share living expenses with her. She had met her at an exercise class a year ago. It would be fun. They shared common satiric philosophies regarding their profession and were delighted that someone else owned up to the same inner thoughts as they. Contrary to many woebegone models Daphne knew, Gissele was cheerful and confidently noncompetitive. Thoughtfully, Gissele reciprocated in boosting Daphne's spirits. When Daphne flew home again, Gissele wished to accompany her. She couldn't wait to get to Paris. Two days before leaving, while she was strolling down West Forty-Seventh Street, a renovation scaffold overloaded with cinder blocks toppled on the exact spot where she was window-browsing. The fourteenth-story impact splattered her skull all over the sidewalk. The incident devastated Daphne. She said that she would never forget Gissele's cliché "If you focus and don't let the outside forces disturb you, there's plenty of work for everyone in this zany business."

Soon after that calamity, Brigitte and Chelsea, two friends of Claudine who Daphne had thought were pals of hers, evaded contact, even though in the past she had lent them both clothes and money. Her on-again, off-again two-year relationship with Rudolph, an attacheé second-in-command to the chargé d'affaires of the Luxemburg delegation to the United Nations, completely dissolved when he avowed his bisexuality. She couldn't allow herself to share him as such.

In a city with over nine million residents, Daphne was starting to feel terribly alone. It was as if an avalanche of upheaval had befallen her. In realty, she felt both unwanted and unwonted. The bad omens were about her, that New York City could no longer be her home. Though she could afford to take the Concorde every two months or so to visit her family, it wasn't enough time spent. The Concorde was seven times more expensive than a regular Air France commercial flight but cut her travel time in half and by almost two thirds on the return flight back to the States. Because she had mal du pays (home-sickness), Daphne had to return permanently to France. She wanted to be around people that spoke her native tongue. Modeling success in America would be sacrificed for her own happiness. Despite prompting from Maxi and Myra, they could not get her to reconsider moving overseas. On condition she return to do special assignments, they referenced her to an agency in Paris.

Not to be a name-dropper, she only did shoots, besides Paris, in the "smaller" cities of western Europe: Amsterdam, Antwerp, Belfast, Bern, Brussels, Copenhagen, Dublin, Edinburgh, Lisbon, London,

Luxemburg, Madrid, Monte Carlo, Oslo, Paris, Rome, and West Berlin. Occasionally, she came back to New York as a favor to Myra and a chance to visit Claudine and Harold for a few days. "I was never a big name on the continent, but I was offered, work and that was what was important to me," she told me.

When her schedule permitted, she took French literature classes at the Sorbonne.

CHAPTER XI

Daphne, or I should say my fabulous feline, returned from the ladies' room with her hair in a plaited ponytail, held in place with a metal slide, crossed softly in front of her right shoulder. Hmm, another different coat on the same cat? I wondered. After kissing me, she continued her account.

"Instead of modeling the latest European designer creations," she said, "I was better known as the face on a can or box in someone's cupboards. My profile was adorned on brands of consumer products throughout the continent."

She laughed that sweet laugh of hers.

"I even posed for a profile impression that's on both sides of a tulip-perfumed hypoallergenic glycerin bar of soap in Belgium. Unfortunately, the soap doesn't float. Fitted with a fish tail, a scaled costume, and my hair lightened, I was the mermaid figure on a Japanese cannery's tuna fish. I rescinded my association with the company when I learned they were unconcerned about killing porpoises in their fishing nets," she expressed with vehemence.

"Wolf's grape juice in West Germany, I'm cloaked in Little Red Riding Hood capote, where the discriminating wolf prefers the purple eight-ounce product in my basket rather than to me. A red bolero-type jacket is worn by me along with a matador hat and carrying a muleta, a small cape, in a 'veronica' posture on the package of a brand of cigarettes in Spain, and alas, I'm the demure peasant girl again, wearing a bodice, on a jar of fancy French button mushrooms," she entertained.

"Ha ha, if my former first-semester freshman classmates from that preppy school could only eat their hearts out with envy. Allow me to judge bon ton, good breeding," Daphne declared with pride. "Never, if at all possible, do I pronounce that college's name, and I've refused to ever list on my résumé that I ever attended there," she indignantly addressed.

Spontaneously deliberating with myself, I came to the conclusion that this lady had done well.

"There are other grocery items, too, I did. My contracts ran from year to year. If they were renewed, I would be compensated accordingly. Regrettably, I wasn't recompensed with endorsing any of the products. My name wasn't associated," Daphne informed me. "Voilà!" She laughed. "The residuals would have been enormous. But I can't complain."

"It appears that you had a good time enjoying that type of consumer-goods modeling," I interjected.

"Definitely. Now, don't think I didn't love beau monde, the fashionable world. I still found time to style wonderful black-tie evening dress or casual sportswear, which I feel most comfortable modeling," she voiced with inclusion.

She laughed that sweet laugh of hers.

"It's still charming in Paris when a wife, with her husband, approaches me at a street market and the woman states that my face is so familiar but not my name. Whew. Thankfully, my anonymity is still preserved in public, I return to them. Their faces go agape when I mention that I've been hiding in their pantry for years. I calm the husband's fears shortly afterward by telling the wife who I am," Daphne waggishly related.

Smiling broadly and rapping the table with my knuckles for reinforcement, I indicated my appreciation for her short narrative.

"In Europe, did you ever find yourself faced again with any precarious situations like the one you experienced that time as a 'runway' model?" I inquired.

"No. There were naughty but nice assignments, but nothing vulgar. I would never do them. There was the time in Cannes when I was doing swimwear for a Swedish fashion journal and it happened to coincide with the film festival. A distinguished American gentleman wearing a blazer and smoking a pipe and surrounded by a bevy of beautiful women was present. A fan of the arts, I supposed. But why were paparazzi on his heels?

"After my shoot was completed, another well-dressed man approached me, claiming he was an associate of the former gentleman. I was asked if I would consider posing au naturel, nude, for *Qui Magazine*, and a roundabout amount of money was mentioned. Flatly I declined without any further consideration. Not that I'm a prude and afraid of my family's reaction. It just wasn't the direction I wanted my career to go. Surely, my mother wouldn't have spoken to me for years had I accepted the offer." She laughed that sweet laugh of hers. "Stanley, I'm not hedonistic either, but there is no problem for me sunbathing topless on a European beach, sans telescopic American tourists. I just don't want to be photographed that way for pay," she matter-of-factly proclaimed.

Could that really have been "Heff"? I marveled at the thought.

I proceeded to light up another Winston and offered Daphne a drag, which she accepted.

"Daphne, I feel stupid," I admitted, "for not realizing that someone who looks as great as you wouldn't be model. I pride myself with being perceptive."

She gently took ahold of my arm and snuggled against my shoulder for a few seconds.

"Silly boy, how would you know if I didn't disclose it? Never would I promptly bring it up until it easily finds itself in the conversation. People, especially men, find my career intimidating if they don't take the time to know me as a person. I'm very happy that you never asked me earlier what my occupation was. Then, I'm always pressed into how much money I make. It pleased me that you were genuinely interested in what I had to discuss.

"Since the topic has been broached regarding modeling, I'm only working part-time and strictly for Maxi's agency. My main concern is raising horses on the farm I purchased with my brother in Mount Plesant six months ago. It's only a few miles away. Partly my idea, my father pushed me sight unseen into the venture. John Henry surveyed the property for us. Besides the investment tax credits…"

She laughed that sweet laugh of hers.

"Whoops. Listen to me ramble about investments when that's your area of expertise," she regretfully quipped.

Sally has kept her well informed, I weighed.

"Besides the investment tax credits and penetrating a new market in the United States, I needed a career change where I could gradually phase out of modeling. The fact that I've been around and loved horses all my life is a natural inclination."

"Isn't your decision a little premature, especially when you're still so young and look so great?"

"Thank you," she returned, "for your vote of confidence in me. Solace, to say in my profession, I'm getting old. Not ancient, just older. Oh, I feel I have a few more good years ahead of me."

"About a year ago, while skiing in St. Moritz, I had a close call, which forced me to reevaluate my lifestyle," Daphne shared.

"What happened?"

"While I was on the expert slopes, the downhill terrain they call the Grand Prix, where my skill level did not belong, my mind was on something else other than the tree I was zooming in on thirty meters straight ahead. Descending rapidly, I wiped out as I tried to veer left with my poles and was going to crash headfirst into the pine tree. Rolling and slewing, I missed serious injury by centimeters. Other than out of breath, I was all right, with the exception of minor scratches. In a business where your major asset is your face and body, I virtually risked losing it all. Going through my mind, as I was sliding, was that I was going to smash every bone in my body and never be able to model again yet want to be seen in public without a scarf covering my face," she tensely denoted. "What else did I want to do, and what was I qualified to do? Remember, Stanley, all this was happening in a flash. I was a very lucky woman," Daphne proclaimed excitedly. "What was I foolishly doing skiing and horse-jumping on other occasions, where I could be jeopardizing the remaining years of my career? I seemed to realize, crying and lying in the snow, that I had been acting cavalierly. No, I wasn't immortal, and I needed to safeguard myself from such self-destructing activities. Seemingly, I matured in a hurry. In discussions afterward with my papa, he focused my attention to working with horses."

She pressed my hand tightly to hers. Not wanting to let her languish further, I redirected to another topic I wanted to pursue beforehand.

"What became of your patron Ruth Weiss?" I queried. "I don't recall you mentioning her."

There was an interval in Daphne's response as she took another puff on my freshly lit cigarette.

"My poor darling expired," she quietly rejoined, "about five years ago. About a year and a half after her fall in front of the museum, senility set in. Doctors later diagnosed her condition as Alzheimer's disease. Her remaining years were spent in an infirmary. Mournfully, I never had the chance to ever meet her again."

"Why?"

"Maxi and Myra thought it best that I didn't. Sometimes I chatted with her on the phone, but after a time, she lapsed into confusion on who I was. Never did I forget her in my prayers. I offered special intentions to St. Bernadette for her."

"Daffy," I said without so much as considering how it sounded, "how much different was your social life once you returned to France?"

"Stanley, I was then a young lady when I came home. A change occurred in me. No longer interested in keeping a low profile as I did in New York, mostly associating with ordinary people, I decided to broaden my horizons. Because of who I had become, I was readily accepted in a higher stratosphere. Besides hanging out with other model friends, I got to meet celebrities in the arts, dignitaries, famous personalities, industrialists, and politicians.

"Through my influential contacts, I got to know some of the countesses, marquises, titled ladies, and princesses of Europe on a nickname basis. I casually dated a baron for a while. He'd send me a gross of yellow roses on my birthday and holidays. Finding out that he made his money by distributing heroin, I told him, 'No more flowers.' Things were going copesetic with an earl, until he sought to use my influence with Papa to fix a horse race at the Prix Foy. Indignantly, I did not insult my father's integrity with such a revelation. A duke proposed to me with a five-karat Kohinor-cut diamond ring. I said no again. The prospect of being addressed Duchess, I favored, but not if it meant being married to that bloody cur. He was always on the fiscal run, helter-skeltering one country ahead of his creditors, leaving behind a mountain of unpaid bills. Without knowing royalty, it's difficult to appreciate that they have the same problems as everyday people, except that theirs are on a higher plane," she believed.

"One sheik who liked to party in Monte Carlo bribed the necessary people to invite me to a charity ball after seeing one of my infrequent cameo appearances on French television. His magic carpet ride consisted of the following: He insisted that I become his fourth bride, though the other three wives were all alive and well but still wed to him. By offering me twice my body weight in gold bullion, he sought to ingratiate himself and for me to voluntarily accept his simple centuries-old social custom. Then, he forcibly twisted my hand, ordering that the deal would be consummated by practicing for our honeymoon in the privacy of his hotel suite, incidentally, across the hall.

"Besides kicking his two attendants in their respective shins, I cuffed him so hard with my free hand that his ruby-banded kaffiyeh fell over his eyes, rendering him farcical. I discovered later that on the London market, gold was being quoted at $570 a troy ounce. It was worth losing the $2,000,000 just to rid myself of him. As I said before, money isn't everything," she ended.

After guffawing and assessing good judgment on her part for declining such lofty European ranks and the bright yellow stuff too, I facetiously informed her of my and my family's tenure with nobility. "Daffy, for twenty-two years, I've known the Italian American princess Vicki Scallopini, heiress to the veal scallopini misfortune. I've listened to the music of Count Basie and Duke Ellington…and I've seen Rex Harrison in *My Fair Lady*." I laughed.

She started to giggle. I'm always impressed with a woman who's amused with my silliness. It showed good taste. However, with Daphne, it wasn't a nervous laughter or a forced "Ha ha ha" that was socially polite. She genuinely enjoyed my dumb jokes. Since I had an appreciative audience, I continued my verbal skit.

"If you think that was something, then let me share with you about the exploits of my great-grandfather. He toured with the heralded Warsaw circus as a high-wire aerialist, supreme, performing the death-defying and never-duplicated quadruple somersault, without benefit of a safety net. His troupe traveled throughout continental Europe, entertaining heads of state," I exclaimed with artificial pride.

Not thinking it was that funny, I wondered why Daphne was so helplessly jolly, pointing at me.

"I'll always know," she said between deep breaths, "I'll always know when you're lying to me, because your nose twitches."

I pinched it with one hand and held my index finger sideways to my lips. I nasally tried to get her to "shh" and to "shush."

"Stanley, that won't help," she declared, "but it'll be our little secret."

With her in such good spirits, I took advantage of the moment to recruit her savvy resourcefulness to reverse the score and avenge John Henry's Gullible's Travels victory. I relayed that it would take time to excogitate a suitable tactical "sting." It was a subversive way on my part to get her phone number. She was enthusiastically responsive to the idea of collaborating with me. Her voluntariness virtually leaped across my lap.

"Oh, I almost forgot to tell you," she fervently ascribed, "that it's fashionable to purchase royal titles. They're available at the right price."

Laughing, I couldn't resist commenting on her statement.

"How much are you willing to pay to be Mrs. Jankowski?" I verbally accosted. "The custom of a dowry should be revitalized."

The effect of my blazing words left Daphne encumbered. With her speechless, her face took on the hue of the Compari in her glass.

When the invisible smoke cleared the air, she laughed that sweet laugh of hers. Apparently, she was well pleased with my bon mot (a clever saying). Sacrebleu. Oh no. Now I was interjecting dismay in French for thinking French. "Soon I'd be conjugating French verbs," I scornfully uttered to myself.

"You are unconscionable, Stanley."

"I know. That's exactly why you are interested."

"What do think happened to your friend TJ?" she digressively solicited.

"I don't know," I answered, "but let's go search for him near the bar."

Before leaving, I peeled off a fiver from my money clip for the happy-faced Leslie Ann.

When we arrived at our destination, we found no trace of TJ, save his baseball hat occupying a free antler space behind the bar. He must be somewhere on the dance floor, but people were wedged in so tightly I couldn't make him out in the crowd. I told Daphne to be on the lookout for the dark-skinned guy without his Yankee cap. She smiled at my statement, knowing that TJ was the only non-Caucasian here. My statuesque feline had a look of concernment about her.

"Something bothers me, Stanley. Or should I call you Mr. Perceptive?" she asked.

"What?" I returned.

"When I greeted you earlier tonight, my exact words were 'Nice to see you again.' Aren't you the least bit curious when and where we first met? And it's incidental with my first visit to the United States."

Now I was confused. I was trying to conceptualize what she was referring to.

"You have an unfair advantage over me. I give up," I told her. "Our eyes met when the big guy guided us to the dining room. He led you into that impromptu pirouette coming in to receive us at the bar. However, technically, we weren't introduced. Humph. I just don't recall. It's difficult to believe I wouldn't remember you," I granted.

I threw my hands up in concession.

"We met fifteen years ago at Sally's wedding to John Henry. I was there too. At the reception, we even danced together in a big circle. You held my hand. Of course you were accompanied by a fair-complected blond girl who occupied your attentions," she recalled.

"Daphne, how were you there?" I inquired suspiciously.

"The first time I arrived in America, I came over with my mother and aunt and uncle for a month's stay to visit their daughter and my cousin Claudine. We stayed with first cousins of my mother and aunt whom I had never met.

"After four years of living in the states, Claudine chose to stay when Uncle Jacque's tenure expired as a chief structural design consultant on the engineering project that his Calais firm was involved with. At Villanova, she had become good pals with Becky Carlyle, who was a hometown high school friend of Sally's. They would visit Sally at Rider College, or Sally would take the New Jersey Turnpike to stay with them. Claudine and Sally hit it off well over the years, so naturally she was invited to her wedding. Since I had arrived one week before, Claudine inquired if there was an extra seat for me. Sally was agreeable. So I attended my initial American wedding and met you. You left a good impression on me. Isn't it a small world, Stanley?" she concluded.

"And getting smaller," I returned, dumbfounded.

"You were very polite to a gawky, pimple-faced kid. I wouldn't expected you to recall me," she said.

Honestly, I wished I could recollect meeting her. I kept to myself. The blonde Daphne was alluding to was Kristine. We had a summer fling, until she went back to college in Ohio. She wrote to me several times, but I never bothered to follow up. It seemed I was always bad that way during that time of my life.

A silly thought occurred to me. I was contemplating what a phenomena it was that people's lives could overlap. How an insignificant meeting with a stranger years ago might be predestined to a chance encounter with the same person years later, leading to a meaningful relationship because of mutual circumstance and a transformation in one or both of you. What if you knew then what was in store for you and no matter how hard you fought, fate would still win? It was crazed thinking.

That was why I was not sharing it with Daphne. She might want to commit me to the transcendentally insane.

"Here's a hypothetical for you. Is it negative of me not to want to look through the crystal ball?" I earnestly implored.

"Yes," she replied, "because it is couleur de rose."

Hmm. Maybe the lady was telepathic after all, I was thinking.

Catching sight of the hatless TJ, we waded through the sea of people cavorting to Jake and the Jayhawks' lively music. John Henry, close by, waved as he saw us. He pointed over to our fraternity brother.

Instead of trying to shout to him in competition with the crowd buzz level, I simply nodded, cognizant where TJ was.

He had volunteered his services on the dance floor to a slim, sweltry brunette cowgirl clad in Levi's and a checkered blouse. Crowned with quail feathers in the band, she sported a dimpled-in-the-brim hat dipped forward, which hid her face but not her contentment.

Daphne and I joined in the merrymaking, and without prompting, she was clapping with her hands over her head, as I was. TJ and his newfound friend moved to our vicinity. I didn't catch her name, but the mystery lady gave us "How dos."

The big guy, with yet a different gal, came over to high jinks with our little group. As the band was cranking out some bad-ass country blues, the six of us were steppin' lively, exchanging and returning to our partners in the process. TJ's cowgirl friend led us by the hand to form a circle, where each of us came out to the center solo, free-styling some "mean," nonchoreographed steps to the encouragement of clapping and whistling. Soon our chain of hands multiplied by four as other couples enlarged the circumference.

I offered a hip-swiveling, knee-jerk rhythm movement that delighted the enveloped throng. It was a parody even Elvis would have been proud of. *Provocative minx* was the definitive description to describe Daphne's actions as she characterized an uncaged go-go girl bouncing and strutting her stuff. John Henry's slow-action mechanical man incited the audience for more windup. The aroused cowgirl had undone the bottom of her shirt. She tied it in the back for a sexy, bare-midriff exposure as a component to her shoehorn-tight, stonewashed jeans. The cowgirl dared to show off her little bluebird tattoo just above her "tuchis." Unencumbered, her straight locks fell shoulder-length as she tossed her Western fedora to a glib wrangler to hold as a transitory keepsake. She was quite the eyeful. Arising from her smug facial expression, with the spotlight on, she was about to step into a steamy workout fitted in her below-the-knee two-toned snake bootery. Noticing TJ's smiling, bugged-eyed demeanor, I tapped him on the arm.

"Perri Belle Brown is her name," he declared, indicating his new friend. "She's a cutie, but I think a little strange."

"No one said you had to buy her, just borrow her for a bit," John Henry smartly butted in, sneaking up from behind. "Hey, TJ, try on the cognomen Perri Belle Bell for size."

"Thanks, wise guy, for being so clever," he cracked. "I wouldn't wish that name on anybody."

Perri Belle didn't disappoint any fellows with her showtime. She broke into a high-stepping, rapid-paced crossover-step routine wiggling her buttocks and shaking her boobies sideways.

Daphne, whom I had my arm around, jovially stepped in front of me, blocking my view path. Likely, in her opinion, I'd seen enough.

The crowd went nuts cheering for an encore. She obliged, waving her hat and exiting quickly with a soft shoe-wiggle-waggle. Grudgingly, TJ was about to be received in what had evolved into an eclipse from its circular beginnings.

"Never follow animal acts, children, or cupcakes," he said, grinning.

"Break a leg," I theatrically expressed.

"You're on, dude," he returned.

That son of a bitch took a running start from beyond the circle and did a flip in the air. Was it something I said? Not. The contingency was electrified. He broke out into his patented hunch-shouldered knife-hand dance. When the big guy called out for his funny Egyptian interpretation of "pharaoh left, pharaoh right," he alternated to each side with feet in motion. TJ's fingers were pointed, with the farthest palms upraised slightly higher than the other running across his body, parallel. Easy for me to say. He performed the request adroitly.

Kinetically, he quantum-leaped, sequencing to his never forgotten, from our days at school, the tight rope.

"Never upstage the star!" I blithesomely yelled out to him.

He certified my caution with a solitary thumb up. On an imaginary line, he gingerly stepped forward, arms spread eagle, balancing himself from descending to a perilous fall. Fearless performer he was, TJ did his stunts without benefit of a net.

Maybe he knew of my great-grandfather's feats in the Warsaw circus? Our daredevil reversed his field and returned the opposite way, almost slipping for the hush of the audience.

Bravo, the handstand in midfloor. Hearing the exclamative cheers above me, I inadvertently turned around an upward, noticing the aerial onlookers from the balcony that John Henry assigned as "hillbilly heaven." One truly needed a parallax view from different perspectives to fully appreciate center ring. For his finale, he beckoned Perri Belle. He cautioned her to be careful tiptoeing across the tightrope toward him. Before picking her up, she blindfolded him with her red bandanna and he lifted her torso on his shoulders. He was now balancing his assistant's extra added weight. She was perched high, waving her plumed hat, while he, ladies and gentlemen, was puffing a cigarette and walking backward. TJ, with both eyes still covered, lowered Perri Belle in his arms and tossed her to his new assistant, John Henry. The three held hands with the lady in between. They gracefully bow amid cheers. "Bravo! Bravo!" I chanted. People around me, including Daphne, took up my exclamation and other forms of ovation, namely, two-fingered whistles.

TJ started to jog over to us, but his new fans wouldn't let him escape. Oh no. A mob of thirty, including the Bea sisters, Leslie Ann, three swampies, and Uncle Miller were now in single-file "tightroping" with TJ in the forefront. To the nth degree, they were following their leader around the room as if they were lemmings. I was waiting any second for John Henry to push the button that opened the trapdoor, ergo, they all fall into the sea. Fully grinning, I elevated my hands palms up. Understanding my wish, Daphne complaisantly grabbed my arm and marched me out, thus becoming numbers thirtysomething on line.

The big guy cut in ahead of me.

"Well, Dr. Frankenstein," I merrily greeted, "you've created a monster."

"Nonsense, cous, that's the worst-case scenario. Take it from your pundit. What we've got here is a genuine folk hero." He chuckled with a wink.

A woeful Daphne informed me that it was getting late and she had to go home. She had to be up early tomorrow to interview a trainer. I understood, though I wasn't pleased either. I'd miss her company more than she realized. Subsequent to her au revoirs (goodbyes) and bonsoirs (good nights) to the guys. Damn this lady. She had me thinkin' French. I escorted her out the door.

The cool air felt good, though the temperature had dropped considerably since our arrival. Inasmuch as my suit jacket was warmer than her shawl, I made her the offer; nevertheless, she asserted that she was fine. Amid the General Motors, Internationals, and other brands of Jeeps and trucks still left in the lot, I figured Daphne owned the spanking-brand-new jet-black Range Rover she was heading for. Nope. I figured wrong. Hers was the hunter-green Corvette directly behind it that I had admired earlier.

"Your middle name is Anne," I guessed from her vanity plates bearing the remembered "DAR."

"No." She laughed that sweet laugh of hers. "It's Antoinette, as in Marie."

I smiled with her humor. It was an awkward moment of parting for me and clumsy for her as she bungled trying to find her keys. When they fell to the ground, we bumped heads trying to pick them up. Compulsively, I held her close to me with my best ursine hold.

"You and your friends are such wonderful characters. Honestly, Stanley, I had a fabulous time," she whispered sincerely.

"So did I."

"Sally told me you would be staying over their place tonight. I'm all for the idea. I wouldn't want anything to happen to you," she said tenderly, clutching me.

"Oddly enough, I didn't know we were staying. It's a refreshing thought to me. There's no flak from my direction. We've been drinking heavily all night. Your thoughtfulness is well received," I said, pressing my lips tenderly on hers.

Just as I thought she should be contented, overtones of solicitude shadowed her expression.

"Looking forward to seeing you at the party in two weeks, even if you bring your bonne amie, sweetheart," she pronounced, accenting every syllable in the last two words.

From the sunken way I felt, her vocal diacritical marks hit their literal point as if by a jackhammer. I was surrendered speechless. It was a blessing in disguise, because no matter what I replied, it was going to come out twisted and she'd feel affronted. If she started boo-booing, then my sinuses might be compelled to react.

"C'est la vie." That is life. She faintly susurrated.

As I proceeded to kiss her good night, she winced from me.

"Before I go home," Daphne encouraged, "I want you to know that you have savoir faire." Good breeding.

Before exiting the parking lot, she blew me a kiss from her car as a finale. I headed back to the Inn, but not without sneaking peeks until her 'Vette vanished out of sight. Checking to search for the folded manila piece of paper with Daphne's phone number, I found it was still there. Squeezing it tightly in my left hand, I felt pumped up and glad to be alive.

CHAPTER XII

Once back inside, I headed in the direction of the bar, obeying Uncle Miller's urgent wave request. As I got closer, he was smoothing out the coarse hairs of his mustache.

"Huh! What a surprise to see you!" he clamored with shocked disbelief. "Only five minutes ago, my nephew was dawdlin' away right here at the stool your leanin' on. He claimed that you and that French wench—and she is a humdinger—left in a hop, skip, and jump to elope. Obviously, it ain't true. Stanley, my apologies. That boy's a damn liar. I said, If you were gettin' married, you sure as hell wouldn't pass up the chance to have your reception here."

Frankly, I stared at him with a "What the fuck are you talking about?" type of look. Under my breath, I was on the verge of interspersing a few choice words about John Henry in the vernacular of four letters. Wait a blessed minute. Uncle Miller's eyes were shifting, and he was holding back from breaking into a grin. "Haw-haws" and "Hew-haws" could be heard from behind the bar that sounded familiar. A head popped up, and it belonged to the big guy. He hopped over to my side.

"This will soothe your feelin's," Uncle Miller said to me as he poured the three of us a drink. "Any second, you were goin' to pop your cork. Stanley, I wanted no parts of that yarn. Your good pal made me do it. Let me say this much: mind you, I'm just simple folk, but from what I observed tonight, that cat Daphne wanted to dig her claws in you."

"And I'm ready," I informed him as I heartily quenched my thirst.

Poor John Henry slobbered on himself after my announcement, and it served him right. He was yakking at himself. Uncle Miller, rejoicing at that, made things worse by intentionally pouring my big cousin's second round on his hand.

"Ah-haw. It's a damn conspiracy," he expressed, banging his dry hand on the mahogany wood. "Let's dispense with the tomfoolery. Give me the sloe gin, Unc."

John Henry took a good, healthy swig through the goosenecked spout, carefully avoiding touching it to his lips.

"Always kill the one you love," he advocated, emptying the four-ounce contents. "By the way, you and TJ are staying with me. That's the law."

"I know."

"How?"

"A friend of your wife's told me," I cavorted.

He was lethargic, I assumed, as my comment passed by without a response. Ostensibly, he was three sheets to the wind, and I was nearly ossified. At thirty-seven, I couldn't slosh them down as I used to, and that was another blessing in disguise.

"I'm drivin'," he seriously stated.

Uncle Miller was leaning on the bar top. While his head was cradled in his palm, resting on his elbow, he delightfully took in his nephew's last utterance.

"Poppycock!" was his outburst as his arm slid down, thumping on the slick wood. He attempted to stand erect but slouched.

"If you're not half-soused, then I'm a nocturnal creature of the night," Uncle Miller screeched.

Imitating a screech owl, he shuttered his eyelids, hooting "To-whit-tu-whoo!"

Unexpectedly, Uncle Miller brought his arms in close to his sides, fluttering his hands in raillery.

"One other thing this ole geezer would like to get off his chest before he goes over to wait on Jim and his wife is this: I'm the law. The drivin' arrangements are already handled."

"You couldn't pay enough to witness a show such as that." I laughed.

I slapped the big guy on the back.

John Henry commented, "That's why he makes the big bucks. He's the ringleader of this carousin' carnival atmosphere we have every weekend."

"I heard that," he said from five barstool lengths away.

John Henry saluted the "spunky" one.

"Well, Stanley, did you ask her out?"

"Who?"

"My aunt Edna. Stop the horseplay. What do you mean who? The friend of my wife. Didn't think I was listenin' before, did you? Just because I'm on my way to bein' shit-faced doesn't mean I don't have my hearin' faculties."

"No, I didn't," I answered. "I have things to work out first with—"

"Samantha?"

"Yes," I said.

"Let me be your Dutch uncle for a minute."

"Then lend me twenty bucks," I humorously demanded.

"Seriously. Sam's all right, but Daf is the gal for you. That woman told me she's crazy about you."

"She said that," I challenged.

"Not only that. She spoke in French you were better than haute couture, high fashion. That's praise, indeed, coming from a model," he jawed.

"I know," I said, beaming with pride.

"You two have somethin' in common," he stated.

"What is it?"

"She's an expatriate livin' in the United States who prefers an honest-to-goodness American man rather than one of those European pansies who need several women 'cause they can't handle one well. You're an American man who, from what I remember, has always been fascinated with international ladies," he delivered on target.

"You're right."

"Then, golly gee, lasso that mare pronto before she gallops off to 'greener' pastures."

"You're right."

John Henry tapped me on the arm.

"Stop tellin' me I'm right. You damn well know I'm right. When have you known me to be wrong? It's selfish on my part too." He smiled.

"How do you mean?"

"Since you'll be practically commutin' from here in my neck of the woods, we'll be seein' a lot of you. You and Daf double-datin' with Sally and me. Let me preface it for you: eats, drinks, and repartee. We'll have a ball!"

We high-fived his plan for us.

"Big cous, I really like that lady. She got to me."

"It shows. Sally caused the same feelin' in me. Had to have her." He slapped his thigh.

"I'm glad it finally happened to you. Nothin' is too good for my best friend."

"Best friend. What am I now, forty-third on your list of best friends?" I bantered.

"No, siree, bobtail. Joe, TJ, or you, it simply depends on whom I'm tellin' it to at the time," he happily said. "Put it this way: if you weren't my best buddy, why would I have set you up with such a beautiful gal who I knew was a perfect match? Enough said on this topic. Stop lollygaggin' and just do it."

I didn't have to capture myself in *The Thinker* pose to understand his drift; catching him straight in the eye, I simply knew he was telling the truth.

My new "best friend" watched as I finally saw TJ through the thinned-out dance floor area seated forty feet away at a wall table. He was hijinxing and talking with Perri Belle and some other folks.

"Did you give him the envelope?" John Henry inquired.

"No, not yet. Tomorrow will be fine."

"So-so with me. Just hold on good and tight to it. There's some serious 'cabbage' in there."

"It's none of my business what the amount is. I've been careful with its contents."

"Then, why, cous, did you throw your jacket on the floor earlier when you were smoochin' it up with Daf?"

My arms shook, and currents of terror zapped my spine.

"Easy, cous, nobody's been blown to smithereens. I was with the Bea sisters when I saw what you did. Probably would have done it myself if I didn't realize the quantity contained. You scared the livin' daylights out of me. After that scene, I had cousin Emmel put two of his dart-playin', part-bloodhound friends keep a watch on you and your clothin' all night. They were even skulkin' you in the parkin' lot before. Never knew they were there, did you?"

"No, I honestly didn't. Don't tell me anything else. You should have handed this transaction directly yourself."

"Let's not nitpick. Have it your way. But a bagman such as yourself is so much better at passin' the buck than me," he joked. "Speaking of TJ, do you think he had fun tonight?"

Before allowing him to change the subject, I gave him a gentle-reminder middle finger for shirking his responsibility.

"Of course, and he met a lovely lady friend."

As I spoke, they ambled to the floor. The cowgirl was showing TJ a form of the Texas two-step.

"She's not so lovely. The lady has her own agenda. TJ and I talked some serious 'turkey' about her before. Have a barrel of fun, but don't fall in love. She's long-term trouble," John Henry sternly counseled.

"What's the scoop on her?"

Inquisitively, I had to know.

"Her name is Perri Belle Brown. She lives up past the old mill by the stream. All three of her husbands dearly departed from natural causes, but just a wee bit too early in their life spans. Some folks refer to her in the appellation the Widow Brown, while others intimate she's as deadly as a black widow spider," he boldly expressed.

"Why?"

"The widow has a preference not only for older gentleman but also for lonely ole geezers who are excessively wealthy. They all exhaled their last breaths while dutifully performin' their connubial obligations in the bedroom."

"So she killed them with kindness. That's the way I'd wish I could go out of this world," I hoped.

"There's another common denominator I've left out purposefully. All three had a history of chronic heart problems. No physical exertion such as marathon sex sessions would have been their cardiologists' warnin'."

"Oh, that's a lot different."

"You betcha, cous. Same modus operandi in all three cases. As sure as my name is John Henry Andrews, that woman fucked those men to death."

After kicking a spoke on the bottom of my stool, I began to incessantly laugh.

"It's true, cous. The widow has gotten away with three murders. That's the personal opinion shared to yours truly from an insurance claims investigator who calls the experiences déjà vu, a medical examiner, and the county coroner, who's my cousin. She's awfully slick. Who can prove malice aforethought? She knows the law better than Oliver Wendell Holmes did. She plays the role of the femme fatal. Poor, sweet Perri Belle, for whom the fates have smiled unkindly, is always the sole beneficiary of her husbands' life insurance, property, stocks and bonds, and hard cash. She might even be absentee owner of a soup factory in Camden. Her new beau, or significant other, since she researched his holdin's, didn't come out tonight to play. Tim's a youngster compared to the others. He's only sixty-eight, but naturally he fits to a tee all her requirements, makin' him a very favorable suitor," John Henry expatiated. "He'll be cremated, too, shortly after the brief closed-coffin viewin' with the standin' picture-framed photo on top. Same procedure the other husbands received. Different pictures, of course, but they all shared the same damn frame, I've heard."

"Why no open casket?" I challenged.

"Too horrible to look at." John Henry grimaced. "Contracture of the lower anterior portion of the head always developed essentially around the mouth region. Believe it or not, it leaves a lateral upward extension of the lips. Doesn't it sound awfully grim?"

"Yes," I answered.

"Until you translate it to mean they died with big grins on their faces," he stated waggishly.

Propped against the bar now, I was still laughing without cessation. I'd like to offer my own two cents' worth of comment, but I couldn't. Satisfied I'd regained my composure, I managed to blurt out, "How can you prosecute a woman for making love to her husband?"

"You can't. She can always say things got so hot and frenzied she never heard him, or, in her case, them, beggin' to stop," he ribbed.

"Big cous, she looks so young. I'd guess about twenty-six."

"Your way off base. Take off the blinders and add thirteen more years. Hey, she's a fox to me too. My eyeballs were poppin' earlier the way she was workin' that steamy dance number. I gave her the once-over a hundred times tonight. If I weren't married to my Sally, I'd spread a rumor about me needin' a pacemaker, and that's exactly what I'd do," he said in oath.

"Just remember the indelible word is *if*," I chided.

"Damn right, Stanley. That's a mighty big *if*," he reconsidered. "An *if* I wouldn't care to find out about." He uneasily laughed.

The big guy straddled over the bar to get us a couple of cold bottles of beer. He signaled if I wanted two, but at this stage in the night, I was lucky if I could nurse one.

"John Henry, what time is last call?" I inquired.

With his back turned to me, he answered, "Check out the shingle by the register."

The shellacked signpost with jagged, severed corners read, "The bar closes when we ain't got no more."

"Technically, however, we stop serving after one thirty," he informed me.

"They only come out at night," I said, referring to Perri Belle.

"Oh, we have our share of characters in the daytime too, yet the distinctive ones seem to congregate much later."

"The pip-squeak talkin' to that gal over there," he told, pointing, "is, in common parlance, a boondoggler with the Army Corps of Civil Engineers. Amply and aptly put, he's a waster of taxpayer money. Like his job, his hobby pursuit is an exercise in futility. He's an amateur numismatist, same as I've been a coin collector for years, except..."

The late-fifty-ish gentleman with the telltale toupee that was speaking with Uncle Miller approached us.

"How do, John Henry? And howdy to your guest," he offered enthusiastically, including handshakes.

His hands were chafed, and his right one felt grimy. I was cognizant of his blistered left thumb that had a crack in the nail.

"Well, I do declare if it isn't Lester King. How are you feelin'?" the big guy asked.

"I'm feelin' fit as a fiddle, after havin' one of your uncle's humongous prime rib dinners. It's the best in the county. Probably in the state too," he sanctioned.

"Lester, this is my best friend, Stanley Jankowski. He's suburbia born and bred, but we're breakin' him in like a new pair of cowhide boots."

By the way he reacted, you'd think that passing remark was the funniest thing Lester ever heard.

"You and your uncle, God bless yas, have a way of really ticklin' my funny bone. Not just ten minutes ago, he had Beth and me in stitches, chewin' the fat with him. I decided to stretch my legs and let your uncle bend my wife's ear for a spell to see what your jabberin' about."

"So you're the antique dealer," I expressed, "that John Henry said I'd meet later."

"In the flesh, unless others are usin' identical names in the same profession," he jocosely remarked.

"You're one of a kind, Lester," John Henry alluded.

He placed one of his bearlike paws around him.

"Stop eatin' humble pie. Stanley, not only are you lookin' at a master craftsman of this or any decade, what we have here is an antique wood forger who's a genius in his field. Lester's specialty is chairs. He can recreate fifty- to two-hundred-and-fifty-year-old ornate designs. All depends on how much collectors are willin' to pay for his furtive agin' process methods. It's serendipitous the way he'll stumble upon the right lathes, woods, resins, and upholstery for that specific time period."

"I don't rightly know what all that means, but it sure sounds like you are butterin' me up," Lester declared.

He slowly shook his head sideways.

"Some of the finest families from some of the finest homes in Far Hills, New Haven, Newport, Scarsdale, Short Hills, Spring Lake, the Berkshires, the Hamptons, Tewksbury, Upper Montclair, and Upper Saddle River, to mention several, have dubiously scooped up Chippendales, Hepplewhites, Windsors, includin' combed-backed styles, wings, and Yorkshires as originals at bargain-basement prices. Seems like somebody spread a rumor several years ago that proved very beneficial to you," the big guy pointed out.

"You know as well as I do, John Henry, that Garrison Cobb is guilty of that slander," Lester acknowledged.

"Yeah, yeah, yeah. He alluded you had a pipeline to all of Doris Duke's antiques stored in her attic at her Hillsborough Township residence that she was bored to tears with and couldn't wait to have evacuated. That was why she called you, Lester, to cart it all away. Must be an inexhaustible supply of old wooden chairs up in that garret or a whole mill crew workin' the graveyard shift, too, to get the production out."

"John Henry, when those out-of-towners ask me if a piece is from her estate collection, I neither agree nor deny. I just give them my famous gap-toothed smile and name my price."

"And they think, 'cause he purposely mispronounces a few words, he's the village idiot. With all the money Lester rakes in and takes to the bank, they should want to be such simpletons."

"Doesn't anyone ever catch on to the ruse?" I interrupted.

"What ruse? You'd need a blue-ribbon panel of expert's experts to debunk Lester and disprove authenticity. He's that damn good. You want to second my opinion? Just go ask Christie's, since 1766, or Sotheby's, both auction houses in New York City. If they're honest, they'll tell you."

"Since your illustrious credentials superseded the finish of the topic of our conversation, I'll tell you what I was jabberin' about. I was just describin' to Stanley the exploits of one of our extraordinary locals, namely, Hubert Matthews," John Henry said.

"Oh yeah, you had to bring him up. Sorriest day of my life was when, without thinkin', I mentioned the old-style-size milk cans to him we have in our basement chock-full with pennies. I said sometime, when I had nothin' better to do, we might dump them out and have a look-see for what he desperately wants to find. Because he's so hell-bent on this impracticable quest, he thinks he's entitled just to come over anytime he so pleases to put them under a lookin' glass. John Henry, I'll swear on my father's grave that screwball Hubert has rung my doorbell at 3:00 a.m. more than once to do penny-searchin'. Don't want him to set foot on my property without callin' first, and certainly not at that hour."

I scanned John Henry for his reaction, and it was nodding approbation.

Lester complained, "It's gotten to the point where it's unlucky to run into him. You just know he's goin' to pester you about goin' through those pennies. Tonight, I saw him before he noticed Beth and me. I was half-tempted to take off my silly hairpiece at our table to camouflage my appearance, hopin' he wouldn't detect me. If he did come over, I was goin' to say, 'I'm not him, but that's his wife I'm datin'.' Beth refused to go along with my gag. I only wear this darn thin' for her," he stated, referring to the faulty head coverage. "That Hubert has one thought in his brain: to find that damn 1943 copper penny. It's a fuckin' mindless ambition that cost him his wife and kids."

"Lester," the big guy interposed, "just one important question I have to ask."

"Shoot, JH. What is it?"

"Why are you tellin' my fuckin' story?" he trenchantly demanded.

"John Henry, I'm sorry," he pleaded. "I didn't know I was blowin' so much smoke and belaborin' the point I wanted to make."

Dancing in place, the big guy was smiling. He started to grin.

"Oh, you damn fool." Lester coarsely laughed. "Why didn't you tell me to shut up sooner? Pick up the story where I left off."

Welcomely, Uncle Miller arrived with three large mugs of coffee.

"Don't forget the dessert, Unc, and I mean liquid," John Henry qualified.

"It's comin'. Hold your horses," he offered figuratively.

Mr. Congeniality returned with three snifters of Sambvca with coffee beans sunk to the bottom. Our master mixologist fired them up with an elongated stick match, as six eyes across from him were intensely gazed.

"Can I drink mine yet, or is someone waitin' to sing happy birthday?" Lester crowed.

My big cousin and I were amused at Lester's earnest solicitation as we blew out the flames and proceeded to sip. Mr. King took a hard drink of his coffee, with gusto.

"John Henry, finish your story," I requested. "What sort of penny was this guy trying to uncover?"

He bumped me on the arm and directed his reply to Lester.

"It's been the rock of ages, since I was tryin' to explain it, but I'll do my best," he caroused.

Simultaneously, Lester covered his mouth with his hand and slumped his shoulders, deadening his excitement.

"Ever since 1909 to present, the US Treasury department has minted Lincoln-head copper pennies. There must be billions in circulation. In the year 1943, the composition of the denomination was changed because copper was needed for the war effort."

"Yes, I've seen them. Weren't they referred to as white, silver, or steel pennies?" I interjected.

"They may have been, and please excuse my expression, *coined*, but they were actually made of zinc. As I've heard the account, eight copper Lincolns were made on purpose but mistakenly placed into circulation. Maybe five have been accounted for, while three are still out there for grabs, scattered among the billions, possibly not even in this country. Findin' such a coin could be worth a million dollars or more to the lucky person who knew what they found and it was authenticated. This numskull Herbert claims to have found a copper '43, then lost it in a gumball machine. He said, 'If I've found one once then, I can find another.' Herbert has contacts in all other forty-nine states sendin' him rolls of pennies. He pays fifty-five cents for a roll. Through some type of geographical scientific approach he claims to have perfected, he swears one of the pennies is in one of the Northwestern states, and as soon as he's pensioned with the government, he's goin' to move there. It's all hogwash to me. I've never heard of anyone being so dedicated to such an impossible mission.

You talk about findin' needles in a haystack! He'd have better luck findin' a penny with Lincoln smokin' a fuckin' cigar."

We enjoyed the merriment of his joke.

"He sounds to me more of an annoyance than someone who's dangerous," I delivered.

"That's true, cous, except every time you see him in here, he wants you to open your cash register to see if you collected any pennies, the same way he's bothersome to every merchant in town. He doesn't listen to the words *later* or *no*. Never does it sink in with him. Perhaps he's just anal-retentive."

"Charlie Haps, vice president of the bank around the corner, calls him a noodlehead. His tellers feel uncomfortable with Herbert's persistence. I guess every locale has their town kook, and he's our very own," the big guy admitted with reluctance.

"If you want dangerous," Lester offered, "that could mean Barty Vance. He's in here tonight, you know. Drinkin' his special type of beer," he claimed, antecedent to unmannerly smacking his lips, while roughly gurgling his coffee.

Hurriedly, the big guy left his stool to investigate the other side of the bar obscured from our position, following the barbarian table manners of his uncle's friend.

"Yeah," John Henry said upon returning, "he's there, mindin' his own business, sluggin' down his beer through a straw and, as usual, havin' a conversation with himself. I didn't see him come in. Lester, I wouldn't call him dangerous anymore. We have more muddleheaded types working at the Inn these days. That incident was over seventeen years ago. He's as calm as a cucumber these days, now with the strength of the tranquilizers that are prescribed for him."

"You don't think he's capable of goin' off his rocker again, John Henry? Maybe this time havin' a conniption with his sister or a stranger who might give him hard looks?" Lester seriously voiced.

He noisily sipped his coffee for the third straight time.

"You're slurpin' that Colombiari brew," John Henry accused, "louder than a crocodilian draggin' his own baggage."

Euphoric rustlings were shared by our trio.

"No way. Forced into livin' under those conditions for all those years, I can't say, nor can you, that we may not have gone off the deep end," the big guy apologized.

"Amen to that, John Henry," Lester voiced before he polished off his cordial.

Attentively listening, I was wonder-stricken. Impatiently, as if a kid brother, I tugged on John Henry's shirtsleeve for clarification.

"Who's Bart Vance, and what terrible thing did he do? And if he's so dangerous, what's he doing drinking beer in here?" I beseeched. "Well, cous, if you give me a Mississippi minute, I'll mention it momentarily," he alliterated with a complacent air.

Glancing over my left shoulder, I found that TJ would soon be participating in our spirited group. The cowgirl was leaving with a woman and two guys. TJ jaunted over and stooped behind the big guy, practically blotting himself from view. Having no idea whether or not he was going to attempt to crawl between his legs, Lester and I chorused consent to be still to his nonverbal command. As John Henry moved and stepped, so did his new shadow follow suit, in tandem. We couldn't help snickering when the big guy twisted in both directions sideways and nobody was there. Lester didn't realize it, but we were witnessing a harlequinade; TJ had cast himself as the non-costumed harlequin empty of wood sword, and our big cousin was unwittingly playing himself as the lovable clown. If he appreciated it or not, Lester and I had front-row tickets to this unrehearsed pantomime. Refusing to give up, John Henry, with both arms akimbo, bent to his knees for a unique upside-down perspective to discover the identity of the prankster. If you asked me for my money, I'd take an impromptu skit such as this, on French toast, any day, to a boring Punch and Judy production anytime and anywhere.

"Cous, what in blazes are you tryin' to do? Now that you're over here, I'd like you to meet a good pal of my uncle's and mine, Lester King," he greeted nevertheless, topsy-turvy. "Lester, this is my… best…friend…TJ," he finished up with a belch.

Lester immediately scanned to me. I responded with a "null" expression. With him strained from too much laughter, ole Lester's face was illuminating a shade rubious and holding on for dear life to his roly-poly paunch hanging over his belt at least eight inches. A grinning Uncle Miller greeted John Henry's new best friend with a duplication of our last indulgences.

"Please, boys, don't kill the man," Uncle Miller pleaded. "He's our seventh in the poker game at the fire hall Sunday. We can't afford to lose him. Possum Lippse can't make it."

"Uncle Miller," I jocundly beseeched, "it seems to me I recall you having mighty strong language about disapproving of gambling. Moreover, you said 'it's the devil's doings.'"

"Well, it may on the surface appear like I got my tongue caught in that ole proverbial cookie jar instead of my hand, but it's a false impression."

While the tip of his protuberance was touching his palate, he was giving me an obliquely eyed stare I was not backing down from. I felt the perception of a light bulb going off in his head.

"By golly, Ms. Molly, my darn nephew was right when he said you have a photoscopic memory," he glibly suggested.

"You mean *photographic*," I corrected his catachresis.

"And that too," he said. "By the way, smarty britches, I've got one of those also, them there memory banks. Just because I disapprove of wagerin' at the Inn doesn't mean it's not okay to sit in on a few hands of cards at the fire hall. As far as the devil is concerned, sometimes you just have to give me, whoops, *him* his due. When I'm on a hot streak, the other players have a devilish time tryin' to take away my winnin's." He cordially laughed.

As a parting shot, he displayed his rolled tongue, and with thumbs in his ears palms straight up, moving tight fingers forward, he included jackass ears for my comical benefit. Wistfully, I kept to myself, *So much for remembering.*

"What's going on?" a perplexed TJ inquired.

He noticed that the big guy, presently straightened up, was foolishly inspecting the rafters overhead.

"You'd have to be a bumpkin to fully appreciate it," I told him, pulling him aside.

"What's he looking for?"

"Oh, probably invisible termites or…possibly, a way out," I said as I unsuspectedly elbowed John Henry in the midsection.

Had I worn fancy suspenders, as some of the clientele were attired, I would have snapped them loudly and proudly, then displayed my thumbs sticking out through them.

"TJ," John Henry proffered, "you came in the nick of time to save your friend here."

"From you."

"No, from Bartholomew Vance. He's over yonder." He pointed.

TJ peeked in the direction of the bar corner where the big guy was alluding to. The standing patrons had cleared from a few minutes ago, and we had a clearer perspective of Barty across from us, far left. Slight of built, he was whey-faced with an irregular part in his wispy brown hair. I predicted he was no older than thirty-three, and he was quenching his thirst with a mason jar of dark beer. You could see his lips moving, talking only to thin air, cautious every other minute he might be under surveillance, perhaps from the thought police. His mood swing soon turned wistful, as if *The War of the Worlds* was playing through his mind.

"All right, let's get down to cases. What did that charmer do?" TJ asked.

"Oh, nothin' much, cous, other than smash to pieces every piece of inventory in his father's store while at the same time bludgeonin' his daddy's face beyond recognition. After, he was institutionalized for twelve years. Sixteen months ago, Barty was released to the care of his sister, Aggie," John Henry relayed.

"Since being here, I feel as if I've crossed over into the time warp of *The Twilight Zone* without the benefit of meeting Rod Serling. Stanley is scaring me with talk of the Jersey Devil before we get here; you try to steal my ring by pulling a Gullible's Travels routine; you let me party with a rich, premeditated husband-killer widow; and if that isn't enough to rattle my nerves, you've got a demented lunatic convicted of parricide who spent a decade in la-la-land whose capacity to adjust to society could unravel any second to recidivism. On top of it all, John Henry, you're asking me now to save Stanley. Just who the fuck is going to save me?" he shrilled.

In a flash of TJ ending his jovial diatribe, John Henry disbelievingly found himself being shimmed up, as if he were a sturdy old maple tree. To his credit, the big guy was laughing as his arms, serving as branches, helped support TJ's weight as his noggin was being pummeled with amiable noogies. Unfortunately, I couldn't slap a high five with Lester, because he'd been reduced to silly putty; the ole boy was coughing, then wheezing, before he finally delivered a maundered frick and frack. "If I don't go to the bathroom now, I'll piss my pants for sure" was the last thing I coherently picked up hearing from him as he ran off, signifying "Later" to his wife as he rushed past her.

From behind the bar, Uncle Miller flicked TJ his Yankee cap. After dusting it off with his hand, he returned it to its rightful place, on top of his own head instead of the elk's.

Uncle Miller brought back seconds on the coffee, and I placed my hand horizontally on my snifter glass, indicating no more snootfuls for me. My two other partners favored more stronger liquid hospitality.

"Just need to wet our whistles a little longer," John Henry boasted to his uncle after winking at me.

"If you wet your whistle any more, it would be submerged," his uncle playfully came back with.

He took a few paces down the bar and did an about-face.

"And another thin', nephew," he said as he reached over the bar top to mildly wiggle John Henry's earlobes, "I'm sure pleased as punch that you're my partner, 'cause I could never afford the giveaways to you as a cash-payin' customer."

Lester, our missing link to this new quartet, anxiously arrived back, sneaking past his wife, who was conversing with the couple sitting next to her and Unc.

"John Henry, guess who I was talkin' to in the stall next to me?" he said in a huff.

"Hmm. Don't tell me Burt Reynolds is back in town," the big guy ribbed. "Only comes in here just to use our latrine. They don't seem to have such things in Jupiter, Florida. Or was it that guy Unc threw out of here one night and told him never to come back? What was his name? I've got it," he rejoiced in remembering. "He went by

Barney Barnes, a.k.a. Chubby. And that's another thin'. Who would want to be referred to as Chubby even though they were fat? The twit had a perversion to hang out half the night in the men's room, comin' out only to get refills at the bar. Folks were joshin' my uncle about him hirin' a porter, and he didn't. Especially some potbellied type paradin' around in a lavender jumpsuit," John Henry cracked.

"Naw, it was Cactus Conrad," he yakked.

TJ and I got our kicks out of the vivid surname.

"Never saw Cactus come in," John Henry stressed. "That ole son of a gun. Where did he go?" He laughed.

"He was hobnobbin' before. Now he's sittin' with his girlfriend and the Bea twins. All kiddin' aside, JH, do you call him Cactus to his face?" Lester inquired.

"Oh, gosh to Betsy, no. I've got too much horse sense for that. He'd get hotter than a hornet if I did that. I call him just plain Ricky. We'll tell the boys about him later," he suggested.

I said, "Instead of a Mississippi minute, John Henry, you're taking a laid-back Southern California hour to finish your damn story about Barty. Shake a leg, will ya?"

Lester looked at John Henry with awe.

"Hot damn," he yelped to Lester, "when I'm wrong, I'm wrong, but when I'm right, boy, oh, boy, I'm fuckin' good. Just what did I tell you, Lester? I said earlier we were breakin' him in to our country-esque mode of expression."

He placed one of his big mitts on my neck.

"Hallelujah," he praised, "we've got ourselves a colloquial convert!"

TJ ripped up nearby napkins into strips and skipped around me, tossing his newly made confetti.

John Henry yakked, "'Cause you're one of us now, I'm obligin' to you."

"That's mighty big of ya, cous," I told him.

"And before you add on largess, let him get on with it," TJ moderately reproofed.

"Just for that, wisecracker, I'm not startin' from the point from when you weren't here. It might psychologically make me feel like I'm talkin' to the conservation captain," he teased.

"Poor Barty. It was somethin' that was bound to happen. I put the blame on his lunkhead father for methodically tryin' to put the boy off the deep end. The father operated an antique clock shop on the other end of town, next to the hardware store. The family made livin' quarters upstairs in a two-bedroom apartment. I remember the place well. Talford, the father, carried all types of clocks, from the most simple mechanical devices to the sublime: alarm, brass, crystal, cuckoo, grandfather, grandmother, hand-carved, kitchen, mantel, musical, regulators, and wall," he cataloged.

"While on display, meticulous care had to be taken in the daily winding of these timepieces, for accuracy. When Barty was old enough, he was given this task, whether he liked it or not. And for the record, he didn't.

"As you can picture, bein' in that shop for five to ten minutes, you could hear some beautiful sounds, with each instrument having its unique resonance. It was an acoustical anthology of bells, buzzers, chimes, clicks, chirps, cuckoos, ticktocks, tones, and tunes. Some of the bigger models, such as the grandfathers, with their metal moon faces, emitted special sounds on the quarter, half hour, and every sixty minutes. It was a pleasant visual and listenin' experience for a while to watch over two hundred clocks runnin' at the same time, but anythin' more could give you a splittin' headache.

"Now, take a child raised under these conditions who wasn't allowed to participate in sports because he had to come home right from school to work at the shop and be subjected to this constant noise. He wasn't allowed to wear earplugs because Talford just simply said no. Accordin' to his father, he had to take it like a little man. Even at night, there was no escape, because sounds came through from the first floor. It wasn't necessary for them to live above the damn shop, 'cause Talford's father had willed them his house just right outside of town. Too far away from work, he said, yet he didn't rent the house out either. Don't ask me why. The family dwellin' there could have served as a nice, calmin' sanctuary for everybody, but Talford, behavin' as if he were Captain Bligh, chose to ignore their pleas. The result of which drove his family batty. The mother, a God-fearin', churchgoin' woman couldn't take the torture anymore and ran away with a travelin' salesman from Smith and Wesson when Barty was about thirteen. Aggie, the younger sister, walked around half-dressed in a catatonic state, holdin' on to her dolly like a zombie. I heard three days before the murder, townspeople witnessed Barty rollin' on the ground in the park. He had dirt in his mouth and was chewin' on twigs. His mind had finally degenerated far away from normal comprehension.

"Oncomin', Talford's demise proved to be as macabre as his sadistic treatment to his own flesh and blood. In an ironic twist of administerin' punishment, Barty bashed in Talford's skull with a gnomon, the raised metal part of a marble-based sundial that casts a shadow. It was always placed near the side slate walkway on the front lawn. The gnomon was the singular measurement of time they owned that didn't make a sound. The sheriff's report suggested that Barty gave his father three whacks for every clock in the store. Neither did he allow any functional piece to be left for sentiment. It appeared as if a demolition derby had run amuck, with Big Bertha-size wheeled rigs, deciminatin' those alarms to the sound of silence," he told.

"They sent him to the 'funny farm' at Ancora, where for your duration it's 'summertime and the livin' is easy,' on strong daily dosages of lithium. Some people there are guests of the state the rest of their natural lives. Totally isolated, I've heard they have underground tunnels traversin' the grounds. Besides a place you wouldn't want to live, well, it's not a place you'd want to visit either. What if you were mistaken for one of them? Presently, Barty lives in Nowheresville with his sister in the house he should have spent his childhood in," John Henry interestingly storied.

TJ and I gave the big guy strange conveyances.

"The post office calls it that because it's an RD address that gets sent to a PO box. It's confusin' because the street is not within our town or Pittstown two miles away. The snafu exits because Quakertown, the village it should be localized, doesn't deliver their mail. So dependin' on the tenth-mile stretch of the road the house is situated on affects which post office they go to, and sometimes the mail winds up in Allens Corner or Cherryville. Since the highway authority is always makin' construction changes, it can get preddy complicated. That's why I'm only explainin' it once." He laughed.

"Speakin' of Barty, directly in terms of his drinkin', the only beer we serve him in here is root. He likes to say he can hold his beer. Who am I to take that privilege away from him? Barty keeps a low profile, and as far as Unc and I are concerned, he can enter the premises anytime he wants. He's not a bother to anyone."

John Henry chuckled to himself.

"It struck me as funny at the time, and I'll share it with yous. About a month ago, he bicycled his way up here on a Tuesday to have his supper at the bar. He ordered one of our generous-portioned blue-plate specials with all the 'beer' he could guzzle down thrown in for free. Now, before I quote what he said, let me preface that children in school want to be doctors, lawyers, rocket scientists, and such when they grow up. My little guy John Henry Jr., because he likes arithmetic, thinks right now, at least, that he might want to be a math teacher. Chagrined or not that he doesn't have an aptitude for farmin', teachin' is an admirable profession, if that's what he really wants to pursue." He paused.

"What's your point?" TJ petitioned.

"Well, if you give me two shakes of a lamb's tail, I'll tell you. Now, where was I? Okay, I've got it. I'm sittin' down next to Barty while he's enjoyin' every mouthful of his dinner.

"'John Henry,' he said, turnin' toward me, 'do you know what I'd really like to be?'

"'No,' I answered, eager for his response.

"'A meatloaf platter, a meatloaf platter. That's what I'd really like to be, a meatloaf platter,' he decisively conveyed.

"That recital placed me between a rock and a hard place whether to laugh or to cry. So in all honesty, I told Barty I was aspirin' to be a hot tom turkey sandwich on pumpernickel with cranberries on the side, but most of the time I felt like fuckin' chopped goose liver. He steadily gazed at me for a three-count with those soulful eyes, bobbed his head, smiled, and extended his hand to me. Barty wanted to say somethin', but he waited till Unc was out of range."

John Henry started to laugh.

"'I've known for some time. Just didn't want him to find out about you,' he said."

We were all reeling at that announcement.

"What else could I do but thank him for his confidentiality? That ole horseface over there," he said, pointing to his uncle, "still doesn't know, 'cause it's top-secret information, classified to only Barty and me."

Poor Lester was in hysterics, and we were not far behind, guffawing.

"Before you hoot and holler too much," the big guy cautioned, "but for the grace of God, walk I."

"Whoa. I can't believe it. Don't turn around now, but isn't that John Henry's Sally sitting over there, hugging and kissing that guy with the red beard who's wearing a visor on his head?" TJ carefully implied out of the side of his mouth.

"I wish I could say you've been smokin' some rope, but you're right. Can't believe what I'm seeing. If the big guy finds out, we'll have a donnybrook in here. The bearded gigolo has buddies, so roll up your sleeves and be ready for some fisticuffs," I prepared.

"What's solacin' you two? Both of you look like you just swallowed grubworms by mistake. What's up? Let your cousin know."

"John Henry, I'm sorry to have to say that…," TJ attempted to dislodge.

"Sally is playing patty-cake with some guy over," I finished, head bowed.

Lester and our big cousin looked over, not particularly perturbed. "So what?" he said calmly. "She's entitled to a little diversion, isn't she? She appears to be havin' a good time, maybe too good of a time, if you ask me, but nevertheless, she's allowed to have fun. What do you think, Lester?"

"Oh, she's havin' a swell time with her new boyfriend," he purposely emphasized to TJ and myself. "They're lovebirds for sure," Lester included.

TJ was biting his lip, and I didn't know what else to say regarding Sally's open affair. Then I noticed Sally lighting a cigarette, and she never smoked a day in her life. She had a bottle of Rolling Rock in front of her, but she always found the taste of beer bitter. Then, there was an indelible sunburst pattern on her bare shoulder. Intrinsically, I knew now this woman wasn't Sally.

"I appreciate the fact," John Henry pointed out, "that he spends his money on her in an establishment partly owned by me. Keeps it in the family that way."

"Hey, Unc!" he yelled over to his senior relative across the bar. "Buy my Sally and her special friend over yonder a round on me."

"That's it, John Henry. Kin or no kin, you're cut off from the bar, even though you're majority owner. Boy, you're startin' to see mirages. I knew that last batch of apple wine I distilled had a kick to it, but I didn't realize how potent it was," he said to himself. "I'll have to start labelin' it as nitro, with a cautionary two-glass limit per customer."

Subsequent to that informal communique, John Henry and Lester were yapping and yowling as if they were penned-up collies awaiting to be walked. A previously stunned TJ immediately understood some hoodwinking had taken place, and I was still yakking over Uncle Miller's comment. John Henry threw his hands straight up.

"That's not my Sally," he swore. "There's a strikin' resemblance, but that's where it ends. She belongs to somebody else."

"Who?" TJ and I replied in unison.

"That's Tanya 'Tessie' Turner, Billy Bob Turner's wife. That's him in the flesh, all cozied up next to her. Recall me bringin' up his name earlier? He's Billy Goat Turner, Sally's ex-fiancé. That damn nincompoop had to go out and marry a woman who physically reminded him of Sally about four years after I fleeced her—I mean, squired her away from him. Sally doesn't take too well to the similarity and gets mighty burned up with Tanya's fixation to copycat any change in Sally's hairstyle. I'd be most grateful if you did a big favor for me and a small one for yourselves by keepin' this situation hush-hush from my better half, that you saw Tanya in the Inn with Billy Bob. You see, I was dancin' with her tonight. What Sally don't know won't hurt me," he pleaded.

For the price of ham and eggs in the morning, we pledged to be tight-lipped. Our silent discretion always had a small price to it. Uncle Miller motioned with his chin for John Henry to inspect his right flank.

"Well, I'll be…!" he exclaimed.

"Corn-frittered," TJ chimed in.

"Yeah, cous. That's Maudie Gavers in the green slacks, with her husband, Matthew. She's a genealogical marvel. The skinny guy is her niece's son, Cyrus Ember, and his wife…"

"Joan," Lester voiced.

"Holy smoke! It has to be a good five years since I've seen them," John Henry told us.

Other than being a nice-looking lady, there wasn't anything particularly special about her, I mused.

"Are you going to share what's so astonishing about her?" I curiously entreated.

John Henry turned to Lester before he answered.

"She's née Maude Fargo, one of Grandma Hannah Fargo's quadruplets. Cyrus's mother is Abagail, granddaughter of Hannah and daughter of Iris, Grandma Fargo's firstborn. As it works out, there's a filial oddity. Cyrus is six months older than Maude. In the decent per-stirpes vernacular, what we basically have here is a situation where a great-grandson is older than the great-grandmother's youngest daughter, his grandaunt. Damn it, the genetic link is feasible, and I know it happened, but why does it seem so unnatural to me?"

TJ and I had mixed expressions without articulating our sentiments.

"That reminds me. See that good ole burly boy with the bushy sideburns standin' by the front entrance? He's out gallivantin' tonight."

TJ and I did a search left near the wooden chief, where a threesome was talking.

"We didn't see him."

"Not there, cousins, to the right side. The dude with the shoestring bow tie on a metal slide, placin' a plug of Burley under his tongue." As a pointer, Lester finally directed us to the right man he called Bo Coles.

"Okay, so what?" was TJ's answer after our weary-eyed hard work.

"He did. He did," the big guy repeated and couldn't help but to chuckle, "the most unthinkably, unconventional thing. He married his fuckin' mother-in-law."

"That's cuttin' off your nose to spite your face," someone exploded with hilarity.

I took the volition to be the one who asked, "Why?"

"Because Bo got so tired of quarrelin' with his wife, he divorced her. He soon realized afterward he was in love with his ex's mother, and she felt the same emotion toward him. Now, everythin's Jim Dandy, except the kids can't figure out why Daddy's married to Grandma and their mommy is his stepchild."

We hooted and howled jubilantly with that disclosure.

Beth slipped away from her bar companions to inspect the stir caused by our motley crew. She seemed to be an amiable middle-aged woman, except with a half-pound of makeup trying to conceal the crow's-feet around her eyes and her wrinkled complexion. Her frosted hair would do her justice if it weren't teased once, twice, ten times too much; hence, what good would have been my constructive criticism if she liked having a Baltimore oriole's nest as a hairdo? I thought.

"Hello, John Henry," she said with a deep voice.

"And how are you, gorgeous?" the big guy returned after hugging and kissing her.

"Everythin' with me is hunky-dory. But more importantly, Mr. Sweet-Talker, how's my yin-yang of a husband behavin' himself?" she loudly bombarded. "Haven't heard him so excited since I told him my mother and her Mexican hairless wouldn't be comin' for an extended visit a few years back."

"Lester didn't make the little Chihuahua feel welcome? Didn't ya, Hoss?" John Henry casually assumed, giving him a cross-eyed frown.

"Naw. I'm talkin' about her Tex-Mex boyfriend. Seems like that's the only thin' Mom and I have in common, bald-headed men," she squealed.

Conspicuously, there was simultaneous broken laughter. Hands were covering mouths, with the exception of Lester's.

"Now, Beth," John Henry gasped after several ho-hos, "why are you callin' your ole man a yin-yang?"

"Don't know," she returned, alarmed the big guy would make such an inquiry. "All I can summon to mind is that I saw the words in some Chinese philosophy book," she stated after her minitrance. "It was confu—"

"Confucius," John Henry tried to elicit anagrammatically.

"Naw, don't know what that is," she said, befuddled. "Just confusin'. Why's the pressure on me? Could you ask him why he's been answerin' to it for over ten years?" she tempestuously answered.

"Son of a bitch, son of a bitch," Lester faintly audibled under his breath.

A mist of forehead sweat broke out on him.

"What's yin-yang mumblin' about, now?" Beth recited out to the group.

"Honeysuckle, darlin'," he said, restrained from anger, "could you please skiddoo to your bar seat near Buster and Millie while I talk shop with the boys? Your preddy little head shouldn't be concerned with the tone of men's business we're discussin'. All right, sugarplum?"

Steadfastly determined not to be harried or hurried, she furiously hurled, "Lester King, when I married you sixteen years ago, ya knew right from the 'I dos' that I don't put up with nonsense. Happily ya understood that ya weren't gettin' any fuckin' 'No, sir,' 'Yes, sir,' wifey. Ya told me never to change. Better make believe I'm not here, 'cause this is where I'm stayin' anchored," she vented with arms folded.

If I continued to watch TJ rapidly gum his lips and raise his eyebrows again, I was going to burst out jubilantly, and the Kings weren't about to find it a wee bit funny. It was a ticklishly dangerous powder keg I didn't wish to ignite; therefore, I intelligently turned to face the platform the band was occupying. *No, it's absurd,* I answered to myself, grinning.

The barraging thought persisted, and I had to ponder if Beth checked in her firearms, or was the derringer behind the bar hers? When I shifted about-face, our brief duration of deadly quiet had stretched to the point of who spoke first between husband and wife was the loser. Like TJ on the spot, which invariably he was, he succeeded in defusing the matrimonial tiff.

"Beth," he said with his hand touching her arm, "allow me the privilege of refreshing your drink. Uncle Miller, set 'em up all around. I'm buying!"

Prim and improper Beth loved to have another sombrero.

Ditto for me on more coffee, and even Unc said that he'd be a moocher for a free cocktail. When our refreshments arrived, our big cous perfected his role as the ultimate MC.

"Never forget, cousins, behind every good man is a better woman, and that's about the best possible thing I can say," he *oratoried*.

Polite clapping was courteously in order, till Unc reared his engineer's cap above his cranium and propounded that his toy train, dubbed the Nightingale, would run a lap in honor of Beth. That was met with yells and hollers, hers being the loudest.

"John Henry," she cried above the crowd, "that's the sweetest thing I've ever heard! I swear you could charm the venom from a hissin' snake."

"I think he just did," I capriciously extended, only to TJ.

"If I had a medal to give, it would be all yours," she remarked to the big guy.

"You payed, and he saved the day," I poked privately to the generous purchaser of the last round.

"Me thinks it stinks," said TJ, the current royal bard of the Inn.

He pulled his shirt up over his mouth to tone down his verbiage.

Perceptive Uncle Miller pointed to the masked man and play-acted as if he were being held up, hands high in the air.

"Enough is enough," TJ lowly projected out of the corner of his mouth in tête-à-tête. "He's already bein' considered as a nominee for some type of Academy Award," TJ joked in a soft tone.

In his haste to get by us, a husky, craggy-faced man with a disheveled mop of curly sandy-colored hair and salt-and-pepper beard brushed against the big guy. There was an unctuous body odor about him.

"Have you seen Tatter or Smitty?" he abruptly asked without any inkling of an "Excuse me." "I'm lookin' for them."

"Not lately," John Henry returned to his questioner with the dirty shirttails hanging out, "but I do recall seein' them give or take an hour or so ago. Go check out the back room. Better yet, see Jonas standin' over there. He was hangin' out with urn."

If there was a thank-you, then there must have been a code of silence about it, because we never heard it. He offered only a disingenuous nod.

"Baa, baa," Beth bleated within earshot of the departing Mr. Unkempt and Mr. Unmannerly rolled into one.

Cringing, neck bowed, he pivoted about 130 degrees, snarling and grinding his teeth.

Her husband had that painted-on "Why'd ya do that for, honeysuckle?" expression on his face.

"He should be ashamed of himself for his beastly behavior," said Beth.

TJ and I voiced agreement.

"Then you guys know about him too," she continued.

"I should say so, the way he just acted," TJ committed, unknowing why our big cousin was holding his side in hysterics.

"It's convoluted," he hailed. "That's not quite…what Beth was alludin' to," he hurled out between deep breaths.

"Why'd they say they knew if they didn't know?" she inquired of her red-faced Lester.

"Woman, just forget it," he begged. "It's not all that darn important."

"But Beth is right," John Henry said kiddingly. "Why did they say that they knew?"

"Cousins," the big guy directed to TJ and me, "the character you just saw here that Beth was baain' is a panderer of sheep, but his only customer is himself. His name is Willie Degnan. Wee Willie to those in the area that know him. In the presence of a lady, I don't know any other way to express it other than that misfit, Willie, likes to get it on with ewes!" he exclaimed.

Lester had marked agitation on his face.

"Get rid of that gloomy puss, Lester. I wouldn't cuss, usin' the four-letter F-word in front of your wife. Get with our happy program and have some fun," John Henry insisted.

He slapped ole Lester on the back. This wasn't the "vote of confidence" Beth's husband wanted.

"It's common knowledge around here what he does to them wooly critters up on his daddy's farm," he depicted. "And that's not the half of it. To top it all off, there's a strange twist to his bestial sexual preference, bein' that Wee Willie suffers from lambdacism, meanin' he can't pronounce the letter *L* correctly. Instead of screwin' lambs, he's doin' it to yams. Shame is," he said, laughing, "years ago, he used to go out with some passable-lookin' women. Now they've been replaced with a four-hoofed alternative."

Our little group was both reeling and reveling from John Henry's depiction. TJ was crying from merriment on the big guy's shoulder. Where I didn't want a drink before, I wouldn't mind having one poured for me now with that latest outburst.

"No decent woman would want anythin' to do with him," Beth, giggling, shared.

She slurred her words in the process and was unsteadily holding her sombrero.

"What's new, Hoss?" said the bass-voiced man of John Henry-sized proportions.

"Heard you were in here, Ricky," JH verbally responded and with a good-measured ursiform hug. You know everybody present except for my two best friends, Stanley and TJ."

We extended our greetings. "Can I buy you one?" John Henry offered to him.

"Give me a raincheck, Hoss. I just came over to pay my respects and get some change for April. She's gettin' lonesome waitin' for me," he said in frolic. "Don't worry, Uncle Miller," he called out, "I don't need any pennies like some people, you know."

Uncle Miller gave the big man a few dollars' worth of quarters, and before he strode off, he delivered "Nice meetin' yas" and "See ya all later."

"Lester," John Henry merrily challenged, "now that he's gone, do you want to tell the boys about Cactus, or shall I?"

"Hoss, how dare you? It's one thin' havin' me standin' here nervously twiddlin' my thumbs while you idly carry on with Beth about a lowdown standin' in the mud while he's doin' it, sheep-fucker, but when you lack the restraint to not wait about tellin' tales about dual-peckered men till my wife leaves, that's when I draw the line. Adios."

Lester picked his wife up from the floor, saying "Upsy-daisy," in a fireman's carriage hold and brought her over to Buster and Millie.

"That's my Neanderthal for you. No sense of humor," Beth voiced deeply with her hands hoisted in midair.

"Please tell me later" could easily be read from Beth's lips as she held her hands in prayer.

"Was it somethin' I said?" John Henry pleasingly solicited. "What's he so prim and proper about? Beth King can duel filthy jokes and foul language with a hard-boiled Marine drill instructor and win," he said, certain.

"What were they babbling about?" TJ interposed.

Before John Henry could answer, sounds of screams, shrieks, and tumult were echoing way from the back room. Spurred on, with megaphone in tow, Uncle Miller rallied his troops.

"Battle stations, JH, battle stations!" he vociferously yelled. "The McCadlin boys are on the warpath again. Call to arms, call to arms!" he repeated.

As if shot from a cannon, the big guy blasted ahead, cutting the most direct route to the battle zone with us in hot pursuit, and an alerted Lester held up the rear flank. John Henry hurdled a chair and nimbly stepped on and off a seated table to avoid shaken customers blocking his way. TJ and I dodged the three bruisers wearing aprons who came out of the kitchen door armed with pots, pans, and a rolling pin. When we arrived at the fight scene, two young men of medium built and height, wearing tank tops without the biceps to go with them, were attempting to slug it out. Both had haircuts cropped short in the front and shaggy in the back. John Henry waved off anybody from barging in the brouhaha. Sliding tables and chairs aside, an assortment of people had enclosed the welterweights in a small rectangle.

"So this was the Inn's version of the main event in the squared circle," I reflected out loud. Methodically, I was rubbernecking for the bass-voiced, microphoned ring announcer with the tuxedo duds

to prep the telecast with a familiarly protracted "Let's get ready…
to…rum…ble!" ditty.

"Because the area wasn't packed," he stressed to us, "I'm allowin'
them to punch each other's lights out before we escort them out the
back door. This way, any third person in won't get hit. They relish
sucker punchin' whoever tries to break their clinch, so they can start
a battle royale. I'd much rather see them get all their licks on each
other than land a rabbit punch on an employee or patron."

"Can you believe that two brothers want to go at each other's
throats like pit bulls at the drop of a hat? Well, we have Ike and Inky,
and I wish some other place would, 'cause it's not profitable runnin'
a beer and a beaten bistro. Between the two, they've probably had
more amateur pugilistic bouts than Muhammad Ali, except theirs
are all barroom brawls with each other, all endin' in draws. Notice
their form. Any astute fight fan can tell they could never dream of
turnin' pro, let alone boxin' Golden Gloves," he cavorted. "See how
they both drop their right hands? They're both suckers for a left
hook. First lucky punch wins. If they only dedicated a little trainin'
to the sweet science, they would know. Won't be long now before
these sparrin' partners run out of gas. No stamina. Ike's arm's weary
already, and the scrappy, often-maligned Inky couldn't knock the air
out of a paper bag at this juncture in the round," John Henry said,
making light of it.

"Ten seconds ago, with his unorthodox southpaw style, Inky
was head-bobbin' and weavin'. He was boxin' from a defensive
crouch, scorin' by doublin' up on his jab and connectin' with a nicely
timed combination. He definitely had a boxer's chance to outpoint
his brother. His fight plan has all but disappeared, from the well-in-
tervaled flurries he was throwin'.

"Abandonin' the right lead for the left, Inky's standin' straight
up, with his feet too close together. Unquestionably, I have to deduct
points on my scorecard, 'cause he's missin' with wild bolo shots and
gettin' pummeled with overhead rights from his pooped brother,"
John Henry said, vividly describing the nip-and-tuck action.

"Cousins, whatever you do, don't blink," the big guy warned,
eye shifting left and right to us, his two bookends. "'Cause Ike is

telegraphin' a right uppercut, as his fist is lowered, thrust firmly from his right hip. Oh my gosh. Oh my gosh!" he shouted again as fast as humanly possible. "After he launches it, he's goin' to be as fuckin' flat-footed as the Statue of Liberty, with a tight fist holdin' the semblance of a torch," he predicted.

While Ike was waiting for his opening, I counted to myself silently, "One thousand one…"

"Hot damn, hot damn," John Henry immediately continued, as excitable as I've ever seen him at ringside. "There's two schools of pugilistic thought on how Inky can counter this big Sunday punch," the big guy analyzed.

Continuing his fast-paced commentary, JH colorfully expressed, "It's goin' against the grain, but it's a beautiful move, pulled off swiftly. Steppin' left, parryin' with his right, he can set up Ike like a sittin' duck, clobberin' him from the blind side with a left cross to the temple."

Ike was getting impatient as I progressed with "One thousand two…"

"For my money!" our big cous exhaled, pounding his chest, hoping that it would help.

His throat was raspy, and he started coughing in quick succession. *Please don't get laryngitis.* I kept still. *Because neither TJ nor I can fill your shoes figuratively and literally with your depiction.* "Thank God," I said under my breath when his voice box came back and for not having to be fitted with size 18 D walk wear.

"For my money!" he coughed out again. "I'd step right, blockin' with my left arm, and from out of the sky throw a sparkin' roundhouse right to his chin with the force of a sledgehammer hittin' its mark dead center on the anvil."

"One thousand three!" I bellowed out loud for my two buddies. After dropping his hands to his side, letting his guard down, Inky flinched to a feigned left jab thrown by his brother. Leaning in, he got caught by Ike right on the button, snapping his neck back, lifting one of his heels straight up off the floor.

Discussing the potential punch in slow motion aside, when the "Real McCoy" landed, it took less than a second, leaving in its wake the expression of doomsday on Inky.

Incredibly, glassy-eyed Inky was still on his feet. He was myopic in trying to shake off the cobwebs. His knees buckled, and he was unable to plant his one foot, which must have felt as if he was stepping onto quicksand, in an attempt to regain his balance.

"Damn it," I said out loud, "this is the nearest I ever want to be to experiencing walking that walk on queer street."

I nudged John Henry.

"The guy's out on his feet."

The big guy couldn't hear me because of the deafening noise level in this bedlam. No different from any other hostile fight crowd, this bunch demanded their pound of flesh and could smell the knockout coming. A group of guys took up the chant of "Down, down, down!" I could detect cheers of "He's goin', he's goin'!" Across the human ring, I heard, "Yes, yes, yes!" and "No, no, no!" Choruses of "Hold on!" were being yelled by the Inky contingency. There was even reverberations of "Cover up, cover up! and "Finish him, finish him!" "Give him a standin' eight count!" a beery set of lungs alongside us discriminated in the midst of the debacle. One young lady shouted, "He's a bum, he's a bum!" and I swore I picked up the sounds of a Bronx cheer. Even my two ringside-aficionado pals, frenzied by the slugfest, were trying to root Inky on. John Henry and TJ roared too little too late, "Get legs!" Before that perfect punch exploded, this bout seemed as if it was innocent "rock and sock 'em" robot stuff. Welcome to the stark reality of the barroom fight game.

The majority of onlookers got their wish when Inky, subsequent to staggering for the umpteenth time, did indeed go down. At precisely the moment it happened, one of the men making up part of the human rope on the far side thundered out "Tim…ber!" to the delight of the electrified audience. Histrionically, as you'd pay to see it, Inky kissed the canvas or, in this case, the dirty hardwood floor, clutching his chin.

"Glass jaw," John Henry remarked, shaking his head.

Guernsey, the cowman from the earlier wrestling match with cous, self-served as referee, counted Inky out at ten, and raised the hand of the winner, who never went to a neutral corner. John Henry checked on the loser, helping him to his feet, informing him that he was banned for a month of Fridays, which didn't sit well with the throng of disillusionists, who booed with catcalls. They probably anticipated Inky making a better showing on next week's fight card.

"Betcha Inky could win a split decision in the return match," offered one juiced-up cowpoke with the cigarette behind his ear, who, from the appearance of his flat-nosed face, had been punch-drunk once, twice, or twenty times in his life.

He was re-enacting the haymaker to his buddies who missed the shot seen 'round the Inn. The big guy gave the four-week heave-ho also to Ike for fighting. He reacted, slightly affronted. John Henry glared at him, conceivably exercising, "What? Do you think you get to stay and come back tomorrow night 'cause you're the fuckin' champ?" Our big cous signaled his troopers to move in on the palookas. Exhausted, they surrendered without whimper and got ushered out the rear entrance without much fanfare.

"Attention, ladies and gentlemen. Attention, ladies and gentlemen. The McCadlins have left the building. Let me repeat, the McCadlins have left the building!" boomed the familiar but amplified vocal chords of Uncle Miller.

He addressed the standing-only crowd vis-à-vis his megaphone as he marched around.

A few people who were actually hiding reappeared from their crouched seclusion underneath their tables.

"Your friend Ricky 'Cactus' Conrad is making tracks this way," TJ said with capriciousness to the big guy.

"That show wasn't bad, Hoss," offered a congratulatory Ricky to John Henry in a snide fashion. "Now, what about a few boxin' exhibitions durin' the early-bird supper hour?" he coarsely howled.

He slapped ole Hoss hard on the back.

"I've got a neighbor friend who might hook ya up with some midget mud wrestlers," he said, continuing his verbal onslaught.

"And, John Henry, they're relatively inexpensive for a cheapskate like you, bein' they charge by the pound."

"Or you can really pack the house," Ricky persisted, "by seein' if a has-been like you can still fit into that ole San Diego football uniform of yours and fight all takers on. Even your wife and kids can get in on the bandwagon sellin' programs."

After I let out a short-winded puckered "Ooh" and hearing the whistling sound emitting from TJ's lips, both of us turned in John Henry's direction to see how he was going to handle this verbal low blow to his family. I was sure TJ wouldn't have any objections if I held Cactus while he pounded away, or vice versa. Suffice it to say that all we might require from him was to endure thirty seconds' worth of corporal punishment to vindicate Sally and the children. It wasn't a nice thought, but then again, he'd proven not to be a nice man. He demeaned the big guy's loved ones, who were special to us too.

"Why don't you take that upon advisement yourself, Cactus Conrad?" John Henry calmly released after nodding to TJ.

"No one gets away callin' me that stupid—"

"I just did," our normally sanguine big cousin abruptly exploded.

John Henry stood nose to nose, violating Ricky's arm's-length space. The blood vessels in his neck had expanded, and he was flexing his massive chest muscles.

"Just who died and made you promoter at the Inn, Cactus? Whoever lit the fire under your ass, Cactus," John Henry strained, "should have cautioned you that you're the one who's goin' to get burned. Assaults on my character, I can digest, but when you insult my family, that's a totally different equation. Cactus, I'd like you to be the first taker on."

He continually poked the large man in the breastbone with his steely finger.

A small gathering took cognizance that Cactus was gritting his teeth and curling his fingers into a fist. Be that as it may, words to the wise for Cactus would be for him to offer his mea culpas (my fault) because his dilatant brown irises hinted of apprehension. Had macropsia set in? I wondered. As long as Conrad kept his big trap shut, he might merit a stand-off, but if he cocked his arm, he was in for a dire country whippin'.

As lady luck would intervene, in the flesh, an attractive, well-toned woman of Amazon-size proportions with cloven nutmeg-colored hair emerged to the forefront. Bedecked in blue denim slacks and jacket with a hot-pink turtleneck top, she favored hoop earrings and profiled a retroussé nose.

"Give my best to Sally and the kids," she vocalized to John Henry with a Snow White-capped smile.

"Be obliged to April," he answered without spinning around, keeping his vision stationary on Cactus.

"Ricky, I overheard your foaming at the mouth to John Henry, and it was pitiful. I'm angry at you," she vented succinctly in a dialect bred originally west of the Rockies. "Before you mutter another word, please listen to me carefully. Desperado, even though you're presently busy up to your elbows with alligators, we need to iron out a misunderstanding," she admonished.

She silently waltzed him away, without so much as a peep by his belt loop.

"What's eating him? He seemed like a swell guy just twenty minutes ago. Then he gets quarrelsome," TJ asked.

"Damn, if I know, cous," the big guy said while massaging the whiskers on the contour of his bottom lip. "When you think you can figure people out, two and two come up five."

"John Henry, what did you start to say about Cactus before at the bar?" I reminded him.

"Oh, he's a polyorchid man," he returned.

John Henry laughed. He realized from our blank expressions we didn't know what he was referring to.

"Bein' honest, cousins, I first heard the term in Doc Mitchell's biology class," the big guy knowledgeably recalled.

That was still no erudite clue to us.

"To put in proper perspective for you, when John Henry Jr. was first learnin' to count, we'd offer him a candy treat and he wouldn't say that he wished to have two but that he wanted 'two ones.' That's a good base one exponential notational description for a youngster,

I'm proud to say. Now, let's apply this to Ricky. Let's just pretend that sheer coincidence brings both of you to the men's room at the precise time Ricky's bladder gets full and it's time for you all to 'drain the geranium.' Now, try real hard now to create a mental picture of this. The three of you, Ricky in the middle, are sharing space at that group urinal…"

We still didn't understand what he was driving at.

"However proud you are, and some of us are prouder than others who might feel a little inadequate of the unit nature endowed you with, the thing your hand's aimin'. But please remember one thing: he's the proudest of you all 'cause he's got…"

Neither one of us had to go back in time, trading places with the young John Henry Jr., to comprehend. "He's got two ones!" the three of us loudly harmonized, contagious with laughter. Carousing, during the hoopla TJ tagged me first, but our unexpected player, the big cousin, simultaneously tapped us, declaring we each owed him a beer. In my case, I wasn't going to be an unhappy camper just because I owed "two ones."

"I still don't get it," TJ quizzically stated, "why you call him Cactus."

"Because the appendage to his main penis resembles the arm of a saguaro cactus. I ought to know, I've peed next to him," he honestly delivered.

His control, all but lost, TJ straddled the nearest table, his belly hurting from the excitement of John Henry's fanciful outburst. I wanted to make a comment, but I was laughing too hard to be understood. People around us thought we had cracked up, and in fact, we had. The big guy was displaying with his fists what he would have done to Cactus, Cactus, Cactus, and I couldn't stop my laughter. He ignored my time-out hand-signaled plea.

"The goddess who saved his butt is April Peterson. She's a veterinarian along with her older sister, via Nebraska, who moved here a few years back. Cactus is her steady. Don't know what woman would envy her selection. The poor thin' has worked with animals so long she succumbed to datin' one too," he insistently guffawed. "One other thing," he added, "the poor darlin' must wear some iffy expressions when Cactus requests some good head. But she does get a choice.

And imagine she's associate vice president of this county's chapter of the Humane Society? Cousins, who protects her?" He was romping.

As I squeezed the right side of my head with my hand, I collected my thoughts.

"John Henry, you have more preternatural beings in here tonight than *Star Wars*. And I'm not talking about President Reagan's devised missile defense mechanism, but the movie," I blabbed.

We couldn't physically take any more boisterous romping. My globes were red and sore from rubbing away the secreted saline, and if TJ didn't lead me back to the bar area, I was going to hemorrhage from excitement. We did just that with our big cous in tow. Uncle Miller set us up with more java and a shooter each to blend with it. If Inky thought he had it tough wobbling to maintain his balance, he had only see me still knockin' 'em down with sea legs.

"War is hell," our bartender said, chuckling, to TJ and me, attributing to the McCadlin hurly-burly. "Reserved your seats for yas," he said with a wink.

He knew that prime real estate at the bar had become cheap, since it was no longer three-deep to get a drink. Without bothering to check my watch, I knew it was getting late, because the crowd was filtering out.

"Does a man proud to see ya boys belt down your liquor, especially since none of yas will be operatin' any American Harvester combines or highway machinery," our fiery host wagered. "Mind ya, for one night you boys were throwbacks to the rowdy gang I hung out with thirty years ago, the only difference bein' that we did it every night and went to work the followin' day hungover. In due regard to the meanin' of survival of the fittest, a few of us died and the rest of us settled down, mendin' our reckless ways. It's ancient history to you boys, but I still have my memories," he recalled.

"Give me another hit, Unc," the big guy asked after making his shot vanish. He wiped away any flavorful residue from his lips with his tongue.

After heeding to his nephew's request, Uncle Miller leaned over to TJ and me, sitting right alongside John Henry.

"Boys, this cadaver next to you, and mind ya, I know how large he is and how much he can consume," he motioned with his right thumb, "would be no match in a drinkin' contest with any swampy over the age of thirty. If I were a bettin' man, and you boys certainly remember how I disapprove of wagerin' at the Inn…"

We nodded.

"I'd bet the ranch on them." He smiled, alternately winking each eye.

"No shit, Sherlock!" bellowed our not-so-stiff comrade.

"Why, they're not human. Swampies can swallow pond scum and not get sick. They have lead-lined stomachs," John Henry made reference. "What about me versus any of them nippin' a little vodka, Unc?" he voiced sharply without the need to benefit from a moment's examination.

"You damn fool!" Uncle Miller laughed hoarsely. "They'd all sign up for that. Two or three blasts each and they'd go on a rampage. Speakin' of swampies and vodka, that reminds me, are you sneakin' any Smirnoff to Big Clemson and Turtle? Because the rest of their clan are askin' me for it too."

"No way, Jose," he returned his answer.

John Henry's fingers, hidden under the bar rail, were crossed for my amusement. Uncle Miller winked at TJ and me.

"Well, even though you're not, I'm just remindin' ya what can happen if ya were. It's bad enough ya allow them to wear that throwin' artillery strapped to their legs. You've got too much invested, and I've got my livelihood at risk. Boys, several years back, when I was in partnership with Chipper Myer, that no-good ole college chum here let the Jones boys on separate occasions drink a quart of vodka each with their hands cuffed behind them. It made no gosh-darn sense, but they drank it straight and they had no choice but to suck it up through a straw. When they emptied the contents, they started bangin' their heads against the wooden door like two batterin' rams and makin' ghastly sounds like wildebeests. I've seen one of them animals on a documentary about South African wildlife, and believe me, they're strange-lookin' creatures. The swampy brothers were more determined about levelin' the place than worryin' about splinters in their skulls," he recollected.

Our senior storyteller left the bar in a huff when a sleepy-eyed waitress with a concerned expression whispered something in his ear. An accommodating gal, named Amy, offered to perform Uncle Miller's function, and the big guy hopped over to lend a hand. After John Henry filled some drink orders at the other end, he traipsed back to our section.

"Hey, John Henry," TJ entreated, "don't look this second, but what's the condition of that guy over there?"

TJ was alluding to the short broad-shaped man with the bulbous protuberance on the tip of his nose. I had meant to inquire about him myself.

"Let's not stare at him," I stated.

"Well, cous, if I'm not supposed to peek, then describe him," the big guy answered back.

"He's got a…" TJ placed a closed fist on the end of his own beak.

"Oh, that's August Gherkins. He's a helluva guy. Ole Auggie has patents on a few inventions. Why didn't you just say the man with the clown nose?" John Henry questioned.

Embarrassed by his own silly gesture, TJ didn't answer, and I had nothing to say.

"That's the layman's title. I'm not sure what the clinical term is for the affliction, but it's fair. In his particular stage, it's the medical opinion not to lance it, for terminal-health reasons. It's a case of not wanting to cut off your nose to spite your face because the consequences might kill you," he relayed.

"Tell us, cous. People can be cruel. Does anyone bust his chops about his deformity?" I piningly invited.

"Hallelujah!" he applauded. "Thank you for askin', Stanley. What goes on elsewhere, I don't know. At the Inn, I'm not runnin' a fuckin' beauty contest for men or for women. What I'm damn proud about in this place is that it is a departure from anyone's bad manners or preconceived notions at home. In our humble establishment, and that includes Unc, 'cause it wouldn't run without him, how you act as a person counts more than what you do and what you look like," he explained. "Amen."

"Well said," TJ noted.

Ditto his annotation as I raised my coffee cup in salute.

"If I may be so bold?" John Henry requested, awaiting our assentation.

Our bodily actions told him to proceed.

"I'll even go out on a limb sayin' that it doesn't matter whether Queen Elizabeth II entered our swingin' doors with her three boys or August Gherkins and his brood. Everybody gets treated the same. The only person allowed celebrity status in here is me," he affirmed as he picture-framed his jaw on three sides with his index fingers and thumbs.

As the big guy's pitiful friend Barty had been talking to no one in particular excepting empty air, much earlier, so presently was John Henry's life imitating art or, in this case, Bart.

John Henry was going into his "If I weren't married to my Sally" jargon. "I'd give you a run for your money with April. But, Ricky, you lucky so and so, I'm not the one she shares her pillow with." Typical John Henry humor, but his best line was about to be offered. "Ricky," he again called Cactus, "for me to have the time to do all the things I'm accused of, you'd have to stretch my days to thirty-two hours long."

"Do you think there's any sliver of truth regarding this bunk about Cactus?" TJ asked.

"Oh, it's improbable, nevertheless probable," I returned, forming my own conclusion. "Naw, what am I saying? It's just got to be bullshit. In any case, as you once said at the Gondolier in Newark, 'we don't need to know!'"

We shared a laugh. Cactus departed shaking hands with a favorable disposition on his puss. John Henry walked back with an *All Quiet on the Western Front* expression, at least for the end of this night. Our acting bartender competently inquired if we'd like a last call.

"Amy, darlin'," the large one projected, "after the usual litany of 'Okay, good people, drink 'em up,' I can dead-bolt the doors and we can drink till dawn."

"You know what I meant," she answered in a provocatively sexy way. Amy's eyelashes appeared to flutter.

"Let's get forty winks," John Henry suggested. He was standing facing his assembly of two.

Rather than a unilateral approach, the decision to go to sleep was met with eclecticism, the only debate being the proper amount of shut-eye. If we stayed, none of us were in much shape to be lending a hand wiping off tables as part of the skeleton crew doing work detail. Amy made our wishes known to Uncle Miller in the kitchen via the intercom on the wall. TJ and I reached in our pockets for some green stuff for her before the big guy led our triphalanx through the front entrance. We could see Emmel and his dart buddies. They scrambled out the side door to bring the vehicles as if they were parking lot jockeys. Uncle Miller met us outdoors to supervise the caravan. While waiting, we admired the stars in the crystal clear sky, and I wondered if that ole full moon hadn't been the precursor on the effect of this night's occurrences. TJ and I thanked Uncle Miller for his "horsepitality." He relished the sound of it. "Will even buy us a brewski," he promised at John Henry's clambake. Our country chauffeurs arrived with the rigs. Two designated drivers pulled up in John Henry's and TJ's trucks, and Emmel returned in his Ford Bronco jeep.

"All this logic is making me confused," I teased Uncle Miller.

"Just for kicks, Stanley, I was goin' to follow in my Blazer. See if my nephew Emmel would foolishly leave his Bronco at John Henry's farm and transport back with me," he said, snickering.

"Thanks for the faith in me," a seemingly ultrasonic-eared Emmel responded after overhearing his uncle get in his dig. He was standing a distance away.

His declaration was met with cheers from the rest of the throng.

Uncle Miller's suggested that the three of us hop in with Emmel and let the two dart buddies follow. We wouldn't hear such a thing. As a matter of fact, we pooh-poohed the idea because we were grateful for our DDs (designated drivers) consideration. We chose to travel shotgun style, double-barreled. Indicating two to a vehicle. Since a lottery would take too long, Uncle Miller picked the traveling companions the Army method: "You two, you two, and you two."

The results: I'd be riding with Emmel, John Henry was matched with Beaver, who suffered from psellism, meaning he stammered. TJ got to go along with Arty, who wore the flashy fishing hat with the front brim creased up with the interesting bobs and lures decorating the crown. I never suspected that water bugs had such sharp-barbed hooks to them.

The departure wasn't complete without Uncle Miller waggishly hollering, "Now, with the whole kit and caboodle out of here, I can finally get some peace!"

CHAPTER XIII

Our motorized caravan journeyed forward. I spoke with John Henry vis-à-vis the citizens band radio Emmel had installed.

JH's handle was Daddy Long Legs. He asked his blood-related cousin to show me his clothing paraphernalia tomorrow morning that he returned with from his Alaskan trek this past spring.

"Can hardly wait," I facetiously implied.

As we climbed the slight grade, the immense farmhouse jutted out to sight with a glint before we reached the crest of the plateau. In the daylight, there was a panoramic view of the valley below. If I ventured a guesstimate on how long it took to get to the big guy's doorstep, it would be under three minutes at the thirty-five miles per hour we were traveling. It didn't have the legendary Georgian elegance of Margaret Mitchell's mansion Tara, but with its second-storied brick-faced addition, the structure was a splendid citadel worthy of the magnanimity found in a Courier and Ives backdrop, especially when snowflakes covered the landscape. Stained robin's-egg blue with white-trimmed miscellaneous-sized windows of bay, bull's-eye (near the third floor), dormer, French, lancet, and oeil-de-boeuf (by the attic) designs added a touch of accentuated rustic grace to the abode.

As you might expect from such a magnificent house, there was a crowing rooster weathervane on one of the cupolas, and if you placed pennants on the pepperbox turret or the other smaller cylindrical tower with the pavilion top covering stretched diagonally across the imbricated hip-and-valley roof, you could find medieval grandeur.

"Leave the keys in the ignitions," our big cousin instructed. "Don't worry, cous, this isn't downtown Newark," he caustically relayed to TJ.

John Henry eye-beamed TJ's Chevy pickup in advance of glimpsing my facial expression. He informed me without so much as a word that TJ might be better off if someone did waylay those wheels. Before heading for the white wraparound spindled front porch of the Andrew's bastion, we thanked the boys for their public service and offered "Good nights." John Henry opened the front door without the restraints of inserting his key.

"You're right, this isn't beautiful downtown Newark," TJ alluded. He jocosely realized that even this former country custom was now only remnant.

Personally, I always revered the walloping antechamber with the cherry-stained wood finish baseboard covering half the length of the wall. Passing through the Tudor-shaped archway, underneath the wishbone-shaped staircase, led one past the blind wall to a king-size kitchen with fireplace, a pantry, and an adjacent dining room. With a barrel-shaped ceiling raised twenty feet high, the width of the herringbone parquet floor was suitable for a half-court game of basketball. In fact, years ago we did just that, after we removed occupying spaced furniture to the flanked larger living room; we chose the one where the bookshelves were aligned, boasting a metal spiral staircase leading to the upstairs hall. While we performed that chore, the big guy set up his adjustable basket with the fiberglass backboard. Ha, John Henry's father thought we were crazy until he saw how good it felt to swish an eighteen -footer. "The boys are just lettin' off a little steam," he said to mollify the missus's reservations.

When we politely declined John Henry's hospitality of a nightcap, there was nothing else left to do but race him up the carpeted dog-legged steps. He took the left side of the staircase as always, and TJ and I took the right. The starting line was the newel post at the bottom of the stairs and the finish was the second-floor landing. Half a length was what I finished ahead of TJ. I took advantage of good inside-rail position and strode two steps at a time. Daddy Long Legs came in dead last, and it wasn't surprising he was holding on to his tummy. I was unsympathetic, but sick to my stomach too. John Henry accused me of cheating. So I took off on set. Needed the good jump start, I reckoned.

He pointed out our respective sleeping quarters. Mine was the green-wallpapered room containing the floral water pitcher in the bowl pottery on the west side of the house I usually got as a guest. TJ was set up in the penthouse room in the attic, the quarters he always preferred. Before retiring, the big guy directed us to the door of his master bedroom. He gave us ursine good-night hugs that would shake the ice cycles off a polar bear.

"If I don't personally serve you guys that big country breakfast as promised or see you off with a marchin' band tomorrow morn', you'll understand that some pressin' matters took precedent, like my beauty sleep. Regardless of that," he said, facing TJ, "tonight I didn't pry, but next time, and that means my party, I'm remindin' you that me and you, cous, are goin' to talk some serious turkey."

"Cousins," he implored with zeal, "stick around five seconds after I close my door 'cause you'll appreciate my duplication of a call and a squishin' sound."

We had no idea what he was up to, but we complied to his whim.

"In the shape he's in tonight, no way is he making love to Sally," TJ gleefully opinioned.

A moment later, TJ and I cracked up to a familiar "Tim…ber" preceding the 275-pound flop to his mattress.

As we walked down the hallway, TJ was shaking his head. "Just hope Sally was way on the other side of the bed."

When my slumber was interrupted, I suspected that it was about 3:00 a.m. My Movado disproved me, indicating that it was actually half past the hour. Probably, it was nothing more than the two women I had on my mind, but if I was going to experience violent regurgitations, I didn't want to awaken anyone else from their repose, save my own embarrassment. Just because I wasn't experiencing airplane spins or having the room move about me did not mean that I could afford such a chance. Finished dressing, I scooted down to the sink in the kitchen after fidgeting with the stuck bathroom door. Thankfully, it was all a false alarm.

After helping myself to a glass of milk mixed with a Coke, and satisfying my nicotine addiction, I closed my eyes on the floral couch in a sewing room off from the pantry. A multicolored afghan served its purpose as my blanket.

My eyelids opened, not to the usual barnyard noises, but to the giggling of children, namely, eight-year-old John Henry Jr., wearing a familiar-looking New York Yankee cap, and his little sister, Katie, who had converted my solitude into a romper room. To them, I was the center of attention, but as Junior's godfather, all I wanted was to roll over and get some more sleep. Notwithstanding, the calico, the tiger, and the battleship-gray tabby cats, mewing and miauling, the kids had placed on top of my pillow wouldn't afford me the luxury. Even Jody, the two-year-old golden retriever, was getting in on the fun. She was pawing my arm and licking my face. Right beside Junior's neat toy fort was a green turtle lying on its plastic domicile, with palm tree overhang, a hamster exercising in its wheel, a parakeet swinging in its cage, and a gander dressed down in doll clothes honking away. When I sat up, a Shetland pony was showing his face in the window. Why, I asked only me, wasn't Cody the squirrel partying with us hoydenish kids?

Next, I mused, they'd be talking, walking pigs and George Orwell would be laughing his ass off on the ottoman catty-cornered from us if it weren't, I double-took, being occupied by cousin Emmel. He was enjoying a morning cup of coffee while steadily watching me.

"Cousin, John Henry said you were a deep thinker, and dang, you are, even while restin'. I was studyin' on you while you slept," he said, outfitted in a fur hat and parka more suitable for a Yukon sleigh dog ride in a blizzard than for the seventy-five-degree June weather we were experiencing throughout New Jersey.

Was he yearning, I wondered, for a bit part in the remake of *Call of the Wild?* Then, where were the huskies resting by the blazing fire and the frightening timber wolves, unless they were coming in on cue?

"What do ya think?" he voiced, on his two feet, allowing me to have a turnaround inspection of his trappings.

Oh yeah, this was what he brought back from his Land of the Midnight Sun trip. Well, Clarke Gable from the original movie version he wasn't, but he was becoming almost as comical as Gable's sidekick, Jack Oakie. I kept to myself. I informed him, "It's definitely you." My assessment pleased him.

"Aren't you a bit hot in your winter gear?" I couldn't help but ask.

"That's why I was sittin' in front of the air conditioner with the settin' on the big snowflake," Emmel smartly declared, matter-of-fact.

"Why didn't you just wait until I awoke, then put it on?"

"That's what I told cousin Emmel," six-year-old Katie volunteered.

Out of the mouth of babes, I was seconded. Emmel simply didn't say a word; he drank slowly from his coffee cup.

"Oops," I expressed as I realized some hard foreign object had invaded the confines of my right loafer while I was hopping on my left shoe, attempting to clutch ahold of the foot that smarted. Attempting to avoid the hamster cage, I fell right on my keister, scaring the other animals but delighting the children, including the big kid still in Eskimo gear sitting on the ottoman. Emmel was clapping as if he were a trained seal.

If I only had a salmon to toss him, I thought. Upon emptying, I discovered Junior had booby-trapped my loafer with two plastic toy soldiers he had sneaked inside. No mistake about it, I avowed, he was a chip off the ole block.

The aroma of good food and badly wanting some coffee had me heading for the kitchen as I left my adolescent gang up to their own mischievous devices. I was thinking, a Bloody Mary eye-opener wouldn't be a bad idea, or a shave and a shower for that matter, but I didn't have the time. Once there, I was greeted by Sally with a hug and kiss. All my best, I extended on her pregnancy before heading off to the lavatory. After a few minutes of washing up, I stepped out. Congratulations were in order for her mother, Mrs. Doylan, who was helping out with preparations, and another woman who I had never met introduced herself as Aunt Edna. I told her, "I feel like I've known you for a long time." When Mrs. Doylan rhetorically inquired if Johnny and Katie disturbed my sleep, what could I answer but "Oh, no"?

"No sugar, extralight, with regular milk" was how I responded to Aunt Edna's solicitation of how I'd like my coffee. She handed me a steaming mug just that way. Before Sally could finish her statement that John Henry's stomach virus precluded him from breakfast, her mother and aunt started to laugh. A second later, Sally and I became part of the reveling.

"When my husband gets himself into that delicate condition," she rompingly described, "he'll hibernate like a bruin till late tomorrow afternoon. My poor darlin' is all tuckered out. Oh, John Henry will rejuvenate in time for Sunday's poker game. Then he'll ask me with sugarcoated sincerity if I feel he looks well enough to play…"

In her haste to finish, she dropped the saucer to her own cup, splattering porcelain in three main directions on the floor. Bending down, I helped to pick up the big pieces while her mother fetched the dustpan and broom.

"All the while, he's biting at the bit for me to say yes," she continued from one knee on the tiled wax floor. "Just for fun, come tomorrow, I'm going to change my response to no. I'll allow him to stew for a few minutes."

"Now, Sally, boys will be boys," Mrs. Doylan said.

The kids ducked their heads in to find the cause of the commotion, and yet once more, TJ sprung out from the nook in the dining area.

"Just a little mishap, TJ," Aunt Edna assured him. "We have an army of help in here already, so go back in and finish your meal while it's hot. Care for another slice of rhubarb pie, TJ?"

"Sure," he rejoined, smiling broadly.

Walking up to him, I parroted her inquiry. As I was about to follow empty-handed, the ladies bringing chafing dishes to the dining room, the phone rang. I took Sally's tray while she answered and managed a head turn when I heard "Hi, Daphne, good morning" from her end.

At the table, there was a spread worthy of visiting dignitaries, and TJ and I just happened to fall in that category. Not just the plain ham-and-eggs promise the big guy didn't welsh on; we were going to feast on bacon, cinnamon toast, crescent rolls, hash brown potatoes, grapefruit halves, pancakes stuffed with blueberries, sausages, scrambled eggs, sliced plum tomatoes, T-bone steaks, and of course, rhubarb pie. And to think Wheaties lays claim to the tag "Breakfast of champions." Not likely. Two pitchers, one of freshly squeezed orange juice and the other filled with tomato, were there for the quaffing. When I spied the fifth of Stoli, it made sense to add a little Russian kicker to my Virgin Mary. *That Sally thinks of everything.* Since I knew who was on the other phone line, the octaves of her hilarity had me suspicious. The others at the table had piqued eardrums.

"Where are the limes?" I mirthfully questioned, supposing it was the sole glitch to my recipe.

TJ held up the small dish to the left of him. He informed me between chews that the Tabasco and the horseradish were on the lazy Susan he quarter-turned with a finger flick. And speaking of him, our future godfather-to-be was being princely, attended to hand and foot. The only thing the ladies had not done for him, it seemed, was cut his steak and feed him. TJ grabbed the moment when Mrs. Doylan excused herself to check on the kids.

"John Henry wasn't joshin' Aunt Edna when he said you were the best cook in the book," he complimented.

"What a nice thing to say," she returned his statement. "Next thing you know," she noted, catching my attention, "he'll be sayin', 'If I weren't married to my Sally, I'd…'"

We laughed with her depiction. My tomato juice cocktail blended with the right secret ingredients was just what the doctor ordered and my physician catered to me. All of us paid notion to the female voice we knew cackling excitedly in the other room, again. As I was prepared to sample a little of this and a little of that, an excited Sally summoned me to the kitchen.

"As you're aware, that was Daphne on the other end. She just rang to find out if you guys made it back safely."

"Sally, couldn't you have said that in the other room?" I teased.

"Yes. No. I'm not very good at the lying game, am I?"

"No, you're not."

"Stanley, Daphne called to find out, specifically, if you made it back all right. She was concerned about you. According to her, you are the beau ideal." Highest standard. "Tell me what happened last night."

"Knowing you as I do, Sally, with intimate details at stake, you wouldn't have allowed John Henry a moment's sleep until he gave you the scoop on Daffy and me."

Sally's eyes lit up on that pronouncement.

"That's why you're so tolerating with the big guy being lax in greeting his houseguests this morning," I insinuated.

"I see. I see," she carried on.

"You know I mean Daphne and me. Daffy was not meant in a pejorative sense, but a term of endearment."

"You're something else," she cavorted. "What's going on between you two?"

Wide smiling, with those cobalt blues of hers up to no good, I suspected I was about to get the needle.

"Is it getting warmer in here, or is it just you? Why are your hands so clammy? Are you hot around the collar, Stanley?"

"Yes," I answered, but to what question, I was unsure.

I smirked. Could have changed the subject abruptly to Tanya "Tessie" Turner, but I gave my word of honor and I liked Sally too much to be a slimeball.

"Then undo another button," she carped. "You tried too hard to cover your tracks if Daffy was just an innocent slip," she accusatively pointed out with glee.

Naively, I looked down at my shirt.

"Why don't you interrogate Admiral Byrd in the sewing room?" I sounded with my back facing her. "Emmel was supposed to have been our watchdog."

"He shows complete loyalty." Sally laughed. "The only trouble is, Emmel's true-blue to John Henry. But I'm working on him with his favorite snack, butterscotch cookies. They ought to loosen him up."

Returning to my seat, Aunt Edna kindly offered to microwave my plate, but I politely passed. I'd lost my appetite. It was good for Jody nestled under my chair as she begged me for more people food again. I settled for extra tomato juice and a Winston. When the ladies questioned what shenanigans Sally was up to, I casually offered them a silent, open-handed "I don't know." Shortly thereafter, our hostess presented herself in our room merrily whistling a top-forty tune and remarked that I was not eating.

"Whom were you rioting with on the telephone, dear? Whatever are you so chipper about all of a sudden?" Mrs. Doylan requested.

Purposely avoiding the responses, Sally kissed her mother on the cheek. She looked my way, but I eschewed eye contact with her. Aunt Edna had no idea what was going on, and TJ was chowhounding his third stack of wheat cakes.

"When are you going to tell me?" Sally's mother bemoaned. "Where is this world going to when a mother can't inquisition her own offspring? And why, for Pete's sake, is my little darling having a private rendezvous in the kitchen with Stanley?" she burbled.

"We don't speak French," TJ recited quietly.

He was taking a moment off from stuffing his face. His line went over the ladies' heads, and I wasn't in such a festive mood to appreciate it either. He grinned and went back to doing what he'd so far done best.

"Mom," Sally overly stressed, "I was just having a little fun building up your curiosity. I was on the telephone with Daphne, or as some people prefer to call her, Daffy."

As soon as Sally said that magic word, I lit up a fresh cigarette even though my other one wasn't out.

"Your French friend Daphne is so lovely and simply a charm. I like her company," Sally's mother verbally applauded.

Aunt Edna reinforced her commendation.

"Dear, I remember you telling me about trying to fix her up with some foreign guy."

What foreigner? I wished to put to Sally. "I'll smack his face," I heard myself say.

"Well, foreign to her. I did, and last night they met for the second time in years."

"Who is this fellow? Do I know him?" her mother continually doubled on her solicitations.

"Assuredly, you do. He happens to be…"

First, it was Sally and then, likewise, TJ who threw arms' length extensions in my direction.

"That Stanley, he only travels first-class with the ladies," TJ quipped.

He was borrowing verse from Louis's assertion and substituting me for Johnny Tangerine's name.

The two older women were caught off guard making funny-shaped Os with their open mouths. One of the two said, "Now we've got it." I didn't know, because my face was buried in my hands. I should have told Mrs. Doylan that contrary to her son-in-law's exceptions, two plus two does equal four, but I skipped it. They were tittering with excitement and anxious for some more good ole-fashioned tidbits of gossip. The two of them volunteered to assist Sally in lifting those "heavy" eight-ounce doilies from the tea wagon to the kitchen. Aunt Edna's motive in pushing the bottle of vodka closer to me before she left was in case I needed another fix, and at this point, I craved it.

"Women. Why's minutia such a big deal to them?" I offered to TJ as the ladies caucussed in the culinary department.

TJ lifted the cover off the steak platter. Even if I wanted a T-bone now, he had made the species extinct. Helping myself to a couple slabs of smoked, sugar-cured, thick-cut bacon, however, wasn't exactly settling for second best. As I eyeballed my gluttonous friend, there was still no discontinuity in his eating. Fulfilling my role as the conduit, I placed the heavy sealed envelope in front of him I had been carrying for John Henry.

"It's from Joe and the big guy," I informed him. "For your auto-related business."

Visibly, I saw his malaise when he opened the contents. As one might expect, it was filled with greenbacks. However, I didn't realize how much money until I visually counted out eighty-seven hundred dollars in crisp one-hundred-dollar bills and possibly a couple oval pictures of William McKinley from the half-stack, before he shoved all of it back in its paper wrapper.

"Last time I ripped apart packets stuffed with money, I felt the walls of Jericho come tumbling down…on my life," he vividly recalled. Shaking his head from side to side, he stated forcefully, "I didn't take hush money then, and I don't accept handouts now. The gesture moves me, but leave this with Sally. Don't need it." He fought back with tears. "When you're ready to, I'll be on the front porch. Damn those guys. They had to do this."

He slumped awfully in that direction. Before barging in, I mannerly rap-tapped on the closed-shut dinette door to give the ladies fair warning I was entering, so they wouldn't feel too badly chattering about me.

"Sally, we're leaving," I told her, standing in the doorframe. "So long magpies," I'd like to say to her mother and Aunt Edna, but instead, I expressed "Thanks" and "See you in two weekends."

Sally walked me out, and I gave her the envelope to return back to John Henry.

"I knew he wouldn't accept it. You four are the most pigheaded men I've ever met, and I've told Daphne that about you."

"Thanks, Sal," I abbreviated.

"Call her," she deploringly shot back as TJ sat on the front railing, waiting.

Something was bothering me since I awoke, but I couldn't put my finger on it. I walked briskly back inside the house on my way to the kitchen. I was on a mission. Looking out the back door off the pantry was my pretense. Purposely, I dropped some change to examine the bottom of the wooden-hinged door. The bell-shaped cutout hole was there, albeit fresh particles of sawdust on the floor. Hmm. Interesting. Why stop now? Opening the pantry, I found peanut shelves piled neatly in a corner. I overheard the women saying I must have a bad case of love pangs. How could they possibly suspect that I was exploring the whereabouts of Cody the squirrel? It was the better idea to keep it quiet than to ask about a fictitious rodent. Had I simply dreamed when I heard the distinct sound of electrical machinery being operated in the kitchen earlier, explicitly, a jigsaw? John Henry must have tiptoed down to cover up his tracks on the story.

When I arrived outside, Sally was talking with TJ by the rosebushes. It was going to be a splendid day. Each of my nostrils took in a dose of fresh country air. If you could only capture it in an aerosol can, you'd make a fortune. Dew was still present on some patches of blue-green lawn grass, and jenny wrens were nesting in a cherry tree, forsaking renting space in the co-op birdhouse. Perhaps the worm rent was too high for the area? I reckoned. Stars and stripes flapped gently on the flagpole, displaying itself proud on this villatic compound. An east-westerly breeze slightly creased a corner, curled it in half, straightened it out, and repeated the sequence. One last smiling farewell from Sally and we were headed northward.

CHAPTER XIV

"**D**id you forget something?" I asked, noticing his baseball cap wasn't about or upon him.

"No. What are you inferring?"

"Your hat."

"I gave that to Junior. It happened to be the one Mickey gave me several years ago," he stated collectedly.

"Do you mean to say that you gave away a cap that Mantle presented you with?" I questioned, a bit ruffled.

"Hell no. Are you crazy? It was Rivers, Mickey Rivers." TJ laughed.

Be that as it may, we drove out by the north corridor, past the chicken coops and twin barns, where the orchards began, taking the gravel road out, turning right to the main thoroughfare.

Three quarters of a mile up the road, I was apprehensive when he turned right again instead of traveling forward.

"Just blazing a new trail out, cous. I got you here in good shape, and you'll return in the same fashion."

What could I have said? Other than "Why are you making a left onto a private road?" if I did. It was a good thing we weren't carrying any half-ton payloads going over the wooden plank pons covering a ditch; ergo, we would have been in it. He turned around in an open field. We continued our prior concourse viewing fields of pasture and tillage as we passed riders on horseback inside a wire-fenced-in plot. Sniffing the air produced the smell of fresh-cut grass as we watched a farmer on his riding mower cutting a campestral tract horizontally.

Viridity surrounded, as we encountered cropping fields of asparagus, cabbage, celery, chicory, endive, and green tomatoes left and right of us. As we were leisurely cruising at the twenty-five-miles-per-hour posted speed limit, a whistle from an oncoming train blew and we stopped thirty feet ahead at the railroad crossing with the red signal and downed gate.

"She can make it under seventy-five if he wants to," I expressed in a falsetto voice, mimicking the front-toothless cowboy from last night.

TJ appreciated my comparison between the model and the genuine locomotive article. It would have turned out beneficial for our northeast destination if he had made a left at the following intersection, but he didn't. Dead ahead was his direction. One stretch of property on my side of the road overgrown with too-tall grass and weeds contained a dilapidated shack. Eighteen feet away, there was an outhouse in similar condition with a crescent-moon air vent on the door. Apparently a reclamation project for Father Time, I thought.

"Sally's right," my driver conversed.

"About you being pigheaded for not taking the money?" I lightly harassed.

"Speaking of the money," TJ said, "the contribution of your friendship is no less rewarding."

He freed his right hand from the wheel and extended it to me.

His words and our shaking hands visibly moved me.

"No. You should call. What's her name? Daphne. Don't be foolish to allow what happened to you and Kerrie to occur again," TJ cautiously replied.

He had to bring up her name, I ruminated. It was only yesterday at the Summit Office, right before he arrived, when the Australian lady's voice brought back those memories for a fleeting minute. I was a hotshot sophomore in the best frat on campus when she arrived from Adelaide, Australia, as a freshman. She was as personal as she was beautiful. Long wavy blond hair was the style she wore and hardly any makeup, because she simply didn't need to with her "fresh as a daisy" features. We seemed to hit it off. With a hundred guys trying to squire her, I became her heartthrob right away. Four great semesters I had with her.

Without knowing all the nitty-gritty, I committed myself too quickly to working the summer of junior year at her grandfather's canneries in Boongarooda and Oobagooma off the west coast of her homeland. Unassumingly, I just wanted to be with Kerrie, spending the month of August touring the opposite coastline up to the Great Barrier Reef and attending a corroboree (native Australian festival). Foolish and twenty-one, I thought it sounded as though it was going to be the grand excursion. The quibbles I was to come back to school with: the Indian Ocean, Coral and Tasman Seas, I swam in them. Great Sandy Desert, yeah, it's great and sandy too. Lake Disappointment, it sure was. The Murray River, it was merry. Loved Melbourne, hated Canberra. Didn't want to leave Sydney and couldn't wait to pack my bags in Brisbane. Toowoomba? Too mucha! The view of the reef in Cooktown, breathtaking. My lyrics were all down pat, until my father clued me in to the fact that I could only leave the country with a limited amount of money I earned there. Simply put, I couldn't afford that. Kerrie was heartbroken when I explained that I'd be staying home working at a factory in Kenilworth and taking an evening course. If I thought her not calling or answering my letters was bad, it got worse—she wasn't registered for the fall when I returned full-time for classes. When I finally got her to speak to me on the telephone in November, she cheerfully informed me that she was engaged to an ex-boyfriend named Willaby or Wallaby, more likely the latter. Kerrie was something special, and I took for granted she'd come back to me.

Joy and relief were the emotions I felt when a couple of miles down the road we approached the yield sign, placing us on the spur road for 579. Had we taken 513 from the get-go, as I suggested, it would have placed us on Route 78 East by now, but that was water under the bridge.

"You look as though you've been through the proverbial knothole. Apparently, you didn't get a good night's rest," TJ surmised.

"No, I didn't."

"Then do a small favor for me and a big one for yourself," he phrased in a matter of speaking of somebody we both knew well. "Catch some z's. The ride back now is a lead-pipe cinch."

His suggestion had some merit. So I took him up on it. I decided to rest my eyes for a few minutes, but eventually I fell prey to a deep sleep.

"Wake up, wake up, you're snoring," I imagined someone making an accusation.

When it happened twice, then thrice, my brain conveyed that it was nonimaginary. It was the voice of my buddy.

"What the heck? Where the hell are we?" I shuddered.

My lethargic eyelids half-closed realized TJ's contraption of a truck was crossing the Lockatong River over Green Sergeant's bridge in the ville of the same last name, the only covered bridge existing in New Jersey.

He ostensibly admitted to taking 579 South and seeing where it would take him. I was laughing, and he didn't have the foggiest notion. The outcome of his trailblazing: We had angled approximately twenty miles off course and formed the shape of a backward letter *C*. It was abstruse that in urbanity TJ had the streetwise savvy of a New York City cabbie; nevertheless, if you took him into a rural environ, he was literally a babe in the woods. What he needed here in the country was some trained corvine creature to fly ten yards ahead of him, signaling with a wing flap for a left or right turn.

"Does our intrastate tour include you changing your middle name from Jefferson to Washington and forging the Delaware River from Stockton only five and a half miles away into Pennsylvania?" I sportively asked. "And let's not try it," I replied for him.

A short ways out of town, we drove smack into a fast-food-type restaurant called Mr. Bumbley Bee, with a colossal plastic bumblebee on its dome and a youth dressed similarly outside, welcoming passing motorists to enter the almost-empty spaced parking lot. My driver said all this behind-the-wheel stuff had given him an appetite. I couldn't believe him. Forty minutes ago, he devoured enough food for a small troop, and now he was ready to wolf again. On the bright side, it gave me a chance to stretch my legs, and then I'd insist on taking over the driving chore. We waved to the adolescent clothed black and yellow in four-winged paraphernalia. TJ didn't seem to mind, notwithstanding that the air inside had the stench of stale honey. It gave me a mawkish feeling. As I observed the surroundings, this joint appeared to be a carbon copy of Mr. Bee, located off the Somerville Circle, except for some noticeable modifications.

There was a live beehive in the left-hand corner of the place. It was contained within plexiglass housing with pinhole air vents, so you could actually view the colony of drones being idle and the workers busy as a bee. Three-inch-in-diameter accordion-shaped rubber hosing attached the covering through a porthole in the window. Realizing it was educational as all hell, I still couldn't escape the fact that if some jerk snapped the tubing, the people in here could get swarmed. Guess what? I asked myself. TJ and I were the people.

Suspended from the ceiling were terra-cotta pots containing clusters of artificial flower arrangements of azaleas, geraniums, and petunias. Pure logic said the bees wouldn't find them entomophilous (insect loving), because they were not melliferous (honey-bearing).

The two older ladies behind the counter were pleasant enough, and they even shared some levity regarding their uniform attire. How demeaning, I was reasoning, that these senior citizens were forced to wear black-and-gold horizontally striped shirts and hairbands with eight-inch-high spring antennas.

Their sandwich offerings were framed directly above us in removeable irregular plastic letters. Some of the selections I didn't find particularly mouthwatering were the standard-fared Mr. Bumbley burger, ditto with cheese; a quarter-pound burger with the agnomen of "the big Bumble," ditto with cheese; the Queen Bee, two quarter-pound patties with lettuce, onions, tomatoes, and a secret sauce; honeybees, an order of curly cue french fries; sand bees, golden delicious onion rings; the swarm, baked beans; the hornet, Taylor ham on a kaiser roll; the yellow jacket, a grilled cheese sandwich; for sixty-five cents extra, you can get it with bacon; and honey-dipped chicken with "special breading."

When TJ ordered two Queen Bees for himself, along with his honeybees and sand bees, it nearly made me puke to imagine that the ingredients of the "secret sauce" he'd be lapping could contain crushed bees, including wings and stingers. Strictly speaking, I opted for a medium orange soda.

Emerging out from a supply closet with two cans of industrial-size ketchup was a morbid-looking character I dubbed the wasp boy. He was one of those people personified by "they only come out at night," who attain subcelebrity status as oddities, as they are picked ahead of normal people in the lines to get in Manhattan's trendy clubs. He had to be in his midtwenties. Together with being pockmarked and scrawny, he preferred his straight jet-black hair slicked back à la Roy Orbison, which contrasted too sharply with his ghost-white pallor. Consequently, it must have been a dye job. Wasp Boy's attire was all black, and in short sleeves he showed off a pair of matching mud dauber tattoos on his forearms. His mother could only but hope they were sponge-ons. With dirt under his fingernails, no more would I allow him to take my food order, let alone prepare it on the grill.

We found a nice, comfortable booth far away from the improvised bee terrarium, and it was startling how close it was situated to the side exit, just in case. Unequivocally, the red stickiness on our table had to be fuckin' ketchup not totally wiped clean. It muddied the view of the pipe-cleaner-made bees with tiny rolling plastic eyes resting in their individual comb cell, inside the hermetically sealed tabletop. TJ was too busy chomping on his sand bees for me to point out the one genuine preserved bee in the aureate hexagon among the factitious. How could it have filtered in? I asked only me. Did the manufacturer place this in on purpose? Or was I seeing things? I tried to catechize. This place made me feel "hopped-up" with opinionatedness. I was overanxious to *be* out of here, and damn it, TJ wasn't finished with that second "secret sauce" sandwich.

Little did I realize my biggest challenge was about to occur as I volunteered to take away the refuse on our tray. This was incomprehensible, I expressed, only to me, not counting the three teenage girls within earshot who were lunching on "yellow jackets" and "honeybees." It was opprobrious, I concluded, lifting up the trapdoor handle. Being dismayed for half a minute, I mentally worked out the theoretical solution. Desperately, I needed the brain trust of toddlers, who were child prodigies in Fisher-Price toys aged five to six who could instruct me on emptying the contents of my rectangular tray into the smaller square-shaped opening of the trash bin. Even if you knew the difference between a rhododendron and a trapezoid, it was still fuckin' impossible not to spill garbage all over the floor. Only if I had a chainsaw. Then I could allow for geometrical sameness. Was it any wonder that I said "No, thanks" when one of the senior ladies double-dutying at the register asked as we were leaving if I wished to purchase a Mr. Bumbley T-shirt, whereupon the bee's face was disproportioned two and a half times the length of its body.

Requisitioning TJ's keys, I wished to take the most direct route out of this area. Proceeding north on Highway 523, we picked up Route 202 at Flemington, heading more easterly. Even before we intersected at this juncture, I'd made my decision. It had nothing to do with the course we had taken but concerning Samantha and me. We were supposed to have a dinner date this evening, but I would have to cancel. Though I was tired and a little under the weather, they were not the reasons I'd give her. I was going to explain to her I didn't want to see her anymore. I'd wish her all the happiness in the world, but we were through. Metaphorically, I'd put the relationship to bed. I wanted to see Daphne tomorrow. Of course, I wouldn't tell Samantha that. It was funny. I hadn't done it yet, and still, I felt so damn good about it.

When we approached Route 22 East past the Somerville Circle, it was 12:55 p.m. Fourteen miles more and we'd arrive to Summit. The traffic was surprisingly light for a Saturday afternoon, which was good for us, as I continued the stretch of straight-ahead road. Even if his truck had cruise control, which it didn't, there were too many spaced lights for it to work effectively.

Though it was a bright, sunny day, it was breezy out. My dark shades were shielding the glare because the driver-side visor wouldn't flap down, but the papers TJ had wedged tight did. He caught me yawning. I was okay. As we were driving away from North Plainfield and entering Watchung, TJ informed me he had to put in a couple hours of work. Knowing today would be a total disaster, I sifted through my pile of paperwork on Thursday and cleaned my messes up. Still, I felt badly he had to labor on the weekend. An idea came to mind. What the hell! Maybe I'd—Yes, can do. It didn't matter to me

I was wearing suit pants. So I'd get grease on them from his auto-related business. Chuckling to myself, I looked over at my friend. He didn't have a clue.

TJ was unconcerned when I purposely missed the jug-handle turnoff for Mountainside, which took you into Summit going up the steep grade. Staying in the middle lane, he took notice when left-lane traffic didn't allow me to exit at Springfield a mile and three quarters up the highway. I didn't take that town's next U-turn either.

This section of Route 22 could be dangerous at times. Instead of a divider, there was an island separating the three lanes east and the three lanes west featuring a variety of diners, fast-food franchises, and stores. Though the fast lane was the left, which was customarily the case on roads, vehicles here could pull out slowly on you in the left lane, and the motorist in front of you in the left lane might slow down for a U-turn. At times, it could be tricky maneuvering.

"Ah, poohman," I faultily expressed.

I purposely avoided the next turnaround for Union. As I diverted his attention to the redheaded gal in the Volkswagen Cabriolet exiting for the Burger King, it enabled me to go beyond the turnoff behind the Flag Ship building on the middle island. He noticed too late.

"Sacrebleu!" I cheerfully expressed. Confound it.

"We don't speak French," TJ familiarly retorted.

I briefly faced my passenger, slowly shaking my head sideways while smiling. Laughing out loud, I took quick peeks at him. He was momentarily perplexed as he squinted his eyes and furrowed his brow.

"Let me get this straight," he said seriously. "I don't speak French, but now you do speak French."

I gestured an up-and-down head movement, not taking my eyes off the road. He was easily biting his lower lip.

"Say it ain't so, Stanley, say it ain't so. You traitor! This philosophical change wouldn't have anything to do with meeting a certain someone last night," he merrily accused.

Again, I slowly shook my head up and down. TJ laughed.

We were approaching the Garden State Parkway underpass.

"What are you going to do now?" TJ inquired. "Take the last U-turn at Union!" he hollered.

"Naw, this hauler is going about six more miles more into Newark, unless you don't think she'll make it. I'll turn her around, then."

He cracked a smile and started laughing.

"Happiness is bein' the only hick," I said.

"Ridin' the only horse," he recited slowly.

"In a one-horse town!" we shouted together.

My right hand caught only air, and he tagged me, calling out "You owe me a beer."

"Let's make it two ones," I offered.

Both of us laughed.

THE END

ACKNOWLEDGEMENTS

Special thanks to Mike Moran, Scott Moran, and the Moran family; Michelle and Jayne Moran, Rick Pierce and family; John and Joanne McGhee; Johnny and Wendy and their families; the Dougherty family: John. Eddie, Cathy, and families. John and Barbara Ponnett; John Jr., John III, Mark, Chloe, Jason, Stephanie, Will, Liam, Levi, and Sloan Shaw; Joe And Cass Ponnett; Joseph and Andrew Ponnett; Jeff and Carol Manzi; Stevie, Charisse, Erik, Astrid, Lin, And Linda Manzi; Jenelle Manzi; Jess, Kate, Lillian and Antonia; Dennis Patti, Carol Shoemaker, Rosemary and Bobby Dermody, Kelly and Da. Allen and Hope Rechtsteiner; Rick and Sue Rechtsteiner; Ricky, Kitty, Patty, and Jim Disario; Ginger English and family; the Manzie family: Lou, Lou Jr., Dee, TJ, Lauren, Linda, Lisa, Len, Lenny, Nancy, Frank, Julie, Mark, Susan, and Robert; the Zalewski Family: Dan, Stella, Laura, and their family; the Holland Family: Jackie, Mike, Chris, Tim; Lou And Catherine Pietronuto and family; Gino, Annie, and Robert Picistrelli; the Antonacci Family; John Freda and Family: Ugo, Betty, Rich, Patrica, Elissa, Danee, and John-Daniel Freda. A special thanks to Nina, graphic artist designer from Austin TX. Thank you to the Office Bar and Restaurant, Winberries, and the Beacon Hill in Summit, New Jersey. Thank you to Seton Hall University and staff, all of Walter's friends and family, as he was loved by so many. In memory of all our aunts, uncles, cousins, and grandparents. Thank you, Jesus. Amen!

ABOUT THE AUTHOR

Walter Zalewski graduated from Seton Hall University in 1977 with a BA in political science.

He was member of the Tau Kappa Epsilon fraternity and remained close to his fraternity brothers until his death. His book is published posthumously by his brother, William F. Zalewski, who also created the paintings for the front and back covers.